Billionaire
BOSSES
PROPOSITIONED BY THE TYCOON

Billionaire BOSSES

COLLECTION

December 2015

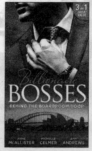

January 2016

February 2016

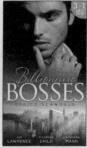

March 2016

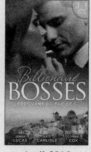

April 2016

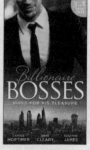

May 2016

Billionaire BOSSES

PROPOSITIONED BY THE TYCOON

DAY LECLAIRE
YVONNE LINDSAY
CAT SCHIELD

First Published in Great Britain 2016
By Mills & Boon, an imprint of HarperCollins*Publishers*
1 London Bridge Street, London, SE1 9GF

PROPOSITIONED BY THE TYCOON © 2016 Harlequin Books S.A.

Mr Strictly Business © 2009 Day Totton Smith
Bought: His Temporary Fiancée © 2011 Harlequin Books S.A.
A Win-Win Proposition © 2011 Catherine Schield

ISBN: 978-0-263-91789-5

24-0216

Printed and bound in Spain
by CPI, Barcelona

MR STRICTLY BUSINESS

DAY LECLAIRE

One

"I need your help."

Gabe Piretti struggled to conceal the intense wave of satisfaction those four simple words gave him, spoken by the only woman he'd ever loved. After twenty-three months he thought he'd be able to see Catherine Haile without experiencing any lingering emotions. Foolish of him to think such a thing was even remotely possible. After all, they'd worked together. Lived together. Tangled hearts and minds and bodies into what he'd once believed an inseparable knot. The passion that erupted between them had been an inferno that even eighteen months together had done nothing to lessen. If anything, it had grown stronger with each day they'd shared.

And then she'd left. He knew the excuses she'd

offered, what she'd said or—even more damning—
hadn't said. For the first time in his life, Gabe "the
Pirate" Piretti had been unable to solve the problem. Not
by hook or crook. Not by demand, nor wit, nor full
frontal attack, nor carefully crafted stealth. When Catherine had left him, he'd lost his anchor. And as much as
he hated to admit it, he'd been adrift ever since.

If she hadn't chosen to come to him today, he'd have
seen to it that their worlds collided in the very near
future. Over the endless months they'd been apart, he'd
given her the space she'd requested. And he had watched
from a distance while she set up her business and professional life on her terms. Keeping that distance had
been the hardest thing Gabe had ever done, harder even
than when he'd swooped in and taken the helm of
Piretti's away from his mother in order to snatch the
business from the teeth of bankruptcy.

Well, now Catherine was back, and he'd find a way
to keep her. She wanted his help? So be it. He'd give it
to her. But the price would be high. The question
was…would she pay it, or would she run again?

Aware that he'd kept her standing, Gabe waved her
toward the sitting area that occupied a large corner of
his office. Liquid sunlight, still damp from a recent
shower, spilled in through tinted glass windows that
overlooked a broad sweep of Seattle, as well as Puget
Sound. The brilliant rays caught in Catherine's up-
swept hair, picking out the streaks of gold buried in the
honey warmth.

"Coffee?" he offered.

After taking a seat, Catherine set her briefcase at her feet and shook her head. "I'm fine, thanks."

He took the chair across from her and tilted his head to one side as he studied her. She wore a chocolate-brown silk suit that shimmered richly over subtle curves, revealing that she'd recently lost weight, weight she could ill-afford to lose. The fitted jacket nipped in at a miniscule waist and ended just shy of a feminine pair of hips. She'd chosen sandals that were little more than a knot of sexy straps with the prerequisite three-inch heels, which she invariably wore to give the illusion of height. The heels also performed double duty by showcasing a stunning pair of legs. Clearly, she'd dressed to impress... or distract.

"It's been a while," he commented. "You've changed."

"Stop it."

He lifted an eyebrow and offered a bland smile. "Stop what?"

"You're mentally undressing me."

It was true, though not the way she thought. He couldn't help but wonder what had caused the recent weight loss, but was careful to hide his concern beneath gentle banter. "Only because I figured you'd object if I undressed you any other way."

A reluctant smile came and went. "What happened to your motto of strictly business?"

"When it comes to work, I am all business." He paused deliberately. "But you don't work for me, do you?"

"And haven't for three and a half years."

His humor faded. "Do you regret your choices, Catherine?"

He caught a flicker of distress before she rearranged her expression into a mask of casual indifference. "Some of them. But that's not what you're asking, is it? You want to know if I had the opportunity to do it over again, would I choose differently?" She gave it serious consideration. "I doubt it. Some things you simply have to experience in order to learn how to live your life…or how not to."

"Some things? Or some people?"

She met his gaze, dead-on. "Both, of course. But I'm not here to discuss our past."

"Straight to business, then."

She continued to study him. He remembered how disconcerting he'd found those amber-gold eyes when they'd first met. Nothing had changed. They were still as intense as they were unusual, seeing far more than he felt comfortable revealing. "Isn't business first how you prefer it?" she asked. "I seem to recall that's practically a cardinal rule at Piretti's. Whenever you buy and sell companies, put them together or dismantle them, it's never personal. It's just business."

"Normally, that would be true. But with you…" He shrugged, conceding the unfathomable. "You were always the exception."

"Funny. I'd have said just the opposite."

Her mouth compressed, a habitual gesture when the spontaneous part of her nature ran up against the bone-deep kindness that kept her more wayward thoughts in check. In the past, he'd taken great delight in kissing those wide, full lips apart and teasing the truth from her.

Somehow he didn't think she'd respond well to that particular tack. Not now. Not yet.

"Sorry," she murmured. "Water under the bridge."

"Quite a bit of water. But not quite enough to break the dam. I'll have to see what I can do about that."

A hint of confusion drifted across her expression, but he moved on before she could question what he meant. In time, he'd find out why she'd left. In time, he'd break through that calm, polite facade and force the fury and passion to the surface. He'd poke and prod until the dam finally broke and the truth spilled out.

"How have you been?" he asked, hoping the mundane question would help her relax.

A hint of strain blossomed across her elegant features. When he'd first met her—and hired her on the spot—he'd thought her delicate. And though her fine-boned appearance gave that impression, he'd quickly learned she possessed a backbone of steel. But right now she seemed more than delicate. She looked undone.

"I'm a little stressed right now," she confessed. "Which is why I'm here."

"Tell me about it," he prompted.

She hesitated, gathering her self-control and wrapping dispassion around herself like a protective cloak. "About eighteen months ago, I started my own business."

"Elegant Events."

He'd surprised her. "How did—" She waved the question aside. "Never mind. You would have made it your business to know what I did after we went our separate ways."

"You mean…after you left me."

The correction escaped without thought or intent, the words whisper-soft and carrying an underlying edge. An edge she caught. The strain she fought so hard to conceal deepened, melded with an old anger and an even older hurt. Her hands curled tight, her knuckles bleached white. This time when she compressed her mouth he suspected it was to control the betraying tremble. Time stretched taut.

"Do you really want to go there?" she asked at last. She pinned him with a single look. "Do we need to deal with the past now? Is that the only way you're willing to help me?"

"It's not the only way."

"Just the way you prefer." She didn't wait for the confirmation. "Fine. I'll make this as straightforward as I know how. You, with your unrelenting need to keep business and personal in separate compartments, gave me a choice. I could work for you or love you, but not both. I, foolishly, chose love. What I didn't realize is that you were already in love. And that love would always come first with you."

"You were the only woman in my life," he bit back.

She lifted a shoulder and smiled in a way that threatened to tear his heart right out of his chest. "Perhaps the only woman, but not the only thing. Piretti's was always your first love. And because of that, it will always be the love you put first."

"You left me because I worked late on occasion?"

he demanded in disbelief. "Because sometimes I was forced to put work ahead of you or our social life?"

She didn't bother arguing, though he could see part of her yearned to. The anger and disillusionment could be read in her expression, the bitter words trembling on the tip of her tongue. She waited until both faded away before speaking.

"Yes," she said with painful simplicity. "Yes, I left you for all those reasons."

"And a host of others?" he guessed shrewdly.

She inclined her head. "And a host of others." Before he could demand more information, she held out a hand in supplication. "Please, Gabe. It's been nearly two years. There's no point in beating this issue to death after all this time. Can't we move on?" She paused a beat, a hint of wry humor catching him by surprise. "Or am I wasting my time coming here today?"

He had no intention of moving on, but he could be patient. Maybe. If he tried really hard. "You aren't wasting your time. If it's in my power to help, I will. Why don't you start by explaining the problem to me?"

She took a deep, steadying breath. "Okay, let's see if I can't keep this short and straightforward, the way you like it. In a nutshell, Elegant Events is an event-staging business geared toward upper-echelon corporations and large-budget clientele."

"Of which there are plenty in the Seattle area."

She nodded. "Exactly. My goal was—and is—to plan and stage every aspect of the event in order to spare clients any and all worry and headaches. They tell me what they want, and I provide it. If they're willing to pay for it, I'll find a way of fulfilling their every desire, and if possible, to exceed their expectations."

"And you do it with grace and elegance and panache."

Pleasure gave her cheeks a hint of much-needed color. "You should write my PR releases. That's precisely our goal. We strive to bring something unique to every event, to set the perfect stage, whether it's to highlight the release of a new product or to create the perfect memory for a special, once-in-a-lifetime occasion."

"Like the Marconi affair tonight."

She shook her head in amused disbelief. "Is there anything you don't know? Yes, like the Marconi affair tonight. You're only ninety once, and Natalie is under tremendous pressure to make her father-in-law's birthday celebration an unforgettable occasion."

Gabe couldn't remember the last time he'd seen Catherine so happy, and that fact filled him with regret. She'd suffered at his hands. It hadn't been deliberate on his part, but that didn't alter the facts. "I don't doubt you'll pull the party off in grand style," he stated with absolute conviction.

"During my years at Piretti's, as well as during the time we were together, I learned a lot about what works, and more importantly, what doesn't. And though I didn't expect the business to take off right away, to my surprise and delight, it did." Energy and enthusiasm rippled through her voice. "We've scored some impressive clients and they seemed pleased with the various events. At least, I thought they were."

Her excitement dimmed and he frowned in concern. "Obviously, something's gone wrong. What's happened to change all that?"

The last of her vivaciousness drained away, leaving behind the tension. "Two things. First, we're losing clients. It's nothing overt. Just contracts I thought were a sure thing have suddenly gone away without any explanation. Everyone's polite and makes encouraging noises, but when it's all said and done, they choose another company."

"And the second problem?"

"Is the most serious." Worry darkened her eyes and turned her voice husky with nerves. "We're on the verge of bankruptcy, Gabe. And I don't know why. I thought we'd been careful with our profit margin, but maybe there's been more waste than I realized. I can't quite get a handle on it. It's not my area of expertise. I can tell something's off, but I can't seem to pinpoint what. I'm hoping you can figure it out and suggest changes to correct the problem before we go under."

He keyed in on one very pertinent word that he hadn't noticed until then. "We?" he repeated.

She hesitated. "I have a partner, someone who prefers to remain anonymous," she hastened to add.

He didn't like the sound of that. "Why?"

Catherine lifted a shoulder. "She just does. Since half the startup money was hers, I respect her desire for privacy."

She. Gabe refused to allow his relief to show that the partner was female rather than a male. It was petty of him, but he couldn't seem to help himself. Not when it came to Catherine. Still, it seemed odd that this partner would want to keep her identity a secret. Maybe he'd do a little digging and see if he couldn't find out what the mystery was all about. "Depending on what I find, that may need to change," he warned. "There's an excellent chance I'll want to meet her."

"I did discuss that possibility with her. She's agreed that if it means the difference between salvaging the business and having Elegant Events go bankrupt, she's willing to meet with you."

"Good decision," he said dryly.

"Agreed." A quick smile flashed. He didn't realize how much he missed it until it was there, reawakening an ache that had been tamped down, but never fully excised. "Tell me what you require in order to get started," she requested.

He forced himself to switch gears. "All bank and accounting records since you opened your doors." He ran through a mental list. "Debts, creditors, cost of goods purchased, billables, write-offs. Your prospectus, past and current contracts, a list of services offered and what you charge for them."

"In other words, you want a copy of everything." She reached for her briefcase. Pulling out a thick folder, she handed it to him. "I have most of that information with me."

He nodded. "Excellent. I'll go over what you brought and have Roxanne prepare a list of anything more I might need."

A shadow swept across Catherine's face, evaporating so swiftly that he'd have missed it if he hadn't been looking straight at her. "I'd hoped to keep my problem strictly between the two of us. Would you mind if we leave your assistant out of this? Is that possible?"

"Possible, but not probable. Roxanne is privy to most of what goes on around here."

"And what she isn't privy to, I'm certain she makes it her business to find out," Catherine commented blandly. "How else can she provide you with everything you need?"

Okay, he knew a minefield when he saw one. "I'll leave Roxanne out of the loop."

"And if she asks?"

His eyes narrowed. "Are you questioning how I run my business? Considering why you're here…"

"No, I—"

"I didn't think so." He relented. "But if it will make you feel better, should the subject come up in conversation, I'll simply explain that you and I are an item again."

Alarm flared to life in Catherine's eyes. "Excuse me?"

"After all, it won't be a complete fabrication." He smiled in anticipation. "In fact, it won't be a fabrication at all."

She tensed, like a mouse finally noticing the trap. She'd been so busy nibbling at the tasty hunk of cheese that she'd been oblivious of it. Until now. "What are you talking about?"

"You never asked my price for helping you."

She inhaled sharply before lifting her chin. "How foolish of me. I'd forgotten what a pirate you are, Gabe."

"That's me," he agreed lazily. "A pirate to the bone."

"So what's your price? What do you want?"

He gave it to her hard and straight. "You. I want you, Catherine. Back in my life. Back in my apartment. And back in my bed."

She shot to her feet. "You've lost your mind. You can't possibly think I'd agree to such a thing."

He regarded her in silence for a long moment before responding. "I guess that depends on how badly you want to save your business."

"Not that badly."

He stood and closed the distance between them. "Liar."

"Whatever there was between us is over, Gabe. Dead."

She was so small compared to him. So delicately put together. And yet she vibrated with sheer feminine outrage, with a strength and power he found irresistible. It was one of the qualities he'd always admired about her. Where most women looked for ways to make themselves as appealing to him as possible, Catherine had never played those types of games. He'd always known where he stood with her. Those gloriously unique eyes of hers could slay him with a single look, or melt him with the fire of her passion. Right now she was busy slicing and dicing him in every imaginable way.

"I know you'd like to think that what we shared is dead and buried." He allowed his amusement to show. "But you've forgotten one small detail."

"What detail?" she demanded.

"This…"

He slid his arms around her and locked her close

against him. He remembered the feel of her, the perfect way her body fit his. She had a pixie-lean figure with delicious curves her trim business suit only hinted at. But they were there, and they never failed to arouse him. Unable to resist, he cupped her face and drew her up for a kiss. She didn't fight as he expected, but neither did she respond. Not that he expected instant capitulation. That would take time.

For now, her full, generous mouth did no more than accept the teasing pressure of his. Gently, oh so gently, he teased his way past that sweet barrier, knowing just how she liked to be touched. Caressed. Taken. He'd missed the taste of her, the feel of her, the subtle scent of her. He missed the sharpness of her mind, and yes, even the sharpness of her tongue when she felt wronged.

He missed the quiet evenings when they'd sit together on his balcony sipping a glass of local merlot while day slid into night and Puget Sound came alive with the twinkling lights from the boat and ferry traffic. How they would slip from soft, sweet conversation to a soft, sweet tangle of arms and legs and lips. How their clothes would form a silken pathway from the balcony to the bedroom. And then the night would go from that softness, that sweetness, to something fiery and demanding. Something that branded their connection on every fiber of his being.

No matter how hard he tried to cut off that part of himself, that part indelibly linked to her, it would have been easier to rip out his heart and soul. He couldn't live without her. And he wouldn't. He'd been one of the living dead for long enough. He refused to spend another minute without Catherine in his life. And if it meant that he had to use blackmail to get her there, then that's what he'd do. Because once he had her back, he'd do whatever necessary to keep her.

With a soft moan, her lips parted and he slid inward. For a split second she surrendered to him, taking all he had to give. Her body flowed against his and her lips moved with familiar certainty, nibbling hungrily. Her fingers slid into his hair and gripped, anchoring them together. And her heeled foot inched upward, hooking around his calf in a practiced maneuver. He recognized the signal and responded without thought. Cupping her bottom, he lifted her so she could wrap those incredible legs around his waist. The instant he did, she began to fight free.

"No!" She wriggled from his hold and took several stumbling steps backward. "This isn't happening."

"It's too late, Catherine. It already happened."

He saw comprehension burn in her eyes. He also caught an infuriated acknowledgment that their feelings for each other weren't anywhere near as dead as she claimed, though if he didn't miss his guess, that fury was aimed more at herself than at him. She closed her eyes, effectively shutting him out.

"Damn," she whispered.

"Does that kiss prove my point, or is another demonstration necessary?"

She yanked at the hem of her suit jacket and with an exclamation of annoyance, shoved button through hole where it had come undone. Then she tugged at her skirt and smoothed her hair. What he'd ruffled, she swiftly unruffled. Then she regarded him with undisguised irritation. "You've made your point," she retorted. He could only imagine the amount of effort it took to look at him. "You do realize that I believed it was over between us, or I'd never have approached you."

"That's rather naive of you since there's not a chance in hell this will ever be over between us, sweetheart."

Her chin shot up. "There shouldn't have been anything left. I figured at most we'd have to kick over some of the ashes just to satisfy our morbid curiosity. I didn't expect to find any lingering embers."

"I don't doubt that for a minute."

"This—" She waved an all-encompassing hand to indicate him, herself, and the kiss that still heated their lips. "None of it changes my mind about our relationship. I'm not coming back home."

Home. The slip hung in the air for a timeless instant. He didn't reply. He simply smiled knowingly.

Swearing beneath her breath, she shot toward the couch and gathered up the file she'd given him and stuffed it inside her briefcase. Tossing the strap of her purse over one shoulder, she spun around to face him. He deliberately stood between her and the door. Not that that stopped her.

"I'm leaving," she warned. "And I'm going around you, through you or over your dead body. But I am going."

"And I'm going to make certain that doesn't happen. Oh, not today," he reassured her at her unmistakable flare of alarm. "But very soon I'm going to be around you, through you and—trust me—your body will be far from dead when I'm over it." He stepped to one side. "When you change your mind about needing my help with Elegant Events, you know where to find me."

She crossed the room, circling just out of reach as she headed for the door. Her hand closed over the knob, and then she hesitated. "Why, Gabe?" she asked quietly, throwing the question over her shoulder. "Why the conditions?"

"The truth?"

"If you don't mind."

The words escaped in a harsh undertone, the brutal honesty making them all the more devastating in their delivery. "Not a night passes that I don't ache for you, Cate. Not a morning dawns that I don't reach for you. I want the pain to end. The next time I reach out, I want you there."

Two

It took every ounce of self-possession for Catherine to exit Gabe's office without it looking as though she were attempting to escape the fiery pits of hell. Worse, she'd completely forgotten about Roxanne Bodine, aka Satan's handmaiden, whose sharp black eyes made note of the distress Catherine wasn't quick enough to conceal. A mocking smile slid across sharply flamboyant features.

"Not the reunion you were hoping for?" Roxanne asked in a honeyed voice that contained just a whiff of a southern drawl. "If you'd bothered to ask, I could have warned that you were wasting your time. You let that fish slip off your hook nearly two years ago, and he's none too eager to slip back on again."

"Maybe you should tell him that," Catherine retorted, then wanted to kick herself for revealing so much.

Roxanne could deliver taunts with needle-sharp precision. But she wasn't the type of woman who took them well. Nor did she appreciate the implication that Gabe might be interested in getting back together with the rival she'd worked so hard to rid herself of.

"Some women don't understand the concept of making a graceful exit." Roxanne stood and stretched a figure as full and lush as Catherine's was petite and fine-boned. She settled on the corner of her desk with all the lazy grace of a true feline. Then she proceeded to sharpen her claws on the nearest available target, in this case, Catherine. "Seems to me you'd have more pride than to come crawling back. You're just asking to get kicked to the curb again."

All her life Catherine had chosen discretion over a more overt approach. She'd been the good girl. Quiet. Polite. Turning the other cheek when required. But enough was enough. She didn't have anything to lose anymore. "I don't know how I'd survive without you looking out for my welfare, Roxanne," Catherine said with a sunny smile.

"Maybe that's your problem. Maybe instead of looking out for me, you should be looking out for yourself."

"Oh, don't trouble yourself on my account. I'm like a cat," she said, stating the all-too obvious. "I've been blessed with nine lives and I have a knack for landing on my feet."

Catherine planted a hand on a trim hip. "And yet here you are still sitting behind a desk…like an alley cat meowing at the back door waiting to be let in. I'd have thought with me out of the way, you'd have found a way in by now. I guess that's one door you can't quite slink through."

Fury turned Roxanne's face a deadly shade of white while two patches of harsh red streaked across her sharp cheekbones. "You think I made your life a misery before? Try me now. This is my turf, and I'll do whatever necessary to defend it."

Catherine made a sweeping gesture. "Go right ahead. But while you're so busy staking out your territory, maybe you should consider one small detail that you seem to have overlooked."

That stopped her. "I haven't overlooked a thing," Roxanne insisted, just a shade too late.

"No? How about this. You know your boss. When he wants something, he doesn't let anything stand in his way. Gabe wants, Gabe takes." Catherine allowed that to sink in before continuing. "You've worked for him for…what? Two and a half years? Three? And yet you've never been taken. I'm willing to bet you can't even get him to sample the goods. If he hasn't been tempted in all that time, what makes you think he ever will?"

She didn't wait for a response. If there was one thing she'd learned since opening Elegant Events, it was when to pack up your knives and leave. Without another word, she swung around and headed for the elevators. The instant she stepped into the car, she checked her back. To her relief she didn't find any of those knives sticking out of it.

Yet.

* * *

"So, fill me in on every detail. How did it go?" Dina Piretti asked eagerly. "You didn't have to tell him about me, did you?"

Catherine set down her briefcase just inside the front door and shot Gabe's mother an uneasy glance. "No, he still hasn't discovered that you're my partner," she reassured her.

Dina released a sigh. "I hear a 'but' in there."

"But it didn't go well," Catherine confessed. "I'm afraid we're on our own. We'll either have to figure out where the problem is ourselves, or we'll have to hire an outside consultant to advise us. A consultant other than your son."

Dina stared in patent disbelief. "No," she stammered. "You must have misunderstood. I can't believe Gabriel refused to help you. Not you."

Catherine hesitated. She had two choices. She could lie, something she not only hated, but didn't do well. Or she could tell Gabe's mother what her precious firstborn had demanded in exchange for his help. Neither option held any appeal.

"I need a drink," she announced. Maybe while they fixed a pot of coffee, some stroke of brilliance would come to her and she'd figure out a third option. "And then we'd better get to work. The Marconi birthday party is tonight and I have a dozen phone calls I need you to make while I head over there and supervise the setup."

Dina led the way to her kitchen, though she hardly needed to considering the two women spent a good deal of their workday together in its comfortable confines.

When they'd first conceived Elegant Events it had been right here, in Dina's Queen Anne home, sitting at her generously sized bleached oak kitchen table. Since then, they'd filled the emptiness of the huge house by converting several of the rooms into an office suite, one that had so far escaped Gabe's notice. The division of labor worked to each of their strengths. Catherine manned the front lines, while Dina ran the business end of things. Right now the older woman wore her shrewdest and most businesslike expression.

"You're being evasive, Catherine. That's not like you. Tell me what went wrong. Oh, wait. I'll bet I can guess." A broad smile flashed, one identical to Gabe's. When they'd first started working together that smile had caused Catherine untold pain. Even now it stirred a twinge that wouldn't be denied. "Gabriel put those patented Piretti moves on you, didn't he?"

Catherine deliberately turned her back on her partner. "One or two," she admitted. Dumping fresh coffee beans into the grinder, she switched it on, relieved that the noise of the machine made conversation impossible.

The instant the machine shut off, Dina jumped in. "It was just the same with his father. I never could resist him." A hint of sorrow appeared in her eyes and cut faint grooves beside her mouth. Not that it detracted from her startling beauty, a beauty she'd managed to pass on to her son, if in a slightly more masculine form. "Funny how much I can still miss him after all this time."

Catherine abandoned the coffee and wrapped her arms around Dina. "From everything you and Gabe have told me, he was an incredible man. I only wish I could have met him."

"He'd have adored you." Dina pulled back and forced a smile. "You've evaded answering me long enough. What happened? Why did Gabriel refuse to help?"

"He didn't refuse," Catherine told her. "He just put a price on his help that I'm unwilling to pay."

"Ah." Understanding dawned. "He wanted to get back together with you, didn't he?"

"How did you…?" Catherine's eyes narrowed. "Did you speak to him before I went over there?"

"I haven't spoken to Gabriel about you in months. I haven't spoken to him at all in the past three days," Dina insisted. She crossed to the coffee machine and made short work of starting the brewing process before turning to face Catherine. "I am, however, a woman, and I know my son. He's still in love with you."

No, not love, Catherine almost said. Lust, maybe. But he'd never truly been in love with her. Not that she could explain any of that to Dina. "He said that he'd only help if I moved back in with him."

"Naturally, you refused."

"Naturally."

"Because you don't have feelings for him anymore, either."

Catherine didn't dare answer that one. Instead, she regarded Dina with troubled eyes. "I know you've always hoped that we'd work out our differences, but that's not going to happen. You understand that, don't you?"

It was Dina's turn to look troubled. "I've never wanted to push for answers you weren't ready to give. I gather something went horribly wrong between you. You were so ill during those early weeks after the two of you broke up that I didn't have the heart to ask. But I always thought that you and Gabriel would work it out. You were so right together. So in love." She swept that aside with a wave of her hand. "Never mind. You were absolutely right to refuse him. It was quite rude of Gabriel to put conditions on his help."

Catherine smiled in relief. "You're not upset?"

"I'm disappointed." She poured them both a cup of freshly brewed coffee, putting an end to the subject. "Why don't we forget about all that for now and get down to business? I suggest we double- and triple-check that everything's in place for tonight's affair. We can't afford any errors."

No question about that. Between their financial woes and the contracts they'd lost, there was added urgency on getting every event perfect. The next several hours flew by. Much to Catherine's relief, the intensity of the work didn't allow for thoughts of Gabe to intrude. Every ounce of concentration and effort went into putting the finishing touches on the Marconi event. More than ever she needed tonight to be a stunning success, for Natalie Marconi to rave about Elegant Events to all of her closest friends—and more importantly, her husband's business contacts.

By nine that night the party was in full swing, and Catherine worked behind the scenes, keeping everything running with smooth efficiency, while remaining as unobtrusive as possible. Having a half dozen walkie-talkies that kept all the various stations in touch with each other certainly helped with speed and communication, not to mention coordinating the progress of the party. But she always faced last-minute glitches, and tonight proved no exception.

This time around the band showed up late and the caterers underestimated the amount of champagne necessary to fill the flutes of the several hundred people who'd come to toast the Marconi patriarch. Both problems were corrected before anyone noticed, but it took some fast maneuvering, a flurry of phone calls and an exhausting combination of threats and pleas.

Catherine paused by the doorway leading outside to the staging area and, for what seemed like the fiftieth time that night, examined the checklist she'd posted there. Every aspect of the evening was listed and carefully initialed by the responsible party once it had been dealt with. She'd found the list a lifesaver on more than one occasion since it kept everyone up to date on the progress of the event, and ensured accountability. Only a few boxes remained blank. The birthday cake. A few catering chores. And, of course, the post-party cleanup.

Satisfied, she had started toward the kitchen to speak with the caterers about the cake when she felt a telltale prickle along her spine. She turned, not the least surprised to discover Gabe lounging in the doorway behind her.

For a split second, all she could do was stand and stare. That's how it had been the first time she'd seen him, too. One look stole every last ounce of sense and sensibility. He stood a full six feet two inches, with mile-wide shoulders, topping a powerful, toned body. He'd encased all that potent masculinity in formal wear, which turned his body into a lethal weapon that no woman had a chance of resisting. But it was far worse than that. Gabe Piretti also possessed the striking features of an angel coupled with the burning cobalt-blue eyes of a devil. And right now he had those predatory eyes fixed on her.

It wasn't just the raw, physical impact of the man, Catherine was forced to admit. Perhaps for some women that would be sufficient. Maybe his looks, along with the embarrassing number of digits that graced his bank account, would satisfy. But she'd always wanted something else in the man she chose as her own. She wanted a heart and a mind that worked in sync with hers. For a brief time, she'd found that with Gabe. At least, she had until he made it clear that money was his god, and what she had to offer was only icing to fill in the cracks of his multi-layered cake.

Maybe he hadn't caught her helpless reaction to his appearance, though why she even bothered to indulge in such pointless speculation, she didn't know. One glimpse of the amusement gleaming in his eyes put paid to that forlorn hope. How could she have forgotten? Gabe could read people at a single glance. It was part of what made him such a good deal-broker. No one pulled anything over on him.

Except Roxanne.

"Should I even bother to ask what you're doing here?" she asked.

A half smile eased across his mouth. "I was invited."

"Of course." She didn't doubt that for a minute. "You neglected to mention it when I saw you this morning."

He lifted a shoulder in a careless shrug. "Must have slipped my mind." His attention switched to her mouth. "I believe I was preoccupied with more important matters at the time."

"Speaking of more important matters, I have to work right now. So if you'll excuse me…" She started to press past him, but he shifted just enough to make it awkward. "Gabe, please," she whispered. "This is a really bad idea."

"I'm afraid I have to disagree with you about that." When she made another move to pass him, he pressed her against the wall, locking her in place. Tucking a loosened curl of hair behind her ear, he allowed his fingers to drift from the curve of her cheek to her mouth. And there, he lingered. "Just give me one more minute."

"Forget it, Gabe. I can't be caught necking with the guests."

"I just want to talk to you. You can spare a minute to talk, can't you?"

One minute. Sixty seconds of sheer heaven. She couldn't resist the temptation, not when those devil's eyes promised such decadent delight. "You can have thirty seconds. But no kissing the help," she warned.

His smile came slow and potent. "You look stunning tonight. That shade of bronze turns your eyes to pure gold."

It took her precious seconds to find her voice and respond with anything approaching normalcy. "I look quietly elegant," she corrected in far too husky a voice. "I work hard at looking quietly elegant so that I fit in with my surroundings without standing out."

He regarded her in amusement. "I gather standing out would be inappropriate."

"It would," she assured him.

Just another few seconds and then she'd step away from him. She'd step away and force her mind back to business. Just another moment to feel the powerful press of his body against hers. To gather up his unique scent and allow it to seep into her lungs. To lower her guard just this one time and surrender to the stir of memories, memories of what once was and what could have been, if only…

She snatched a deep breath, forcing herself to address the mundane and irreverent. With luck it would help her regain her sanity, something she'd clearly lost. "I don't want to wear something too flashy, any more than I want to wear clothing too casual for the occasion. I want the attention on the event and the participants, not on me."

"I can see your dilemma." He continued to stand close, so close that she could feel the softness of his breath against her skin. "There's only one small problem with your scenario."

"Which is?" she managed to ask.

"You could be in a burlap sack and you'd still outshine every woman here."

She shouldn't allow his flattery to affect her. And maybe she wouldn't have if she hadn't witnessed the flare of passion in his eyes and heard the ring of sincerity in his voice. She weakened, just for an instant, her body and heart softening. Yielding.

It was all the invitation he needed. He leaned into her, pressing her against the wall. And then he consumed her. If she thought the kiss they'd shared earlier had threatened to overwhelm her, it was nothing compared to this one. He knew just how to touch her to decimate every last ounce of control. He breached her defenses and slipped inside with an ease that shook her to the core.

And in that moment, he turned her world upside down.

She heard a harsh groan and couldn't tell if it emanated from his throat or hers. All she knew was that it sounded primal and desperate. She'd gone without this for too long, she was forced to concede. She'd been stripped of something she hadn't even realized she needed. He was her air. Her heartbeat. Her sustenance and her reason for being. How had she survived all this time without him?

Unable to help herself, she wrapped herself around him and gave. And then she gave more, putting all the longing and hope and despair into that one single kiss. She had no idea how long they stood there, their breath coming in urgent pants, hands groping, bodies pressing.

Perhaps she'd never have surfaced if she hadn't suddenly felt a tingling awareness that they were being watched. Shoving at his shoulders, she pushed him back, or tried to, for all the good it did her. The man was as immovable as an oak, and because of his height, he blocked her view of whomever had witnessed their embrace. All she caught was a fleeting glimpse of red.

"Playtime's over," she managed to say.

It took him a minute to release her and another one after that for her to recover her equilibrium and attempt to walk down the hallway. Thank God she'd worn sensible shoes. If she'd tried to maneuver on her usual heels, her shaky legs would have pitched her straight onto her backside. He must have picked up on the results of his handiwork because his rumble of laughter followed her down the hallway, as did he.

"Seriously, I need to work, Gabe," she said, attempting to dismiss him. She gave her walkie-talkie a cursory check to make sure she hadn't accidentally bumped the volume knob. To her relief, she saw that it was on and working just fine.

"I won't get in your way. I have a legitimate reason for following you."

"Which is?"

"I need to watch how your run your business. Just in case."

"Just in case…what?" she asked distractedly.

"Just in case you change your mind and ask for my help."

She stopped dead in her tracks and faced him. "That isn't going to happen. I can't meet your price." She shook her head. "Correction. I *won't* meet it."

He only had to lift a single eyebrow for her to consider what had happened just moments ago, and realize that her claim rang a little hollow. "Time will tell," he limited himself to saying.

She waved him aside with an impatient hand and

looked around, not sure where she was or how she'd
gotten there. What the hell had she been going to do
when he'd interrupted her? She was utterly clueless. With
an irritated sigh, she turned on her heel and headed back
the way she'd come. Giving the checklist another cursory
glance, she stepped outside. She'd do a quick walk-
through and inspect each of the various stations. Then
she'd touch bases with the caterers— She snapped her
fingers. The caterers. That's where she'd intended to go.
She needed to coordinate the presentation of the cake.

She spared Gabe a brief glance. If she turned around
yet again, she'd confirm how thoroughly he'd rattled
her, which would never do. No point in giving him that
much of an advantage. Instead, she'd keep moving
forward and circle back once she'd ditched him. She
crossed the beautifully manicured lawn toward Lake
Washington, pausing at the demarcation between grass
and imported white sand. She took a moment to gaze
out across the dark water. And all the while a painful
awareness surged through her.

"You've done an incredible job, Catherine," Gabe said
quietly. "The gondolas are a particularly special touch.
I'm sure it reminds Alessandro of his home in Italy."

Catherine smiled at the sight of the distinctive boats
and the gondoliers manning them, all of whom were
decked out in their traditional garb of black slacks,
black-and-white-striped shirts and beribboned straw
hats. Some were even singing as they rowed, maneuvering the distinctive single oar with impressive skill and
dexterity as they ferried passengers around the section

of the lake cordoned off for their use. Channel markers
fashioned to look like floating fairy lights turned the
scene into a romantic wonderland.

"It was something Natalie said that made me think
of it," Catherine explained. "I was a bit concerned about
lake traffic, but we were able to get permission to use
this small section for a few hours tonight. I even sta-
tioned security personnel in private craft directing
boaters away from the area."

"Smart, though there's a no-wake zone through here,
isn't there?"

"There's supposed to be." She shrugged. "But you
know how that can go."

Satisfied that the guests were thoroughly enjoying
their small taste of Venice, she turned her attention to
the buffet station set up on one side of the sweeping
lawn. The caterers she'd chosen specialized in authen-
tic Italian cuisine and had gone all out for the evening's
festivities. Graceful tents of silk and tulle surrounded the
groaning tables. With a stiff breeze blowing from off the
lake, the tents served the duel function of protecting the
food and keeping the fuel canisters beneath the hot
dishes from blowing out. Adjacent to the tents, linen
draped tables dotted the area, the silver cutlery and
crystal glassware gleaming softly beneath the lighting.

Catherine gave the area one final check, and was on
the verge of returning to the kitchen when she caught
sight of Roxanne. The woman stood chatting with
Natalie, while her gaze roamed the crowds, clearly
searching for someone. Catherine could make three big,

fat guesses who that someone might be and they would all center on the man standing beside her.

"I didn't realize you brought your assistant with you," she said to Gabe.

He followed her gaze and shrugged. "I didn't. I believe she's a friend of Natalie's daughter."

As though aware of the scrutiny, Roxanne homed in on Catherine…and Gabe. And then her lips curved in a killer smile, a horribly familiar one that, in the past, warned of coming trouble. Offering her hostess a quick air kiss, she excused herself and made her way toward them, undulating across the grass with her distinctive catwalk stride.

She looked fabulous, Catherine reluctantly conceded, dressed in traffic-stopping red. The bodice of her skin-tight dress bared a path of bronzed skin straight to her equator while her skirt barely covered the assets composing her southern hemispheres. She shot Catherine a challenging look, before wrapping herself around Gabe.

"Since we're not on duty…" She moistened her lips before planting a lingering kiss on his mouth. Then she pulled back and laughed up at him. "See what you've been missing? I did tell you."

He regarded his assistant with indulgent amusement. "A shame I have that rule about not mixing business with pleasure," he replied easily. "Otherwise, you'd be in serious trouble."

"Some rules are made to be broken. And in case you didn't notice, I excel at trouble." Her dark eyes sparkled. "Don't you agree?"

"That you excel at trouble?" He inclined his head. "Absolutely. Unfortunately, my rules are written in concrete. I never break them, no matter how tempting the offer."

It was a gently administered rebuff and maybe if they'd been alone, Roxanne would have taken it better. Unfortunately, Catherine's presence heaped humiliation on top of embarrassment. Deciding it was time to make a tactful retreat, Catherine offered the two her most professional smile.

"If you'll excuse me," she murmured, "I'll leave you to enjoy the party while I get back to work. If there's anything I can do to make your evening more pleasant, please don't hesitate to let me know."

With that, she made a beeline for the kitchen. Damn it. Roxanne would not appreciate her witnessing that little scene with Gabe. She could only hope that by making a swift departure, she dodged any sort of bullet fired off as retribution. She couldn't afford for anything to go wrong tonight. If Gabe's precious assistant decided to even the score a little, it could cause serious trouble for Elegant Events. Catherine managed a full dozen steps before she was caught by the arm and swung around.

"You don't want to leave now," Roxanne insisted in an undertone, anchoring her in place. "The party's just about to get interesting."

Catherine's eyes narrowed. "What are you talking about?" she demanded.

Roxanne simply smiled. "Wait for it.... Ah, right on cue."

The roar of multiple engines echoed from across the lake and a pair of bullet-shaped motorboats bore down on the area reserved for the gondolas.

Three

Catherine stared in horror. "Oh, no. No, no, no."

"Now, *that* doesn't look good," Roxanne observed with a well satisfied smile. "Maybe this part of the lake wasn't the best place to put your little boats."

At the last possible instant, the invading crafts cut their engines, sending huge swells careening among the gondolas, overturning three of them and swamping most of the others. Shrieks of panic echoed across the lake as guests, dressed in their party finery, tumbled into water that still clung to its springtime chill.

While Roxanne sauntered back toward the house, Catherine yanked her walkie-talkie from a holster clipped to the belt at her waist and depressed the mike. "I need everyone out to the lake. *Now.*" She ran toward the shoreline, even as she barked orders. Off to her left, she saw Gabe flying across the lawn toward the water, as well as several of the other men present. "There's been an accident with the gondolas. There are guests in the water. Everyone drop what you're doing and help. Davis…call marine patrol and have them dispatch emergency vehicles immediately."

Within minutes, guests and staff alike were pulling people from the water. "I want the gondoliers locating those guests who were in their individual boat," Catherine called out. Comprehension was instantaneous and the gondoliers immediately started rounding up and organizing their passengers to confirm that everyone who went into the lake had come safely out of it. "Make sure every guest is accounted for. Report to me as soon as you've counted heads."

Natalie appeared at her side. A combination of tears and fury burned in her eyes. "How could you let this happen?" she demanded. "My father-in-law is out there. My grandchildren are out there."

"Try and stay calm, Natalie. I'll have everyone accounted for in just a few minutes," Catherine attempted to reassure her.

"Calm! Don't tell me to be calm." She hovered along the edge of the grass, desperately scanning the crowd of soaked guests for family members. Tears fell as she spotted them. "If anything happens to my family or friends as a result of this, I will sue you six ways to Sunday!"

"I'm sorry, Natalie. Truly, I am. We've called the King County Marine Unit. They're on their way. The area is posted. I had boats anchored just outside the warning buoys to help direct lake traffic away from this section, but they simply drove straight through." She gestured toward the motorboats responsible. "If the marine unit catches these guys before they disappear, they'll take the appropriate action. In the meantime, all my staff is down there helping people ashore. We're going to need towels, if you have them."

"Of course I have towels," she snapped. "But that doesn't change what's happened. This is an unmitigated disaster. I was warned not to hire you, Catherine. But I liked you. You told me you could do the job and do it perfectly. You knew how important this was to me—"

Catherine never heard the rest of Natalie's comment, perhaps because it ended in a shriek as water seemed to explode around them. Sprinkler heads popped up across the lawn and shot drenching sprays over the guests, the tables and the food. Within seconds, those who hadn't been thrown in the lake were as thoroughly soaked as those who had been.

People fled in all directions. Natalie's daughter tripped over a peg anchoring one of the tents and knocked a billowing section into the hot dishes. The flame from the fuel canisters leapt onto the material and raced hungrily across the silk and tulle. If it hadn't been for the sprinklers, the entire area would have turned into an inferno.

Catherine ran to the tent, yanking at the burning section in an attempt to pull it to the grass and extinguish what flames the sprinklers weren't reaching. She felt the scorching heat lick at her hands. She'd barely managed to knock the awning to the ground, where the flames subsided with a smoky hiss, when an arm locked around her waist and swept her clear of the area. The next thing she knew she was tumbled to the grass and rolled repeatedly. She struggled against her attacker, even managing to connect with a fist to an iron-hard jaw before his hold loosened. Shoving her sopping hair from her face, she found herself pinned to the ground, nose-to-nose with Gabe.

Catherine fought for air while tears of outrage welled up in her eyes. "What the hell are you doing? Why did you tackle me?" She couldn't seem to make sense of what was happening. "I was trying to put out the flames."

"So was I. You were on fire, Catherine." He snagged the sleeve of her dress and showed her the scorch marks. Then he ripped the seam of her sleeve from wrist to shoulder and checked her skin for burns. He didn't find any, and an expression of undisguised relief flashed across his face. "Looks like I caught it in time. Another minute and you'd have been on your way to the hospital."

"I…I thought I was being attacked."

"So I gathered." He waggled his jaw from side to side. "That's one hell of a right hook you have, by the way."

She buried her head against his shoulder and fought for control. Everything had happened so fast, she couldn't make sense of it all. "I don't understand any of this, Gabe. The fire… Dear God, the tent went up so fast. If anyone had been nearby—"

He wrapped her in a tight embrace. "Easy, honey. Everyone's safe. And everyone made it out of the water without injury. Best of all, the marine unit has the boaters corralled."

She could feel her emotions slipping and struggled to hang on. Hysterics wouldn't help. Not here. Not now. She needed to keep a level head until she could get home and crawl into some dark hole. "Who were they?" She forced herself to pull free of Gabe's protective hold even though it would have been so much easier to cling. She fought her way to her knees. "And how did the sprinklers turn on? I checked them myself. They're not scheduled to start up until morning."

"I don't know." He soothed with both voice and touch. "Let's take everything one step at a time, sweetheart. I know it looks bad, but we'll figure out what happened and why."

She knelt there, soaked and shivering, as she scanned the area. Tables were overturned, chairs upended. Shards of shattered crystal and china glittered under the outdoor lights. The other tents had also been knocked askew by fleeing guests, though miracle of miracles, they hadn't caught fire as this one had. But the buffet tables had all tipped. Food littered the grass in soggy heaps. Along the outskirts of the property, people were milling, looking shell-shocked.

Dear heaven. Catherine bowed her head, defeat weighing heavy. "I guess I won't need your help saving my business, considering that my career is now officially over."

"Not necessarily." Compassion rippled through his voice. "I've turned around companies in worse predicaments."

For a split second she felt a resurgence of hope. She lifted her head to look at him. "Do you really think Elegant Events can recover from this?"

"We'll never know until we try."

Catherine took a deep breath. "In that case…" It would seem she only had one remaining option. "I don't suppose your offer from this morning is still on the table?"

Not a scrap of triumph showed in his voice or expression. "It was never off."

Early morning sunshine flooded Dina's kitchen and turned the glass insets of her cabinets into polished mirrors. "You don't have to do this, Catherine," Dina protested. "You don't have to acquiesce to whatever terms Gabriel foisted on you during a critical moment. Considering the circumstances—"

"Considering the circumstances, yes, I do," Catherine insisted. "I've always been a woman of my word, and that's not going to change just because I was under pressure last night. If anyone can salvage something from the Marconi disaster, it's Gabe. Trust me, we need someone of his caliber if we're going to keep Elegant Events from becoming known as Deadly Disasters."

Catherine leaned a hip against the countertop and tried not to think about the previous evening. It was bad enough that she'd spent the entire night with various highlights rampaging through her head. It was time to focus on solutions for the future, instead of dwelling on unalterable past events. But she couldn't seem to help herself. In the wee hours of the morning she'd reached a few unpleasant conclusions. Though she refused to accept blame for the boaters—that she could lay firmly at Roxanne's doorstep—the other incidents were the ones that troubled her the most.

It had been her initials on the checklist beside the detail that read "change the time on the automated sprinklers." She distinctly remembered doing so. In fact, she'd checked the digital read-out a second time before the party started, just to be certain. She tapped her fingers on the countertop. Maybe she'd made a mistake. Maybe she'd pushed p.m. instead of a.m., even though at the time she'd been very careful to avoid just such a mistake.

And then there'd been the tent peg. She couldn't blame that one on Roxanne, either. She'd seen Natalie's daughter trip over the anchor rope and uproot the peg. Granted, the wet ground might have loosened it. But it was her responsibility to make certain such incidents didn't happen. Period. That was the entire premise behind her business.

"I know what you're doing, and you have to stop it, Catherine." Dina crossed to her side and gave her a swift hug. "You're going to drive yourself into exhaustion over something that wasn't your fault, and that's not going to help. Let's deal with one issue at a time, starting with…" She pulled back. "What, exactly, did you promise Gabriel, if you don't mind my asking?"

"That I'd move in with him." Just saying the words

was hard enough. She had no idea how she'd be able to handle the reality of living with him again. "I promised I'd stay with him until he figured a way to turn Elegant Events around. Though after last night—"

"As you said yourself, if anyone can do it, it's Gabriel."

"I don't doubt he'll be able to figure out why the business is losing money."

"It is his specialty," his mother admitted. "When he took over Piretti's he nailed the financial end of our problems and plugged the leaks within a month. He's only gotten better since. He can take apart a company and put it together again better than anyone I've ever seen. He's even better at it than his father."

"That's what I'm counting on. It's our other problems that he's going to find a bit more difficult. If we can't figure out why we're unable to nail certain key contracts, how can he? And now, after the Marconi incident, that may not even matter. Somehow we're going to have to come up with a dynamite scheme to rebuild our reputation." She eyed Dina grimly. "I'm expecting a slew of cancelations the minute word gets out. And I doubt our contract is sufficiently bulletproof to keep them from walking."

"Gabriel might be able to talk them around."

"Someone better be able to."

"So what's the next step?" Dina asked. "Where do we go from here."

Catherine rubbed at the headache pounding against her temples. "I have a meeting with Gabe in just under an hour. We're supposed to discuss strategy. I'd like you to continue to man the office, if you don't mind. You've always been incredible at sweet-talking the customers when they call."

Dina's smile flashed. "I give great phone."

For the first time in what seemed like forever, Catherine laughed. It felt wonderful, almost a purging. "Yes, you do," she agreed. "If you would do your best to give unbelievable phone today, I'd be grateful."

"Anything I can do to help. You know that."

"Yes, I do." She caught Dina's hand in hers. "How can I thank you for all you've done? Not just for today, but for every day over these past two years."

The older woman shook her head. "There's nothing to thank me for."

"Please. Let me say this." Tears filled Catherine's eyes, as unexpected as they were unwanted, no doubt the result of exhaustion. "You took me in at a time I desperately needed someone. And you took me in despite the fact that I was leaving your son. You let me live here and took care of me during those first couple of months until I felt well enough to find my own place. Not only have you been a friend, but you've been the mother I never had."

"Oh, sweetheart, now you're going to make me cry. No one should lose their mother, especially not at such a young, impressionable age. If I've been able to fill in for her, even in the smallest capacity, I'm more than happy to do it. I just wish…" She caught her lip between her teeth, her expression one of intense guilt. "I have a confession to make."

"Let me guess. You weren't being altruistic when you took me in all those months ago? You did it because you were hoping Gabe and I would eventually patch things up?"

"You knew?"

"Let's say I suspected."

"I hope you're not offended."

Catherine shook her head. "Not at all." With a small exclamation, she wrapped her arms around the woman she'd once thought would be her mother-in-law and gave her a fierce hug. "Thank you for everything. Just don't get your hopes up about me and Gabe. It's only temporary. After a few months he'll realize that my leaving two years ago was inevitable. We simply aren't right for each other."

"I'm sure that's precisely what you'll discover. And I'm so sorry you've been forced into this predicament."

"Dina?"

"Yes, dear?"

"You do realize that your kitchen cabinets have glass insets, don't you?"

"Yes. I chose them myself."

"And you also realize that in this light, the glass acts like a mirror?"

"Does it?"

"I'm afraid it does. I'd have an easier time believing you felt badly about my moving back in with Gabriel if I couldn't see you pumping your fist in the air."

"I'm not pumping my fist," Dina instantly denied. "I'm giving you a totally sympathetic, albeit enthusiastic, air pat."

"I can still see you. Now you're grinning like a maniac."

"I'm just trying to put a happy face on your moving back in with Gabriel. Inside, I'm crying for you."

Catherine pulled back. "It's temporary, Dina. We're not back together again."

Dina's smile grew wicked. "Try and tell Gabriel that and see how far it gets you."

Forty-five minutes later, Catherine swept off the elevator at Piretti's and headed for Gabe's office. She'd dressed carefully in a forest-green silk suit jacket and matching A-line skirt, completing the ensemble with a pair of mile-high heels. It was one of her favorite outfits, mainly because it served as a complementary foil to her hair and eyes. The formfitting style also made the most of her subtle curves.

She'd spent the drive into the city planning how best to handle the upcoming encounter with Roxanne in the hopes it would take her mind off a far more serious issue—her upcoming encounter with Gabe. Though she'd agreed to move in with him, she hadn't agreed to anything beyond that. Before she packed a single bag, she intended to set a few ground rules, which put her at a disadvantage right off the bat. Gabe, she reluctantly conceded, was one of the best negotiators she'd ever met and if she had any hope at all in gaining the upper hand, she'd need some leverage.

To her surprise, Roxanne was nowhere in sight. Considering how hard Gabe's assistant had worked at turning the Marconi party into a grade-A disaster, perhaps she'd taken the day off to get some much-needed rest and restock on what must be a dwindling supply of venom and spite. Well, they'd have their little chat soon enough, Catherine decided. She'd make certain of that. It wouldn't matter all that much if it waited a day or two.

The door to Gabe's office was open, and Catherine paused on the threshold. He stood in profile to her in front of a bank of windows overlooking Puget Sound and she drank in the sight while heat exploded low in her belly and fanned outward to the most inconvenient places. For a split second her vision tilted and she saw, not a captain of high finance and industry, but the captain of a pirate ship.

At some point, he'd shed his suit jacket and rolled up the sleeves of his snowy shirt, exposing the bronzed skin of his forearms. His tie had long ago been ripped from its anchor around his neck and discarded, and he'd unbuttoned his shirt, revealing the broad, powerful chest she'd so often rested her head against. With his feet planted wide and his hands fisted on his hips, all he needed was a cutlass strapped to his side to complete the image. As it was, he barked out orders with all the arrogance of a pirate. But instead of it being to a crew of scallywags, he had a wireless headset hooked over his ear.

"Tell Felder the offer is good for precisely twenty-four hours." Gabe checked his watch, which told her that those hours would be timed to the minute. "After that, I won't be interested in restructuring, let alone a buyout,

regardless of how he sweetens the pot." He disconnected
the call and turned to face her, not appearing the least
surprised to find her standing there. "Right on time.
I've always appreciated that about you, Catherine."

She waded deeper into his office. "I have a lot to
do today, so I didn't see any point in wasting either
of our time."

"*We* have a lot to do," he corrected. "I've rescheduled
my appointments today so we can formulate a tentative
game plan for Elegant Events."

She made a swift recalibration, mentally rearranging
a few appointments of her own. "Thank you. I appreciate your taking the time."

"It's what we agreed to, isn't it?"

He tilted his head to one side and the sunlight made
his eyes burn a blue so brilliant and iridescent, it scattered every thought but one. She was moving back in
with this man. Soon she'd share his life in the most
private and personal ways possible. Share his home.
Share space he'd marked as his. And though he'd never
come right out and said it, she didn't have a single doubt
that he also expected her to share his bed.

It had seemed so natural before. Hasty breakfasts
that combined food and coffee and brief, passionate
kisses that would—barely—get them through the day
before they were able to fall on each other again in the
waning hours of the evening. Long, romantic dinners,
though those became more and more rare as work
intruded with increasing frequency. The heady, desperate, mind-blowing lovemaking. The simple intimacy of

living with someone day in and day out. She'd experienced all that with him. Wanted it. Wanted, even more, to take their relationship to the next level. Instead, they'd been unable to sustain even that much of a connection.

How could she go back to what hadn't worked before? How could she pretend that their relationship had a snowball's chance in hell of succeeding when she knew that it didn't. What had happened in the past colored too much of the present for them to ever go back. She bit down on her lip. They couldn't even forge a new, different sort of bond. It simply had no future, only a very brief, very finite now.

"Catherine?" He stepped closer. "It is what we agreed, isn't it? My help in return for your moving back in with me?"

"Gabe—" she began.

His expression hardened. "Reneging already?"

"No. I made a promise, and I'll keep it." She met his gaze, silently willing him to change his mind, to see the impossibility of his plan ever succeeding. "But you need to understand something before we take this any further. Whatever you have planned, whatever you hope to accomplish by forcing us together again, isn't going to work. You can't force a relationship."

He smiled his angel's smile while the devil gleamed in his eyes. "And you need to understand something as well. It won't take any force. All I have to do is touch you, just as all you have to do is touch me. That's all it will take, Cate. One touch and neither of us will be able to help ourselves."

She shuddered. "Then I'll have to make certain that one touch doesn't happen."

"It's already happened. It happened the minute you set foot in my office yesterday. It happened again last night during the party. You're just not willing to admit it." He reached out and tucked a loosened lock of hair behind her ear before trailing his thumb along the curve of cheek. He'd done that last night. And just as it had last night, a shaft of fire followed in the wake of his caress, forcing her to lock her knees in place in order to remain standing. "At least, you're not willing to admit it…yet."

His touch numbed her brain, making logical thought an impossibility. It had always been that way. Even so, she fought to remember what she'd planned to say to him. "We haven't set up ground rules," she managed to protest. "We need to negotiate terms."

"The terms are already set. We live together, fully and completely, with all that suggests and implies," he stated. "Now stop delaying the inevitable and let's get to work."

She lifted an eyebrow and stepped clear of his reach. It was like stepping from the deck of a ship riding turbulent seas to the calm and safety of dry land. It only took a moment to regain her balance. "Strictly business?"

He regarded her in open amusement. "Here and now, yes." He leaned in. "But what happens tonight will have nothing to do with business."

The breath stuttered in her lungs as an image of them flashed through her mind. Naked limbs entwined. Mouths fused. Male and female melding into the most intimate of bonds. How the hell did he expect her to work with that stuck in her brain?

He must have known what she was thinking because he laughed. "Don't feel bad. You're not the only one."

"Not the only one…what?"

"Who's going to find it difficult to concentrate on business today."

"That's a first," she muttered.

His amusement faded. "Not really. It just hasn't happened for a while. Not in about twenty-three months." He took a deep breath and shoved his fingers through his hair. "If your situation weren't so serious, I'd say to hell with it and have us both blow off work."

Interesting. "What would that accomplish?"

"It would give us an opportunity to get our priorities straight," he explained. "Because this time I intend to fix what went wrong."

A deep yearning filled her at the thought, one that shocked her with its intensity. Pain followed fast on its heels. He'd waited too long to compromise. Now, when it didn't matter any longer, when regaining what they'd lost had become an impossibility, he was willing to change. "We can't afford to blow off work and you know it."

"Unfortunately, we can't, no. At least, not today. And since we can't…" And just like that he switched from lover to businessman. "Let's see what we can do to salvage Elegant Events."

It took her a moment longer to switch gears. "After last night's fiasco, I expect cancelations," she warned. "A lot of them."

"You have contracts with your clients?"

"Of course. I'm not an idiot, Gabe." She closed her eyes. "I'm sorry. That was uncalled for. Blame it on exhaustion."

He let it slide without comment. "Set up appointments with those who want to cancel. Tell them that if they'll meet with you and give you a full thirty minutes of their time, and you still can't reach an amicable agreement, then you'll happily refund their deposit."

Catherine paled. "You realize what that'll mean? We'll go under if I can't salvage more than seventy-five percent of our current bookings." She rubbed a hand across her forehead. "And even that number might be wishful thinking. It could be closer to ninety."

"I can give you a more accurate figure once I examine the accounts. Who's in charge of them?"

"My partner."

His eyes narrowed. "Ah, the mysterious co-owner. You realize you can't keep her identity hidden after last night. Schedule a meeting with her. If we're going to turn your business around, I'll need to know everything about it from the ground up. And that includes whatever you can tell me about your partner."

Catherine reluctantly nodded. "I'll arrange it. What's next?"

"Next, I called Natalie Marconi, and she agreed to see us in…" He checked his watch. "An hour and a quarter. You'll be expected to tender an abject apology." He held up a hand before she could interrupt. "I know you took care of that last night, but it needs to be done again in the cold light of day. I doubt anything we do or say will help, but—"

"But we need to try."

He picked up his tie from where he'd draped it over his desk chair. "Exactly."

She shot Gabe a keen-eyed look. "Somehow I suspect she would have refused to see me if you hadn't placed the call." She didn't wait for him to confirm what she already knew. "Just so you're aware, I plan to give her a full refund."

Snagging his suit jacket, he shrugged it on. "How bad a bite is that going to take out of your reserves?"

She didn't want to think about it. "A big one," she admitted. "Not that it matters. It has to be done."

"Agreed." A hint of sympathy colored the word. He guided her from his office out into the foyer and paused beside Roxanne's vacant desk. "Let's see if meeting with her won't help you retain a small portion of goodwill."

"Where's your assistant?" Catherine asked casually while he scribbled Roxanne a quick note. At least, she hoped the question came across as casual. Considering what she'd like to do to his precious assistant, she was lucky it didn't sound as though she was chewing nails.

"In the field. I've spent the past six months negotiating a takeover of a plant that manufactures boat engines. It'll dovetail nicely with another company I own that custom-designs yachts. Right now we outsource quite a number of components. I'd like to change that."

"So you're busily acquiring businesses that manufacture those outsourced components."

"Exactly." He propped the note on Roxanne's computer keyboard before walking with Catherine to the bank of elevators. "Roxanne is working to set up a meeting to hammer out the final details. For some reason the owner, Jack LaRue, has been dragging his feet, and I need to find out why and resolve whatever issues remain. Roxanne has a way of…" He shrugged. "Let's just say, she can motivate people to stop dragging their feet."

"Got it."

The elevator doors parted and they stepped inside. "You've never cared for her, have you?" he asked.

What was the point in lying after all this time? "No."

"Is it because she took over your job? Or is it a woman thing?"

Catherine stared straight ahead and counted to ten before responding. "Call it a clash of personalities."

"Sorry. I don't buy that. What's the real reason?"

She faced him. "The truth?"

"No, I want you to lie to me."

Catherine released her breath in a frustrated sigh. "I resented having to go through her to speak to you. I resented that she had the power to decide which of those messages she'd deliver and when she'd deliver them. I also resented the fact that she didn't just want to take over my job, she wanted to take over my place in your life. Is that reason enough?"

Four

Before Gabe could respond, the elevator doors parted and Catherine exploded from the car. Her heels beat a furious tattoo across the garage surface, a beat that echoed the anger chasing through her. She hadn't realized until then how long those words had choked her and how badly she'd wanted to speak them. But now that she had, she realized they wouldn't make the least difference. He wouldn't believe her now any more than he had two years ago. When it came to Roxanne, he was as blind to her true nature as every other man.

Catherine paused beside Gabe's Jag and struggled to regain her self-control. How the hell did Roxanne do it? It wasn't just her looks. Plenty of women had incredible bodies, as well as faces that could have graced a god-

dess. Maybe it was the body combined with a Machia-
vellian brain that would have done Lucretia Borgia
proud that gave Roxanne such an edge.

Gabe opened the car door and waited while Catherine slid in before circling the car and climbing behind
the wheel. Instead of igniting the powerful engine, he
swiveled to face her. "I'm sorry. I had no idea she was
such a problem for you."

"She isn't a problem. Not any longer."

"And I'll make certain of that. When you call, I'll
give her strict instructions to put you straight through,
even if I'm in a meeting."

"You don't have to do that."

"Yes, I do."

It took Catherine a moment to steady her breathing.
"Why, Gabe?" she whispered. "Why couldn't you have
done this before when it first came up? Why now when
it's far too late?"

His jaw firmed, taking on an all-too familiar stubborn
slant. "It's not too late." He started the engine with a
roar. "You walked out on me for good cause. I admit
there were problems. Serious problems. This time
around, I intend to fix them."

The drive to the Marconi estate took just under an
hour. A maid, all starched and formal, escorted them to
an equally starched and formal parlor that overlooked
the scene of last night's disaster. Catherine didn't doubt
for a moment that the uncomfortable choice of venue
was deliberate.

"I'm not quite sure why you're here," Natalie said,

once they were seated. She made a point of not offering them refreshments by pouring herself a cup of coffee from the gleaming silver service on the table at her side and taking a slow, deliberate sip. Her coldly furious eyes moved from Catherine to Gabe and back again. "I'm particularly in the dark about your presence, Gabe. It's Ms. Haile who owes me both an explanation and an apology."

"You're absolutely right, Mrs. Marconi." Catherine spoke up before Gabe could. "I do owe you an apology, and I can't begin to express how sorry I am that your party was ruined." She opened her purse, removed a check and placed it on the delicate coffee table that served as a buffer between her chair and Natalie's. "This is a full refund."

Twin spots of color chased across Natalie's cheekbones. "You think throwing money at me is going to fix this?"

"Not at all. I think refunding your money is the least I can do to compensate for my part in what happened. I'm sorry the security detail I hired was unable to intercept the intruders. I contacted the authorities this morning, and they informed me that the young men on the boats received an invitation from an unidentified woman. They're continuing to look into it in the hopes of pinning down precisely who extended the invite, in case you wish to pursue the matter. The boaters involved have volunteered to recompense your guests, as well as the gondola company, for any damages incurred."

"That will certainly help," she reluctantly admitted.

"And the sprinklers? That mistake is one hundred percent your fault."

Catherine inclined her head. "I accept full responsibility for that. I promise you, I double-checked to make sure they'd been disengaged for the evening. I can't explain how they were switched back on."

"I can. You're incompetent."

"Natalie," Gabe said softly.

"Well, what other explanation is there?" she retorted defensively.

"I can think of three. One, there was a power interruption and the device returned to its default setting. Two, someone accidentally changed the time. Or three, someone did it deliberately as a prank." He paused to allow that to sink in. "There were a lot of youngsters there last night who might have considered it quite a lark to have the sprinklers go on in the middle of the party and watch the mayhem from a safe distance."

Natalie sat up straighter, her eyes flashing. "Are you accusing someone in my family?"

"I'm not the one making accusations." He let that hang. "I'm simply pointing out that there are alternative explanations."

"Catherine's initials were on the checklist as the one responsible for resetting the sprinklers. I saw them there myself."

"Which means she did reset them. Why else would she have initialed it? Twice, I might add." Natalie fell silent at the sheer logic of his question. He pressed home his advantage. "You'd have more cause to point fingers if it hadn't been checked off because then you'd know she'd overlooked it."

Natalie dismissed that with a wave of her hand. "And the tent going up in flames? We could have lost our house. People could have been seriously injured, or worse."

"Your daughter tripped over the line anchoring that corner of the tent. I saw it happen. I'm sure if you ask her, she'll admit as much, especially since she twisted her ankle as a result and your son-in-law had to carry her to safety. There is no negligence here, Natalie. It was a simple, unforeseeable accident."

"On the other hand," Catherine inserted, "the point of hiring an event planner is to foresee the unforeseeable and take precautions."

Gabe turned on her. "In hindsight, what could you have done differently to prevent those accidents from happening? You'd already checked the sprinkler system. Twice. That section of the lake was posted and patrolled. And the tent was securely anchored."

Natalie released her breath in a sigh. "All right, all right. You've made your point, Gabe. I don't see how Catherine could have possibly foreseen any of those eventualities. I wish she could have, but I like to consider myself an honest and fair woman. And honesty and fairness compel me to admit that no one could have anticipated such a bizarre string of events." She looked at Catherine, this time without the anger coloring her expression. "Thank you for returning my fee and for your apology. Up until all hell broke loose, the event was brilliantly planned and executed."

Catherine stood. "I appreciate your understanding. I'd say I look forward to doing business with you at some point in the future…" She offered a self-deprecating smile. "But I have a feeling I might find a cup of that lovely coffee poured over my head."

Natalie managed a smile as well. "Good try, my dear, but there's little to no chance of my being quite that forgiving."

Catherine shrugged. "It was worth a try." She held out a hand. "Thank you for taking the time to see me."

"You can thank Gabe for that. I'm not sure I would have agreed if not for him." Her gaze swept over him, filled with pure feminine appreciation. "For some strange reason, it's impossible to say no to the man."

Catherine released a sigh of exasperation. "So, I've discovered," she murmured.

After leaving the Marconi residence, Gabe handed Catherine a business card for a transportation firm, along with the key to his apartment. "I've made arrangements with this company to move your belongings over to my place. Just call them when you're ready."

"I won't have that much," she protested, as they headed back toward the city. "Just a couple of suitcases."

He pulled onto the floating bridge that spanned Lake Washington and negotiated smoothly around oncoming traffic. "I want you to feel like you live there, not like you're a temporary guest."

"I am a temporary guest," she retorted. "The only one who doesn't realize that is you."

He didn't bother to argue. But when he pulled up in front of her apartment complex, he parked the car and exited at the same time Catherine did. He followed her across the sidewalk and up the stairs leading to the vestibule.

"You don't need to come in," she informed him over her shoulder. "I'll call the moving company if that will satisfy you."

One look at his set face warned that she wouldn't get rid of him that easily. "You'd rather have this discussion out here on a public street?" he asked with painful politeness.

"In all honesty, I'd rather not have this discussion at all," she replied.

"I'm afraid that's not one of the options available to you."

She hated when he donned his business persona. There was no opposing him. "I've agreed to your terms. What more do you want?" He simply stood and stared, and she released her breath in an irritated rush. "Fine. Let's go inside."

She led the way, choosing to take the steps to her second-floor apartment, rather than the elevator. She paused at the appropriate door and unlocked it. "Would you like a cup of the coffee Natalie didn't offer us before you leave?"

He lifted an eyebrow. "Here's your hat, what's your hurry?"

Her mouth quivered in amusement. "Something like that."

"No, what I want is to clarify a few things." He paced through the confines of her tiny living area, studying first the view, and then her furnishings. "Cozy."

"I don't require a lot of space." She dropped her keys in a green blown-glass bowl on a table near the front door. "Probably because I don't take up anywhere near as much room as you."

He turned. "Sometimes I forget how small you are. It must have something to do with that strong, passionate personality of yours."

The compliment knocked her off-kilter, and she didn't want to be off-kilter. She folded her arms across her chest. "Do you really think it's going to make the least difference to our relationship whether I move two suitcases' worth of possessions into your place or two truckloads? Possessions won't keep me there. Not when our relationship falls apart again."

He ignored that final barbed shot. "Having personal possessions around you will make you feel more comfortable. And maybe if you're more comfortable, you'll be more inclined to work through our difficulties rather than run from them."

"I didn't run the first time, Gabe."

His jaw tightened. "Didn't you? It looked like running to me. It felt like it. One minute you were there and the next you were gone. No warning. Not even a phone call."

"I left a note," she retorted, stung.

"I remember." He stalked closer. "I got home after forty-eight straight hours of a brutal work crisis that could have meant the end of Piretti's and found it waiting for me."

"What do you mean…that could have meant the end of Piretti's?" she asked in alarm. "I thought it was one of your takeovers on the verge of imploding."

"No, it was an attempted coup staged by Piretti's former board members, the ones I'd kicked out after staging my own coup. Not that it matters." He returned to his point with dogged determination. "What you did was cold, Catherine."

"You're right, it was," she conceded. "And I'm sorry for that. Someday ask me about the brutal forty-eight hours I experienced leading up to that decision. It was cold because I was cold. Cold and empty and—" She stemmed the flow of words before she said too much. She wouldn't go there with him. Didn't have the emotional stamina, even now. Even after nearly two years, she couldn't face the memories with anything approaching equanimity.

"And what? You were cold and empty and…what?" he pressed.

"Broken. Sick and broken."

She forced the words out, then busied herself opening her briefcase and removing the file on Elegant Events that she'd offered Gabe the day before. His hand dropped over hers, forcing her to set the papers aside.

"Is that why you went to stay with my mother? Because you were sick and broken?"

"I didn't have any other family," she whispered. "I didn't have anywhere else to—"

His grip gentled. "You don't have to justify it. I'm relieved that you felt comfortable going to her."

"Really?" She searched his expression, seeking reassurance. "I'm surprised you didn't give her a hard time about taking me in."

His head jerked as though she'd slapped him. "Was I such a bastard that you think I'd do such a thing to you? I'm relieved to know you had a place. To know you were safe." Then he asked the one question she dreaded most. "You said you were sick. What was wrong with you?"

"Nothing that a little tender loving care couldn't cure."

"Care I didn't offer you."

She met his gaze dead-on. "No, you didn't."

"That's going to change." He waved aside her incipient response. "I know you don't believe me. Only time will convince you otherwise, and I'm hoping the next few months will do just that."

There was no point arguing, not when he was right. Only time would give them the proof they needed...proof that they *didn't* belong together. "Fair enough."

"Call the number on the business card, Catherine," he urged. "They've been paid regardless of how much or how little you bring. And all you have to do is point out the things you want transferred. They'll pack, load and transport, and then reverse the process once they get everything over to my place."

"Thank you," she said with in a stiff voice. "That's very generous of you."

He frowned. "Don't. Please, don't."

She closed her eyes for an instant. "I'm sorry. We've

been apart so long, and—" She shook her head in bewilderment. "I don't know how to handle this."

"Then I'll show you how to handle it. It's easy." He cupped her face and feathered a kiss across her mouth. It was soft and gentle and drove every ounce of common sense straight out of her head. "See how easy?"

"I still don't—"

She never completed the sentence. She never even completed the thought. It faded away, forever lost. His mouth returned to hers, and the tenor of the kiss changed, grew more potent. He slipped a small demand into the embrace, urging a response she was helpless to resist. So she didn't resist. After that it seemed such a small step to go from reluctant response to active participation. To meet his demand and make one of her own. To give. To take. To nudge up the heat ever so slightly.

She felt the tilt, the inner shift from submission to aggression. She slid her arms across his chest and shoved at his suit jacket. She caught the whisper of silk as it slipped away. Not breaking contact, she yanked his tie from its mooring, ripping at the knot until it followed the same path as his jacket. Plucking at the buttons of his shirt, she finally, *finally*, hit hot, firm flesh.

Heaven help her, but he was built. Her mouth slid from his and traced a pathway along his corded throat and downward. She felt the groan vibrating beneath her lips and smiled. She remembered that sound, the pleasure it gave her to be the cause. To thrill at the knowledge that her touch could drive a man of Gabe's strength of will to lose total control.

Even now she felt him teetering on the brink and caught herself hovering there as well. She had just enough awareness to realize she had a choice. She could finish what she'd started, or she could pull back. Part of her, the part that longed to feel Gabe's hands on her again and experience anew that incredible rush when their bodies joined, urged her to continue. But there were too many issues between them for her to give in so quickly and easily.

As though sensing her hesitation, he gave a push of his own. "I've missed you, Catherine," he murmured roughly. He followed the tailored line of her suit, reacquainting himself with familiar territory. Fire splashed in the wake of his touch. "And I've missed this."

She wouldn't be able to hold out much longer. It was now or never. With a reluctant sigh, she pulled back and felt the first tiny shudder of her common sense returning. "You don't fight fair," she complained. She gave his chest a final nipping kiss and stepped clear of his embrace. "I guess you think this proves your point."

"If I could remember what the hell my point was, I'd agree with you. But since every ounce of blood has drained from my head to places lacking brain cells, I don't think that's going to happen." He lifted a sooty eyebrow. "I don't suppose you remember what my point was?"

"Can't say that I do."

He grinned. "Liar."

She cleared her throat. "It might have been that living together again will be like riding a bicycle. Once we start pedaling, the moves will come back to us."

"I have to admit, I don't remember that part of our conversation, but it sounds good to me." His eyes sharpened, the blue growing more intense. "The business card. The movers. Your doubts."

She smiled with something approaching affection. "Ah, there he is. Back to business-as-usual."

His mouth twitched in an answering smile. Not that it kept him from staying on target this time round. "How about this. Have the movers take less than I'm asking and more than you want. Is that a reasonable compromise?"

"Yes."

"Does that mean yes, you'll do it?"

She nodded. "I should be there well before dinnertime."

Satisfaction settled over him. "Perfect. I've arranged for something special for tonight." He tapped the tip of her nose with his index finger. "And no, I didn't mean anything sexual, so don't go all indignant on me."

"Hmm." She tilted her head to one side and scrutinized him through narrowed eyes. "Despite your assurances, I somehow suspect you'll get there later, if not sooner."

"You can count on it." The promise glittered like sapphires in his gaze and gave the hard angle of his jaw an uncompromising set. "But in this case I was actually talking about dinner."

"You don't have to do anything special," she protested.

He hooked her chin with his knuckle so they were eye-to-eye. "Yes," he assured her. "I do. I'll see you about six."

The rest of the day flew by. Giving in to the inevitable, she phoned the movers. She barely hung up the phone before two burly men arrived on her doorstep. It was almost as easy as shopping on the Internet. They were user-friendly, and all she had to do was point and click. In no time they had far too many of her possessions packed and carted down to their moving truck. Just as Gabe predicted, the other end of the procedure proved equally as painless.

The one uncomfortable moment came when they asked where they should put her clothing. She briefly debated whether to direct them to one of the spare bedrooms, or to Gabe's master suite. Considering the close call she and Gabe had experienced back at her apartment, it seemed pointless to take a stand she suspected wouldn't last more than a single night. Even though she knew that nothing would come of their relationship—that nothing *could* come of it—she might as well enjoy the fantasy while it lasted.

The instant the door closed behind the movers, she finished the few unpacking chores she preferred to see to herself. Then she took a leisurely tour of Gabe's penthouse suite. It felt peculiar to be back again. Part of her felt right at home, as though she'd never left.

There was the table where she used to sit and keep track of their social calendar and plan the parties that had become her specialty. And in the window seat over there, she and Gabe would curl up together on a quiet Sunday morning over a steaming cup of coffee while they watched the rain pound the city. And over there… How many times had they entertained guests in the living room? Gabe would sit in that enormous chair he'd had specially designed, and she'd squeeze into a corner next to him.

Of course, there were a few changes. A different set of throw pillows were scattered on the sofa. She came across a gorgeous wooden sculpture that hadn't been there before. It was of a woman in repose and made her itch to run her fingertips along the graceful, sweeping lines. The drapes were new, as were a pair of planters on either side of the front door.

After delaying the inevitable as long as she could, she gathered her nerve and entered the bedroom, only to discover this room showed the most changes of all. The previous bed and furniture, darkly masculine pieces, had been removed, and Gabe had replaced them with furnishings made with a golden teak heartwood that brought to mind sailing ships from the previous century. Catherine couldn't help but smile. Nothing could have suited him better, though she couldn't help but wonder why he'd replaced his previous bedroom set.

To her surprise, the changes brought her a sense of relief, as though all the old, negative energy had been swept clean. Checking her watch, she realized that Gabe would be home in just under an hour and if he'd planned something special for their dinner, maybe she should consider dressing for the occasion.

She took her time primping, finally settling on a casual floor-length sheath in an eye-catching turquoise. For the first time in ages, she left her hair loose and flowing, a tidal wave of springy curls that tumbled down her back in reckless abandon. She touched up her makeup, giving her eyes and mouth a bit more emphasis.

She'd just finished when the doorbell rang, and she went to answer it, fairly certain it was whatever dinner surprise Gabe had arranged. Sure enough, it proved to be a small catering company that she'd used for a few of her events. She greeted the chef by name and showed her and her companion to the kitchen.

"Gabe said we were to get here right at six and serve no later than six-thirty," Sylvia explained. "It'll only take a few minutes to unload the appetizers and get them heated. In the meantime, I'll open the wine and let it breathe while Casey sets the dining room table. She'll be serving you tonight."

"Thanks," Catherine said with a warm smile. "I'll be in the living room. Gabe should be home any minute."

Or so she thought. By six-thirty, she'd nibbled her way through any number of appetizers that she was certain should have tasted like ambrosia, but for some reason had the flavor and consistency of sawdust. At a quarter to seven Sylvia appeared in the doorway. "Should I hold dinner a little longer? I'm afraid to wait too long or it'll be overcooked."

"Hold off for fifteen more minutes. If he's not here by then, you can wrap everything up and stash it in the fridge."

"Oh. Oh, sure. We can do that."

Catherine flinched at the unmistakable pity in the other woman's voice. "Thanks, Sylvia. I'll be in the bedroom if you need me."

Keeping her chin high, she marched to the master

suite and gently closed the door. Then she proceeded to remove her belongings and transfer them to one of the guest bedrooms. Why, oh why, had she allowed herself to believe for even one single second that he'd changed? Nothing had changed. Business always came first with Gabe and it always would.

From deep inside the apartment the phone rang. More than anything, she wanted to ignore it. But it would only make matters worse if she allowed the answering machine to take the call so that Sylvia and Casey could overhear whatever excuse Gabe cared to offer for his delay.

She picked up the bedroom extension. "Hello?"

"I'm sorry." Gabe's voice rumbled across the line. "This wasn't how I planned our first night together."

She held on to her self-control by a shred. "I'm sure it wasn't."

"You're furious, and I don't blame you. That deal I told you about earlier came to a head. Roxanne managed to get LaRue to the table, and this was the only time he'd agree to."

"I'll bet."

"It's going to be a while. I'll be home as soon as I can."

She heard the unspoken question and answered it. "I promised I'd be here, and I will. The rest we'll negotiate in the morning."

He swore softly. "This will be the last time."

She shook her head in disbelief. He still didn't get it. "You think it will, Gabe. That's part of the problem. You always think that next time will be different. But it never is, is it?"

She didn't wait for his response, but hung up. She needed to inform the caterers that their services wouldn't be required. But first, she needed a moment to herself. A moment to grieve over the death of a tiny blossom of hope that had somehow, at some point when she wasn't looking, managed to unfurl deep in her heart.

Five

It was two in the morning before Gabe keyed open the lock to his apartment. Catherine had left a light burning for him, the one by the sculpture of the sleeping woman—a sculpture whose gentle curves and sleek, soft lines reminded him vividly of her. It was why he'd bought the damn thing, even though he suspected it would torment him every time he looked at it. And it did.

Turning off the light, he headed directly for the bedroom, pulling up short when he realized Catherine wasn't there. For a single, hideous moment, he flashed back on the night she'd left him. His gaze shot to the dresser, half expecting to see another crisp white envelope with his name neatly scripted across the front. Of course, it wasn't there. Nor was the dresser. Within a week of her departure, memories too painful to bear had him replacing every stick of furniture in the room.

Stripping off his suit jacket and tie, he went in search of Catherine. He found her in the spare bedroom farthest from the master suite. She sat at a small antique desk by the window, her head pillowed in her arms, sound asleep. She wore a long, sweeping silk nightgown in a stunning shade of aqua, covered by a matching robe.

Gabe silently approached and glanced at the papers littering the desk beneath and around her. They were accounting records, he realized, and he tugged free a few of the sheets. As he glanced down the rows and across the columns, a frown knit his brow. Hell, she was skating precariously close to disaster. First thing tomorrow, he'd take a closer look at this and see just how close to the edge she'd come and what it would take to turn it around…assuming that was even possible.

Tossing the pages aside, he circled the desk and gently tipped her out of the chair and into his arms. She stirred within his hold, but didn't awaken until he reached their bedroom and eased her onto the bed. She stared up at him in confusion, her golden eyes heavy with exhaustion and brimming with vulnerability.

"What…?"

"You fell asleep at your desk."

He saw the instant her memory snapped back into place, watching with keen regret as her defenses came slamming down. She bolted upright. "What am I doing in your bed? How did I get here?" she demanded.

"You're in my bed because it's where you belong,"

he explained calmly. "And you got here because I carried you here."

"Well, you can just carry me back, because I'm not staying."

He toed off his shoes without saying a word. Then he proceeded to strip. He was one article of clothing away from baring it all when she erupted off the bed.

"You're not listening, Gabe. I'm not sleeping with you."

"Then don't sleep," he retorted mildly. "But when we go to bed, we'll be doing it together."

She shook her head, and her sleep-tangled curls danced in agitation. "You stood me up tonight. You promised me this time would be different and then you stood me up." The vulnerability he'd seen earlier leaked through her defenses, nearly killing him. "You can't do that and then expect me to—" She waved a hand in the direction of the bed.

"Just for my own edification, is this how I'm supposed to react when the shoe is on the other foot?" he asked.

That stopped her, if only for a moment. "What do you mean?"

"I mean that your business is as demanding as mine. Most of your events take place in the evening or on the weekend when I'm off work. Having spent the past two years building up your business, you know there are times when the unexpected arises and you have no choice but to deal with it."

"Damn you!" She glared at him in frustration. "I'm not in the mood for your brand of logic. You can't turn this back on me."

"I'm not trying to. I'm trying to make you see that every once in a while something like this is going to happen. We'd better learn to deal with it starting right here and right now. Tonight was on me, and I'm sorry, Cate. I'm more sorry than you can possibly know. I wanted your homecoming to be special, and instead it was a nightmare. But you tell me how to handle it the next time or how I should react when you're the one calling with the last-minute emergency."

He could tell she was at a loss for words. The fire died, leaving behind pain and confusion. "I was looking forward to tonight so much," she confessed.

The admission hit and hit hard. "So was I." He stripped off his shorts and tossed back the bedcovers. Then he held out his hand. "Robe."

When she didn't immediately comply, he simply took matters into his own hands. He flicked buttons through holes with ruthless efficiency before sweeping it from her shoulders.

"Don't," she whispered. "Please don't."

If she'd used anger against him, or that ice-cold wall of defiance, he might have ignored her request. But he couldn't resist her when every scrap of defensive armor lay shattered around her and unhappiness coursed from her in palpable waves.

"Okay, sweetheart," he said in a husky voice. "It's okay. We'll just sleep."

He gathered her close, locking her against him, and his eyes shut at the feel of her body curving into his. This time she didn't protest when he urged her toward the bed. How long had it been since he'd had her head pillowed on his shoulder and felt those crisp, wayward curls tickle his jaw? How long had he waited to have that silken skin flowing over his, her small, perfect breasts pressed against his side? He'd craved this, just this, for endless, torturous months. Now that he had her back in his arms he could afford to be patient. As much as he wanted to make love to her, this would do until the time was right. He could give her some space while they worked through their issues.

"Are you asleep?" she asked.

"Not yet."

"Did you make the deal?"

He smiled. It was a start. He could be satisfied with that.

Gabe woke at first light and realized that this time he wasn't dreaming. This time it was real. He held Catherine safely tucked within his arms, tight against his side, the rhythm of her heart and breath and sleep-laden movements perfectly synchronized with his. He'd always considered her an elegant woman, small and delicate. But not here. Not now. Not when she abandoned herself to sleep and was at her most unguarded. Then he saw through all the defenses and shields to the very core of the woman. Mysterious. Powerful. Gloriously female.

She'd entwined her body around his, all slender shapely arms and legs. Even in sleep she clung to him, a delicious, possessive hold that cut through all the conflicts and difficulties that separated them and simply lay claim. In the real world she dressed with style, presented herself with calm self-confidence. She'd always impressed him with her cool, professional demeanor. But here in their bed she revealed a passion that never failed to set him on fire.

He traced the planes of her face, reveling in the sensation of warm, silken skin, skin covering a bone structure of such purity that it quickened his breath and annihilated reason. He thought he would forgot, that over the long months they were apart that time would steal precious memories. But it didn't. He knew each curve, remembered them all, would have recognized the feel of her, even if he'd been blind.

She was back. Granted, it wasn't out of choice. But in time, that would change. He'd make sure of it. His fingers trailed downward, across a pale shoulder, sculpting the feminine dip and swell of waist and hip. The hem of her nightgown had bunched high on her slender thighs, offering him a tantalizing view of the shapely curve of her backside. He'd missed waking up to this. Would she still moan if he caressed those sinewy lines with his fingertips?

He put thought into action and was rewarded with the lightest of sighs, one of undeniable pleasure. She shifted against him, softening and opening. Her head tipped back, spilling golden curls across their pillow, offering up the long sweep of her throat. He buried his mouth against the hollow at the very base and at the same time cupped her breast through the thin layer of silk covering it. It felt warm within his palm, the nipple a small perfect bud, ripe for the plucking. He grazed the tip. Once. Twice. The third stroke had her stirring with his name on her lips, the sound escaping in a strangled cry of sheer need.

There wasn't any just-woke-up confusion about Catherine. There never had been. She went from a dead sleep to aroused woman in the blink of an eye. Her arms circled his neck and she pulled him in for a hot, hungry kiss. He didn't need further prompting. He rolled over on top of her, sinking into her warmth.

He'd planned to give her a moment to adjust to both his weight and his embrace. But she took the initiative. Hooking a leg around his waist, she anchored him close and deepened the kiss. In this area they'd always been in perfect accord, each the perfect mate for the other. Her lips parted and he delved inward, stoking the heat. He could feel her tremble in response to his touch, feel her heartbeat pounding against his palm, and his own pulse caught the rapid-fire rhythm and echoed it.

Need ripened between them, escalating with dizzying speed. As though sensing it, she ended the kiss with a small, nipping tug of his bottom lip. "Not so fast." The request was half plea, half demand. "Give me time to think."

"Forget it, Catherine. No more waiting. This is all that matters," he told her fiercely. Once again he plied her lips with small, biting kisses while his hands traversed sweetly familiar pathways that had been left unexplored for far too long. "This is what's important. What we feel right here and right now."

"I wish that were true." Her breath hitched when he reacquainted himself with a particularly vulnerable curve of skin, just along the outer swell of her breast. "But we can't just forget what came before. What about my reasons for leaving you? What about all the empty space during the time we were apart? As enjoyable as it will be, knotting up the bedsheets isn't going to make all our problems go away."

"But it'll ground us," he maintained. "It'll give us a common base from which to work." He swept his hand across her heated flesh to prove his point, watching as her eyes glazed and her breath exploded. "We were meant to be together."

She managed to shake her head, but he could see the effort it took her. If he pressed, she'd cave. And though parts of him wanted her any way he could have her, the rational part of his brain preferred her willing, not fighting regrets. He leaned in and gave her another wickedly slow, thorough kiss before easing back.

She eyed him in open suspicion, while she probed her swollen lips with the tip of her tongue. "Are they smoking? They feel like they're smoking."

He choked on a laugh. How did she do it? How did she take him from overwhelming hunger to heart-melting amusement with one simple question? "Your lips aren't smoking, but your tongue is. Just a little around the edges." He leaned in. "I can show you where. Make it all better."

Now it was her turn to laugh. "I'll just bet." She closed her eyes. "You make it impossible to think."

"Then don't." He couldn't keep his hands off her. "Just feel."

"That's not smart. Nor is it safe."

"I won't hurt you, Cate."

He felt the tremor that shook her, the quiver of re-membered pain. "You already have," she whispered.

"Let me heal some of that hurt."

His offer provoked tears and they glittered in her eyes like gold dust. He didn't know if he'd said the right thing, or the wrong. He just knew it was honest, welling from the very core of him. Her arms slid up along his chest in response and she cupped his face. This time she initiated the embrace. It was her lips that sought his and slid like a quiet balm over his mouth. She probed with a delicacy unique to her, dancing lightly. Sweetly. Tenderly.

Just as he'd reacquainted himself with the dip and swell, the remarkable texture and scent, now so did she. Her hands cruised along his back, testing far harder planes and angles than those he'd examined. "This is where you carry it," she told him between kisses. "The weight of your responsibilities."

He trailed his fingers along her shoulders, scooping up the narrow straps of her nightgown and teasing them down her arms. "I'm strong. I can take a lot of weight."

"Not right now. Right now I want you right here. With me. No responsibilities. No interruptions. Just the two of us."

Didn't she understand? "There's nowhere else for me to be." And he'd find a way to prove it.

He painted a series of kisses along the lacy edge of

her nightgown where it dipped low over her breasts, and nudged the flimsy barrier from his path. He nearly groaned at the feel of satiny skin against his mouth and cheek. Her breasts were glorious, small, firm, and beautifully shaped, but then so was she. He caught her nipple between his teeth and tugged ever so gently, watching the wash of color that blossomed across her skin and turned her face a delicate shade of rose.

"Your eyes have gone dark," he told her. "Like antique gold."

"They haven't gone dark." Her breath escaped in a wispy groan. "They've gone blind."

"You don't need to see. Just feel."

More than anything, he wanted to make this perfect for her. To heal some of what had gone before. As much as he wanted to take her, to bury himself in her warmth and create that ultimate joining, this first time would be for her. He'd give her slow. He'd give her gentle. And he'd give her the healing she so desperately craved.

He danced with her, danced with mouth and hands and quiet caresses, driving her ever higher toward that elusive pinnacle. The air grew thick and heavy with need, tightening around them until all that existed was man and woman and the desire that bound two into one. He drove her, ever upward, knowing just how to touch, just where to stroke until her muscles clenched and she hovered on the crest.

And then he mated their bodies, kissing away the helpless tears that clung to her lashes like a dusting of diamonds. Slow and easy he moved, sliding her up and up and up, before tipping her over and tumbling down the other side with her. For a long time afterward they clung to each other, wrapped together in a slick tangle of limp arms and legs.

"I can't remember how to breathe," he managed to say.

"Funny. I can't remember how to move." She opened a single eye. "If I breathe for you, can you move for me?"

"I'll get right on that." He groaned. "Tomorrow, maybe."

"Okay." She fell silent for so long he thought she'd gone back to sleep. Then she asked, "Why, Gabe?"

"Why, what?" he asked lazily.

She opened her eyes, eyes clear and bright and glittering like the sun. "You were always a generous lover. But this morning... This morning was a gift."

He grinned. "Then just accept it and say thank you."

"Thank you."

"You're welcome."

"It makes me wonder, though..." A small frown creased her brow, like a thundercloud creeping over the horizon. "Where do we go from here? What do you want from me?"

He answered honestly. "Whatever you're willing to give."

She absorbed that, turned it over in her mind, before nodding. "That's easy enough. I can't give you permanent, but I can give you temporary. We can enjoy each other these next few months. I don't have a problem with that."

His jaw tightened. "And then?"

Something about her easy smile rang false. "Then we go our separate ways, of course. We tried living together once. It didn't work, remember?"

How could she lie beneath him and act as though what they felt was transient? Didn't she feel the connection, the way their bodies fused one to the other? The way their minds and spirits were so evenly matched? "What if a couple months isn't enough?" he argued. "It wasn't last time."

He watched her pick and choose her words and his suspicion grew. She was hiding something, keeping a part of herself locked carefully away. "We were different people then. We had different goals in life. You wanted a woman who would take care of the social end of your life. Someone who would nurture you and your home. At the time, I thought that would be enough to satisfy me, too."

"Is this about your career?" Relief swept through him and he almost laughed. "You think I object to you running your own business?"

"No...at least, not yet. But I have a feeling the time will come when you'd expect me to set it aside in order to fulfill more pressing obligations."

"More pressing obligations," he repeated. His eyes narrowed. "Are you talking about children?"

She refused to meet his eyes. "I don't want children, Gabe. I want a career. You made it crystal clear to me before I left that you were planning on a large family, just like the one you had growing up."

He sat up and thrust a hand through his hair. "Is that

why you left?" he demanded in disbelief. "Because you didn't want to have a baby?"

"You were pressing for one."

"Damn it, I asked you to marry me."

"I remember," she retorted. "It was a beautiful proposal…right up until work reared its ugly head. Roxanne's call cut me off midsentence, do you even remember that?"

He fought to recall. She'd been crying. They'd been tears of joy, of that he was certain. She'd been shaking and laughing while those tears had slid down her face. And she'd said something…. Hell. What had it been? "You had something you wanted to tell me." He shrugged. "I assume it was, 'Yes, darling, I'll marry you.' Or did I get even that wrong?"

"It doesn't matter, anymore, does it? Because you left." She spoke carefully, as though holding those long-ago emotions at a cautious distance. "You left me there with the beautiful flowers and an uneaten dinner congealing on the plate. You left me with your gorgeous ring and empty promises echoing in my ear. Because when it came right down to it, your top priority was and always will be Piretti's. So you left, explaining without saying a word where our relationship rated in the grand scheme of things, and you didn't come home again. Not that day. And not the next."

"Hell, Catherine. You may not have known about the attempted takeover two years ago, but I explained all this to you yesterday at your apartment. What was I supposed to do? Let Piretti's go under? Let those bastards take my business from me?" He stood and yanked on his clothes. "And I did come home. I came home to find a stilted little note from you and the ring you'd cried such pretty tears over sitting on my damned dresser."

If nothing else, their lovemaking had opened a wide crack in her defenses, allowing him to see all she'd kept buried before. And what he saw was pain and fear and vulnerability. "Why would you expect anything else, Gabe? Do you think I'm some sort of plaything that you can pick up and discard when it suits you? Did you ever wonder what I did while you were off running your empire? Or did you simply stick me on a shelf and forget about me until it was time to come home and pick me up again? I don't go into hibernation like one of your damn computers."

"I never said—" He thrust a hand through his hair and blew out his breath, fighting for calm. "Is there a reason we're dredging all this up again? I know what happened. And I know that you wanted more from our relationship than I could give you before. I'm willing to do that. But I don't see the point in re-hashing the past."

"If not now, then when?" She tilted her head to one side. "Or were you hoping it no longer matters and move on?"

"You're good at pointing the finger, Catherine. And I'm being as honest as I know how. I screwed up. I made mistakes. But if we're going to go there and dig into all that muck, then you have to be honest, too."

Her eyes widened. "Meaning?"

"Meaning... I'm willing to continue this conversation when you stop lying and tell me what really happened. Why did you really leave me?"

She shook her head in instant denial. "I don't know what you're—"

"Bull. Just cut the bull, will you?"

He snatched a deep breath and fought for control. For some reason his gaze landed on the bedside table. A cell phone sat there, not his. He eyed it for a long minute as he considered how and when Catherine had left it there. And then he knew. She hadn't taken the bedroom at the end of the hallway when she'd moved in the previous day. She'd moved her things in here with him, at least initially. He could make a pretty accurate guess when that had changed and why. Crossing the room, he picked up the phone and tossed it to her.

"Call your partner," he instructed. "Have her meet us at Piretti's in an hour."

"Excuse me? We were in the middle of a—"

"An argument?" he shot at her.

"A discussion."

Right. "Well, it's one we're going to set aside until you come clean. Until then, it's off the table."

Indignation shot across her face and reverberated in her voice. "Just like that?"

He inclined his head. "Just like that." He deliberately changed the subject. "I saw some of your financial records last night. And I did a quick scan of the documents you provided when I returned to the office yesterday. You told me your partner handles the books?"

"Yes, but—"

"Then I want to meet her. Now." She opened her mouth to argue again, and he cut her off without compunction. "You came to me for help," he reminded her. "This is how I help."

"Okay, fine. I'll call her."

"I'm going to shower. You're welcome to join me."

"Another time, perhaps."

He managed a smile. "I'll hold you to that." He started toward the bathroom, then paused. "The breakup in our relationship? It wasn't about children or careers, Catherine. There's something else going on. I just haven't figured out what, yet. But I will. And when I do, we'll do more than put it back on the table. We're going to have this out, once and for all."

Six

They accomplished the brief ride from the apartment to Piretti's in silence. Catherine appeared a little paler than Gabe liked, but whether it was the result of the upcoming meeting with her partner, or because of their argument, he wasn't certain. Perhaps a bit of both.

Roxanne was already at her desk when they arrived, and he watched with interest as the two women exchanged a long look. Another brewing problem, one he needed to think about before determining how best to resolve it.

They entered his office just as Catherine's cell phone rang. "Excuse me a minute," she murmured. After answering the call, she listened at length, her expression growing more and more concerned. "Thanks. I'll take it from here."

"Problem?" he asked once she'd disconnected the call.

"I have the Collington wedding scheduled for a week from tomorrow. The bride just called in to cancel our services."

"At this late date?"

Catherine shook her head. "Obviously, she heard about what happened at the Marconis' and it's panicked her. Di—my partner managed to get her to agree to meet with me for lunch."

"I'll go with you."

To his surprise, she didn't argue. "Normally, I'd be able to handle it. Brides are often in crazy mode by now. I'm used to it."

"But trying to calm her down after hearing about everything that went wrong with Natalie's party…"

"Will prove challenging. Fortunately, I have an ace in the hole." She smiled, the first natural one she'd offered since their argument. "You. You've always had a way about you, an ability to smooth ruffled feathers."

"I'll do my best." He checked his watch. "Your partner is late."

"Maybe she hit traffic."

"You're sure she's coming?"

"She was in the city when she called me just now."

Right on cue, voices reverberated through the thick wooden door panels, one irritated, clearly Roxanne. Gabe winced. His assistant wasn't at her best this morning. The other, a voice he'd known for every one of this thirty-three years, snapped back with impatient authority. His office door banged open, and his mother paused with her hand on the knob.

"I know the way into my own son's office, Roxy," she informed Gabe's assistant.

"It's Roxanne."

"Well, maybe when you've worked here awhile I'll remember your name."

Gabe could see his assistant visibly struggling to hang on to her composure. She managed it. Barely. "He has a meeting scheduled, Mrs. Piretti. And just to set the record straight, I've worked here for three years, as I'm certain you're well aware."

"Huh. Could have sworn you were one of those annoying temps." With that Dina slammed the door in Roxanne's face. Turning, she offered a broad, delighted smile. "Gabriel, Catherine. It's so good to see the two of you together again. Give me a minute to just stand here and enjoy the view."

Gabe's lips twitched. "I'm sorry, Mom, but Roxanne was right. We're waiting for Catherine's business partner to join us in order to—" He broke off as the connection clicked into place, a connection he would have made long ago if he hadn't been so distracted by the apprehensive woman standing at his side. "No. Oh, *hell,* no. You're not… You can't be—"

Dina stuck out her hand. "Dina Piretti, co-owner of Elegant Events. So good of you to help us with our small financial crisis."

* * *

The meeting didn't last long. The minute Dina exited the room, Gabe turned on Catherine. "My *mother*? You dumped me, and then you went into business with my *mother*?"

Catherine struggled not to flinch. "Really, Gabe. I don't see what one thing has to do with the other."

"You don't see—" He forked his fingers through his hair, turning order into all-too-attractive, not to mention distracting, disorder. "You must have suspected I wouldn't like the idea considering that the two of you have been careful to keep me in the dark for nearly two years now. Why is that, Cate?"

She planted her hands on her hips. "You want logic? Fine. Here's some logic for you. I didn't want to see you. If you knew I was in business with your mother, you wouldn't have been able to stay away. Worse, you might have tried to interfere, or…I don't know—" She waved a hand through the air. "Tried to protect her from me and stopped us from doing business together."

"You're damn right I would have stopped you from doing business together," he retorted. "But not for the reason you think. It isn't my mother I would have wanted to protect. It's you."

That stopped her cold. "What are you talking about?"

"I told you that I had to step in and take over Piretti's," he began.

"Right." He'd never gone into details, other than to inform her that it had been one of the toughest periods in his life. But she'd been able to read between the lines. "After your father died."

He shook his head. "Not exactly. After he died, my mother took over."

That caught her by surprise, not that it caused her any real concern. "So? She's brilliant."

"Yes, she is. What I never told you before was that she brilliantly ran Piretti's to the verge of bankruptcy. That's when I seized control."

Uh-oh. That didn't sound good. "Seized. You mean—" She struggled to come up with a more palatable word. "Took charge."

His mouth tightened. "No, I mean I swooped in and instigated a hostile takeover. You've teased me often enough about my nickname, but you never came right out and asked where I got it." He lowered his head and rubbed a hand along the nape of his neck. "Well, that's where."

She approached and rested a hand on his arm. She could feel the muscles bunching beneath her fingers, his tension palpable. "I can't believe you'd have done such a thing unless it was absolutely necessary. What happened, Gabe? Why were you forced to such extremes?"

He stilled. "Catherine." Just her name, spoken so softly, with such a wealth of emotion behind it. He lifted his head and looked at her. The intensity of his gaze mesmerized her, the shade of blue so brilliant it put the sky to shame. "You show such faith. Not a single doubt. Not a single hesitation. How can you think what's between us is temporary?"

"I know you." The admission slipped out on a whisper. "I know what sort of man you are."

"I'm hard and ruthless."

"True."

"I take apart companies."

"And put them back together again."

The smallest hint of a smile played about his mouth, easing some of the tension. "Or make them a part of Piretti's."

"Well, you are a businessman, first and foremost." Sorrow filled her. "And that's why I say our relationship is temporary. Because Piretti's isn't just a place where you work. It's who and what you are."

The tension stormed back. "There hasn't been any other choice. I had to take the business away from her."

She drew him over to the couch and sat down with him. "Explain it to me," she encouraged.

"You are right about one thing. My mother is a brilliant business woman. When it comes to numbers and accounting and contracts, there's no one better."

"But…?"

"But she's too damn nice."

"Yeah, I hate that about her, too," Catherine teased.

The grin was back, one identical to his mother's. "That soft heart means people can take advantage of her."

"And they did."

He nodded. "After my father died she began staffing Piretti's with friends and family. Nepotism became the byword."

Catherine tried to put herself in Dina's shoes. "It

probably comforted her to have loved ones around at such a time."

He started to say something, paused, then frowned. "Huh. I never considered that possibility, but looking back, you may be right."

"I am right. Dina told me so one evening." Catherine interlaced her fingers with his, needing to touch him. She suspected he needed the physical contact as well. "I think it was on the fifth anniversary of your dad's death. She was having a rough night, and we talked about all sorts of things. It was one of the few times she mentioned Piretti's."

"Taking the business away from her nearly killed her." Pain bled through the words. "I did that to her. I did that to my own mother."

Catherine frowned in concern. "Were her friends and family members incompetent?"

"Not all. Those who were took gross advantage. She paid them ludicrous salaries for jobs they, at best, neglected, and at worst didn't perform at all. They'd put in a few hours and then take off. That forced Mom to hire more people to do the jobs that weren't getting done."

"Which explains why you refuse to mix business and pleasure." It explained so much. "Couldn't you have simply come in and cleaned house?"

"If she'd let me, yes. But there was the board of directors to consider."

Understanding dawned. "Let me guess. The board comprised those individuals who were taking advantage of her. And they weren't about to let you mess with the status quo."

"Got it in one."

Compassion filled her. "So the only solution was for Gabe 'the Pirate' Piretti to raid the company."

"I cleaned house, all right. Starting right at the top with my mother and working down from there."

"How did Dina handle it when you took over?"

"She was furious. She wouldn't even speak to me. So, I abducted her."

Catherine's eyes widened. "Excuse me? You what?"

"I loaded her into my car, protesting all the way, and took her off to a resort and forced her to deal with the situation. Of course, the daily massages and mai tais— heavy on the rum—didn't hurt. It also helped that I brought along the accounts and forced her to look at the bottom line." He shot her a cool look. "I've considered using the same approach with you in order to get to the bottom of some of our issues."

She released his hand and swept to her feet. "It wouldn't have worked."

His eyes narrowed. "And there's that secret again, right smack-dab between us." He rose as well. "How many mai tais would it take to pry it out of you, Catherine?"

She shook her head. "There's nothing to pry out. I told you. Your view of marriage and what you want from it are a hundred and eighty degrees different from my wants and needs."

"You know one of the qualities that makes me such a good pirate?" He didn't wait for her to respond. "I'm excellent at reading people."

She took a step backward. "Not all people."

"You'd be surprised." He followed in the path of her retreat. "For instance, it only takes one look for me to know that you're lying. You're keeping something from me, and all the denials in the world aren't going to convince me otherwise."

"Too bad. You'll just have to live with it."

"For instance…" He trapped her against one of the huge picture windows overlooking the sound. Brilliant light encased them, sparkling over and around them. "I know for a fact that you've always wanted children. You told me so yourself."

She forced her gaze to remain steady, to be captured and held by his. "Long ago. In another lifetime. But I've changed since then. My wants and needs have changed, as well." She forced out a laugh. "I find it ridiculous to have to explain this to you, of all people. You, who puts business ahead of everything and everyone. Why is it acceptable for you and not for me?"

"Because it's not true."

He leaned in. Even with layers of clothing separating them, she could feel the heat of his body, feel the sinful contours that were so potently male. And then he made it so much worse. He slid his hand low on her abdomen, his fingers spread wide across the flat surface. She shuddered beneath his touch, her belly quivering in response. Liquid heat pooled, stealing thought and reason.

"Are you telling me you don't want any children at all? Not even one?"

She forced out the lie. "No, not even one."

A lazy smile crept across his mouth, one that told her

he didn't believe a word of it. He dropped his head, his mouth brushing along the sensitive skin of her throat, just beneath her ear where her pulse skipped and raced. "You don't ever want to give birth?" The question burned like acid. "You don't want to feel your womb swell with our baby? Feel the flutter of new life? Sing and talk to him while he grows and becomes? Encourage his passage from his safe little nest into a world just waiting for his arrival?"

Dear God, make him stop, she silently prayed. She fixed her eyes on a point just over his shoulder and took a long, calming breath. "That's what you want, isn't it?"

"More than you can possibly imagine."

One more slow breath and she'd worked up the courage to shift her eyes to his. It took everything she possessed not to respond to the rich warmth of those impossibly blue eyes. "Then I suggest you start looking for someone who can give that to you. Because it's not going to be me." She spread her hands across his chest and nudged him back a few inches. "Look at me, Gabe. Look at me and tell me I'm lying to you. I won't give you a child. Not ever. Is that clear enough for you?"

His hand slid from her abdomen and he stepped back. "Quite clear." His face fell into hard, taut lines. "And quite honest."

"Thank you for recognizing it." She twitched her blouse into place and smoothed her skirt. "And thank you for admitting as much."

The phone on his desk gave a soft purring ring. He

crossed to answer it. Listening a moment, Gabe said, "Put him through." Then he covered the receiver. "I'm sorry, but I have to take this call."

She slipped behind her most professional demeanor. "Of course. I'll wait for you in the foyer."

He stopped her just as she reached for the doorknob. "Catherine? If you think our discussion has changed my mind about our relationship, you're wrong."

She glanced over her shoulder. "Why? Because you think at some point in the future I'm going to change my mind?" She could see from his expression that was precisely what he thought. A smile escaped, one of infinite regret. "Let me clue you in and save both of us a lot of time and grief. I won't."

And with that, she escaped his office.

Closing the door behind her, Catherine took a quick breath. As long as her day was progressing so well, she might as well keep the streak going. The time had come to deal with Roxanne. Either they came to terms here and now or Catherine would take action. But never again would she step back and take it on the chin. Never again would she allow this woman to cause harm to her business or make her life the misery it had been during those earlier years.

She paused by Roxanne's desk, fully aware that she'd been noticed and equally as aware that she wouldn't be acknowledged any time soon. It was unquestionably a power play, one Catherine intended to commandeer.

"Hiding behind that computer screen isn't going to

make me go away. All it does is confirm that you're afraid to look me in the eye." It was the perfect gambit, Catherine thought with some satisfaction, causing Roxanne's head to jerk up and anger to flare to life in her sloe eyes. "You and I are going to get something straightened out."

"You're the one who needs to be straightened out. I—"

"I'm not interested in what you have to say," Catherine cut her off smoothly. "It's your turn to listen. Or shall we have this conversation in Gabe's office?"

"And talk about what?" she demanded. "Your whiny complaints about his favorite assistant? He's too logical to give them any credence."

"It's because he's so logical that he will." She gestured toward Gabe's closed door. "Shall we find out which of us is right?" She wasn't the least surprised when Roxanne didn't take her up on the offer.

"Where do you get off, threatening me?" she asked instead. "You have no idea who and what you're taking on."

Catherine planted her palms on Roxanne's desk and leaned in. "I know precisely who I'm taking on, and, sweetie, I knew what you were from day one. Now you close your mouth and listen very carefully, because I'm only going to say this once. If you mess with me or my business ever again, I will see to it that your career as you currently know it ends. I will make it my mission to introduce you to hell on earth."

"You don't have that power," Roxanne scoffed.

"Watch me."

Gabe's assistant leaned back in her chair and folded her arms across her chest, a smug smile playing about her generous mouth. "Is this about your little disaster at the Marconi party?"

"No, this is about *your* little disaster at the Marconi party. Specifically, the boaters whose advent you were so eager for me to witness."

Roxanne's smile grew, slow and catlike. "You can't prove I had anything to do with that."

"Can't I?" Catherine straightened and thrust her hand into her purse. Retrieving her cell phone, she flipped it open. One press of a button snapped a digital picture of Roxanne. Another press had it winging its way to Catherine's e-mail account.

Roxanne straightened in her chair. "What the hell did you just do?"

"I've e-mailed myself your photo. When I get home, I intend to print it off and hand-deliver it to the King County Sheriff's Marine Unit. They have some very contrite boaters who are eager to point the finger at the person who invited them to the Marconis' party and encouraged them to make—how did they phrase it? Oh, right. A splashy entrance." Roxanne turned deathly pale, and Catherine smiled. "Nothing to say? How incredibly unlike you."

It was too much to hope the silence would last. Roxanne recovered within seconds. "So what if I extended an invitation? It's their word against mine how it was phrased."

"You be sure to explain that technicality to Natalie Marconi…right after you explain your side of things to

Gabe. I doubt either of them will be terribly sympathetic considering the damage done."

"They won't believe you." An edge of desperation underscored the statement.

"Oh, I think they will. And once Natalie finds out you were behind the boat incident, I don't think it'll take much of a nudge to convince her to ask around and see if any of her guests happened to notice a very striking guest in an attention-grabbing red dress hanging around the sprinkler controls. I guarantee someone will have noticed you. That's what happens when you work so hard to be the center of attention. Sometimes you get it when you'd rather not have it." Catherine gave that a moment to sink in. "This ends and ends now. You keep your claws off my business. More importantly, you keep your mouth—and every other body part—off my man. And you stop setting up business appointments that interfere with our life together."

Roxanne fought to recover a hint of her old cockiness. "Spoiled your first night together, did I?" She released a sigh of mock disappointment. "Such a shame."

"Gabe more than made up for it this morning." That wiped the smile off her face. "I'm giving you precisely one week to convince Natalie that someone else is at fault for the events of last night, someone other than Elegant Events. You have seven days to convince her that somebody other than me sabotaged that party."

Roxanne's eyes widened in panic. "Have you lost your mind? How do you expect me to do that?"

"I don't know, and I don't care. You've always been fast on your feet and quick to spin a story. Find a way."

"What if I refuse your…request?"

"It wasn't a request. In one week's time, I act. I start with the sheriff, and I end with a lawyer. And somewhere in between—one night in bed, perhaps—I'll wonder out loud whether you're the type of person Gabe wants representing Piretti's. Seeds like that have an uncanny knack of taking root."

"If I do what you want…" The words escaped like chewed glass. "What then?"

"Then you have two choices. Option number one, you can behave yourself and toe the line. For instance, I have an event coming up this next weekend, assuming Gabe and I can salvage the account. You are not going to interfere with that event in any way, shape or form. If anything goes wrong, just the least little thing, I'm putting it on you. I don't care if it decides to rain that day, it'll be your fault. If Mt. Rainier turns active and dumps ash all over Annie Collington's special day…your fault. If anything goes wrong, I promise, I will bury you for it."

One look at Roxanne's face told the story. She'd planned to do something. Catherine could only imagine what that might be. "You said I have two choices," she replied. "What's my other one?"

"You can pack up your brimstone and find a new boss to screw with."

"You can't fire me. Only Gabe can."

Catherine smiled in real pleasure. "Now, that's my favorite part about our little dilemma here, because you're right. I don't have that ability. So I thought of the perfect way around that small stumbling block. You see, men always have so much trouble deciding on the perfect wedding gift for their bride." Not that he'd asked. But Roxanne didn't have to know that. "Lucky for Gabe, now I know exactly what I want. And I guarantee he'll accommodate my request."

"You bitch!"

Catherine's amusement faded. "You're damn right. I'm through playing nice. And in case you still have any doubts, let me assure you that the benefits of bitchdom keep adding up." She gave it to her, chapter and verse. "If you try and start any more trouble after you leave Piretti's, people will immediately conclude that it's sour grapes on your part. And if they have the least little doubt, I'll be sure to explain it first to them, and then to my lawyer." She released her breath in a happy little sigh. "See how simple all this is?"

"This isn't over, you—" She broke off and to Catherine's shock, huge tears filled her eyes. "Oh, Gabe. I'm so sorry you have to see us like this."

He stood in the doorway, his gaze shifting from one woman to the other. "Problem?"

"Not yet," Catherine said.

She kept Roxanne pinned with a hard look. She held up her phone as a pointed reminder and then made a production of returning it to her purse. It was a subtle warning, but it seemed to have a profound effect. Satisfied that they understood each other, Catherine turned and offered Gabe a sunny smile.

"No problem at all," she assured him. "Roxanne and I were simply coming to a long-overdue understanding."

He folded his arms across his chest. "That explains the tears."

"Exactly," she stated serenely. "Tears of joy. We're both all choked up with emotion."

"Uh-huh. So I see." She wished she could read his expression, but he'd assumed the indecipherable mask he wore during his most intense business negotiations. "Roxanne? Anything to add?"

His assistant ground her teeth in frustration, but managed a hard, cold smile. "Not a thing. At least, not yet."

"Excellent." He inclined his head toward the elevators. "Ready, Catherine?"

"As ready as I'll ever be."

"Then off we go before you cause any more tears of joy."

Seven

Catherine gave Gabe directions to the little café just north of the city, where arrangements had been made to meet with the bride-to-be. Annie Collington, a bubbly redhead with a smattering of freckles across the bridge of her upturned nose, appeared tense and unhappy.

Introductions were made, and Annie smiled at Gabe with only a hint of her customary zest. "I recognize you, of course. I think your photo is on everything from the society page to the business section to the gossip magazines."

"I wouldn't believe a word of anything except the gossip magazines."

She twinkled briefly before she caught Catherine's eye and her amusement faded. "Do we really have to do this?" she asked miserably. "I've fired you, now that's the end of it. Nothing you say is going to change my mind."

Before Catherine could respond, Gabe stepped in smoothly. "Why don't we sit down and have a cup of coffee and a bite to eat while we figure out how best to settle this?"

"Please, Annie." Catherine added gentle pressure. "Your wedding is only eight days away. You have such a beautiful day planned. You don't want to make any rash decisions that might jeopardize it."

"That's precisely what I'm trying to prevent," Annie insisted. "I heard about the Marconi party. It was a disaster. I can't have that happen at my wedding."

"And it won't," Gabe assured her. Without even seeming to do so, he guided them to the table the hostess had waiting for them, seated them, and ordered coffee and a platter of house specialty sandwiches. "May I make a proposal that might help with your decision?" he asked Annie.

"Gabe—" Catherine began.

"No, it's okay," Annie interrupted. "He can try."

Catherine fell silent, struggling to suppress an irrational annoyance. After all, Gabe was just trying to help, even if it did feel as if he'd swooped in and taken command of her meeting. Still, she didn't appreciate him seizing control like…well, like a damn pirate.

"How about this, Annie?" Gabe was saying. "If you agree to continue to use Catherine and Elegant Events as your wedding planner, I will personally guarantee that your wedding goes off without a hitch."

"You can't do that," Catherine instantly protested.

"You can do that?" Annie asked at the same time.

"I can, absolutely."

The coffee arrived in a slender, wafer-thin porcelain urn hand-painted with an intricate pattern of wild red strawberries and crisp green leaves. After aiming a dazzling smile of dismissal in the direction of their waitress, Gabe took over the chore of pouring fragrant cups for the three of them. The delicate bits of china should have looked small and clumsy in his large hands. But instead he manipulated the coffee service with an impressive dexterity that made him appear all the more powerful and male. He made short work of the chore, and Catherine could see that she wasn't the only one dazzled by the way his raw masculinity dominated and subdued the fussy bit of femininity.

"Let's see if this offer doesn't appeal," he said as he handed Annie her cup. "If you're not one hundred percent satisfied with your wedding, I'll personally see to it that you're refunded every penny."

She accepted the coffee with a smile. "That doesn't exactly guarantee that it'll go off without a hitch," she pointed out with impressive logic.

"True," Gabe conceded, while Catherine silently steamed at his high-handedness.

She didn't want or need anyone to guarantee her ability to pull off this wedding. She was capable. Competent. She knew the business inside and out. But with one simple offer, he'd reduced Elegant Events in the eyes of her client to a struggling start-up in need of a "real" businessman to back its ability to perform successfully.

Gabe relaxed in his chair, very much in charge. "I may not be able to guarantee that nothing will go wrong if you honor your contract. But understand this, Annie. There is one thing I *can* guarantee." He paused to add weight to his comment. "Your wedding will be an unmitigated disaster if you try and do it on your own at this late stage. You're just asking for trouble attempting to be both bride and coordinator."

Annie gnawed on her bottom lip. Clearly, the same thought had occurred to her. "I might be able to pull it off," she offered.

"You think so? Then I suggest you consider this…"

He turned the full battery of Piretti charm and business savvy on her and Catherine watched in amused exasperation. Annie didn't stand a chance against him, poor thing. She hung on his words, her eyes huge as she tumbled under his spell like every other woman who'd come up against those devilish blue eyes and persuasive personality.

"After what happened at the Marconi party, Catherine is strongly motivated to make certain your wedding is perfect in every regard, if only to prove that her reputation for excellence remains intact."

Catherine shot Gabe a quelling glare. Not that it did much to quell him. The man was unquellable. "I can't go into specifics about what happened," she explained to Annie, deftly assuming control. "But I want to assure you that the problems we experienced were not a result of anything I did wrong, but for the most part caused by some mischief maker out to amuse him- or herself by turning on the sprinklers. On top of that there were a few boaters who crashed the party. I know this is a stressful time for you. And I don't doubt you're under tremendous pressure."

"My mother's insisting I get rid of you," Annie admitted. "And since she's the one paying…"

"If you'd like me to meet with her and address her concerns, I will."

Annie gave it a moment's thought before shaking her head. "No, that won't be necessary. One of the agreements Mom and I came to about the wedding was that it was my wedding. I get to make the decisions." Her gamine smile flashed. "She gets to pay for them."

Catherine responded with an answering smile and gave one more gentle push. "In that case, I hope you'll decide to honor our contract." She kept her eyes trained on Annie's, hoping the younger girl would see Catherine's sincerity, as well as her determination. "I promise to do my absolute best for you."

"But Gabe's guarantee stands, right?"

Catherine gritted her teeth. "Gabe's guarantee stands."

"In that case…" Annie beamed. "Okay."

"Then it's settled? We move forward?"

"It's settled. You can stay on as my event stager." Her attention switched to Gabe and she shot him an impish look. "Although I have to admit I'm almost hoping something does go wrong so you're stuck footing the bill."

He leaned in. "I'll see what I can do to sabotage

something," he said in a stage whisper. "Something that won't cause too much trouble, but just enough to get you off the hook."

Annie giggled. "Nah, don't do that. It would only make me feel guilty, afterward. If you can make sure there aren't any screwups, that's all that matters to me."

"Gabe won't have to worry about it," Catherine inserted smoothly. "That's my job." She leveled Gabe with a single look. "And it's a job I do quite well."

Lunch sped by, though afterward Catherine couldn't have said what they talked about or even what they ate. While part of her was grateful for Gabe's assistance—after all, he'd rescued the account, hadn't he? The other part, the major part, was hands-down furious.

"Go on," he said the minute they parted company with Annie and were walking toward his Jag. "What's eating you?"

She didn't bother to hold back. "I realize you're accustomed to being in charge, but I'd appreciate it if you'd remember that this is *my* business."

He paused beside the passenger door, key in hand. "You resent my offering to guarantee a successful event?" he asked in surprise.

"To be blunt, yes. I felt like a teenager purchasing her first car and needing Daddy to cosign the loan agreement."

He considered that for a minute. "Perhaps it would help if you examined it from a slightly different angle."

She folded her arms across her chest. What other angle was there? "What other angle is there?"

"I'm a businessman. It goes against the grain to lose

money." He thought about it, and added, "It more than goes against the grain."

"Then you better hope everything proceeds without a hitch, because otherwise you'll be on the hook for…" She silently performed a few mathematical gymnastics and named a total that left him blanching. "Weddings don't come cheap," she informed him. "Especially not ones I stage."

"Why don't they just buy a house?" he argued. "It would last longer and one day show a return on investment."

"Fortunately for Elegant Events that doesn't occur to most couples."

He brushed that aside. "My point is…my offer to guarantee your success shows the extent of my confidence in you and Elegant Events. I don't back losers, and I don't have any intention of paying for Annie's wedding. Nor will I have to because I know you. I know you'll do an outstanding job."

Catherine opened her mouth to reply and then shut it again. "Huh."

He closed the distance between them, trapping her against the car. "I have faith in you, sweetheart. There's not a doubt in my mind that Saturday's wedding is going to be a dream come true for our young Annie. And I think it's all going to be thanks to you."

"You really believe that?" she asked, touched.

The intensity of his gaze increased. "I've always believed in you, and one of these days you're going to let me prove that to you."

She barely had time to absorb that before he lowered his head and caught her mouth in a kiss so tender it brought tears to her eyes. He believed in her, had done his best to demonstrate that today. And what had she given him in return? Doubt. Mistrust. Secrets. As much as she feared attempting that first, wobbly step to reestablish their relationship, maybe it was time to take a small leap of faith. Gabe was reaching out. Maybe, just maybe, she could do the same.

And with that thought it mind, she surrendered to the embrace and opened herself to possibilities. Opened herself to the dream.

The next week flew by. To Gabe's amusement, he realized that Catherine was doing just as he'd predicted. She threw every ounce of energy, focus and determination into making Annie's wedding as perfect as possible. She double- and triple-checked every detail. Then she checked again. She ran through endless scenarios of potential problems that could crop up, endless possibilities that might occur at the last instant. She knew she'd be under intense scrutiny, that any tiny flaw would be blown up into a major catastrophe. Annie's mother, in particular, was already proving a handful with endless phone calls and demands. And yet Gabe noticed that Catherine dealt calmly with every problem and complaint, not allowing her demeanor to be anything other than polite and reassuring.

"You're driving yourself to exhaustion," he told her toward the end of the week. He sank his fingers into the rigid muscles of her shoulders and worked to smooth out the knots and kinks. "You don't want that exhaustion to show, and the best way of avoiding that is to get some sleep."

Catherine nodded absently. "You're right. I'll join you in a minute. I just want to go over the seating chart one final time."

Without a word, he lifted her into his arms and carried her—protesting all the way—into the bedroom. "The seating chart will still be there in the morning, as will the menu and the flower order and the final head count. There's nothing more you can do tonight other than fuss."

"I do not fuss," she argued. "I organize."

"Sweetheart, I know organizing. That wasn't it. That was fussing."

She sagged against him. "You're right, you're right. I'm fussing. I can't seem to stop myself."

"That's what I'm here for."

He lowered Catherine onto the bed and in less than thirty seconds had her stripped and a wisp of a nightgown tugged over her slender form. Then he tucked her under the covers. He joined her ten seconds later, but by that time she'd already fallen sound asleep. Thank God for small miracles, he couldn't help but think. Sweeping her close, he brushed her hair back from her brow and planted a gentle kiss there. Satisfied that he'd accomplished his goal with minimal effort, he cushioned her head against his shoulder and allowed sleep to consume him as well.

As the end of the week approached, Gabe kept a

weather eye on Catherine, ensuring that she ate properly and caught as much sleep as possible. She tolerated his interference, seemed amused by it, even. Perhaps she understood that it originated from concern. And that gave him hope that maybe this time around they'd get their relationship right.

By Friday morning, the day of the reception, Catherine's calm had vanished and her nerves had shredded through her self-control. "Anything I can do?" he asked over breakfast.

She shook her head. "I have some paperwork to take care of this morning—"

"You and I both know it's all in order."

She flashed a brief, tense smile. "True. But I'm going to review it, anyway. Late this morning I'll head over to Milano's and finalize the arrangements for tomorrow's reception. Joe's outstanding at his job, so I don't doubt everything will be perfect, but—"

"You'll feel better after making sure." Gabe nodded in complete understanding. "What about tonight's rehearsal dinner?"

"That's the responsibility of the groom's family, thank goodness. Once the rehearsal is out of the way, I'll come home." He could see her do a mental run-through of her to-do list and wondered if she even noticed that she'd fallen into the habit of calling the apartment "home." "I want to try for an early night, which shouldn't be a problem. There will be a few last-minute phone calls to make before turning in, just to confirm everyone knows what time they need to show up tomorrow."

He covered her hand with his. "No one will dare be late."

She relaxed enough to offer a genuine smile. "You're right about that. It's not wise to tick off a woman clinging to the edge of a cliff by a fingernail."

His grin faded, replaced by concern. "That bad?"

She hesitated, then shook her head. "Not really," she confessed. "I've got two or three fingernails firmly dug in."

Maybe he could help with that. "I want to escort you to the wedding tomorrow, Cate."

She stared blankly. "I'll be working."

"I understand. But I'd like to be there to offer moral support, as well as give you another set of hands should there be a snag."

A frown formed between her eyebrows. "People will think I can't handle my own business," she argued.

"I'll keep a low profile."

"Right," she said in exasperation. "Because, goodness knows, no one in Seattle will recognize Gabe 'the Pirate' Piretti."

He tried another tack. "My presence might help keep Annie's mother in check."

"I can handle Beth," Catherine grumbled.

"I don't doubt it. But it might force her to think twice before causing trouble or throwing a fit over some trifling problem."

Catherine turned white. "There will be *no* trifling problems. There will be *no* problems at all."

Hell. "That's what I meant to say," he hastened to reassure her. "I'll just be your muscle."

To his relief, she relaxed ever so slightly, and her smile flashed again. "Fine. You can be my muscle. Muscle remains in the background and blends in with the wallpaper."

"Got it. I can do wallpaper."

Catherine simply shook her head in open amusement. "Good try, but you couldn't do wallpaper if your life depended on it."

He lifted her hand and kissed it. "Why, thank you, darling. Allow me to return the compliment."

She visibly softened. "You don't have to come, Gabe. I won't need help."

"You're right, you won't. But I want to be there for you."

She debated for a few seconds before nodding. "Fine. This one time you can come."

He struggled to appear both humble and grateful. If she hadn't been so distracted, she wouldn't have bought it for a minute. "I appreciate it." That decided, he pushed back from the table. Bending down, he tipped her chin upward and gave her a slow, thorough kiss. "I'm off to work. If you need me, call my cell."

She stopped him before he'd gone more than a half dozen steps. "Gabe?" When he turned, she smiled in a way that had his gut clenching.

"Thanks."

The day of Annie's wedding proved perfect in every regard. The weather couldn't have been prettier. Everyone showed up exactly on time. And best of all, the entire affair ran like clockwork. To Catherine's relief, her nerves settled the minute she stepped foot in the church. She fell into a comfortable rhythm, orchestrating the progression with an ease and skill that impressed even Annie's mother.

There were the expected last-minute glitches. Someone stashed the bridal bouquet in the wrong room, causing momentary panic. The ring bearer managed to get grass stains on his britches during the ten seconds his mother wasn't supervising him. And one of the bridesmaids caught her heel in the hem of her gown and needed last-minute stitching. But other than that, the flow continued toward its inevitable conclusion, slow and smooth and golden.

Once the ceremony began, she had a moment to catch her breath and stood in the vestibule with Gabe, watching the timeless tradition of sacred words and new beginnings. It never failed to move her, and this time was no different.

"We never quite got there, did we?" Gabe said in an undertone.

It had been a long day. An exhausting week. Perhaps because of it, the question struck with devastating accuracy. "No," she whispered. "We never did."

The couple had reached the point where they were exchanging their vows, promises to love and cherish through good times and bad. When she and Gabe had hit those rough patches, she hadn't stuck. She'd run.

"We're not going to ever get there," he informed her in a quiet voice. "Not the way we're going. In order for a couple to marry, they have to trust each other. And we don't."

She fought to keep the tremble from her voice. "I know."

He leaned in, his presence a tangible force. "We have a choice, sweetheart. We can walk away now. No harm, no foul." He let that sink in before continuing. "Or we can do what we should have done two years ago. We can fight for it."

Would he still feel the same way if he had all the facts at his disposal? She doubted it. And now wasn't the time to find out. "I don't trust easily," she admitted. "Not anymore. I've spent two years building up walls."

"There are ways around walls. Chinks and cracks we can squeeze through. If it doesn't work out between us, you can always seal up all those cracks again."

"True."

"Are you willing to try, Cate?" His hands dropped to her shoulders and he turned her to face him. "Will you give it an honest try?"

She wanted to. Oh, how she longed to do just that. "I'd like to. But there are things—"

His mouth tightened for a telling moment. "I'm well aware there are 'things.' I'm not asking you to explain until you're ready."

A wistful smile quivered on her lips and she shook her head in a combination of affection and exasperation. "I know you, Gabe. What you really mean is I can explain when I'm ready, so long as I'm ready on demand. Am I close?"

He conceded the observation with a shrug. "We can't resolve our differences until I know what the problem is."

He had a point.

"Will you give me a little more time?" Time to see whether their relationship had a shot at working before she unburdened herself. "I need to be convinced we can straighten out our previous problems before introducing new ones. I need to be certain it's real."

"It is real. But if time is what you need, I'll give it to you. For now." He held out his hand. "Shall we make it official?"

"You have a deal, Mr. Piretti."

She took the hand he offered, not the least surprised when he gave it a little tug. She allowed herself to sink against him. Then she lifted her face to his and sealed the agreement in a long, lingering kiss, a kiss that spoke to her on endless levels. The gentleness of it made a promise, one that she longed to believe, while the strength and confidence had her relaxing into the embrace. It contained an unspoken assurance that she could lean on him and he'd be there to gather her up. That she could tell him anything and everything and he'd understand. But there was another quality underlying the kiss, the strongest quality of all. Passion. It ribboned through the heated melding of lips, barely leashed.

"Cate…" Her name escaped in a harsh whisper, one filled with need. "How can you deny this? How can you doubt?"

"I don't deny it." It would be ridiculous to try, not when he could feel her helpless reaction to his touch. "But—"

"No, Catherine. No more excuses." He cupped her

face and fixed her with a determined gaze. "Make a choice. Right here, right now. Give us a chance."

She'd spent two long, lonely years getting over Gabe. Out of sheer protection, she'd shut that door and locked it, and she'd been determined to never open it again. Now here she was, forced to deal with all that she'd put behind her. Gabe didn't just want her to open that door to the past, he wanted to storm through.

She shivered. What would happen when he uncovered the secrets she kept hidden there? Would it make a difference? Or would a miracle happen? Was it possible for them to come to terms with the past? To readjust their priorities and choose each other over their careers? Or would they slowly, relentlessly slip back into old patterns?

There was only one way to find out. With the softest of sighs, Catherine closed her eyes and surrendered to the dream. "All right. I'll give us a chance."

Eight

It had become almost a ritual, Catherine decided. The long elevator ride to the executive floor of Piretti's office building, the brisk sweep across plush carpeting toward Roxanne's desk, the brief feminine clash of gazes and then the welcome that waited for her on the other side of Gabe's door.

Unlike the previous week, this time Roxanne stopped her, putting an unwelcome kink in the ritual. "Did she call you?" Her usual honeyed accent was missing, replaced by a tone both tight and abrupt.

Catherine paused. "If you mean Natalie, yes, she did."

Coal-black eyes burned with resentment. "That ends it, then?"

"That's entirely up to you."

She didn't wait for a reply but gave Gabe's door a light tap and walked in. He stood in his usual position at the windows, talking on his headset, and she could tell he hadn't heard her knock. She didn't think she'd ever tire of seeing him like this, a man in his element, captain of all he surveyed.

A hint of melancholy swept over her. He deserved so much more than she could give him. It was wrong of her to take advantage of him. Wrong of her to allow him to believe, even for this brief span of time, that they could forge a future together.

Even knowing all that, she couldn't seem to help herself. He'd asked her to try, and she intended to do precisely that, all the while knowing that she'd never have to reveal her secret because their relationship would never get that far. They'd hit a stumbling block long before it was time for true confessions.

The muscles across his back flexed the instant he became aware of her, and his head tilted as though he were scenting the air. He turned his head, his focus arrowing in her direction, and he smiled. Just that. Just a simple smile. And she melted.

What was it about him? Why Gabe and only Gabe? His personality was a big part of it, that forceful, take-charge persona that never saw obstacles, only challenges. But it wasn't only that. His intelligence attracted her, those brilliant leaps of insight and the instant comprehension of facts and figures, people and events. And then there was that raw sex appeal, his ability to ignite her with a single touch. She closed her eyes. Or a single look. Just being this close to him left her drunk with desire, the need for more a craving she'd never quite overcome.

"I'll get back to you tomorrow," he murmured into his headset, before disengaging. "What is it, Catherine? What's wrong?"

She forced herself to look at him and accept what couldn't be changed. "Nothing's wrong," she replied calmly. "In fact, something's very right."

He lifted an eyebrow and pulled off the headset, tossing it aside. "Good news? I'm all for that. What happened?"

"I had a call from Natalie Marconi this morning. It seems she's had a change of heart. She's discussed the situation with a number of her friends and decided that Elegant Events did a marvelous job, after all, and that the series of catastrophes that occurred were neither our fault, nor could we have prevented them."

Instead of appearing relieved, Gabe frowned. "That's a rather dramatic turnaround, considering her attitude the day after her party. Do you know what prompted it, other than a bit of time and conversation?"

Catherine prowled across his office to the well-stocked wet bar adjacent to the sitting area. Gabe got there ahead of her and poured her a glass of merlot. "Thanks." She took an appreciative sip. "From what I can gather, the suggestion has been made that someone deliberately caused the problems at her party in order to make Elegant Events appear incompetent."

"Interesting. And why, according to Natalie and her cronies, would someone do that?"

"Natalie is of the opinion that it's one of my com-

petitors." Her comment caused surprise to bloom
across his face and his frown to deepen. "Apparently,
she'd been warned prior to the party not to hire me, but
chose not to listen to the advice. She thinks the incidents were retribution."

He puzzled through that, his head bent, his fists
planted on his hips, before shaking his head. "I don't
like this, Catherine. It doesn't feel right to me. Just off
the top of my head, I can think of a half dozen methods
for undercutting someone in the business world that are
far more effective than ruining a client's party. There are
way too many risks setting up the sort of problems you
experienced. Too many chances of getting caught. Too
many potential witnesses who could point the finger in
your direction. It's sloppy and nowhere near as effective as, say, undercutting your prices." He shook his
head again. "No. This sort of reprisal, assuming it is a
reprisal and not a series of unfortunate accidents, feels
personal, not business related."

Unfortunately, he was right. It was personal. One
more thing bothered her and bothered her a lot. She
didn't care for Roxanne blaming other event planners.
They were innocent in all this, and if the gossip ad-
versely impacted their business, she'd have to find a way
to set the record straight. Worse, she'd have to assume
a small portion of the blame, since she'd ordered
Roxanne to correct the problem, without putting any
conditions on how she went about it.

Gabe seemed to reach a decision. "Let it go for now,
Catherine. If Natalie is willing to forgive and forget, and

better yet, give you a glowing recommendation, it can only help."

She stilled, eyeing him with open suspicion. "I know you, Gabe, and I know that expression. You're planning something. What is it?"

"Not planning," he denied. "But I do intend to poke around a bit. Kick over a few rocks and see if anything slithers out. If Natalie is right and someone is trying to destroy your business, I want to know about it. And if it's personal, I damn well intend to get to the bottom of it." A grimness settled over him and had her stiffening. Anyone who saw his expression at that moment wouldn't question how or why he'd acquired his nickname. "And if I find out it's deliberate, there will be hell to pay."

Catherine considered that for a moment and decided it worked for her. She hadn't asked for his help. She hadn't so much as hinted in that direction. Nor had she anticipated him offering it. If Gabe chose to do some kicking and came across a certain snake wearing a smirk and a tight red dress, it wouldn't hurt her feelings, nor would she feel terribly guilty about the resulting fallout.

"Fine. Let's forget about all this for now and move on." She checked her watch and nodded in satisfaction. Five on the dot. She set aside her wineglass. "Time to go," she announced, crossing to his side.

She'd caught Gabe off guard and suppressed a smile at his confusion.

"Go?"

"Absolutely. Time to clock out or whatever it is you

do when you power down the mighty Piretti conglomerate. We have plans."

"Hell, I didn't realize. Sorry about that."

He reached for his PDA and she took it from his hand and tossed it aside. "You won't find the appointment in there."

That captured his attention. "What are you up to?" he asked, intrigued.

"It's a surprise. Are you interested?" She started toward the door, throwing an enticing smile over her shoulder. "Or would you rather work?"

He beat her to the door. Opening it, he ushered her through and didn't even glance Roxanne's way. "Close down shop" was all he said as they headed for the elevators.

It proved to be a magical evening. They strolled along the Seattle waterfront, taking in the sights with all the excitement and pleasure of a pair of tourists. There'd been a number of changes since they'd last taken the opportunity to visit. New, intriguing shops, refurbished restaurants, a small plaza that hadn't been there before.

Catherine couldn't recall afterward what they talked about. Nothing life-altering. Just the sweet, romantic exchanges a man and a woman share while establishing a relationship. The swift, intimate touches. The eye contact that said so much more than mere words. The flavor of the air, combined with the texture of the season, mingling with the unique scent of the man at her side. She knew it was a bonding ritual, and that she had no business bonding with Gabe. But she couldn't seem to help herself.

Eventually, they arrived at Milano's on the Sound, Joe's newest restaurant. He'd asked her to drop by some evening and see if it wouldn't be an acceptable venue for one of her future events. They entered the restaurant, a trendy building at the far end of one of Seattle's many piers, and Gabe lifted an eyebrow.

"Is this business or pleasure?" he asked in a neutral voice.

"Not really business," she assured him. "I'll come back another time to check it out more thoroughly, but not tonight." She caught his hand in hers. "Tonight's for us."

One of the aspects that she loved about Joe's restaurants was that he designed them with lovers in mind. She had never quite figured out how he pulled it off, but through the clever use of spacing, angles and elegant furnishings, he managed to create little clandestine nooks that gave the diner the impression of utter privacy.

The maître d' remembered her from the many events she'd scheduled at Milano's downtown restaurant, and clearly recognized Gabe. He greeted them both by name and, with a minimum of fuss, escorted them to an exclusive section reserved for VIPs. A deep-cushioned V-shaped bench faced windows overlooking Puget Sound and allowed them to sit side by side. And yet, because it was angled, they were still able to face each other.

"I'm curious," she said, once they were seated. "Would you have been angry if I'd chosen to eat here in order to check out the restaurant, as well as have a romantic dinner with you?"

"Not if you'd told me that was your intention." He accepted the wine list from the sommelier and after a moment's discussion, placed their order. Out on the Sound, a ferry plied the white capped chop, heading toward Bainbridge Island while the Olympics rose majestically against the horizon. "I think one of the problems I'm having is deciding how, when and where to separate business from pleasure."

She conceded his point with a wry grin. "Don't feel bad. So am I."

He regarded her in all seriousness. "How am I supposed to handle it, Catherine? I'd like to tell you about my day. It's a big part of who I am and what I enjoy doing. I want to share that aspect of myself with you. And I'd like to tell you about the progress I've made on your accounting records." He watched the ferry as it headed out, and the bustle of a tug returning to port, before switching his attention to her. "But I'm hesitant in case I cross that line, especially since I haven't quite figured out where you've drawn it."

"I haven't," she insisted, turning to face him more fully. "I think that's something we should discuss."

"Fine. Are you willing to discuss it here and now?"

Good question. She'd planned this as a romantic evening rather than a business meeting. But with two high-powered careers, finding a balance was paramount. "Let's discuss work over wine and then see if we can't move on from there."

He gave a brisk nod. "Agreed."

She almost laughed at the mannerism. It was so Gabe

Piretti, master negotiator. "Okay, here goes. Have you had a chance to look at my accounts?"

"I have."

He seemed troubled, so she gave him a gentle bump. "Did you find something wrong? Dina is always so meticulous, I can't believe she made a mistake."

"No, everything looks in order. It's just…" He hesitated. "You remember I told you that Natalie's deduction about a competitor being responsible for your problems felt wrong?" At her nod, he continued. "Your books appear in order. But they feel wrong to me. Off, somehow."

"Have you spoken to your mother about it?"

He shook his head. "Not yet. I need time to go through them a little more thoroughly first. I've been a bit distracted because of this upcoming buyout, so I haven't been able to give it my full attention." The wine arrived, was poured and tested, then accepted. "When's your next event? I want to make sure I schedule it in my PDA."

She played with the stem of her glass. "Two days. It's a small one. Under normal circumstances I wouldn't have taken the contract, but with all the problems I've been having, I didn't dare turn them down."

"Smart."

"After that there's a charity function later in the week. And Dina tells me that some of the people who called after the Marconi party wanting to cancel have changed their minds. It's clear that word is getting out, though I suspect some of the turnaround is thanks to your mother's way with people." She shifted closer to Gabe. "You're like that, too."

He draped his arm around her, and she rested her head on his shoulder. "Dad wasn't. He tended to be gruffer. No nonsense."

She toyed with her wineglass. "I've seen that side of you, too, particularly when it comes to business."

"It runs down the Piretti line." A slow smile built across his face and a distant look crept into his gaze. "It'll be interesting to see which of our sons and daughters carry on that tradition. Or maybe they'll be more like you. More passionate. Determined to take on the world."

"Oh, Gabe," she whispered.

He stiffened. "Damn. Damn it to hell." He gave a quick shake of his head. "I'm sorry, Catherine. That wasn't deliberate, it just popped out. I wasn't thinking."

"Don't. Don't apologize." She eased from his hold. "Don't you see, Gabe? It's part of who you are. Part of what you come from. You're a Piretti. Your family has been in this part of the country since the first settler felled the first log. You told me yourself that Piretti's was originally a sawmill."

"Times change," he said with a hint of imperiousness. "Now Piretti's is what I say it is."

"Your empire was built on a foundation of those who came before you," she argued. "You may have changed the scope and context of your family's business, but it's still a family concern."

"It's *my* concern," he corrected. "Where it goes from this point forward is wherever I choose to steer it."

"And in another thirty years?" she pressed. "In another forty? Who steers it then, Gabe?"

"In another thirty or forty years I'll have an answer for you," he replied with impressive calm. "Or maybe I'll follow Jack LaRue's example and sell out. Retire and live large."

"I can't believe you could simply let it all go after working so hard to build it up."

"Watch me."

She didn't believe him. "I know you, Gabe. You still want children. That little slip tells me that much. And it doesn't take a genius to see what course of action you've set. You think you'll be able to change my mind."

"Cards on the table, Cate?"

She snatched up her wineglass. "Oh, please."

"I do want children. Either you'll change your mind about that, or you won't. But understand this…" He paused, his face falling into uncompromising lines. "If it comes down to a choice between you and children, I choose you. Is that course of action clear enough for you?"

He didn't give her time to say anything more. He took her wineglass from her hand and returned it to the table. And then he pulled her into his arms and kissed her. Kissed her in a way that had every other thought fleeing from her head. Kissed her with a thoroughness she couldn't mistake for anything but total, undiluted passion. Kissed her until her entire world was this man and this moment.

"No more excuses," he growled, when they came up for air. He bit at her lip and then soothed it with his tongue. "No more barriers. I may have forced you to move in with me, forced you into this devil's contract, but you accepted the terms and by God, you'll honor them. I won't have you walking away from me because of some trumped-up excuse."

She fought for breath. "It's not an excuse."

He swore. "Anything and everything you use to shove a wedge between us is an excuse, and I'm not having any more of it. Try me, Catherine. Keep trying me. Because I swear to you, I will wipe each and every obstacle out of existence before I'll ever let you go again. I made the mistake of letting you run last time. This time I will follow you to the ends of the earth. I will follow you to hell and back, if that's what it takes."

She buried her head against his shoulder. "You're wrong, Gabe. You just don't know it yet. Next time, you won't just let me go. You'll throw me out."

Gabe couldn't help but notice that the tenor of their relationship changed after that. There'd always been barriers between them, but now they were so high and clear that he found himself stumbling over them at every turn. Despite that, two things gave him hope.

For one, Catherine continued with their impromptu dates, constantly surprising him with tickets to a play or dinners out or a picnic in their bedroom. Some occasions were brief, barely an hour, slipped into a narrow window in their schedules. Others were longer, partial days where they'd escape from work and spend endless hours enjoying each other's company. It made him realize that they could change. They could work around two diverse and demanding schedules.

The other thing that gave him hope was the nights they shared. For some reason, when they slid into bed and then into each other, all their differences, all their conflicts, faded from existence. There they joined and melded. There they found a true meeting of mind and body and spirit.

Later that week, he surprised her by showing up at one of her events, a charity fund-raiser for pediatric cancer patients. He'd expected to find her in her usual position, quietly in the background directing and coordinating the smooth progress of the affair. Instead, he found her sprawled on the floor, reading to a crowd of children from a Mrs. Pennywinkle picture book.

Tendrils of her hair had escaped its orderly knot and a succession of curls danced around her forehead and cheeks and at the vulnerable nape of her neck. Her eyes as she read were golden warm and sweetened with a soft generosity. There weren't any barriers here. Here he found her at her most open and natural. He'd seen her like this other times, almost invariably around children, and he shook his head in amusement. How could she claim to never want a child of her own when he could almost taste her longing, and could see the sheer joy she experienced light up the room?

She must have sensed him on some level because her head jerked up, like a doe sensing danger. Her gaze shot unerringly to his and for a brief second she shared that same openness with him that she'd shared with the children. And then the barriers slammed into place. He stood for a long moment, staring at her. It just about killed him that she felt the need to protect herself from him, and a fierce determination filled him.

Somehow, someway, he'd break through those defenses. He'd win back her trust, and this time he'd do everything in his power to keep it. He approached, keeping his demeanor open and casual. Leaning down, he gave her a light, easy kiss, one that elicited giggles from their audience.

Catherine handed the book over to one of her assistants and excused herself. Not that the children let her go without a fight. She was swamped with hugs before they reluctantly allowed her to leave.

He helped her up, drawing her close long enough to murmur in her ear, "Have I told you recently how beautiful you are?"

Vivid roses bloomed in her cheeks. "Don't exaggerate, Gabe."

He tilted his head to one side. "You don't believe me, do you?" The idea intrigued him.

"I'm attractive. Interesting looking, perhaps." She stepped back. "But I'm not beautiful."

"You are to me," he stated simply.

To his amusement she changed the subject. "I didn't expect to see you here. You never mentioned that you might attend."

"I've been on the board of this particular charity for a number of years, but I wasn't sure I could get away." He cut her off before she could ask the question hovering on her lips. "And no, I had nothing to do with hiring you. That's handled by a subcommittee. I did discover, however, that you've waived your usual fee and donated your services."

She shrugged. "It's for a good cause."

"Thank you." He could see her slipping back into professional mode and didn't want to distract her. "I'll let you get on with your duties. One quick question. What's your calendar for tomorrow look like?"

"I thought I might need a day off after the fundraiser, so I kept it clear."

That suited him perfectly. After a few days of allowing Catherine to take the lead with their romantic outings, Gabe was intent on trying his hand at it. "Keep it that way, if you would."

She brightened. "You want me to plan something? Or shall we wing it?"

"I'll take care of everything. You just show up."

He gave her another swift kiss and then left her to focus on her event, though periodically through the afternoon he caught her glancing his way with a speculative look. Since they'd started in with the dates, he'd discovered that she preferred to keep their outings moving, no doubt so they wouldn't have another incident like the one at Milano's.

Come tomorrow, he intended to change all that.

All Gabe told Catherine in advance was to wear a swimsuit underneath her shorts and cotton tee and prepare for a day in the sun. When he pulled into Sunset Marina the next morning, she turned to him, her eyes glowing with pleasure.

"We're going for a cruise?"

"I thought we'd take a ride through the Chittenden locks and onto Lake Washington. Or we can wander around the Sound, if you prefer."

"It's been ages since I've gone through the locks. Let's do that."

The day became magical. In those precious hours, Gabe didn't care about the secrets that divided them, or the past or the future. The now occupied his full attention. It turned into one of those rare Seattle days where the Olympics stood out in sharp relief to the west and the Cascades held up their end to the east, with Mt. Rainier dominating the skyline in between. But as far as he was concerned the best view was the pint-sized woman who lazed across his foredeck. A hot golden sun blazed overhead, causing Catherine to strip down to her swimsuit, while a warm summer breeze stirred her hair into delightful disarray.

Eventually, she joined him on the bridge, handing him a soft drink and curling up in the seat next to him. She examined her surroundings with unmistakable pleasure. "I gather this is one of the custom-designed yachts your company manufactures."

"One of the smaller ones, yes." He shot her a swift grin. "It's not a Piretti engine…at least, not yet. I'm hoping to pin Jack LaRue down soon. Then maybe I'll have time to dig into your bookkeeping records and give them the attention they deserve."

She shrugged. "I'll leave that to you. It's definitely not my area of expertise, although it sure is Dina's."

"Mom has a talent for it," he agreed.

"I guess that's why it surprised me that she didn't catch on to... What was the name of that guy who proposed to her a few months after your dad died?" She snapped her fingers. "Stanley something, wasn't it?"

The question hit like a body blow. "Are you talking about Stanley Chinsky?"

She hesitated, reacting to his tone. "Um. Did he head Piretti's accounting department at some point?"

"Yes. He was also a board member." Outrage filled him. "That bastard had the nerve to propose to Mom?"

Catherine made a production of sliding her can into one of the drink holders, her gaze flitting away from his. "I gather she never mentioned it."

"No, she didn't."

Catherine released a gusty sigh. "I'm sorry, Gabe. I didn't realize or I'd never have said anything. She told me about it that night we had our heart-to-heart."

"Did she also tell you that Stanley attempted to rob her blind during his tenure as our accountant?"

"Actually, she did. I think she blamed herself to some extent," Catherine offered. "She thought her refusal of his proposal may have provoked his retaliation."

"The hell it did. He started stealing from us the minute my father died. If he proposed to her, it was only in the hopes of covering up his little scheme."

Catherine offered a tentative smile. "Dina did say it was a pretty clever one."

"It was. It took me forever to figure out—" He broke off. "Son of a bitch. Son of a *bitch*. Why the hell didn't I see it?"

"See what?"

He turned on her. "This is your fault, you know. If I hadn't been so distracted by you, I'd have seen it right off."

"Damn it, Gabe. Seen *what?*"

"What my mother's been up to." He turned the boat in a wide arc and goosed the throttle. "The reason you're going bankrupt is that my dear mother has been skimming the accounts."

Nine

It took several hours for Gabe and Catherine to work their way back from Lake Washington to Shilshole Bay and safely dock the boat at the marina. They arrived on Dina's doorstep just as dusk settled over the city. She opened the door with a wide smile, one that faded the instant she got a good look at their expressions.

She stepped back to allow them in. "I'm busted, aren't I?"

"Oh, yeah," Gabe confirmed. "Seriously busted."

Her chin shot up. "Actually, I expected this confrontation quite a bit sooner. I'm a little disappointed in you, Gabriel."

"And you'd have gotten this confrontation sooner if I hadn't been so distracted by Catherine."

Dina nodded. "I have to admit, I was counting on that."

They stood in the foyer, the three of them as awkward and uncomfortable as strangers. Gabe thrust a hand through his hair. "What the hell is going on, Mom? How could you do such a thing to Catherine? She trusted you, and you betrayed that trust."

In response, Catherine eased her hand over the tensed muscles of his arm. "There's a good reason, Gabe. There has to be."

Dina smiled her approval. "Why don't I make a pot of coffee while we chat?"

"Chat." Gabe stared at her in disbelief. "This isn't some sort of afternoon social. Coffee's not going to fix this. This is serious. This is jail-time serious."

An expression not unlike Gabe's settled over her face, one of ruthless determination. "If you want your questions answered, then we'll do it over coffee. Because I'm not saying another word, otherwise."

He turned to Catherine. "I'm sorry about this. I swear I had no idea."

She simply shook her head. "Let's hear her out."

Dina linked her arm through Catherine's and drew her toward the kitchen. "Don't worry," she whispered. "It's not as bad as it seems."

"No, it's worse," Gabe broke in, clearly overhearing. "You and Stanley can have adjoining cells."

"Catherine isn't going to turn me over to the authorities," Dina replied with calm certainty. "Not after I explain."

"This better be one hell of a good explanation."

Dina made short work of the coffee. The entire time, she chatted about anything and everything except the reason they were there. Pouring coffee into mugs, she carried them to the table. "You both have had some sun today," she commented, spooning sugar into her cup. "It's nice to see that you're spending so much time together and working things out between you."

"Mom." Just that one word. Quiet. Fighting for patience. But with an underlying demand she couldn't mistake.

She gave her teaspoon an irritable tap against the porcelain edge of the mug and released her breath in a sigh. "All right, fine. Ask your questions."

Gabe reached for Catherine's hand and gave it a reassuring squeeze. "You skimmed money out of the Elegant Events accounts." He didn't phrase it as a question.

"Yes, I did." Dina leaned back in her chair and took a sip of coffee. "I'm sorry, Catherine, but you made it quite easy. I highly recommend you take a few accounting courses so no one else takes advantage of you in the future."

Catherine lifted an eyebrow and to Gabe's disbelief, he caught a hint of amusement at his mother's outrageous suggestion. Though what she could find amusing about any of this he had no idea. "Why, thank you for your advice, Dina. I'll get right on that," she murmured.

Gabe stepped in again. "You used the Chinsky method, I assume."

"Oh, yes. Stanley was an excellent teacher. I just

followed his example and did to Catherine precisely what he'd done to me." She shrugged. "And then I waited."

This time, he reached for his mother's hand. "Are you hurting for money? Has something happened that you've been afraid to tell me? Whatever it is, I'll do everything in my power to help. You know that, don't you?"

Tears welled up in Dina's eyes. "Oh, Gabriel. You have no idea how much your saying that means to me. You've always done your best to look out for me." She gave him a misty smile. "But it's not about the money, dear."

"Then, what?" Catherine asked. She caught her lip between her teeth. "Is this because I left Gabe? Is this some sort of payback?"

Dina inhaled sharply. "You think I did this out of revenge? Oh, no, sweetheart. Never that. I love you as though you were my own daughter. How could you doubt that?" Her gaze, bird bright, shifted from Gabe to Catherine. "No, I did it to help the two of you."

"To help us," Catherine repeated, confusion overriding every other emotion. "How does driving our business into bankruptcy help?"

"Think about it. What did you do once you realized we were having financial difficulties?"

"I tried to drum up more business. I economized. I worked to reduce overhead and increase—" She broke off and closed her eyes. "Of course. I went to Gabe."

"There you go." Dina patted her hand. "I knew you'd get there eventually. Just as I knew that if our finances became serious enough and you couldn't see any other option available to you, you'd eventually go and ask Gabriel for help. I have to tell you, I was quite impressed by your determination not to give in. I almost had to scrap the entire plan."

"But I caved before you had to."

She beamed. "Exactly."

"Are you telling me," Gabe gritted out, "that you set up this entire scam, put Catherine through hell and back, as a matchmaking scheme?"

Dina tilted her head to one side in a mannerism identical to Gabe's. "I'd say that pretty much covers it, yes. And it worked, didn't it? You two are back together and looking happier than ever. If I hadn't stepped in, you'd still be apart and miserable." She tapped her index finger against the tabletop. "And before you lose that infamous Piretti temper of yours, let me tell you that I'd have done almost anything, risked just about any consequence in order to give you the opportunity to work out your differences. You taught me that, Gabriel, when you abducted me. You didn't care what ultimately happened to you as a result of your actions, so long as we patched up our relationship."

Gabe wrestled his temper under control, with only limited success. "I believe the expression is…hoisted by my own petard." And didn't that just bite? Another thought occurred to him. "And are you also behind the sabotage of her reputation?"

Dina's mug hit the table with a crack. "Absolutely not. How can you think I'd do such a thing?"

"Oh, hell, Mom. I don't know. Maybe because you stole from her?"

She sniffed. "That's different. The money didn't actually go anywhere. It's safe and sound. Catherine's name is even on the account where I have the funds stashed. So, technically, it probably isn't embezzlement."

"Technically, when I kill you it won't be murder because there's not a man alive who wouldn't consider it justifiable momicide." Okay, so maybe his temper wasn't totally under control.

"That's enough, Gabe," Catherine said, stepping into the fray. "It's time to go."

For the first time, Dina's smile faltered. "Are you terribly angry with me? I really was trying to help."

To Gabe's surprise, Catherine left her chair and crouched beside Dina. She wrapped her arms around the older woman and whispered something in her ear, something he couldn't make out. All he knew was that it made his mother cry, though a single look told him they were tears of happiness. Then Catherine straightened and glanced at Gabe.

"Could you take me back to your apartment, please?" she asked.

Not home, he noted. But to *his* apartment. He could feel the time remaining between them growing short, could almost hear the clock ticking down the final minutes, and his jaw clenched. Now that he'd resolved Catherine's financial issues, and her reputation had regained its footing, he was rapidly running out of leverage for convincing her to stay with him. Did she want to return to his place because she planned to pack up and return to her apartment?

If so, he'd better come up with a new plan for convincing her to stay...and fast.

Gabe's tension was palpable the entire drive to his place and Catherine didn't dare say a word in case it was the wrong word, one that set off whatever was building inside him. She waited quietly while he inserted his key in the lock and shoved open the door, allowing her to enter ahead of him.

The interior lay in utter darkness and thundering silence, a silence broken only by the harsh sound of their breathing. She switched on the lamp by the wooden sculpture of the sleeping woman and trailed her hand along the fluid lines. It had become a habit to caress the small statue whenever she entered the apartment.

"I bought that after you left because it reminded me of you," Gabe said.

"Does it?" She took another look. She couldn't see the similarity herself, but then she had no idea what she looked like when asleep. She could only hope it was this graceful. "Why would you do that when our relationship was over?"

"Because it wasn't over. It isn't over."

She couldn't miss the implacable tone, the underlying statement that he planned to do everything within his power to convince her to stay, even after all the problems at Elegant Events had been resolved. And he was right. It wasn't over between them.

Not yet. Not tonight.

"And when our business is concluded?" She glanced at him over her shoulder. He stood in shadow, making it impossible to read his expression. But there was no mistaking the look in his eyes. A look of utter ruthlessness. "You aren't going to honor your promise and let me go, are you?"

"No."

She nodded to herself. "I didn't think so."

In a single supple movement she snagged the hem of her T-shirt and pulled it up over her head. The scrap of cotton fluttered to the floor, a pale flag of surrender against the gray carpet.

"What are you doing?" The question escaped, abrasive as sandpaper.

She unsnapped her shorts and shimmied out of them, letting them pool at her feet before stepping clear of them. "What does it look like I'm doing?"

"It looks remarkably like a striptease." He reached for her, but she evaded him. "Why, Catherine?"

Reaching behind her, she unhooked her bathing suit top and let it slip away into the darkness. "Why am I taking off my clothes? Why aren't I packing up and moving out? Or why did you never come after me when I left? Why did your mother have to go to such extremes to throw us together again?"

He ignored all her questions, but one. "Are you staying?"

She hooked her thumbs in the scrap of silk anchored to her hips and slid it off. She headed for the bedroom, turning at the last minute to say, "It would be a shame to let all Dina's hard work go to waste, wouldn't it?"

He caught up with her in the hallway. Without a word, he swept her high into his arms and carried her into the bedroom. The world spun dizzily around her right before the bed reached up to cushion their fall. Still he didn't speak. But she found that words weren't necessary. Not when he said it all in a single kiss.

His mouth closed over hers, first in tender benediction, then in something else. She sensed he wanted to be gentle, but this wasn't a night for gentleness. Something fierce and desperate and raw erupted between them. It was as though they'd been stripped to their bare essence, all polish and sophistication shredded, with only an elemental need remaining.

"I can't hold back tonight," he said in between kisses.

"I don't want you to."

He gathered her up and spread her across the silk bedcover, anchoring her wrists above her head with one hand while shaping her lean contours with the other. And then he feasted on what her striptease had bared. His mouth captured her breast. While the light nip and tug shot her skyward, his hand slid to her hip and then through the crisp triangle of curls. He cupped her, and with one slow, torturous stroke with his clever, clever fingers he had her erupting.

"No," she moaned. "I want more. I want you."

"And you'll have me," he promised. "Patience, sweetheart."

"You be patient. I'll have you now."

She fought free of his hold and pushed at his shoulders, rolling him onto his back. He didn't put up much of a struggle, but then she didn't expect him to. It was her turn to explore. Her turn to taste, then devour. Her turn to sculpt lines as graceful as the wooden statue he'd compared her to. But his lines flowed with a far different type of grace. His body was hard and crisp and honed. And utterly, gloriously male.

She started at the top of him, with that face that was just a shade too pretty for his own good. Sooty brows. Eyes of cobalt blue that pierced mere skin and bone and arrowed right through to the heart and soul of her. A nose, straight and proud. His jaw, a stubborn block of granite that once set could rarely be shifted. And his mouth.

She fell into his mouth, moaning at the endless sweep and parry of his tongue that never failed to send her heart tripping and racing like a sprinter's. And still, it wasn't enough. More, more, more. She wanted to explore every single inch and give to him the way he'd so often given to her.

His throat moved convulsively as she kissed her way along it and she could feel a harsh groan building there, rumbling against her lips. "Not in control now, are we, Piretti?" she teased. "Looks like there's a new pirate in charge of the pillaging and plundering."

"Pillage any more of my plunder and I'll go digging for your buried treasure."

She choked on a laugh and skittered downward. "Not yet. I have other plans for you first."

Like his amazing chest. It had driven her crazy the entire day, watching him helm his yacht in just a pair of white gauze, drawstring pants slung low on his narrow hips. He truly had a spectacular physique, with powerful arms roped with muscle and yards of deeply tanned, lightly furred chest. And when he'd bent down to adjust one of the boat fenders or secure the lines, the sight of his tight, rounded flanks almost brought her to her knees. All she could think about throughout those endless hours was giving that drawstring of his a little jerk. Now she could.

She made quick work of it, loosening the waistband and delving inside. She followed the plunging line of crisp, dark hair until she hit her own personal treasure. He felt hot to the touch, that peculiar combination of sleek overlying steel one that never failed to amaze, even as it aroused. She wanted to give to him, give something special. So first she touched; then she tasted.

The groan finally escaped his throat, an eruption of sound, followed by an eruption of movement. He dragged her upward, flipped her, and with a single swift plunge mated them one to the other. Energy shot through her, a tense expectation that hovered just out of reach.

"I'm sorry." The words were torn from him. "I'm so sorry."

She cupped his face, forcing that wild blue gaze to fix on her. "Why are you sorry? How can you possibly be sorry when we're here, together, like this?"

"My mother was wrong to force you into this. I was wrong to force you."

Catherine could barely hang on. "This isn't wrong." It was perfect. It was heaven on earth. "It never was and never could be."

The breath burned from his lungs. "You didn't take her apart as you had every right to do. I don't know what you said to her, but it made her so happy."

In a smooth flow of movement, Catherine cinched his waist with her legs and pulled him in tight. "You want to know what I said?" She gave herself up to his helpless movements, caught the rhythm with him and rode the storm. "I told her thank you."

They shattered then, falling apart in each other's arms. Catherine stared blindly up at him, knowing that she'd never be able to gather up all the pieces again, never be able to put them together the way they were before. She'd done the unthinkable that day.

She'd fallen in love with Gabe again.

"Why did you leave me?"

In the exhausted fallout from their lovemaking, the question caught her completely off guard and utterly defenseless. No doubt he'd planned it that way. "Do we have to do this now?"

He rolled over to face her and lifted onto an elbow. His expression was so serious, so determined. "Something happened, didn't it?"

"Yes."

"Something more than my giving work priority at the worst possible time."

"Yes," she whispered again.

"What happened?"

"Please, Gabe. Tonight was so special, I don't want anything to ruin it. I owe you the truth. I know I do. And I'll give it to you, I promise."

He swept wayward curls from her face, his gaze one of infinite compassion. "You thought this moment wouldn't come, didn't you? That our relationship would fall apart and spare you whatever it is you need to confess."

"Yes." She sat up and snagged the sheet, wrapping it around herself. It was a telling gesture. She took a minute to think through her options, aware of him tamping down on his impatience so she had that opportunity. "Do you know what the weekend after next is?"

She could see he didn't care for the abrupt change in subject. "What's that got to do with anything?"

"The date," she continued doggedly. "Do you know the significance of the date?"

He paused to consider, then nodded. "It'll be two years to the day that you left."

"I want you to take four days off—just four days— and go away with me that weekend. You choose the spot. Someplace special."

He left the bed, his movements uncharacteristically jerky. "Are you serious?"

"Quite serious. If you'll do that, I'll answer any and all questions you put to me. And I'll answer them unconditionally." She hesitated. "But I think I should warn you that you're not going to like what you hear."

He snagged a pair of jeans and yanked them on. He'd never looked more potently male than in that moment.

His hair was rumpled from their lovemaking, and traces of fierce passion still cut across the planes of his face. Even his body was taut and scented with aggression. The predator had escaped from beneath his civilized cloak and he was on the prowl.

"Why all the drama, Catherine? Why not just come clean here and now?"

She looked around with wistful affection. "I don't want any more ghosts haunting this place than there already are. And I want to deal with our issues on neutral territory. Either we're able to put it all behind us and move on." She swallowed. "Or we call it quits."

"Son of a—" He thrust a hand through his hair. "You think next weekend is going to end our relationship, don't you?"

A vise tightened around her throat, and she had to force out her answer. "Yes. Please, Gabe. I want—I need—this time beforehand."

"All right, fine. I'll arrange to take that weekend off and give you the time you're asking." He stalked toward the bed. Perhaps it was his partial nudity. Perhaps it was the distracting gap in his jeans. Perhaps it was simply that he still had a prowl to his step. Whatever the cause, she'd never seen him more intimidating. "But hear me, Catherine, and hear me well. I won't let you go. Whatever this secret is, we'll work our way through it."

"I want to believe that."

He rested a knee on the mattress and cupped her face. "All you have to do is let me in. All you have to do is trust me. I'm not going to walk away from you. We will figure this out, after which I'm going to propose to you again. And this time I won't let anything inter-fere. No phone calls. No business. And no secrets."

Tears overflowed, spilling with helpless abandon down her cheeks. "I'm afraid."

"I know you are." He feathered a kiss across her mouth. "But there's nothing I can do about that, no way to reassure you, until you're honest with me."

The next several days passed as though on wings. With each one that slipped away, Catherine saw the death of her dreams approach with lightning-fast speed. Her days became overloaded with work, necessary if she was going to take the next weekend off to be with Gabe. But the nights…

Seated at the small desk in her bedroom, Catherine set her current checklist aside as she paused to consider. The nights overflowed with a passion unlike anything that had gone before. It was as though Gabe were determined to put some indelible mark on her, to prove that what existed between them could never be lost. Would never end.

But all things ended.

She shivered at the thought, then forced herself to return to work, scanning the checklist for any minor details she might have overlooked. At her elbow, the phone rang and she picked up the receiver. "Catherine Haile," she said, still focused more on work than the caller.

"May I speak with Mr. Gabe Piretti, please?" The voice was young, female and friendly.

"I'm sorry, he's not available," Catherine said absent-mindedly. "May I take a message?"

"Hmm. Maybe you can help me. This is Theresa from Très Romantique. I'm calling regarding the reservations he made with us."

Catherine put down her checklist and perked up a little. "Actually, I can help you with that."

"Lovely." Relief sounded in her voice. "When Mr. Piretti originally booked with us, he requested a suite."

"Did he?" Catherine murmured, pleased by his thoughtfulness.

"But when he changed the dates, the room was switched from a suite to a standard king. I took Mr. Piretti's original reservations myself, and I remember how adamant he was about wanting that particular suite. So, before I let it go, I just want to double-check that my associate didn't misunderstand his request." Theresa lowered her voice. "She's new, and I'm in charge of training her, so it's my head if a mistake is made. Besides, it would be a shame for him to lose that room, if it's the one he actually wanted. It's absolutely gorgeous."

Catherine frowned. "I'm sorry. Run that by me again. He changed the dates? We're not booked for this next weekend?"

"No, ma'am. It's been switched to one week later. One moment, please...." A muffled conversation ensued and then Theresa came back onto the line. "Kaisy says she remembers something about a work conflict. Fortunately, due to a recent cancelation, that particular suite is available both weekends. So if you could just confirm which room we should be holding...?"

The hell with which room. Right now all that mattered

was which date. "Theresa, could I get back to you on that?" Catherine asked as calmly as she could manage. "I need a few hours to check into it."

"I'm afraid I can't hold the suite past five today," she explained. "Would that give you sufficient time?"

"That will be fine," Catherine replied. "Thank you for calling."

She returned the receiver to its cradle using the greatest of care, and closed her eyes while despair swamped her. How could Gabe make that change without consulting her first? He knew. He knew how important this weekend was to her, that she'd planned to speak frankly about what had happened two years ago. Why would he undermine all that?

They'd grown so close over the past month. They'd finally learned to trust, had slowly, but surely, dealt with their differences. She'd witnessed the change in him. Understood why Piretti's was of such importance to him, just as he'd accepted the importance of her career. And this was what it came down to.

When everything was said and done, all his fine promises to reorganize his priorities were just so much talk. He hadn't changed, not really.

She fought for calm as she considered her options. Last time she'd run. Last time she'd been ill and her only thought had been to hide somewhere safe while she licked her wounds. But she wasn't the same woman she'd been two years ago. Catherine shoved back her chair and stood.

This time she'd fight back.

Ten

Catherine had little memory of the drive across town to Piretti's headquarters. Little memory of parking her car in the underground lot, or taking the elevator straight to the top using the special coded key card Gabe had given her that allowed her direct access to the highest of the high.

She only woke to her surroundings as she strode, rapid-fire, across the plush carpet toward Gabe's office. Roxanne sat at her desk, smiling that smug smile of hers, and it took every ounce of self-control not to ball up a fist and plant it right in that pouty red mouth. Did she know? Catherine couldn't help but wonder. Did that explain the delighted look in her eye, one that said she would relish every minute of the scene about to unfold?

She swept past Roxanne's desk and thrust open Gabe's door without so much as a perfunctory knock. He was in a meeting, not that she gave a damn. She slammed the door closed behind her.

"Did you cancel our plans for this weekend?" she demanded.

Everyone froze. All eyes swiveled from her to Gabe. "Gentlemen…" He jerked his head toward the door. "Clear the decks."

There was a minor scrambling toward the exit, like rats deserting a sinking ship. The last man overboard pulled the door shut behind him as gently as though it were made of Waterford crystal. Catherine knew she was handling this badly, but she was too furious to care. She tossed her purse onto the chair in front of Gabe's desk, considered sitting and elected to stand. Gabe rose to confront her. Annoyance, bordering on anger, glittered in his blue eyes.

"What's going on, Catherine?"

To her horror she felt tears pressing into her throat and behind her eyelids. She'd planned to maintain her cool, to use a hint of self-righteous anger to carry her through a difficult conversation. Instead, she could feel herself crumbling. She balled her hands into fists, and fought for control.

"I had a phone call less than an hour ago from Très Romantique informing me that you'd called and changed our reservations from this week to next due to a work conflict." Her control wobbled, but she fought back. "I know you probably don't think there's any difference between one week and another. But it mattered—*matters*—to me. I thought you understood." She looked him dead in the eye so there'd be no mistaking her feelings on the matter. "So, here's the bottom line. When I need you, I need you. It can't always be at your convenience. Sometimes life happens and it ends up happening during a meeting or during a negotiation or…or—" To her horror, her voice broke.

"Catherine—"

She waved him off. "No!" She snatched a quick, calming breath, relieved to feel the press of tears ease just enough for her to speak. "No, Gabe. Things have changed. *I've* changed. I'm not handling our little crisis the way I did two years ago. I'm not going to remain silent any longer. I'm not going to sit by the phone waiting for your call. I'm not going to leave you a note. And I'm damn sure not going to run. This time I'll have my say."

Some indefinable reaction shifted across his expression, one she couldn't take the time to analyze, not if she wanted to get through this.

"I'm listening."

But for how long? And how would it ultimately affect their relationship? "I don't care if this weekend interferes with business issues. I need you. Not last weekend. Not the weekend after. *This* weekend."

"Why?" he asked quietly.

She simply stood and stared at him, her grief and sorrow leaking from her in an unstoppable stream. "The date."

"It's the two-year anniversary of the date you left me. I got that part."

She caught a glimpse of the emotion behind that subtle shift in expression, a hint of anger combined with a wealth of pain.

"What I haven't been able to figure is why you'd want to go out of your way to commemorate the occasion."

She could feel the blood drain from her face. "Commemorate? You thought—" Oh, no. No, no, no. "Oh, Gabe, that's not it at all. I'm so sorry you thought so. I don't want to commemorate it."

His eyes closed briefly and he swore beneath his breath. "Aw, hell. You planned to replace the memories, didn't you?" Circling the desk, he pulled her close, and with that one simple touch, the fury and tension drained away. He cupped her face and turned it up to his. "You're attempting to superimpose new memories, happy memories over top of what went before."

She stared at him, her chin trembling. "How could you think otherwise?"

He gave a half-humorous shrug. "It happens. And it's going to happen again, especially when we miss a small step…such as the one where you explain your plan in advance."

She was an idiot. She'd assumed he'd understand without her having to go there. "Sometimes I forget you don't read minds." She let the sigh pour out of her.

"Is that why, Gabe? Is that why you changed the date? You thought I planned to rub salt in the wound? Is that really something you believe I'd do?"

"Listen carefully, Catherine...." He lowered his head and feathered a brief kiss across her mouth. "I. Didn't. Change. The. Date."

It took her a moment to process the words. "But...but I had a phone call from Theresa at Très Romantique. She said you did."

"She's mistaken." He edged his hip onto his desk and reached for his PDA. "Let's get this straightened out, shall we?"

Tapping with the stylus, he brought up the information he needed and then placed a call. A few minutes later he was connected to Reservations. It never ceased to amaze her how cleanly he managed to cut straight through to the heart of the matter, explaining the problem in a few short sentences. He listened for a while to what Catherine could only presume was Theresa's chronicle of events.

"Got it. I'll be certain to tell your manager how much I appreciate your thoughtfulness in calling about the suite, especially since it's clear that the error was on my end. I also appreciate your reinstating the original reservation. In the meantime, could you check with Kaisy and ask her specifically who changed the date? Not at all. I'll wait."

His gaze shifted to Catherine and she shivered. She'd only seen that look in his eye once before, when he'd discovered an employee had been cheating him. She never forgot that particular expression, just as she hoped never to see it again.

"Thank you, Theresa. That's precisely what I needed." He disconnected the call and then punched a button on his desk phone. "Roxanne, would you step into my office for a moment?"

Catherine released her breath in a slow sigh. Of course. How incredibly foolish of her not to have suspected as much. You could paint a leopard purple, but there were still spots lurking under all that dye. Roxanne could no more change her character than a leopard could change from a predator to a rabbit, regardless of threats and coercion.

How it must have chafed to toe the line. And when the opportunity arose to try for one more bit of mischief, she probably found it too much to resist. One more petty little slap, especially if she sensed how much it would hurt. Another thought occurred. Maybe she believed that Catherine couldn't change her spots, either. Maybe she thought that history would repeat itself, and Catherine would run, rather than tackle the problem head-on.

She and Gabe both waited in silence until Roxanne slithered into the room. Catherine scrutinized her closely. Today she'd chosen to project a far different image. She wore a beautiful ivory high-neck dress with tiny pearl buttons down the fitted bodice. A demure touch of lace gave the dress an almost bridal appearance. The entire ensemble was reminiscent of the turn of the previous century, right down to the Gibson Girl manner in which she'd piled her hair on top of her head. She carried a steno pad and pen, held at the ready.

"How can I help you, Gabe?" she asked sweetly.

"Answer a question for me, Roxanne."

She kept her dark gaze trained on her boss, completely ignoring Catherine. "Of course." She smiled, projecting the perfect amount of flirtatious innocence. "Anything at all. You know that."

"I had a reservation at Très Romantique. It's been changed. Do you know anything about it?"

"I do," she responded calmly. "I was going to tell you about it after your meeting ended, but..." She shot Catherine a swift, chiding glance. "I hadn't counted on Ms. Haile disrupting things."

He forced her back on point. "Explain what happened with the reservation."

"Certainly. I had a call from Mr. LaRue. He said that he had some sort of scheduling conflict and that Wednesday was no longer convenient to sign the final contracts. He insisted we change it."

"Insisted?"

She sighed. "Oh, Gabe, you know how he can be. He was adamant. I did my best to change his mind, but he wouldn't be budged. Only one other date would do and that happened to be during those days you had me block off. When I argued, he said it was then or never." She shook her head in distress. "What could I do? I told him I'd check with you and then thought maybe I could help you avert a blowup with Catherine by calling Très Romantique to see if they had any availability for the following week. I'm so sorry I failed. Clearly, Catherine isn't open to compromise."

"You canceled my reservations without checking with me first?"

She hesitated for a split second. "Of course not. I explained the conflict and had the girl hold the room for both dates. She agreed to do so until I had a chance to check with you." Her eyes widened. "Oh, no. Don't tell me she didn't do as I asked?"

"The girl's name is Kaisy. And that's not how she remembers the conversation going down."

Catherine had to give Roxanne credit. She didn't react to the comment by so much as a flicker of an eyelash. Nor did she deviate from her story. If anything her shock and indignation increased. "Then this Kaisy misunderstood. Either that or she's trying to cover up her mistake."

Gabe smiled. "Well, that explains that," he said smoothly.

Roxanne relaxed ever so slightly, even daring to shoot Catherine the tiniest of looks from the corner of her eye, one glowing with triumph. "Is there anything else?"

"I think there might be. Just give me a minute." He picked up the phone and stabbed out another number. "Gabe Piretti here," he replied to whatever greeting he received. "Is the big man around? Yes, I would, thanks."

Another brief pause. "Jack? I'm putting you on speaker, is that all right?"

"Sure…." His voice boomed into the room. "Not another change to our meeting, I hope?"

"Actually, that's why I'm calling."

Gabe fixed his eyes on his assistant, pinning her in place. She turned ashen. The shade clashed with her pretty little ivory dress, Catherine decided. Not at all a good color combination for her. She should have stuck with jewel tones. Besides, ivory was just going to draw attention to the boot print about to be inflicted to her curvaceous derriere.

"I'm looking at a note that Roxanne left me about the change to our meeting date," Gabe continued. "Was our original time inconvenient?"

"Hell, no. Roxy said it was bad for you."

Roxanne opened her mouth to interrupt and with one vicious look, Gabe had the words dying before they were ever spoken. "That's what she told you? That I wanted it changed?"

"Yup. Had it right from those sweet luscious lips of hers. I have to admit, I wasn't too happy about it. If she weren't so pretty with her apology, I would have raised holy hell."

"And why's that, Jack?"

"Because I was planning on ditching town the minute I cashed your check. Had a nice little vacation all planned out to kick off my retirement. Wife's none too pleased, either. Hasn't stopped pecking at me since I broke the news to her."

"I'll tell you what, Jack. Let me make a few adjust-ments at this end so you can go ahead and keep those plans. I wouldn't want to upset Marie."

"That's damn decent of you, Gabe. Think I'll tell her I ripped you a new one and you agreed to switch it back. You don't mind if I make myself the hero of the piece, do you?"

"Go right ahead. My best to Marie, and I'll see you Wednesday, as originally planned." He cut the connec-tion. "You're fired, Roxanne. I've just buzzed for security. They'll help you clear out your desk. Then they will escort you to payroll, where I'll have a two-month sev-erance check cut for you."

"Please, Gabe," she said in a soft, penitent undertone. "Don't I get a chance to explain?"

He didn't hesitate. "No." Hard. Cold. Absolute. "You stood here in front of me, looked me dead in the eye and lied. You changed those dates for one reason and one reason only. To hit out at Catherine. No one does that to my woman and gets away with it."

"If you'd just let me explain," she pleaded, huge tears welling up in her eyes, "you'd see this is just a big mis-understanding."

"You're right. My misunderstanding. I knew what you were when I hired you. I thought I could use that to my advantage. But I'd forgotten the cardinal rule. If you pick up a snake, expect to get bitten."

The tears dried and fury replaced her contrition. "I'll sue you. If you fire me, I'll sue you for every dime you have."

Gabe slowly climbed to his feet. "Try it, Roxanne. Please. I want you to. I'm asking you to." That gave her pause, and he smiled. "You were getting the axe today, no matter what."

"*What?*" Roxanne and Catherine asked in unison.

He spared Catherine a brief glance. "You should have told me, right from the start, and spared us both two years' worth of grief." Then he returned his attention to Roxanne. "I did a little digging into what happened at the Marconi party. And the strangest thing kept happening. Your name kept coming up. So you go right ahead and make your next call to a lawyer. Make sure he's a really good one. Because my next call is to the King County Sheriff's Department. And just so you know, unlike Catherine, I play hardball. I will see to it that her name and reputation are restored and that you are forced to take responsibility for your actions."

Without a word, Roxanne spun on her heel and forged a swift path across his office. She'd barely reached the door when Gabe stopped her. "Once you get your legal issues straightened out, I suggest you consider a fresh start somewhere else, Roxanne. Someplace far out of my reach." He let that sink in before adding, "And just so you know, I have a long, long reach."

She swung around at that, aiming her vindictiveness straight at Catherine, where she knew it would do the most damage. "You may think you've won, but you haven't. Not when he finds out the truth. When he discovers you're damaged goods, he'll end your affair."

Then she switched her gaze to Gabe. "I did a little digging of my own. Placed a few phone calls. Maybe pretended to be someone I wasn't in order to get all the juicy tidbits I needed. Has your lovely bride-to-be warned you that she can't have children? If you marry her, it's the end of your branch of the precious Piretti line. I hope you two have a really great life." And with that, she slammed from the room.

Silence reigned for an endless moment. Catherine stood, frozen in place. She had to say something. Anything. But it was just a fight to continue breathing. The ability to speak was a sheer impossibility.

"Catherine?"

She shook her head and held up a hand in an effort to fend him off. Not that it stopped him. He crossed to her side and, catching her off guard, scooped her up into his arms and carried her to the sitting area by the windows. There he lowered her onto the couch and followed her down, aligning their bodies one to the other. Catherine had no idea how long he held her, murmuring words of comfort and sharing his warmth until the trembling gradually eased.

"I'm sorry, Gabe," she said at last. "I should have told you right from the start."

"She wasn't lying, was she?"

Catherine shook her head. "I can't have this conversation. Not like this. Not with you touching me." She tried to push him away, attempted to put some small amount of distance between them. Not that it worked. "Gabe, please. I can't do this."

But he didn't listen. If anything, he held her closer. Put his hands on her. Warmed her. And refused to let her go. "Shh. It's all right, sweetheart."

"No! No, it's not all right. It'll never be all right."

"What happened? Tell me what happened."

She caved, shrinking into herself. She couldn't put this off any longer. Couldn't hide from the truth, no matter how badly she wanted to. Time to face him and end it. Time to finally and completely face it herself. Time to shatter both their worlds. "It was the night you proposed," she said dully. "You asked me to marry you and I was going to tell you something, remember?"

"I remember."

"I was going to tell you I was pregnant with our child. I'd been hugging the secret to myself for two full weeks, waiting for the right time."

He went rigid in her arms. And she saw those gorgeous eyes light up with almost boyish wonder and excitement. Then the light extinguished as realization set in. "Oh, God. Something went wrong. What happened? Was there an accident?"

Exhaustion filled her. "Not an accident, no. The doctors said it was a spontaneous abortion. Something was wrong with the fetus. I lost the baby." Her voice cracked. "Oh, Gabe. I lost our baby."

He cradled her close and simply held her, waiting out the tears. "Was Roxanne right? Are you unable to have more children?"

"I don't know how she found out. Who knows?

Maybe she called the doctor and posed as me. I wouldn't put anything past her."

"Catherine, please. What happened?"

She'd avoided answering his question and they both knew it. But the time had come to give it to him straight. "The 'how' doesn't matter, does it? The bottom line is, yes. She's right. I can never have children. I was crazed after I lost the baby. That's when I left you. But the bleeding wouldn't stop." Her face crumpled. "A few days later I had to have a partial hysterectomy."

He hugged her close. "I'm sorry. I'm so sorry, Cate. That's what you meant when you said you were broken."

"Did I say that?" She couldn't remember.

He closed his eyes and leaned into her. "Oh, Christ, honey. Where the hell was I when you were going through all that? It was that damn lawsuit, wasn't it?"

"I called you from the hospital," she offered softly. "I'm guessing you didn't receive any of the messages."

"No." Just that one word. But it said it all.

"Do you understand now why I would only agree to a temporary affair?"

He tensed. "Don't tell me you buy in to Roxanne's load of crap."

"She didn't say anything I hadn't already realized for myself."

He raised himself up onto an elbow so he could scrutinize her expression. "You think I'd end our relationship because you can't have children? You think I wouldn't marry you tomorrow because of it? Are you kidding me? Do you honestly think so little of me?"

"You've always wanted a big family," she stated unevenly. "We had endless discussions about it. Piretti's has been in your family for generations. You want children to carry on the name."

"Right, so?"

"So we can't have children!"

"Yes, Catherine, we can. It's called adoption."

"But they wouldn't be your flesh and blood."

That drove him from her arms. "What the hell kind of a man do you take me for? Do you really think me so shallow?"

She stared mutely, shaking her head.

He snatched a deep breath and gathered up his self-control. "Tell me something, sweetheart. Do you need to have a child grow in your womb for you to love and raise a baby as though it were your own?"

"No, but—"

"Neither do I. Neither does any man on this planet, since we don't bear children."

"I do know my basic biology, Gabe."

"I'm relieved to hear it. Think, Cate. Men can't experience what women do during those nine months they carry a child. And yet we bond with our baby when it's born, even though it didn't come directly from our own bodies. How is that any different from what will happen when we adopt?"

She shook her head again, unable to answer. Afraid to believe.

"And what if this had happened after we married? Do you think me the sort of man who would divorce you because of it?"

She started to cry then. How could she love this man so dearly and not have seen the truth? Not have seen all the way to the very heart of him? How could she have given Roxanne so much power? It wasn't Gabe who was guilty of not having enough faith. She was the one to blame.

"I'm sorry, Gabe. I should have trusted you."

"I won't argue that point. But I didn't give you a lot of reason to trust me, not while I had my priorities so screwed up."

For the first time in two long years, she could see clearly. "If I'd come to you about Roxanne two years ago, you'd have fired her then, wouldn't you?"

"Yes. I had no idea she'd become such a problem for you, or she would have been replaced within the hour."

Now for her biggest concern. "Where do we go from here?" she asked.

"That's an excellent question." He returned to the couch and took her into his arms, rolled on top of her so she was deliciously cushioned beneath him. "First off, we keep our weekend reservation at Très Romantique."

A small smile crept across Catherine's mouth and she could feel the beginnings of something precious sprouting inside her. Hope. Hope was taking hold and putting down roots. Deep, unshakable roots. "And then?"

"Then we make sure we've cleared away every last

secret, every last doubt and every last concern while I
explain to you, slowly and clearly, just how much I love
you."

She threw her arms around him and held on for all
she was worth. "I love you desperately, Gabe."

He closed his eyes and she felt his tension drain away.
"You have no idea how long I've waited to hear those
words again."

And then he kissed her. It was a soft caress, unexpectedly gentle. A benediction. A promise. He kept it simple,
the passion tempered and muted. And yet it was a kiss
Catherine would remember for the rest of her life. It
melded them, heart and mind, body and soul. With that
one kiss, all doubts faded, replaced by certainty. This
was her man, just as she was his woman. Whatever the
future brought, they'd face it together.

It was a long time before Gabe spoke again. "After
we have everything settled between us, I'll need to speak
with someone at Elegant Events." He shot her a wicked
grin. "I have it on good authority that they're the best
event stager in town."

A smile flirted with Catherine's mouth. "As a matter
of fact, they are."

"I'll need to speak to their top event specialist," he
warned.

"I happen to know she has a very busy calendar.
But she might find room for Gabe 'the Pirate' Piretti.
If he asked nicely." She tilted her head to one side.
"Tell me. What would you need with a top-notch event
specialist?"

"I need her to plan the wedding of the year."

"Why, Mr. Piretti," she protested indignantly. "That sounds like you're asking me to mix business with pleasure. I thought we had rules about that sort of thing."

"The hell with the rules."

She pretended to look scandalized. "No more strictly business?"

He shook his head. "From now on you are my business—first, last, and foremost."

And he proceeded to prove it in a very efficient, if unbusinesslike manner.

* * * * *

BOUGHT: HIS
TEMPORARY
FIANCÉE

YVONNE LINDSAY

New Zealand–born to Dutch immigrant parents, **Yvonne Lindsay** became an avid romance reader at the age of thirteen. Now married to her 'blind date' and with two surprisingly amenable teenagers, she remains a firm believer in the power of romance. Yvonne feels privileged to be able to bring to her readers the stories of her heart. In her spare time, when not writing, she can be found with her nose firmly in a book, reliving the power of love in all walks of life. She can be contacted via her Web site, www.yvonnelindsay.com.

To my fellow authors—Day, Emily, Sandra, Michelle and Catherine—and to the fabulous editorial team who've worked with us, thank you all for being such a wonderful group. It's been an absolute pleasure!

One

He was just as heart-stoppingly gorgeous as the first time she'd laid eyes on him. And those lips…

Margaret Cole stepped into William Tanner's office and couldn't tear her gaze from her new boss's mouth as he introduced himself as CFO of Cameron Enterprises— the company that had bought out Worth Industries. She'd heard he was from New Zealand originally. She wondered briefly if his home country's British colonial background was responsible for that slightly stiff-upper-lip way he had of speaking. Oh, Lord, there she was, fixated on his lips again. And no wonder. That very mouth had claimed hers in a kiss that had seared her senses and made her toes curl only six short weeks ago.

Even now she could remember the pressure of his mouth against hers, of the way her blood had suddenly heated, then rushed through her veins. The sensation more exhilarating and intoxicating than anything she'd ever experienced before.

She'd wanted more then, and she wanted more now, but men like William Tanner were pretty much off-limits for a girl like her. Especially a man who probably paid more for a single cut of his neatly trimmed dark brown hair than she spent on her own hair in a year. Not that he appeared vain. Far from it. With his casual elegance he probably never thought twice about the cost, never had to. Nor the price of the tailored business suit that fitted the width of his shoulders and now hung open, revealing his flat stomach and lean hips. Even with the two-inch heels on her sensible pumps boosting her height to five foot nine, he stood a good five inches taller than her.

Maggie found herself nodding and murmuring in response to Mr. Tanner's invitation to sit down. She really needed to gather her wits about her, but for the life of her she just couldn't. Every cell in her body vibrated on full alert. Did he recognize her from behind the elaborate mask she'd worn? She'd certainly recognized him—although, on that night, she hadn't had any idea of who he was until after the kiss that had surpassed her every fantasy.

The second he'd arrived at the company Valentine's Day ball, she'd felt his presence like a tangible thing. He'd entered the room alone, standing for a moment in the doorway, his dark costume fitted to his body, his cloak swirling gently around him. Her eyes had been instantly drawn to him. Dressed like Zorro, he was the perfect foil to her Spanish lady and it hadn't taken him long to find her and swing her away in his arms to the dance floor. They'd danced the minutes until midnight together, and he'd kissed her just as the countdown to unmasking had begun. But then someone had called his name, and as he'd taken his lips from hers she'd realized exactly who he was.

Her behavior that night had been completely out of character. She would never in a million years have believed she could feel so much so soon, for a man she'd never met before that night. A flush of heat surged through her body at the memory. A surge that came to a rapid halting crash as she became aware that he clearly awaited a response to something he'd said.

She cleared her throat nervously and fixed her gaze on a point just past his ear.

"I'm sorry, could you repeat that please?"

He smiled, no more than a smooth curve of his lips, and her internal temperature slid up another notch. This was insane. How on earth was she going to work for the man when she couldn't keep her wits about her in his presence? She'd be out of here in two seconds flat if she couldn't perform. He had a real reputation for being a hard-ass. She could deal with that. He hadn't gotten where he was at the age of thirty-one without that particular character trait, she was sure. Focused people didn't scare her—she admired them—but in his case she had to admit that she admired him just a little bit too much.

"Are you nervous?" he asked.

"No, not exactly. Perhaps a little surprised at my appointment—not that I'm complaining about it."

"I was merely commenting on your length of service with Worth Industries. You're what, twenty-eight, and you've been with Worth for eight years?"

Even his voice was a distraction. Rich and deep and with a texture that sent a tiny shiver of longing down her spine. And his accent. A little bit Upper East Side and a little bit Kiwi. The combination and inflections in his tone did crazy things to her insides.

"Yes. My whole family has worked, or does work, for Worth."

"Ah, yes, your brother—Jason, is it?"

She nodded. "And my parents, too, when they were alive. They were both on the factory floor."

"That's quite a loyal streak you're showing there."

Maggie shrugged. "Not really. Especially when you consider that Worth Industries—I mean, Cameron Enterprises—is the major industry and employer in Vista del Mar."

This promotion to Mr. Tanner's executive assistant, even in its temporary capacity, since he'd been seconded to Vista del Mar short-term only to complete financial viability studies, was not only unexpected, but the increase in income would prove very welcome. Paying off her brother's college tuition was an ongoing cost for both Jason and her, and one they looked forward to seeing the end of. Even with Jason working here for the past two years and contributing to their monthly expenses, including the payments on the small house that had been their home from childhood, the college loans had remained a yoke around their necks. Maybe now, with her promotion, they could plan for a few luxuries for themselves—within reason, of course.

"Have you never wanted to branch out? Go further afield with your work?" he asked, leaning back against the edge of his desk.

Go further afield? She was afraid if she told him the truth he'd laugh at her. Ever since she was a child she'd had a map of the world pinned to her bedroom wall—a round red pin pressed into every city or country she wanted to visit. For now, she contented herself with travel books and DVDs. But one day she'd fulfill those dreams.

William Tanner awaited an answer. *Wow, way to go on impressing the new boss,* she thought. So far she'd let her mind wander, what, how many times?

"Travel isn't my priority right now," she said firmly, and sat a little straighter in her chair.

He gave her another one of those smiles and she felt it all the way to the pit of her belly. She'd travel to the ends of the world with *him,* she thought and allowed her lips to curve into an answering smile.

"There may be some travel involved in your position with me. Will that be a problem?"

"No, not at all. I have no dependants."

While that was technically true, and she and Jason shared their family home, the habits of ten years were pretty darn hard to break. Besides, she still felt a deep sense of responsibility toward her younger brother. He'd gone through a very rocky time after their parents died. Guiding his decisions had become second nature, although she knew he sometimes resented her continued interest in his whereabouts and friends.

"I'm glad to hear it." He shoved his hands into his trouser pockets and pushed up off the desk edge, pacing over to one of the floor-to-ceiling windows that looked out over the Cameron Enterprises corporate campus. "You mentioned you were surprised to be given this position. Why is that?"

Maggie blinked several times behind her glasses. Surprised? Of course she was surprised. For eight years she'd been virtually invisible to her peers and certainly invisible when it had come to her previous applications for promotion.

"Well…" She chewed her lip for a moment, choosing her words carefully. "As you said, I've been here quite a while. I guess I thought that no one ever saw me as capable of rising to a position such as this. That's not to say that I don't think I am capable—nothing could be further from the truth. I've worked in several departments here and I believe my experience makes me a valuable asset to any of the executives."

He laughed. "You don't need to convince me, Margaret. You already have the job."

She felt a heated blush rise from her chest to her throat before flooding her cheeks with color. Now she'd be all blotchy. She forced herself to remain calm and focused instead on the fact he'd called her Margaret. No one called her that. Since she was a little girl everyone around her had called her Maggie, and she hadn't really minded much. But hearing her full name from his lips made it sound special, particularly with the way he spoke with that slightly clipped intonation. Yes, as the executive assistant to the CFO of Cameron Enterprises, she would be called Margaret. She replayed the syllables in her mind and let a small smile play across her face in response.

"Thank you, I do know that. I just want you to know you won't be sorry you chose me."

"Oh, no, I know I won't be sorry," he replied.

Will looked across his temporary office at the woman he'd specifically requested be brought to him. It was almost impossible to believe that behind those owlish, dark-framed old-fashioned glasses and the poorly fitted suit lay the siren who'd infiltrated his dreams every night since the masquerade ball. But it was definitely her. Even with her long black hair scraped off her face and dragged into a knot that was tight enough to give *him* a headache, there was no denying the delicate line of jaw and the fine straight nose were those of his Spanish lady.

His gut tightened in anticipation. He'd waited quite long enough to revisit that kiss. Tracking her down hadn't been the easiest thing he'd ever done, but he wasn't known for his tenaciousness for nothing. The trait had stood him well over the years and gave him an edge that saw him succeed where others failed. And he would succeed with the delectable Ms. Cole—he had no doubt about it.

She'd done a runner on him the night of the ball, but not before enticing him in a way no other woman had—ever. He wasn't a man to be denied, not under any circumstances—

especially not when his reaction to her had been very obviously mirrored by the object of his attention.

And here she was. He blinked. It really was hard to believe they were one and the same woman. She fidgeted in her chair—a reminder that it was up to him to do something about the silence that now stretched between them.

"Tell me about your time here. I see from your file that you spent some time in the factory before moving into office work?"

"Yes," she replied, her deceptively prim lips pursed slightly as she appeared to choose her next words carefully. "I started in the factory, but the shifts made it difficult for me to be available for my brother before and after school. I requested a transfer into admin and learned what I know now from the ground up."

"Available for your brother?"

A cloud filled her dark brown eyes and she took her time before responding.

"Yes, that's right. Our parents died when I was eighteen and for the first couple of years afterward we got by on a small insurance policy my father had left us. Of course, that wasn't going to take care of us forever and Jason was still in school so it made sense that I find work. Worth Industries was pretty much the only place that was hiring at the time."

None of this was news to him but it was good to know his sources had been accurate in their dissemination of information.

"That can't have been easy for you."

"No, it wasn't."

Again, a careful response. One that answered, but failed to give any details. Clearly his Ms. Cole was one to keep her cards close to her chest—and what a chest. Even the unbelievably unflattering cut of her suit failed to hide the lush curves of her body. For someone who appeared to actively want to hide her attributes, she still maintained deliciously perfect posture. It was that very upright bearing that confirmed his first impressions of her had been spot on. Margaret Cole was all woman, with the type of figure that would have seen her painted on the nose cowl of every fighter plane in aviation history.

Will forced his thoughts back to the business at hand.

"And I see you've been here, on the financial floor, for the past five years."

"I like numbers," she said with a small smile. "They tend to make better sense than other things."

He smiled back; he felt exactly the same way. His eldest brother, Michael, worked in human resources back in New York. To this day the problems Mike faced and relished each day made Will's head ache. He'd rather face a root canal than that. There was comfort in the cohesion of working with numbers. The defined parameters, yet with infinite possibilities were the types of challenges he excelled at. Which brought him very squarely back to the woman seated in front of him.

"Most of what you'll be doing for me will probably fall outside the usual reports and things you've been doing for middle management here."

"I enjoy a challenge," Margaret answered back.

"I'm glad to hear it. Here, let's get you started on something I've been working on." He reached across his desk and grabbed the file that lay in solitary splendor on the highly polished surface. "Take a look at that and give me your first impressions."

Margaret accepted the file from him and he saw her forehead wrinkle into a small frown as she concentrated on the report. He leaned his hip against his desk and simply watched her as her lips pursed while she read through the columns. Did she give everything in her life that intense concentration? he wondered. The prospect was both intriguing and enticing and occupied his thoughts as she thumbed methodically through the pages.

She must indeed have had a good head for figures, because she closed the folder after about ten minutes and looked him square in the eye.

"It would seem that the figures don't match up. The error margin isn't large, but it's consistent."

Her quick discernment gave him a punch of delight. Not only beautiful under that frumpy disguise, but sharply intelligent, too. The knowledge made him look forward all the more to what he'd planned.

"Good," he replied as he took the file back from her. "I think we're going to work very well together. Tell me, what would you recommend if you had discovered such an anomaly?"

"Well, I'd probably suggest a deeper audit of the books—see how long this has been going on. Then perhaps a more specific check as to who has been involved with the accounts and has access to the funds."

Will nodded. "That's exactly what we have done in this case."

"So this is an ongoing investigation?"

"It's pretty much wrapped up, with the exception of one or two things."

"That's good to hear," Margaret said. "It's too easy for people to be tempted these days. Too often a little responsibility puts a person in a position where they think they're entitled to help themselves to something that's not theirs."

"Yes, well, in this case we're certain we have the culprit lined up. He will be facing a disciplinary panel later this afternoon."

"Disciplinary panel? You won't be firing him?"

"Whether we choose to fire him or not has yet to be decided. Which kind of brings me to you, really."

"Me? In what way?"

Confusion clouded her features and for a moment Will almost felt sorry for her. He knew that what he had to say next would probably rip the rug right out from under her.

"Just how close to your brother's work habits are you?"

"Jason? What? Why?"

Understanding slowly dawned on her and all the color in her face slowly drained away. If she hadn't already been seated, Will had no doubt she'd be dropping into the nearest chair by now.

"*Jason* is the one you're investigating?"

"He is." Will leaned back against his desk again and caught her gaze with a rock-hard stare. "How much do you know about what he's been up to?"

"Nothing! No! He couldn't, *wouldn't* do such a thing. He loves his work. There's no way he's capable of doing something like this. Seriously, I…"

"So you have had nothing to do with it?"

Her features froze. "Me? No, of course not! Why would you even think such a thing?"

Will shrugged. "Stranger things have happened, and you know the saying. Blood is thicker than water."

A fact he knew all too well. It was that very fact that had him in this situation with Margaret Cole in the first place. Rather than take his time, relishing her pursuit and letting it play out to its natural conclusion, his father's latest edict forced him to speed things along somewhat. If Will didn't show some sign of settling down soon, his father would sell the family sheep station back in New Zealand rather than transfer it into Will's ownership as he was supposed to have done over a year ago when Will had turned thirty.

Each of the Tanner sons had received a massive financial

settlement on their thirtieth birthday, but Will had said that rather than money he wanted the farm. His father had agreed, but that agreement seemed to now be laden with conditions Will wasn't prepared to meet. Not in truth, anyway.

It wasn't the fact that he wanted or needed the land—goodness only knew he had little enough time to travel back to his home country these days. But the farm was such a vital part of his family heritage that he couldn't bear to see it carved up into multiple parcels of "lifestyle" farms, or worse, fall into corporate or foreign ownership. The very thought that his father could so cavalierly cast off something that had been a part of all their lives was no laughing matter. That Albert Tanner was using the farm as a bargaining chip showed how very determined he was to see his youngest son settle down.

And, above everything else, it was the knowledge that his father was deeply disappointed in him that rankled. That and the fact that both his parents and his brothers couldn't seem to understand that while love and marriage were at the forefront of their minds, it wasn't at the forefront of his. Not now, maybe not ever.

"Blood might be thicker than water but there's no way I'd ever condone such a thing. Jason can't be behind this. It's just not like him. Besides, he only holds a minor position in accounting and he wouldn't have access to be able to do this."

He had to admire her loyalty to her brother. Will's digging had discovered that Jason had a none-too-smooth history, going back to when he was just a teen. While his records had been sealed by the courts because of his age at the time, money had a convenient way of finding people with a truth to tell. Jason Cole's habit of petty theft as a teenager could easily have escalated over the years into something far more sophisticated. And yet, despite everything, Margaret still believed he wasn't involved with this current situation. Well, he hated to shatter her illusions, but the truth was there in the report. The numbers didn't lie. He pressed home his advantage.

"But you have higher clearances, don't you?"

"Not for this kind of thing and even if I did, I would never share that information with anyone. Not even my brother."

She was so puffed up with righteous indignation and outrage he was tempted to tell her he believed her. But any softness would remove the leverage he needed right now.

"I'm very glad to hear it. The fact remains, however, that your brother is most definitely involved. All our evidence points to him. However, there is a chance he may not be prosecuted over this."

"A chance? What chance?"

Will took a deep breath. This had to go right so he needed to choose his words very carefully, indeed.

"I have a proposition that will protect your brother's position here and ensure news of his activity won't get out, nor will it be permanently recorded on his file should he leave to work for another company."

He saw the hope flare in her eyes and felt a momentary pang of regret that he had to manipulate her in this way. A pang he rapidly quashed.

"What is it? What do we need to do? Seriously, we'll do anything to protect Jason's position here."

"It's not so much what the two of you can do, although he'll definitely have to clean up his act. It's more to do with what you can do."

"Me? I don't understand."

"Your appointment as my executive assistant is a two-pronged affair. On the one hand, I need someone with your acumen and your experience to be my right hand while I'm here." He paused for a moment before continuing. "On the other, I need someone—*you,* specifically—to pose as my fiancée."

"Your what?" she gasped, shooting to her feet, her shock clearly visible on her mobile features.

"You heard me."

"Your fiancée? Are you crazy? That's just ridiculous. We don't even know one another."

"Ah, but we do."

He crossed the room in a few long strides, coming to halt directly in front of her. The light scent she wore, something floral and innocent and totally at odds with the sensual creature he knew lingered under her proper exterior, wafted on the air between them. Will lifted his hand and traced one finger along the enticing fullness of her lower lip.

"Let me enlighten you."

He didn't give her so much as a split second to react. He closed the short distance between her lips and his. The instant his mouth touched hers he knew he'd been right to pursue this course of action. A powerful thrill pulled through him as her lips opened beneath the coaxing pressure of his, as her taste invaded his senses and held him in her thrall. It was all he could do not to lift his hands to her hair and free it from that appalling knot and drive his fingers through its silky length.

Reason fought for supremacy and he wrenched his lips from hers in a force of will that surprised even him.

"See? We do *know* each other, and I believe we could be quite—" he paused again for effect "—convincing together."

Margaret took a couple of steps back from him. She shook from head to toe. Desire? Fear? Perhaps a combination of both he decided, watching the play of emotions across her face.

"No." She shook her head vehemently. "No, I will not do it. It's just wrong."

"Then you leave me no choice."

"No choice? In what?"

"In ensuring that a recommendation is made that formal charges be laid against your brother."

Two

"That's blackmail!"

Her heart hammered in her chest as the finality of William Tanner's words sank in. Surely he couldn't be serious?

"I prefer to call it a basis for negotiation," he said smoothly, as if he did this sort of thing every day.

Who knew? Maybe he did. All Maggie knew was that her usually well-ordered world had suddenly been tilted off its axis. Jason had been on the straight and narrow for years. The trouble he'd gotten into as a teen now well and truly behind him. Surely he can't have been so stupid as to dip into company funds?

She went on the attack. "You're mad. You can't do this to me—to us!"

"If by 'us,' you're referring to your brother and yourself, rest assured, I can and I am. Margaret, your brother took a risk when he started playing in the big boy's league. Embezzlement is never a good look on a résumé. Sure, this is only a beginning, but who is to say he wouldn't get more daring if I hadn't picked this up in our audit?"

Maggie watched William in horror. She processed his words as quickly as she'd processed the information in the damning report on her brother's activities. Whether Jason was guilty or not, it was doubtful that he'd escape from this without some serious scars. The last judge he'd stood before in court had made it quite clear that he was being given one final opportunity to clean up his act—and he had. She didn't want to even consider what might happen if he went before the courts again.

If what William said *was* true, then it was just as well that Jason be stopped now. But, in her heart of hearts, she didn't want to believe a word of it.

"No, he wouldn't. He promised—" She cut off her words before she gave Mr. Tanner any further ammunition to use against her brother.

"Margaret, please, sit down. Clearly this news has come as a shock, and why wouldn't it? I understand you campaigned quite hard for your brother to be given the position he now occupies."

The innuendo in his voice left its mark. He'd already intimated that she could be linked to the fraudulent activity. As innocent as she knew she was, mud had a habit of sticking. She wouldn't have a position here for long if there was any suspicion she was involved, especially not with the corporate restructuring that was rumored to be in the works. Rafe Cameron's determined takeover of Worth Industries, and almost instant rebranding to Cameron Enterprises, had left everyone feeling a little precarious with respect to their jobs. It still wasn't certain what his plans were for the company, and fresh rumors arose each day about the likelihood of the factory work being outsourced to Mexico or, worse, the whole company being moved closer to Cameron's home base in New

York—which would mean the loss of almost all their jobs. Several top-level executive heads had already rolled, or been ousted on the basis of early retirement. And then there was the steady stream of Cameron's own people coming into those key roles, William Tanner being one of them. A shiver ran down her spine.

She swallowed back the words she longed to say. The words that would set William Tanner straight on exactly where she stood on matters of honesty and loyalty. Common sense held her back. Granted, it had been six years since Jason's last run-in with the law. She'd lost track of the number of times she'd been called to the local police station to collect him after he'd been picked up for one misdemeanor or another, in the first couple of years after their parents died. But then the trouble had started to get worse—so much so that Officer Garcia could no longer let Jason go with a stern lecture and a promise of dire things to come.

The first—and last—time Jason had been locked up he was eighteen. The experience of being charged as an adult, with all its long-term ramifications, had finally opened his eyes to his behavior. He'd promised her that would be the only time, and that he'd learned his lesson, big-time. He even swore on their parents' graves that he'd stay away from trouble for the rest of his life. She'd believed him—believed *in* him—so much so that she'd increased the mortgage over the home they'd grown up in so she could borrow the money necessary to send him to college out of state. Somewhere he could start afresh. Somewhere he could grow into the man she and their parents had always believed he would be.

Was it possible he'd thrown that all away?

"Look—" William butted in on her thoughts "—the way I see it, we'd be doing each other a favor."

"A favor?" she repeated dully.

What kind of favor saw her lose everything she held dear?

She'd fought long and hard to maintain her dignity through years of adversity and a lack of recognition. She had always aspired to do better—to be more. Now it appeared that everything she had ever done had been for nothing. Now she was expected to *prostitute* herself to save her brother.

"In return for you doing this for me, and believe me, you will be very well compensated, I will ensure that your brother receives nothing more than a reprimand. Obviously he'll be under close supervision. If he keeps out of trouble, this transgression will be removed from his staff record and he'll have a clean slate once more."

"And if I don't?"

"You will both be escorted from the premises immediately and I imagine that we can arrange for the police to be waiting for you at the front door. It'd probably take some time to go to trial, but I can assure you that if it did, there would be no question of Jason being found guilty."

William Tanner's voice was adamant. Each word a cold steel nail in the coffin of what had been her dreams.

"How long?" she asked.

"How long what?"

"How long would I have to pretend?"

She injected enough distaste in her voice to make William's eyes narrow as he appeared to consider his answer.

"Don't think this would be a walk in the park, Margaret. If you take this on you will have to be convincing in your role." When she didn't reply, he continued. "My father has put some pressure upon me to follow in my brothers' footsteps and find a good woman to settle down with. At this stage of my career that is the furthest thing from my mind. He's withholding something that is rightfully mine over this issue, and the situation is distressing my mother. I would need you to be my fiancée until I'm assured that the transfer of ownership of property back in New Zealand takes place. Basically, until my family calms down again and continues to act reasonably."

"So there's no finite term on this?"

Margaret could feel the walls closing in on her now. With his open-ended proposal and the continued threat of Jason losing his job hanging overhead, this would be a total nightmare. One from which she was afraid she might never awake. And yet this morning had started so promisingly with the inter-office communication confirming that she'd been promoted to being Tanner's EA. For Margaret, the only way from a position like this was up and her summons to report to his office this afternoon had been something she'd been looking forward to all day.

"Obviously this won't go on forever. It's not as if we'll be getting married."

He said the words as if the entire prospect of marriage was completely abhorrent to him.

"Let me get this clear. You want me to pretend to be your fiancée for an undetermined period of time. In exchange you'll recompense me and you will ensure that Jason doesn't lose his job."

"That Jason doesn't lose his job over *this* incident. Should he push his boundaries and try something a little more sophisticated there will be no more second chances."

No more second chances. The words were exactly what the judge had said when Jason had been brought before the court. She'd never been certain if it was the judge's words or the night he'd spent in the county jail's holding cells that had been the catalyst he'd needed to finally want to break free from the creeps he'd been hanging out with. She hadn't cared much at the time. All she'd been concerned with was getting her brother back on an even keel. It had cost her far more than money to do so and she wasn't about to jeopardize things now.

Margaret knew she wasn't in a position to argue, but never in her wildest dreams had she imagined she would be forced into something like this. It wasn't enough that the man had infiltrated her private thoughts and fantasies in the six weeks since the Valentine's Day ball. Now he would control her days as well.

"Why? Why me?" she whispered.

He reached out a finger to trace her lips.

"Because you intrigue me, Margaret Cole. You intrigue me very much."

Despite her distress, she reacted to his caress as if it was a touch of lightning. Her lips parted on a sharply indrawn breath and deep to her core she felt the sizzling awareness of his touch.

"Margaret," he continued, "if you truly believe your brother to be innocent in this, you owe it to him to allow him to prove it. He can't do that if he's suspended pending further investigation, can he?"

Blood pounded in her ears, almost drowning out his words. Her chest tightened with anxiety. What choice did she have? In her heart she knew that Jason could not have done what he was being accused of, but the evidence said differently. She did owe him the chance to prove his innocence. If she didn't accede to Mr. Tanner's demands, all the hard years of work she'd put into Jason, and all the effort he'd made to clean up his act and make something of himself would be in vain.

She drew in a shaky breath.

"I'll do it," she said, the words little more than a whisper. She stood up and raised her head to meet William Tanner square in the eye. "I'll do it," she repeated, more strongly this time.

Will could barely hold back the rush of excitement that spread with molten heat through his body. She'd agreed. For a few moments there he'd thought she'd refuse—that maybe she'd throw her brother to the wolves and to hell with the consequences. He should have trusted his initial research. Margaret Cole was intensely loyal. Everyone had spoken highly of her, from the factory floor workers who still remembered her parents all the way through to the middle management for whom she'd provided secretarial support. As hard as he'd tried, he hadn't been able to unearth the smallest speck of dirt on his elusive masked Spanish lady—except for what her brother had handed him on a platter.

And now, she was his. All his.

"I'm glad to hear it," he said with a quick smile. "I believe it would be best if you went home now. I'll talk to you in the morning about your instructions."

"Instructions?" A spark of fire burned in her eyes.

"As to your new duties, of course. You haven't held an EA role before so I don't expect you to fall immediately into place. And then, of course, there are your extracurricular duties to discuss as well."

A tremor ran through her body. Was it revulsion? He doubted it. Not after the way she'd reacted to him during that all too brief kiss a few minutes ago and especially not after he'd seen the fire leap to life in her eyes as he'd traced the soft fullness of her lower lip with only a fingertip. With her response being so instinctive, so honest, he knew the next few weeks, even months, would undoubtedly be as pleasurable as he'd anticipated from the moment he'd laid eyes on her.

He took a step toward her and tried to tamp down the disappointment he felt when he saw her flinch. Sure, he knew she'd be reluctant. What woman wouldn't under these circumstances? But he had her exactly where he needed her and she couldn't run away.

"I don't need to remind you that this matter between us is completely confidential. Of course there will be questions when news of our 'engagement' leaks out, but I'm hoping we can keep them under control if we keep our stories straight."

"Jason and I share our home. I have to tell him, at least."

"I'd prefer you didn't. Obviously I can't stop you two from discussing the accusations against him, but the more people who know our engagement is a sham the more likely it is to be exposed."

"Don't you understand? Jason and I live together. I can't hide the truth from him."

"Then you'll have to convince him that you're doing this for love."

"Believe me, he won't have any trouble with that. He knows I love him."

"No. Not him. *Me*."

To his surprise, a throaty laugh bubbled from her. As delectable as the sound was, the reason behind it wasn't. He bristled, going on the defensive.

"Is that so very hard to believe?" he pressed. "Don't you think you'll be able to act with credibility?"

"No, please, you misunderstand me." She sobered instantly, the moment of hysteria passed even though traces of moisture still lingered in the corners of her eyes. "You don't know me or you wouldn't ever have suggested we could fake our engagement. I don't go out, I…"

Her hesitation hung in the air between them.

"Yes, you…?"

She threw her hands up, gesturing to herself. "Well, look at me. I'm hardly the kind of woman you'd go out with under normal circumstances, am I? I don't move in your circles, I'm…I'm me." She shrugged her shoulders dramatically, as if that was sufficient explanation for everything.

"Do you want to see who I see when I look at you, Margaret?"

He kept his voice steady and pitched low. Her nervous

movements stilled at his tone and he saw her brace herself, physically and mentally, for whatever it was that he had to say.

"I see a woman who hides her true self from the world. Someone who has a deep inner beauty to match the exterior. Someone who would go so far as to sacrifice her own happiness for that of a loved one. I see a woman who doesn't realize the extent of her own potential, at work or in play. And I see a woman I am very much looking forward to getting to know, intimately."

The flush that spread up her throat and across her cheeks was as intriguing as it was enticing. Was she really so innocent that she blushed at his suggestion? She hadn't thought this fake engagement was going to be purely for appearances, did she? There had to be fringe benefits—for them both.

"So you're going to force me to have sex with you, too, are you?" she asked, her voice wavering slightly.

"Oh, no," William replied. "I won't have to force you at all."

Margaret was still shaking when she made it to her car in the back row of the staff car park. She shoved her key in the door and gave it the customary wiggle she needed to do before turning it and opening the door. She clambered inside and put her key in the ignition. Since her car had been stolen a year ago, both the door lock and the new ignition barrel hadn't been quite in sync with the key. She'd been lucky that when the car was recovered a few miles from home that it was still drivable. One of Jason's friends, an auto mechanic, had done the minor repair work for her at cost. It hadn't been the same since then, though. One day it would let her down, but hopefully not any day too soon.

She rested her head on the steering wheel. It wasn't the only thing that wasn't the same anymore. How could she look at Jason now without worrying about whether he was getting himself into trouble again? No matter what William Tanner had dictated, she would tell Jason the truth about their arrangement. Provided he agreed to be sworn to secrecy, that is.

Maggie wasn't looking forward to what kind of state he'd be in when he got home after the disciplinary panel today, but she knew he wouldn't be happy with her "engagement." With a sigh, she straightened in her seat, started up the car and headed for home. She might find some answers there, or at least some solace in being surrounded by their parents' things.

Grief lanced through her with a sharp, searing pain. Ten years since the accident that had taken both their lives and it still hurt as much as it had when the police had come to the door to give them the news. Where would they be now, she wondered, if her parents hadn't died that day?

She shook her head. There was no point in dwelling on the past. The present, that was what mattered. Making every day count. Meeting the obligations she'd shouldered when she'd made the decision to forgo college and focus on raising Jason alone. At eighteen to his fourteen it had been a monumental decision—one she'd frequently questioned as she'd faced each new trial. But the Cole family had never been quitters. They stuck to their own, through thick and thin. No matter the cost.

By the time Jason arrived home, an hour later than usual, her nerves were tied in knots. The sound of his key being shoved in the front door, followed by the heavy slam as it closed, did not augur well for a rational discussion.

"Are you okay?" she asked as he came through to the kitchen where she was reheating last night's Bolognese sauce and meatballs.

"It's un-freaking-believable," he said. "I've been accused

of stealing, but not quite enough that they're going to take my job from me. I'm on some kind of big-brother probation."

"I know," she said, struggling to keep her voice calm.

"You know? And you didn't think to tell me? Give me any prior warning?"

His voice was filled with confusion and accusation. Inside, her heart began to break.

"I couldn't. I was only told of it right before your meeting with the disciplinary panel."

Jason dragged his cell phone from his pocket and waved it in her face. "Hello? You could have texted me."

"I didn't have a chance. Seriously, you have to believe me. I would have, if I could."

He dropped into one of the bentwood kitchen chairs, the old wooden frame creaking in protest as he threw his weight against the back of the seat and shoved a hand through his dark hair. Unbidden, tears sprang to Maggie's eyes. Times like this he reminded her so much of photos of their father when he was younger. All that intelligence, energy and passion. All so easily misdirected.

She dropped down on her haunches beside him.

"Tell me. What did they say?"

He looked up at the ceiling and swore softly under his breath. "You know what they said. They're accusing me of taking money, but they don't have absolute proof it was me. Anyone could have made that trail go in someone else's direction. I've been framed. I wouldn't do something like that."

Her stomach knotted at the almost childlike plea in his voice. A plea that she, above all others, would believe him.

"Did you, Jason? Did you do it?"

He thrust himself up onto his feet. "I can't believe you can even ask me that. I promised you I'd be clean after that last time and I have been."

"Mr. Tanner showed me the evidence, Jason. He said everything pointed to you."

She felt as if she was drowning. She wanted to believe Jason, really she did. But William Tanner had been very convincing. So convincing she'd agreed to participate in his charade to save Jason's job.

"So you'd rather believe him than me? Is that it? Are you still so goo-goo eyed after that one kiss at the ball that you don't want to believe your own brother?"

"Jason, that's uncalled for," she replied sharply, but she felt the betraying flush stain her cheeks.

Her brother had teased her mercilessly about the kiss he'd witnessed at the ball, until he'd learned exactly who it was she'd been kissing. William Tanner was a man to be feared. No one knew exactly what his recommendation would be for the now defunct Worth Industries, and the rumors that the business could be wound down here in Vista del Mar had buzzed around the staff like a swarm of angry bees.

"I don't believe it," he said, staring at her as if she'd grown two heads. "Even though he's accused me of being dishonest, you still have the hots for him, don't you?"

"This isn't about me." She tried desperately to get the conversation back on topic. "This is about you. I asked you, plain and simple, Jason. Did you do it?"

"It doesn't matter what I say now," he said bleakly. "You're never going to believe me, are you? I'll never be good enough, never be able to prove to you that I'm trustworthy again. Don't wait up for me, I'm going out."

"Jason, don't go. Please!"

But his only response was the slam of the front door behind him, swiftly followed by the roar of his motorbike as he peeled out of the driveway. Margaret raised a trembling hand to her eyes and wiped at the tears that fell unchecked down her cheeks.

If Jason was guilty of what Tanner had accused him, then she would continue to do every last thing in her power to protect him, just as she always had. But if he was innocent, what on earth had she let herself in for?

Three

Maggie was beyond worried by the time morning came. Jason hadn't been home all night. Around four she'd given up trying to sleep and had done what she always did in times of stress—clean. By the time seven-thirty rolled around, the bathroom sparkled, the kitchen bench gleamed and every wooden surface in the house shone with the glow of the special lemon-scented polish their mother had always used.

The scents were in their own way a little comfort, Maggie thought, as she finally peeled off her gloves and wearily went into the kitchen to put on a pot of coffee. She could almost feel her mother's soothing presence in the background.

The growl of Jason's bike as he pulled into the driveway had her flying to the door. She yanked it open, then froze in the doorway. Uncertain of whether or not he would welcome her relief at seeing him home safe and sound.

He came to the door slowly, his face haggard and showing a wisdom beyond his years.

"I'm sorry, Maggie," he said, pulling her into his arms and hugging her tight. "I was so mad I just had to put some space between me and here, y'know?"

She nodded, unable to speak past the knot in her throat. He was home. That was all that mattered for now. She led him inside, pushed him into one of the kitchen chairs and set about making breakfast. As she broke eggs into the pan he started to talk.

"At least I still have my job."

"Yes, you do," Maggie replied. He still didn't know her news, she realized. He wouldn't be happy when he knew. She took a steadying breath. "Speaking of work…"

"What?" Jason asked sharply, picking up on her unease instantly.

"I got a promotion yesterday." May as well transition into this slowly, she thought.

"You did? That's great." Although Jason said the words, the lack of enthusiasm in his voice spoke volumes. "Ironic, huh? The day I get a final written warning and supervision, you get bumped up the ladder. So what are you doing?"

"I've been offered an executive assistant position. It's only temporary for now, but I'm hoping it'll lead to better things in the future." Much, much better things.

"That's cool, Maggie. Who to?"

She stiffened her spine. He wasn't going to like this one bit.

"William Tanner."

"You're kidding me. That insufferable jerk? He was the one who headed the panel yesterday. You didn't take it, did you?" Realization dawned slowly. "You did. That's how you knew about what happened to me."

"I had to, Jason. He didn't leave me any option."

"What? He forced you to take a promotion? You should

have told him to stick it where the sun don't shine." He made a sound of disgust and shook his head.

"Jason, he was going to go to the police over you."

"But I told you I didn't do it."

"All the evidence points to you, Jase. Unless you can prove otherwise, he holds all the strings, including mine." Maggie sighed and reached out to ruffle his hair. "It's not so bad, really. I get a raise in salary."

She balked at telling him the rest of Mr. Tanner's demands. He'd totally flip if he knew.

"I still don't like it. I don't trust the guy," Jason grumbled as he gently swatted her hand away. "You had better not have agreed to work for him to keep my job safe."

She couldn't answer him. She heard his sound of exasperation.

"You did, didn't you? How, in all that's logical, did you agree to that?"

"There's more to it," Margaret started, only to be cut off by her brother.

"Oh, yeah, sure there is. With men like him there always is. So what is it? Is he looking to pick up where you two left off back in February? Is that what it is?"

"Something like that. You can't tell anyone, Jason. Promise me you won't say a word of this to anyone."

"Yeah, like I'm going to shout to the rooftops that my sister is sleeping with her boss to save my job?"

"I'm not sleeping with him! Might I remind you that I have *you* to thank for putting me in this position in the first place? He's asked me to stand in as his fiancée, only for a short time while he sorts something out."

"His what?"

Maggie was saved from further explanation by the interruption of their phone. She lifted the receiver and cradled it between her ear and shoulder as she dished up Jason's scrambled eggs.

"Margaret, it's William Tanner."

She'd have recognized his voice anywhere. The tiny hairs on her arms and up the back of her neck prickled with awareness, her whole body tautening in response.

"Good morning," she replied as coolly as she could. She reached across the table and put Jason's plate in front of him before retreating to the living room.

"Look, I know it's early, but I wanted to catch you before you went into the office and wasted yourself a trip."

"Wasted a trip?"

Didn't he want her anymore? While a part of her sagged with relief, another leaped into full alert. Did this mean that they were going to fire Jason anyway?

"I need you to meet me here at the Vista Del Mar Beach and Tennis Club. I'll let them know at reception that I'm expecting you. How soon can you be here?"

Maggie knew that Rafe Cameron's team of executives involved in the takeover were being put up in the guest accommodations at the club. Her friend, Sarah Richards, worked there in the main restaurant and had commented on the influx of long-stay guests. Maggie took a quick glance at the mantel clock her father had been given for thirty years' service at Worth Industries. If she was quick getting ready, she could make it by eight-thirty, traffic permitting.

"By half past eight," she said into the phone, mentally cataloging her wardrobe to decide on what to wear today.

"See if you can't make it sooner."

Before she could respond, she realized she was listening to the disconnect signal on the phone. "Right, sure thing, boss, anything you say," she said as she hit the "off" button and took the phone back through to the kitchen.

"Problem?" Jason asked through a mouthful of egg.

"No. I just need to meet Mr. Tanner at the club this morning."

"Maybe he wants to check out your forehand before you start working for him," he commented snidely.

Maggie remained silent. She had no idea what he really wanted her for. It could be anything. Yet, strangely, the thought didn't strike fear into her heart. Instead, there was a fine shimmer of anticipation. She clamped down on the feeling before it could take wings. Whatever she was to meet him for was not optional—she needed to remind herself of that. He had her between a rock and a hard place. What she wanted, what she *really* wanted, had no significance beyond keeping Jason out of prison.

Will straightened his tie before checking his Rolex. She was late. Not exactly the most auspicious start for their first day of work together. He crossed the sitting room of the self-contained beachfront suite that was his temporary home and waited out on the terrace overlooking the Pacific. Waves rolled in with steady force, pounding the sand of the perfectly groomed beach before sucking back and starting all over again. He smiled. Even here, he was reminded of his family. Relentless. Well, they'd have to take a step back when they found out about Margaret, that was for sure. Although it wouldn't do for them to discover her too soon. If he was to suddenly produce a fiancée within a month of his last argument with his father it would only look suspicious.

A timid knock at the door barely caught his attention. Ah, she was finally here. He opened the door wide to admit her.

"Traffic bad?" he asked as she entered on his bidding.

"I'm sorry I'm late. Yes, some contractors hit a water main on my street just after you called. It was chaos getting out of there."

She looked flustered, although for someone who'd probably

missed her morning shower because of the issue with the water main she still managed to come across in her usual competent manner. Competent being the kindest way to describe the shapeless beige suit she wore today. He fought back a grimace.

"Is there something wrong?" she asked.

"No, nothing that can't be rectified today, at least," he responded.

Why did she dress in such awful clothing? he wondered. He'd caught a glimpse of her hourglass figure in the gown she'd worn at the ball, felt the lush fullness of her curves when he'd kissed her. Even now his hands itched to push away the serviceable fabric of her jacket and shape themselves to her form.

"What would you like me to do today?" she asked.

She stood perfectly straight and tall in her sensible pumps, awaiting his instruction. Will toyed with the idea of what would happen if he asked her to disrobe and burn the clothes she wore right now, but discarded it for the foolishness it was.

"As my executive assistant, and as my fiancée, there will be certain expectations."

She blanched at his words. "Expectations. Right. Perhaps we'd better discuss those now."

"Trying to call the shots, Margaret? That's a little late, don't you think?" he teased.

"I think you should know, there are some things I absolutely won't do," she answered with a defiant tilt of her chin.

"I'm sure there are," he responded smoothly, deciding to err on the side of caution for now. "But I hope those things don't include shopping."

"Shopping? For you?"

"No. For you. I'm sure what you're wearing was perfectly serviceable for your previous position but I expect a little more from my immediate staff. Besides, as my fiancée, people will certainly have something to say if you continue to dress in—" he gestured at her from shoulder to feet "—that."

She stiffened at his words. "I have a very careful budget, Mr. Tanner. And I try to buy clothes that won't date."

Won't date, he thought. How about won't get past first base altogether.

"I don't expect you to pay for these new items, Margaret. Consider them a fringe benefit. I have an image consultant coming to meet us shortly. Paige Adams—you may have heard of her. I understand she comes highly recommended. She'll take us out this morning to start getting you prepared for your new role."

"I'm going to spend the whole day shopping?" she asked, her eyes wide with surprise.

"Probably not the whole day, no. I'm sure Ms. Adams will have some other things up her sleeve to make your transformation complete."

"And will you be accompanying us on this…this expedition?"

She made it sound like an unwelcome hunting trip.

"Until about two. I have meetings this afternoon that I can't get out of so I'll have to leave you in her hands at that stage but I will see you for dinner tonight."

"Do I get any choice in this?"

There was that delicious hint of steel in her voice, as if beneath the timidity she really did have a will of iron. For some reason, Will found that incredibly appealing. Would she be like that in the bedroom? he wondered. Would she be sweet and compliant, then take control? Take him? An unexpected flood of heat suffused him, sending blood to his groin in a torrent of need.

"Oh, yes. You will have a choice." He hesitated and saw the way her shoulders relaxed, how her chest filled with air, the way her generous breasts moved beneath the serviceable fabric of her suit jacket, before continuing, "Up to a point."

"I won't let you dress me to look like some whore."

Ah, there it was again. That edge of strength. Will forced himself to rein in the urge to cross the distance between them and show her just how good it would be to let him take charge. Too soon, he reminded himself.

"Don't worry, that's the furthest thing from my mind," he said.

A knock at the door interrupted the weighted silence that spread between them.

"That'll be Ms. Adams."

He crossed the carpeted sitting room of his suite and swung open the heavy wooden door.

Margaret stood exactly where he'd left her. Focusing on each inward and outward breath. This was going to be so much more difficult than she'd anticipated. Yesterday it had sounded so simple. Work as his executive assistant. Pretend to be his fiancée. *Keep Jason out of jail.*

But the thought of William Tanner selecting her clothing, of him grooming her so specifically for the role she'd agreed to take on, sent a shiver of caution rippling through her. How would she stand it? She, who so carefully chose her work attire from Time Again, a thrift store supplied by the more affluent areas in town. Everything she bought was good quality, if a little dated. Did it really matter that much?

Imagining him waiting outside the dressing room as she tried on items of clothing for *his* approval made her uncomfortable just thinking about it. Uncomfortable, and something else. Something that went deeper than the idea that a man would have the final say on what she wore and how she looked on a daily basis. Something that sent a throb of longing from a place deep inside of her—a place she'd ruthlessly controlled and held in submission from the day she'd assumed guardianship of Jason.

She had responsibilities. Sure she'd had the occasional boyfriend, some had even become lovers—she was, after all, only human. But she'd never allowed herself to take a step beyond that—to allow herself to fully engage her feelings. Right now, she had the distinct impression it was going to be a whole lot more difficult to keep that distance from William Tanner.

"Meet Paige Adams."

William's voice interrupted her thoughts and Margaret forced her concentration back to the moment. She'd been fully prepared to dislike the woman on sight, in a petty attempt to assert herself over Will's directives, but it was difficult to summon a shred of antipathy toward the vibrant young woman now standing before her. Her skin was fresh and smooth and a friendly smile wreathed her face, while her unusual violet-colored eyes shone with delight.

Dressed in a sharply tailored suit that shrieked the kind of designer chic Maggie had always wished she could pull off, and a pair of high-heeled pumps that wouldn't go astray on a show like *Sex and the City,* the woman exuded both confidence and an air of affluence with effortless ease. Her well-styled hair, tamed into a neat chignon, was a shimmering pale blond that complemented the milky tone of her smooth skin. From the look of her she probably never had to worry about how she'd looked a single day in her life.

"Ms. Adams, I'm Margaret Cole," Maggie said, deciding to take the upper hand and not allow herself to be presented as a victim to the slaughter.

"Margaret, please, call me Paige. I'm delighted to meet you. Would you excuse me?" she asked and reached for the buttons on Maggie's jacket. "I like to see what I'm working with right from the start."

Maggie stiffened as Paige's fingers nimbly flew over the solid metal buttons fastening the front of her jacket. She wore only a thin blouse beneath the confining garment. A blouse she'd only chosen because she never—absolutely never—took her jacket off in the office. An early developer, she'd learned at a very young age how best to hide what made her a magnet for undesirable attention from males of all ages. Starting with her sixth-grade classmates when she'd changed from a gangly stick insect to a curvaceous boy-magnet in the space of a few months.

Maggie's eyes flew to Will's face as Paige handed him the jacket with a distracted, "Hold this." Would he be the same as so many others? Would he forget she was actually a person and not simply a body?

His sherry brown eyes met hers as Paige appraised her project with a critical eye. Maggie waited for the moment when his eyes would drop, as every man's did, to her breasts. But he never wavered, not even for a moment, and when Paige took Maggie's jacket from him and helped her back into it, Maggie felt a bone-deep relief. Maybe being around him wasn't going to be so difficult after all.

"This is going to be wonderful," Paige said enthusiastically. "How long did you say we have?"

"We have a dinner reservation for seven-thirty this evening," Will said in response.

"Oh, that's less time than I thought. Never mind, I can do this." She reached out and gave Margaret's hand an encouraging squeeze. "*We* can do this. You're great material to work with. You won't know yourself when I'm done. Trust me."

Strangely enough, Maggie did. Despite Paige's air of command and immaculate appearance, there was a warmth about her that drew Maggie in immediately.

Paige turned to William and said, "Shall we go then?"

"Certainly." Will bowed his head slightly, a bemused smile curving his lips and revealing the slightest dimple in his right cheek. "I'm at your disposal for the next few hours, then I have to head back for some meetings and leave you two to it."

Maggie felt a frisson of disquiet that he'd be accompanying them. It wasn't something he hadn't already told her, and since he was paying for everything it made sense he'd want a say in what his money went toward, but the prospect of parading before him made her incredibly nervous. She, who never tried to draw attention to herself, would now be the very center of attention. Attention from a man who she found almost irresistibly attractive.

Her pulse picked up a notch as he placed a warm hand at the small of her back and shepherded her before him as they left his suite. The action strangely intimate, and totally unsettling at the same time.

If she felt this disconcerted by something as simple as a touch, the next few hours were going to be excruciating.

Four

Excruciating didn't even begin to cover it, Maggie realized as she ducked back into the dressing room for the umpteenth time. It was as if she didn't even exist in a personal sense. She tugged off the midnight blue cocktail dress Mr. Tanner and Paige had both agreed wasn't her most flattering choice of the day and reached for a black sleeveless gown, pulling it over her head with a huff of frustration. Between the two of them she felt as if she were little more than a mannequin, right up until she shoved her feet in the matching high-heeled, black pumps that Paige had insisted she try on with the dress, and stepped outside the dressing room.

Her two torturers were sitting on the velvet-covered loveseat in the foyer of the dressing rooms, their heads together—each a perfect foil for the other—until they became aware she was standing waiting for their comment.

"Oh," said Paige, for once seemingly at a complete loss for words.

Maggie looked at William's face and her breath held fast in her lungs at the expression she saw there. The skin across his cheekbones tautened and his eyes widened and glowed in obvious appreciation.

"That's a definite," he said in a voice that sounded as if he struggled to force the words from his throat.

"Yes, it certainly is," Paige agreed.

Will rose from the seat and walked across the thick carpet to where Maggie stood nervously.

"Here, why don't we try this, just to soften things a little?"

He reached up to remove her dark-framed glasses from the bridge of her nose then folded them and tucked them in his breast pocket. He reached for Maggie's hair and pulled the pins from her habitual tight knot. Maggie felt her scalp rejoice as he tousled her hair loose from its constriction.

"Oh, yes, that's much better."

There was a note to his words that forced her to look at him, to allow her eyes to connect with his and see, without a doubt, what he was thinking. Desire flamed like a living, breathing thing and her skin tightened in response. Her breasts felt full and heavy and ached for his touch. Maggie swallowed against the sudden dryness in her throat. She was imagining things, surely. He'd said "fake" fiancée, hadn't he? But right now the expression on his face was anything but fake. His need for her was there in all honesty. A jolt of sheer lust shot through to her core, taking her breath completely away.

"Will you wear this for me tonight?" he asked.

"If you want me to," she replied, the words stilted, near impossible to force through her lips as she acknowledged the depth of feeling he aroused in her.

"You look beautiful. Nothing would give me more pleasure than to escort you looking like this. I'll be the envy of every man in the restaurant."

He smiled then, and Maggie felt her lips curve in response.

It was not so much a smile of pleasure as it was of satisfaction. For once she really felt beautiful. The admiration so clear on Will's face was a salve to her feminine soul. While she wasn't quite ready to examine how that admiration affected her on a basic level, she had to answer to the sensualist who dwelled deep within her. To deny that was nigh on impossible.

The sound of someone clearing their throat dragged Maggie's attention back to her surroundings.

"Okay, well we have a few more places to go before we're done. We've barely scratched the surface, really."

"I'll get changed," Maggie said and turned back into the dressing room.

"Here, you'd better take these," Will said, removing her spectacles from his pocket and handing them back to her.

Maggie shoved them back on her face and closed the door behind her. Faced with her own reflection in the private cubicle, she caught her breath. With her hair a loose tumble around her ivory shoulders and with the low scoop of the gown exposing the swell of her breasts she could see why Will had reacted the way he had. She scoured her memory. He hadn't dwelled on any one part of her, though. She hadn't, not even for a split second, felt uncomfortable under his perusal. She turned slowly and eyed her reflection in the mirror.

The dress was cut to perfection. If it had been made for her it couldn't have fit any better. The way it curved into her narrow waist and flared at her hips before finishing just above her knees made the most of her every attribute in a way she'd never dreamed. She skimmed her hand over the fabric before reaching for the invisible zipper sewn into the side seam. Her fingertips tingled as they slid over the fine weave. She'd never dreamed of having anything that made her feel as beautiful as this dress did. And there was still more to come.

Well, not if she didn't snap out of her reveries and get to

it, she reminded herself tersely. Even so, as she shimmied out of the dress she couldn't help but run her hands over it one more time before taking it out for Paige to add to the others William had already approved.

When she was going to wear all these garments absolutely boggled her mind—so far not one of them was suitable for the office. Aside from her regular coffee dates with her friend Gillian and the occasional catch-ups with Sarah when she wasn't working, she had little social life to speak of. All that was obviously about to change dramatically.

When she came out of the dressing room Paige was standing alone.

"Mr. Tanner had to leave early," she said, "so it's up to just us girls now."

For a split second Maggie was swamped with a sense of relief that she wouldn't have to face his minute examination of every garment and pair of shoes she tried on. But the relief was instantly tempered by the realization that it was his very approval she looked forward to every time she stepped from behind the dressing room door.

God, she was pathetic. The man was virtually blackmailing her to act as his fiancée and here she was *missing* him? How swiftly she'd fallen under his spell. Maggie needed to get her act together, and fast.

She summoned a smile and answered Paige, "That'll be fun. What's next on the agenda?"

"First we'll get these boxed up, except tonight's outfit, of course, and then I'd suggest lingerie and lunch. I'm starving, aren't you?"

Paige laughed as Maggie's stomach rumbled its own gentle response.

Later, at lunch, Paige mapped out the rest of their afternoon.

"I think we've got you covered for most social eventualities but I'd like to see you in some more feminine work wear. As soon as we're done here we'll power shop our way through some suits and then I have managed to squeeze in an appointment for you with an optometrist."

"But I can see perfectly well with these glasses," Maggie protested.

"Yes, I'm sure you can. But seriously, wouldn't you rather wear contacts? Then we can get you some super sexy sunglasses as well."

"Contacts?" Maggie wrinkled her brow. "Don't they irritate, though?"

"Not the ones these days. Let's see what they suggest, hmm? And if you're uncomfortable with contacts maybe we'll just choose some different frames for you. Something a bit softer that makes the most of your bone structure."

Maggie sat back in her chair. She'd always been too scared to try contacts before but she had to admit she was very much over the frames she'd been wearing for the past few years. One day, once all Jason's student loans were squared away, she'd maybe consider Lasik eye surgery, but that was still some time away.

"Okay, I'll give them a try," she said, making up her mind.

When Paige Adams talked makeover, she really meant *makeover,* Maggie thought later as she studied her reflection. Not only was she now wearing contact lenses, which didn't irritate her eyes, but, at the day spa at the Tennis Club, she'd been treated to a body wrap and facial, along with a pedicure and manicure. Right now, she felt both boneless and pampered. The crowning glory had come when she'd been shown to another section of the beauty spa where her hair had been subjected to a deep conditioning treatment and a restyle which saw the ends of her hair brush softly to her collarbone in soft, dark and lustrous tresses.

She barely recognized herself. The makeup artist who'd taken some time to show her how to make the most of her cheekbones and eyes had exclaimed loudly and often over how exquisite her skin was. By the time her cape was removed and the new polished and pampered Margaret Cole was revealed, even Paige let loose a long, low whistle of appreciation.

"Oh, yes," Paige said with a knowing smile. "Mr. Tanner is going to be very pleased indeed."

She cast a glance at her watch.

"We'd better get you dressed and up to his suite. It's almost seven-thirty and he doesn't strike me as the type of guy who likes to be kept waiting."

Butterflies suddenly massed in an attack squadron in the pit of her stomach. No, Will Tanner most definitely wasn't the type of guy who liked to be kept waiting.

Paige picked up the garment bag that held the black cocktail dress William had so admired, as well as the tissue-wrapped selection from the lingerie store that Paige had insisted she wear beneath it.

"Here, slip into these and let's see how gorgeous you look."

Maggie felt as if she were trapped in an alternate universe. These kinds of things just didn't happen in her world. The shopping, the makeover, the sheer quality of the stockings she slid up over her waxed and polished legs—it was like something from a dream. By the time she slid the dress carefully over her hair and makeup, and tugged the zipper closed, she was feeling a little light-headed.

She laid a hand against her stomach in a bid to quell her nerves but they simply wouldn't be suppressed.

"Everything okay in there?" Paige asked from outside the cubicle.

"Y-yes, I'm fine."

"So come on out and show us the final result," Paige coaxed.

Maggie took a deep breath, pushed her feet into the high-heeled, black pumps and took a quick look in the mirror. It wasn't her. It couldn't be. She gave herself a tentative, somewhat secretive, smile in the mirror. Even the lush ruby red painted lips didn't seem like her own.

The glamorous creature staring back at her was not the same Maggie Cole who'd left home this morning already feeling as if she was at the end of her tether. No, this was the kind of woman she'd always wished she could be but had never had the courage to reach for. This was *Margaret* Cole.

Strangely, the nerves jumping about in her belly settled and a sense of calm descended over her. She could do this. She could be the woman William Tanner needed her to be. She'd do it for Jason and, even more importantly, for herself.

Margaret closed her eyes and turned from the mirror, mentally leaving her old self behind. From now on she was Margaret Cole, fiancée and executive assistant to one of the most powerful men in Cameron Enterprises.

Both the staff of the day spa and Paige were full of praise for the final effect and it was with a sense of deep accomplishment that Margaret blushingly accepted everyone's compliments. In her hand she clutched a vintage beaded evening bag, a gift from Paige whose violet eyes had swum with tears of pride as she'd given it to her.

"Here, a little something from me," she'd said, giving Margaret a careful hug. "Now don't go all mushy on me or you'll ruin your makeup."

Margaret took the admonishment and with everyone's cheers of good wishes ringing in her ears, she approached the accommodation wing.

* * *

Will inhaled the aroma of the New Zealand Pinot Noir he'd had shipped from his cellar in New York to Vista Del Mar and anticipated savoring the myriad complex flavors that promised to dance across his taste buds. He was struck by the similarities between the simply labeled, yet award-winning wine, and the woman who was about to join him.

Today he'd caught glimpses of the siren she promised to be. The siren he hoped to have warming his sheets before too long. The siren who'd appease his father and ensure the land that had been in his family for two centuries would remain that way. He wanted the farm with a need that went soul deep. A need that had nestled in his heart from the first school holiday he'd spent tagging along behind his grandfather as he'd labored day in, day out, on the soil he loved above all other things. Even now he could still feel the strength of his grandfather's gnarled, work-worn hand holding his as they'd strolled across the fields. It had never been about the money for the old man. He'd always said there was an energy about the land that gave back to him four-fold what he put into it. And even on those rare school holiday visits, Will had understood what his grandfather had been talking about. It was a type of magic he didn't want to lose. Ever.

And now he didn't have to lose it. Margaret would undoubtedly ensure that his dream became a reality. The cost of today's exercise, already emailed to him by the ever-efficient Paige Adams, was a small investment as far as Will was concerned. One he'd make sure paid off in full.

A knock at the door made everything inside him tighten in anticipation. Slowly, deliberately, he placed the crystal wine goblet on the coffee table and went to open the door. He didn't even stop to check the peep hole. He knew to the soles of his feet exactly who stood on the opposite side.

A twist of his wrist and the door swung open to reveal

Margaret in all her glory. And what glory. For the first time in his living memory, William Tanner was speechless. His eyes feasted on the virtual stranger framed in the doorway. Every feminine curve displayed to absolute perfection. Her hair a shining swath of black silk that made his fingers itch to run through it. Her makeup so perfect that with her ivory skin she almost looked like a grown-up china doll.

Every cell in his body rejoiced. She was flawless elegance and beauty personified. Finally, he found his voice.

"You look amazing," he said, reaching for her free hand and drawing her inside to twirl her around slowly. "How do you feel?"

"Like Cinderella," Margaret admitted, with that small smile playing around her lips.

The type of smile that alluded to so much more going through her mind than the few simple words she'd spoken.

"I'm beginning to regret making the booking for dinner at Jacques' tonight," Will said.

"Oh? Why is that?"

"Because I don't know if I'm ready to share this version of you with anyone else."

He couldn't help the note of possession in his voice. She was Galatea to his Pygmalion, and he wanted to keep her all to himself. To explore every facet of her transformation, and then to remove each layer of her new sophistication before laying the true Margaret Cole bare to his eyes and to his hungering body.

Margaret dipped her head shyly and Will had to acknowledge the stark reminder that while, externally at least, Margaret was everything he needed in a female companion, beneath the luxurious trappings his money had provided she was still a small-town girl. Albeit a small-town girl with a magnetic appeal that threatened to scramble his wits.

He forced his lips into a smile.

"But don't worry. I'm not going to be quite so selfish as to keep you all to myself. Not this time, anyway."

"I'm pleased to hear it. I've been looking forward to dinner."

"Would you like a glass of wine before we go? I'm sure Henri will hold our table a little longer."

Margaret nodded; the movement a sensual inclination of her elegant neck. Oh, how he looked forward to exploring every inch of her starting with that spot right there in the hollow of her throat.

"I'd like that," she said.

Will stepped away from her before he did something stupid, like obey his instincts and ruffle up some of that poise she wore like a cloak around her.

"Do you like red wine? I have an excellent Pinot Noir open."

"I can't say I've tried that variety before but I'm willing to give it a go."

He picked up the bottle and poured a second glass of the bright ruby-colored liquid.

"Here," he said, handing her the goblet. "Smell it first and tell me what comes to mind."

Margaret took the glass from him, and lifted it to her nose. She closed her eyes and inhaled gently, all her senses focused on what he'd instructed her to do. Her eyes flew open.

"I can smell plums and berries. Is that right? It makes me think of summer and long lazy days."

"That's spot on. You have a good nose. Now taste it and let me know what you think."

She pressed the glass to her lower lip and tipped it gently, allowing a small sip of the beverage to enter the soft recesses of her mouth. Will felt as if he'd received a punch to his gut as he watched, totally mesmerized, while she swallowed then licked her lips. It was nothing more than a swift dart of her tongue over the plump fullness of her lower lip but it was enough to send his blood pumping through his body with a velocity that almost made him dizzy.

"It's good. I can taste the fruit now, and something else. Something woody?"

"Again, you're right. Well done."

Good grief, was his hand shaking? he thought as he reached for his own glass and took a slug of the wine he'd so anticipated only a few short minutes ago. He couldn't believe she affected him so deeply and in such a short period of time. He cast her another look. She wasn't exactly unaffected herself. There was a fine blush of color along her cheekbones that hadn't been there when she'd arrived and she certainly hadn't had enough wine to justify a flush of heat to her face.

This attraction between them was something else.

"Tell me about the rest of your day," he prompted. "I see Paige has certainly earned her fee."

Margaret filled him in on the shopping they'd done after he'd left.

"You two covered a lot of ground today. I have to say, I like the contacts," Will commented.

"I thought I'd have more trouble getting used to them but I was pleasantly surprised. Of course I haven't tried to take these out or put in a new set yet."

Margaret laughed. The sound that bubbled from her as rich and complex as the wine in his glass. His nerves were already stretched to breaking point. Desire for her clouded rational thought. He really needed to get a grip. He wanted nothing better than to keep her all to himself, all night long. But that was impossible, he reminded himself. They needed to be seen in public for the news to filter back to his parents in New York, as he knew it eventually would.

Will was startled to discover she was an amusing companion over dinner. There was a sharp intelligence to her that he'd underestimated when he'd seen the Miss Prim version of Margaret Cole in the workplace.

Everything went fine through the course of the evening until a group of several couples came into the restaurant. The men were managers who had survived Rafe's takeover of Worth Industries. One of them nodded in Will's direction, a quizzical look on his face as he studied Will's companion, until recognition dawned. Then something less pleasant and more lascivious soon followed as the man's stare traveled down the smooth ivory column of Margaret's throat and lower, to her décolletage.

An unexpected rush of possessiveness, and an urge to protect her from such shallow and insulting interest, suffused Will. He noted she'd paled under the other man's scrutiny before very calmly replacing her cup of decaffeinated coffee back onto its saucer. At first glance he wouldn't have known how the man's look had upset her, with the exception of how pale she'd grown. But now she tucked her hands into her lap where they knotted in her heavy linen napkin, twisting the fabric over and over.

He made a point of staring at the manager until the man's fixed look lifted from Margaret's chest and he slowly came around to making eye contact with Will. It didn't take much, a mere narrowing of Will's eyes, a cooling in his expression, but the guy got the message.

"Shall we go?" Will asked, eager now to remove her from prying eyes and speculation.

His actions were in direct contrast to what he thought he'd wanted. Even the interest shown in them by the chance meeting with the gossip columnist from the *Seaside Gazette* when they'd arrived hadn't drawn this overwhelming urge to shelter Margaret from unwanted interest in their so-called relationship. He hadn't stopped to consider the ramifications of this quite far enough and he made a silent vow to be more careful of her reputation in the future. While he wasn't above using her for his own purposes, he certainly didn't want to see her become the butt of gossip and innuendo in the workplace.

"Thank you, yes, I'm ready to go," Margaret replied with the new mantle of decorum she wore around her like a cloak.

The only telltale sign of her discomfort showed in the crumpled napkin she placed on the table as she rose from her seat and gathered her evening bag.

Neither of them had drunk more than a glass of wine at dinner, but Will was still glad he was using a driver for the evening. It gave him the chance to observe Margaret a little closer, to watch her mannerisms. So far today he hadn't been able to fault her, which was great as far as convincing his parents she was the real deal. They'd see through his farce in a blink if he went out with someone who lacked common courtesy and manners.

As Will handed her into the wide bench seat in the back of the limousine he caught a glimpse of lace-topped stockings before she smoothed her skirt down over her shapely thighs. Lust hit him, hard and fast. The rational side of his mind told him his reaction was no better than that of the accounts manager he'd frozen out in the restaurant. But the less rational side of him, the side that had seen Margaret at the Valentine's ball and known he'd stop at nothing to have her, reminded him he'd kept a lid on his burgeoning passion all through the exquisitely presented meal they'd enjoyed at the restaurant.

He'd been the perfect gentleman, the perfect host. But now, in the close confines of the car and with the privacy screen firmly in place, his mind ran riot on all the things he wanted to experience with Ms. Margaret Cole.

Five

Margaret sat beside Will on the cool leather seat as the car pulled smoothly away from the entrance to Jacques'. It was as if they were cocooned together in a protective bubble and she found the sensation vastly more reassuring than that moment when the manager from accounting had recognized her at the restaurant with Will. The awful assessing look in his eyes had made her feel sick to her stomach. It was exactly the kind of look she'd spent most of her life trying to avoid.

What made it worse was that his wife worked in HR, and she was an inveterate gossip. Margaret wouldn't be at all surprised to discover she was the main topic of water-cooler conversation before nine o'clock tomorrow morning.

She looked out the window at the passing scenery, but her eyes failed to register her surroundings. All she could do was silently castigate herself for being such an idiot. Who did she really think she was? She'd allowed herself to foolishly be seduced into thinking she could belong in this world. But it took far more than clothing and clever makeup to make that leap. Realistically, she was nothing but a tool in a very elaborate game designed by Will Tanner. And she'd become a shamefully eager participant.

It *had* been fun to dress up like this tonight. To allow her senses to be wooed by the glamour of the clothes she wore, the sensuality of allowing the woman she kept buried deep inside to come out. But, as much as she wished for it to be real and true, it wasn't her.

The final vestiges of the fantasy-like qualities of today's activities faded away. Tonight she had to go home, and no doubt face the silent accusations of her brother. Or not so silent, given Jason's propensity to speak his mind. She grimaced at her reflection in the glass. He wouldn't be happy with this new version of her, especially given the man who had engineered it all.

And then there was tomorrow. Work. The word echoed in her mind. She sent a silent prayer of thanks to Paige for the consideration with which she'd helped Maggie choose her new work wardrobe. While the clothing was more fitted than she usually wore, it did nothing to overly emphasize her obvious attributes. At least she wouldn't be subjected to the kind of look she'd experienced in the restaurant.

Strange how one man's gaze upon her could make her feel uncomfortable—dirty, even. Yet another's lit a slow burning fire deep inside of her that even now, beneath all her concerns, still simmered.

She started as she felt Will's warm fingers wrap around her hand where it lay in her lap. He laced his digits through hers and drew her hand to his lips, pressing a brief kiss against her knuckles.

"I'm sorry the evening had to end that way, Margaret."

"It wasn't your fault."

"No, it wasn't, but I'm angry you had to feel uncomfortable for simply being you. Beautiful."

His words were like a balm to her soul, but she knew she shouldn't, couldn't, accept them.

"No, I'm not beautiful." She put up her free hand to silence him as he made to protest. "I'm not just saying that so you can argue the point with me. I know my limitations. And speaking of those limitations—" she gently withdrew her fingers from his clasp "—we have to discuss how we're going to conduct this arrangement at work."

Will eyed her carefully in the darkened compartment, his silence stretching out between them uncomfortably. Eventually, he cleared his throat and spoke, "It's simple, isn't it? You'll act as if you're both my fiancée and my executive assistant."

"But it's all so sudden, our *engagement*. Don't you think people will talk? Are you sure that's what you want?" she protested.

"No one will dare discuss our relationship behind your back, or to your face, for that matter. You can be certain of that, Margaret. I will ensure you aren't made a topic of casual discussion."

"You can't hold back human nature. People will talk."

"Not if I threaten their jobs, they won't," he growled in the darkness.

"Please don't. After you've gone back to New York I still need to be able to work with those people."

He breathed a sound of irritation before inclining his head in agreement. "Okay," he said begrudgingly. "I won't threaten anyone's job, but I will make it clear that our relationship is no one's business but our own."

Good luck with that, Margaret thought with a wry smile. "Thank you. Now, in the office? Is it to be common knowledge that we're…an item?"

"Yes," Will said, sitting up straighter as if he'd come to a decision. "I think that'll put a halt to conjecture right from the start. Which reminds me, we need to get you a ring. Damn, I should have thought of that today. People will think it's strange if you're not wearing one."

Margaret's breath caught in her throat. A ring? She hadn't even thought that far. Just the thought of what Jason would say when she arrived home with her new wardrobe was enough to send a cold chill of foreboding down her spine.

"Is that really necessary? Couldn't it wait a while? After all, everyone is going to think this is a whirlwind affair as it is."

"I want you wearing my ring for your protection if nothing else, Margaret," Will said solemnly. "No one will dare question our relationship that way. Let's stick as close to the truth as possible. If anyone asks, we can say we met at the Valentine's ball and have been seeing each other ever since, on the quiet of course, but now we've decided to bring it all out in the open. Will that cause any problems for you amongst your friends?"

Margaret thought for a few moments. Her closest friends, Gillian and Sarah, would be surprised but happy for her, provided they believed this engagement was the real deal. Jason was the only fly in the ointment. His objections were already the hardest to bear.

But she was doing this, all of this, for him. To keep his job safe. To keep him, hopefully, out of the courts and out of jail. The lingering remnants of enjoyment she'd taken out of the day soured on her tongue.

How could she have lost sight of that? How could she have let her delight—in her new look, her new wardrobe, in simply spending time with a handsome man who made her the center of his attention—overcome her responsibilities toward her brother? Her parents would be ashamed that she'd allowed herself to be so easily swayed from the seriousness of the situation she and Jason now found themselves in. *She* was ashamed.

She saw they were pulling into the driveway at the Tennis Club. She reached forward and tapped on the glass, which slid down to reveal the driver.

"Could you let me off here, please? My car's in the car park over there."

Margaret gestured toward where her car sat in isolation in the back row. The old vehicle seemingly ostracized from its shiny later-model companions parked in the next few rows. The limousine glided to a halt.

"Are you sure you don't want to stay here at the club? I can arrange a room for you if you prefer not to stay in my suite," Will said with a look in his eyes that sent a flush of warmth unfurling from the pit of her belly.

No matter how much she pilloried herself today, just one look from him was enough to start that slow melt deep inside her.

"No, I have my own home. I'd like to keep it that way."

"Have you always been this fiercely independent?" Will asked with a smile.

"Since my parents died, I suppose. It's become a habit," she admitted.

Will exited the limo ahead of her and turned to help her out.

"Maybe it's time you shared some of that load you carry," he commented.

Was he criticizing Jason? She felt herself bristle automatically in defense of her younger brother, words of justification on the tip of her tongue, before she reined herself in.

"I can manage just fine," she finally said, a little more sharply than she'd originally intended but it got the point across.

Will walked her over to her car and stood to one side as she fiddled with her key in the door lock.

"Trouble?" he inquired.

"No, it's okay. It just requires a bit of finesse to get it to work," she said as the key finally engaged with the tumblers inside and the door unlocked.

"I suppose you have all today's shopping in there, too?"

"Yes."

"A bit risky given how easy your car would be to break in to."

Will's comment stung. So what if she didn't have one of the latest models off the production lines of American driving excellence.

"I would have thought the security here at the Tennis Club would ensure that my parcels are quite safe. Besides, they're in the trunk so it's not as if anyone can see them on display."

"No, but anyone could have seen you put them in there, and it's not as if it would take someone with a MENSA-rated IQ to figure a way into your car," Will pressed. "I don't like the idea of your security being so easily compromised. Tomorrow I'll see you have another car to use." At her gasp of shock he continued, "Don't argue with me, Margaret. I need you to have something reliable to get you to and from work and other appointments you'll be undertaking with me. It makes sense that I put a car at your disposal."

Margaret couldn't think of a single argument that would sway him. Will stepped forward and tipped her chin up with one finger.

"Are you angry with me now?" he asked.

Conscious of their audience, the driver still waiting for Will in the limousine that idled a short distance away, Margaret shook her head. She wasn't angry, exactly. But there was a sense of frustration that he'd put her in a position where she couldn't refuse. A sense of frustration that was spilling over in all areas of her life with the power and force of a tidal wave.

"Looks like I'll have to remedy that, won't I?"

Before she could summon a protest Will kissed her—his lips gentle, yet persuasive. A tiny sigh of capitulation eased from her throat and he took the action as an opportunity to deepen their embrace. Without realizing what she was doing, Margaret wound her arms over his shoulders, the fingers of one hand driving into his short hair and cupping the back of his head as if she couldn't quite get enough of him.

When his tongue brushed against hers she felt her body ignite. She leaned into him, pressing her breasts against the hardness of his chest, letting her hips roll against his in a silent dance of torment.

And then, just like that, he broke contact. As if he'd proven his point that no matter what she did, or thought, or said, she was his for the taking. Whenever and however he wanted her. It should have galled her to realize it, but instead she worked on trying to calm the thrumming desire that wound through her.

"Sweet dreams," he whispered against her mouth. "I will see you in the morning."

She nodded and got into her car, her hand trembling a little as she fitted the key to the ignition and fired the car to life. Will pushed her door closed and stood to one side as she backed out and began to drive away. A flick of her eyes to her rearview mirror confirmed he stayed there, watching her, until she hit the driveway that led to the main road.

She had no idea how she was going to handle this over-whelming effect he had upon her. None at all. While every cell in her body bade her to give in to it, to him, logic told her that it would only lead to heartbreak—her heartbreak.

* * *

She'd slept surprisingly well after the turmoil in which she'd ended her evening. Thankfully, Jason had been in his room, the lights off but the sounds of his TV filtering through the closed door. She hadn't wanted to disturb him. Hadn't wanted to face his recriminations—especially when he saw the number of bags she'd brought in from her car.

Now, all she had to do was decide on what to wear to work today. She skimmed her hand over the hangers in her wardrobe before settling on a 1940s-inspired dress with a deep collared V-neck and three-quarter sleeves. The large black and white hounds-tooth pattern of the fabric drew attention to the design of the dress, rather than the person wearing it, and she and Paige had been in total agreement about it the second she'd stepped out of the dressing room. A wide black belt at her waist finished it off and after brushing her hair and applying a light coating of makeup, Margaret went through to the kitchen.

To her surprise, Jason was already there.

"You were late home last night," he said as she reached for the carafe and poured herself a mug of coffee. "Work late at the office?"

"No, I had dinner out. I didn't disturb you when I came in, did I?"

He barked an ironic laugh. "Disturb me? Well, that all depends on who you had dinner with, doesn't it?"

"Why would it depend on that?"

"You were with him, weren't you? And look at you this morning. That's new. Did he buy it?"

Margaret flinched at the accusation in Jason's voice. She drew in a leveling breath and chose her words carefully.

"Mr. Tanner and I agreed that my old wardrobe was perhaps lacking a little for my new role. He very kindly offered to rectify that."

"Your new role, huh? And what exactly is that role to be, Maggie? How long before he has you warming his sheets?"

"How dare you speak to me like that?" she flung back. "I'm not like that and you know it."

"Yeah, but the sister I know doesn't stay away from her desk at work all day long, doesn't ignore her cell phone and doesn't sneak in late at night trying to avoid me, either."

Her cell phone. Oh, God, she hadn't even thought to check it all day and she'd been so rattled by the time she got home it hadn't even occurred to check it then.

"Did you need me for something?" she asked as calmly as she could.

"That's not the point. You're not behaving like yourself. What's going on?"

Margaret chewed at her lower lip. How was she going to approach this without aggravating the tenuous thread she and her brother had between them at the moment?

"I'm sorry. I was distracted."

"By him."

Jason spoke the two words as if they were poison on his tongue.

"Yes, by him. But, Jason, I only took this job to keep *your* job safe. I know you don't like it but that's the way it is. We can't afford for either of us to lose our jobs. You know as well as I do that working for Cameron Enterprises is the only thing keeping our heads above water."

"I don't like it, Maggie. He's only been in your sphere for two days and already he's changing you. It's not just your clothes, but your hair and…" He peered closer at her face. "Are you wearing contacts? What's with that? Weren't you good enough for him the way you were?"

"As his fiancée I'll be expected to look a certain way. I could hardly argue when he covered the bill for every-thing."

"Everything? So I expect we won't be seeing any more serviceable white cotton in the laundry?"

Jason snorted, the sound grating on Margaret's nerves. Oh, it was all so easy for him, wasn't it? To sit in judgment of her when she was doing this for him. If he hadn't been tempted… A slow-building anger began to well inside her. She'd done her best all these years and it was never going to be enough. Well, it was time he faced some truths.

"Keep your mind out of the gutter for once, Jason, and try to focus on someone that isn't yourself."

The sharpness of her voice made him sit up in his chair, a look of surprise on his face. Never, not even when he'd been a sulky teenager, delivered home by the local police, had she spoken to him this way. She forced herself to soften her tone. It wouldn't serve any purpose to antagonize him, anyway.

"Look, William Tanner and I are, for all intents and purposes, engaged."

"You're mad. No one is going to believe it."

"They'll have to." Maggie crossed her fingers behind her back and hoped for the strength to get herself through this. "If anyone asks you can tell them that we've been seeing each on the quiet for almost two months and it's…it's become something a lot bigger than either of us expected.

"The news will no doubt be all around the office today, we were seen out at dinner last night together and a reporter from the *Gazette* was there, too. We have to keep our stories straight about this, Jason, before the gossip mongers get ahold of it."

"Well, don't expect me to welcome him here with open arms. I can't stand the man."

"I know. And don't worry. I won't be bringing him here."

"So you'll be going to him. You'll be at his beck and call at work and on your own time?"

His words couldn't be more true but she couldn't tell him the truth.

"That's right, and that's my choice, Jason. A choice I made for us both. Remember that."

And it was her choice. One she wished she'd never been pushed into making, but there was no going back now.

Six

"I've got tickets to a live show tonight. Are you interested? We can head into San Diego after work and I thought we could stay over—make a weekend of it. How much time do you need to pack a bag?"

Margaret sat up straight in her chair, her hands stilling on the keyboard where she'd been typing up a report for Will. They'd been working together for three days, excluding the day he'd taken her shopping, and every night they'd had dinner together either in his suite or in one of the multitude of restaurants dotted along the coast. Each night he'd done no more than kiss her good-night, and each night she'd gone home, her body aching for more. To all appearances they were very much the engaged couple but, for Margaret, it was growing more difficult each day to separate the truth from reality—even with Jason's brooding silences and fulminous looks when they crossed paths at home.

A weekend solely in Will's company? The idea both thrilled

and terrified her in equal proportions. Jason would be scathing, she had no doubt. But the prospect of spending forty-eight hours alone with Will Tanner was infinitely preferable to the stifling atmosphere at home—for more reasons than one. She'd no sooner had the thought than she instantly felt disloyal. It wasn't Jason's fault he was so unhappy. But why should they both be miserable? Margaret took a deep breath and answered.

"I'd love to go. When do you need me to be ready?"

"If you're finished with that report you could head home now and I'll pick you up in," he flicked a look at the understated yet expensive watch he wore on one wrist, "say two hours. That'll give us plenty of time to drive in, check into the hotel and have a bite of something to eat. The show starts at eight and we can have a late supper afterward."

"Do you want me to take care of the hotel bookings?" she asked, reaching for her phone.

"Already done," Will said, meeting her gaze for the first time.

There was something in his eyes that made her forget what she was doing and her hand hovered, outstretched over her telephone, before she realized what she was doing and pulled it back. Snapping back to reality didn't change anything, though. If anything it made the sudden pulse of excitement that swelled through her all the more overwhelming. Had he arranged one room, or two? She'd find out soon enough.

She forced herself to break the silent, loaded connection between them and turned her head toward her computer screen. A quick flick of her fingers over the keyboard and the document was sent to the printer.

"I'll be ready to leave in a few minutes. Do you need my address?" she asked with as much composure as she could muster.

"No, I have all your details."

Not surprising, given his investigation of her and Jason. The reminder should have been a wake-up call for her to get her head out of the clouds but she chose to ignore the frisson of warning that infiltrated her overheated mind.

They were going away together for the night. Away from the prying eyes of the office. Away from the simmering resentment that clouded every conversation she had with her brother. Just the thought of it was enough to make her feel lighter, happier.

It only took a few minutes to check the printed report, then copy and bind it for the meeting Will had organized for Monday morning. She locked the reports away in her cabinet and let Will know she was on her way home.

Not even the spiteful comment from one of the accounting staff that reached her ears on her way out the door, about it being nice to be the boss's fiancée and be able to leave early on a Friday, was enough to take the polish off the hours ahead.

By the time she heard Will's knock at the door of her home she was ready. The April afternoon had turned quite cool after the spring sunshine of earlier in the day and, as a result, she'd probably packed far too many clothes but, she consoled herself, better too much than not quite enough.

She swung open the front door and her breath caught fast in her chest. She hadn't seen Will dressed casually before, at least not in anything like the green-gray sweater he was wearing now with a pair of sinfully sexy jeans. Words failed her as her eyes took in the subtle breadth of his shoulders and the way the sweater fit snugly across his chest. The lean strength visible beneath the ribbed woolen knit made her mouth dry and she swallowed hard.

"All ready?" Will asked, his mouth quirking up in a half smile.

"Well, I'm all packed," she said, gesturing to the small

suitcase she had standing in the compact entrance to the house.

"Shall we head off then?"

"Sure, just let me check I've locked everything up securely first."

Margaret shot around the house, double-checking all the doors and windows were closed and that the note she'd left for Jason was where he wouldn't miss it. By the time she swung her key in the deadlock of the front door, Will had already put her case in the trunk of his midnight-blue Chrysler 300 and was waiting by the passenger door for her to come outside.

"Sorry to keep you waiting," she said, suddenly shy.

It was ridiculous to feel this way, she told herself. They'd been working together the past week in close quarters, and had spent several hours together outside of work as well. She'd gotten to know him as a man of integrity, quite at odds with the hard-ass attitude he'd been painted with when he'd first arrived for the takeover. He struck her as being fully committed to finding the most workable solution to the transition of ownership from the Worth family to Rafe Cameron. Will was intelligent and insightful. Both qualities Margaret admired greatly.

She'd had plenty of time to think about her earlier perceptions of Will, in particular, plenty of time to rethink her perceptions. He could easily have let Jason go to the wall over the funds that had been so artfully skimmed. Sure, he'd thrown his weight around a bit to get her to agree to act as his fiancée as well, but over dinner last night he'd told her a bit about the reasons behind his need for her helping him. In particular, he told her about the family farm his grandparents had run—the fifth generation of his family to do so—and his father's plans to sell the property if Will couldn't satisfy his wish for his youngest son to settle down.

She'd seen a side of him that no one at the office had seen

before. Certainly a side that no one expected to see from him. By all accounts the whole farming operation was huge and Will's dad was keen to make the most of international interest and sell to the highest bidder. But Will was equally determined the property should remain in family hands—specifically his hands. He'd talked about what the time he'd spent on the farm growing up had meant to him, how it had helped him keep a perspective in life as his parents' wealth had grown in leaps and bounds. His father had never wanted to take over the farm, as had generations of Tanners before him, choosing instead a career in finance. Albert Tanner's acumen had eventually led to him taking a senior management role in New York that had seen the whole family relocate to the other side of the world.

But deep down, Will still felt it was vitally important to maintain that link with his family's past. The reminder that generations of Tanners had hewn a living from what had sometimes been a hostile land, and in bitter conditions, yet had managed to hold on to humor and each other through it all. While he had no plans to actively farm the land himself, he saw no reason why the current method of using a caretaker/manager, with a full complement of staff, couldn't be maintained. And if he was so inclined as to visit every now and then, and muck in with the rest of them, then so be it.

The thought of Will in a pair of muddy rubber work boots—what had he called them? Gumboots?—and sturdy farm gear brought a small smile to her face.

"Penny for them?" Will said, interrupting her thoughts.

"Just thinking about what you told me last night and trying to picture you in a pair of gumboots," she said, a gurgle of laughter rippling from her throat. "Seriously, after seeing you day in, day out in your suits, it's quite a stretch of the imagination."

Will grinned at her briefly before transferring his attention back to the traffic winding in front of them on the freeway.

"Believe it, it happens."

The trip south into San Diego went smoothly, taking no more than half an hour and before Margaret even had time to fully appreciate their downtown surroundings, they were pulling up in front of one of the city's historic five-star hotels and her car door was being opened by liveried staff.

Her heart was in her mouth as they stepped into the grand lobby. She'd never seen anything like it in her life. Crystal chandeliers hung from the ceiling and muted-tone silk carpets made her fear to tread upon them.

"You like it?" Will asked at her side.

"Like doesn't even begin to describe it."

"Wait until you see our suite."

A suite. That could mean two bedrooms, couldn't it? Margaret wasn't sure if she felt a sense of relief, or regret. She didn't have too long to find out, though. They were checked in with supreme courtesy and efficiency and before long were shown to a suite comprising two levels.

While Will tipped the bellboy, Margaret made an exploratory tour. The lower level was made up of a sitting room which opened out onto a wide, furnished balcony. She shook her head slightly. Even the outdoor furniture put that of her humble home to shame. If she hadn't been aware of the two different worlds in which she and Will moved before, she certainly was now. She carried on through the suite and made her way up the staircase, her hand trailing on the black walnut railing.

At the top of the stairs was the master bedroom. Perhaps the door off to one side led to another bedroom, she thought, as she turned the handle and exposed a decadently luxurious marble bathroom. She pulled the door closed again and turned around.

One bed.

One huge, luxurious bed covered in soft pillows and fine bed linens.

Her nerves jangled. It wasn't as if she hadn't spent most of her waking hours during the past week imagining what it would be like to be in Will's arms—in his bed. But facing the potential reality was another thing entirely. Was she even ready for this? In so many ways, no, she most definitely wasn't. However, from deep within her a voice grew stronger, its response to her internal question a resounding "yes." He'd said he wouldn't have to force her, and he'd been so very right.

Will waited on the lower level of the suite as Margaret investigated what the rooms had to offer. Had she noticed he'd only booked one bedroom yet? he wondered. It had been a conscious decision on his part, although if she demurred he had no problem with booking a separate room for her. But it was time he took their so-called relationship to the next level. She was comfortable with him now, physically and socially, although if she was going to convince his parents she really was his fiancée, he needed her to be totally invested in him. He'd hoped to take his time seducing her, but an email from his mother this week had mentioned his father was sourcing realtors in New Zealand who specialized in rural property.

To delay any longer would be cutting things a little too close and he wasn't prepared to take the risk.

He looked up as Margaret made her way back down the staircase to the sitting room.

"Some champagne?" he asked, gesturing to the ice bucket, sweating gracefully on a linen placemat on the coffee table.

She hesitated. Was the objection to their sleeping arrangements going to come now? Will held his breath until she appeared to make up her mind and crossed the room to his side.

"Why not? That would be a lovely way to start the weekend."

He relaxed. Everything was going to plan quite nicely. With deft movements he dispensed with the foil and cage at the neck of the champagne bottle and popped the cork before spilling the sparkling golden liquid into the crystal champagne flutes on the table. He picked them both up and offered one to Margaret.

"To us," he said.

She met his gaze with a serious look in her dark eyes. "To us," she answered and tapped her glass gently against his.

Without breaking their visual connection he lifted his glass to his lips and took a sip. She mirrored his actions, all the time her eyes holding his, and he felt the desire that he'd kept tightly coiled within him all week begin to unravel and take life.

When she took her glass away from her mouth a slight shimmer of moisture remained there. Tempting him. Daring him. He took her glass from her unprotesting hand and placed it back on the table with his own. When he straightened he reached for her, drawing her to him as if the action had been predestined. If he stopped to think about it, it had been—certainly from the moment she'd chosen to protect her brother and his job. But it wasn't time for thinking anymore. No, now it was time to act.

As his lips sealed hers he both felt and heard her surrender to him. It had been the same each time he'd kissed her this past week. The tiny hum she made. It intoxicated him in a way no other stimulant ever could. His whole body focused on the sound, every nerve in his body taut with anticipation.

Her arms tightened around him, as if she could hardly support herself without him, and her kiss was as open and giving as he'd hoped for. He adored the taste of her, the texture of her. It was all he could do to hold on to his wits, to remind himself that this seduction should progress by degrees, not flame out in a flashover of uncontrolled need. But try as he might, his body demanded more. And it demanded it now.

Will reluctantly broke the kiss, noting with pleasure the tiny moue of regret on her lips. He took her hand and led her to the staircase and slowly drew her up the stairs. At the top he took her into his arms again, and this time he didn't plan to let go for quite some time.

The buttons on the silk blouse she wore slid free with ease, and he feasted his gaze upon her soft, smooth skin. Fine white lace cupped her generous breasts and as much as he admired the craftsmanship of the undergarment, it obstructed his view of her just a little too much. He slid her blouse from her shoulders and free of her arms, absorbing her tiny cries with his mouth as he trailed his fingertips over her softly rounded arms, chasing the piece of clothing until it fell to the floor.

All week she'd tormented him with her wardrobe that hinted at, yet concealed, her feminine curves. She was the most sensuously put together woman he'd ever met, yet the most modest at the same time. The juxtaposition was both intriguing and provocative. And now she was all his to discover.

It took the merest twist of the hooks at the back of her bra and her glorious breasts were revealed to him. He smoothed his hands across her ribcage, bringing them underneath the full creamy-skinned globes and cupping them gently, reverently. She gasped as he brushed his thumbs across the deep rose pink tips, feeling them pebble into tight buds beneath his touch.

He trailed small kisses from the corner of her mouth to her jaw as he relished the weight and firmness of her in his hands. When he bent his head lower and caught a tender tip gently between his teeth, a small keening sound broke from Margaret's throat. He hesitated, laving the areola with the tip of his tongue, waiting for her to tell him to stop, but instead he felt her fingers drive into his hair and cup the back of his head, holding him there.

A tremor of satisfaction rippled through him. She wanted this as much as he did. She wouldn't regret a second of it, he promised silently. Not one single moment. He would give and give until there was nothing left.

Later, he couldn't say how they came to be naked and lying together on the bed, flesh burning with heat and need for one another. The details were unimportant. But several things would remain in Will's memory forever.

The way his hands trembled as he explored the dips and hollows of Margaret's lush body. Her unabashed joy in his touch. Her sharp sigh of completion as he brought her to orgasm, the taste of her as he did so. And then, the overwhelming sensation of entering her body, of feeling her clamp her inner strength around him, of drawing her to yet another peak before he tumbled past reason and joined her on that plane where they both hovered, suspended by pleasure, before slowly returning back to reality.

They lay there for some time, legs still entwined, hearts still racing, fingers still tracing one another before Will could put together a single rational thought.

He'd lost track of whether he was the seducer or the seduced. Something had happened while they made love. It had ceased to be something he wanted to do, albeit it had been a task he'd relished. No, somewhere along the line it had become something bigger than that. Something more. Something he didn't want to examine too closely—certainly not now while he had so very much at stake.

And that's what he needed to concentrate on now, he reminded himself. They still had plenty of time before they needed to get ready for the show tonight. It didn't start until eight, and he had plenty of ideas of how they could fill their time until then.

Margaret basked in a rosy glow of supreme satisfaction as they exited the theater. Will had been amazingly attentive all evening so far, and he was an incredibly considerate lover, too. Not that she had a great deal to compare him to, but no one had ever brought her to the heights of pleasure he had. Her arm was tucked through Will's and she felt her sensitized breast brush against his arm as they made their way outside through the press of theater patrons. Even through his suit fabric she could feel the heat of his body, and felt the answering burn of her own.

She'd barely been able to concentrate on the performance of *Fiddler on the Roof,* even though the story was one she'd adored since childhood. All evening she'd been excruciatingly aware of the man at her side. The man who'd bared her for his delectation only a few short hours earlier, when they'd finally gotten around to finishing their champagne, amidst more lovemaking.

If she was a cat she'd be purring right now. It wasn't until her vision was blinded by a sudden bright flash that Margaret became aware they were no longer caught in the throng of bodies exiting the theater, but stood upon the pavement waiting for the car and driver the hotel had arranged for them earlier.

"Don't worry," Will murmured in her ear as she looked around to see where the flash had come from. "It's just some paparazzo looking for some celebrity gossip."

"Well, they won't find much from us, will they?"

"I don't know. The way you look tonight they'll probably print the picture to sell more papers."

Margaret pushed playfully against his chest. "You have to be kidding."

But Will's eyes grew serious as he looked back at her, the smile fading from his face. "Oh, no, I'm not kidding at all. You look sensational."

"Well, if I do, it's all because of you. You made me this way."

Their car materialized through the traffic and pulled up smoothly alongside of them. Will didn't answer, and opened the back door for her to get in ahead of him. Had she hit a sore point? she wondered, as he followed her into the car and they drew away from the curb.

"Hungry?" Will asked.

Margaret realized she was famished. The light snacks they'd eventually brought up to the bed and enjoyed with the balance of their champagne had tided her over but now she was ready for something more substantial.

"Definitely," she said.

"Then it's just as well I've booked us somewhere for supper," he said with a wink.

She looked at him across the semidarkness of the car interior and felt her chest constrict. There was something about him that appealed to her on every level—had from the first moment she'd seen him—and it deepened with every minute she spent with him now.

By the time they were seated at the intimately lit restaurant Will had chosen, Margaret felt as if every cell in her body was attuned to his. She left the menu selection to him, preferring instead to watch him as he perused the choices available to them. He approached their order with the same level of concentration he approached everything. She felt her womb clench in anticipation as she acknowledged he'd applied the same concentration to her and no doubt would again.

She slipped her foot from one expensive high-heeled

shoe and slid her foot up the inside of his calf, secure in the knowledge that no one could see her action beneath the floor-length tablecloth. He didn't so much as flinch, until her toe traced the inside of his thigh—an area she already knew he found incredibly sensitive.

His eyes flicked up to hers and in their sherry brown depths she saw raw hunger reflected there.

"I thought you said you were hungry," Will said, his voice low.

"I am. Very hungry."

She let her foot travel a little higher, until she felt the hardened ridge of his arousal. She pressed against him, smiling as he shifted slightly in his seat. She felt uncharacteristically powerful. She brought about this reaction in him and now she had his undivided attention.

"Do we have time to eat?" he asked.

"Oh, yes, but let's make it quick."

"I promise you, supper will be quick. But as to the rest of the evening…" His voice trailed off as she pressed against him again. "I think I may need to make you pay for this, Margaret Cole."

"I think I'm up for it," she teased, smiling back at him. "Are you?"

"As if there's any question."

His hand shot under the table and captured her foot, his thumb massaging firmly against the arch. She never knew feet could be such an erogenous zone. She was all but a melted puddle of heat and longing.

He released her foot, giving it a soft pat before gently pushing it away.

"I have something for you," he said as he reached into the pocket of his jacket.

"No, Will. Seriously, you've already given me too much."

He shook his head. "This is a very necessary part of our agreement, Margaret."

She stilled. The illusion that she'd foolishly allowed herself to build faded away in increments. She composed herself, damming back the joy she'd indulged in and reminded herself that their whole relationship was merely a pretense.

"Give me your left hand," he instructed as he flipped open the distinctive blue jewelry box.

She couldn't see what he hid inside it but held out her hand as he'd asked.

"Close your eyes," he said, a note of teasing in his voice.

Margaret again did as he'd asked and waited. Her heart jumped a little as his warm fingers captured hers and as she felt the cool slide of metal on her ring finger.

"There, a perfect fit. Do you like it?"

Will continued to hold her hand and as Margaret opened her eyes, they widened in shock at the stunning ring he'd placed upon her finger. Shafts of brilliance spun from the emerald-cut diamonds flanking a large rectangular glowing ruby. The gold band itself was very simple, leaving all its glory to the stones set upon it.

"It's the most beautiful thing I've ever seen," Margaret said, sudden tears springing to her eyes.

More than anything in the world right now, she wished this was for real. That the man opposite her at the table was indeed in love with her and pledging his life to hers. She blinked back the moisture and summoned all the composure she could find.

"I'll take great care of it, I promise you," she said, withdrawing her hand from his.

"It was harder to find than I thought," Will admitted. "But as soon as I saw it, I knew it was you."

His words were like tiny shards of glass tearing at her

dreams. She'd slid into the fantasy of being his fiancée with all too much ease and she needed to remind herself of the truth—that she was simply a means to an end.

Seven

Monday morning saw the return to routine that Margaret craved. Here, in the office, she could focus one hundred percent of her energy on her work. Will was away in meetings all day that day and after the intensity of the weekend, she was all too glad for the space that provided her.

Today she was looking forward to seeing one of her dearest friends, Sarah Richards, for lunch. Although they'd been four years apart at school, never really crossing paths, they'd formed a firm friendship over gallons of coffee in the intervening years. Margaret had been surprised when Sarah had married Quentin Dobbs—she hadn't really thought him Sarah's type at all, despite his long-standing crush on her— but they'd made it all work only to have it ripped apart when he was killed in a motor vehicle accident three years ago. Margaret had always admired Sarah's "take no prisoners" attitude, a legacy of her fiery red hair, she supposed. Sarah worked as a waitress in the restaurant at the Tennis Club and

Margaret had actively steered William from dining there with her. It was one thing to lie to the rest of the world about their engagement, but to one of her best friends?

But Sarah wouldn't be put off. She'd left a message on Margaret's mobile phone, saying she was free for lunch today and could meet her on the Cameron Enterprises campus. Margaret couldn't think of a single decent reason to postpone the inevitable any longer. She checked herself in the polished reflection of the elevator doors as she traveled downstairs to meet her friend. Yes, she'd pass muster. No one could tell just by looking at her that she'd just indulged in the most decadent and sensual weekend of her entire life.

"Oh, my God! You look fabulous!" Sarah gushed the instant she saw her. "What have you been up to? Actually, on second thought, maybe you shouldn't tell me, I'll only get jealous."

Margaret felt her cheeks flush with embarrassment. "Sarah, I'm still the same old me." She laughed uncomfortably.

"Well, yes, I know that. But, wow, I really like what you've done. Seriously, you look amazing. And there's more. You're glowing. It's a man, isn't it? Tell me everything. Gillian said you've been reported on in the *Gazette* as being the mystery woman on the arm of a certain Cameron Enterprises executive, is that true?" Sarah demanded, her green eyes flashing with curiosity. "Although I'm not sure I should forgive you for leaving me to *read* about your love life."

"Over lunch, I promise." Margaret laughed. "Where do you want to eat?"

"How about outside? It's warm enough and I brought a couple of roast beef subs and diet sodas. Sound good?"

Relief flooded Margaret that at least they'd be able to enjoy each other's company in the relative privacy of the campus gardens, without others straining to overhear what she was saying. It felt as if everyone wanted to know her business since her engagement to Will had become common knowledge around the office. Even more so since she'd arrived at work this morning wearing his ring.

"Sounds excellent, thanks."

After they'd settled on a bench Sarah divvied out their lunch. She sighed with unabashed pleasure as she bit into her sub. After she'd chewed and swallowed she turned to Margaret.

"So, he's good in bed, isn't he?" Sarah came straight to the point.

Margaret nearly choked on her sip of soda. "I beg your pardon?"

"He has to be brilliant, seriously. Everything about you is radiant. And look at how you're dressed. I bet he can't keep his hands off you. Who is it?"

Margaret took a deep breath. "William Tanner."

"You're kidding me. The CFO from Cameron Enterprises? One of Rafe's henchmen?"

"The one and only," Margaret conceded wryly.

Sarah sat back against the back of the bench and took stock of her friend. Margaret knew the exact instant her eyes picked up the ring on her finger.

"*You're engaged to him?* And you didn't tell me?"

Sarah grabbed her hand and turned it this way and that in the light, gasping over the beauty of the stones.

"It's all very sudden," Margaret said. "It's taken me by surprise as well."

"You guys haven't known each other very long, are you sure about this? It's not like you to rush into things."

Margaret struggled to find the right words. Words that wouldn't come across as a blatant lie. Finding the balance between the truth and what would satisfy her very astute friend was not going to be easy.

"It's different from anything else I've experienced," she

finally managed. "We met back in February—you remember me telling you about that kiss at the Valentine's Day ball?"

Sarah nodded, the expression on her face silently urging Margaret to continue.

"Well, it kind of grew from there. We just went to San Diego for the weekend. It was out of this world."

Suitably distracted from having to delve into the whys and wherefores of the engagement, Margaret told Sarah about the weekend she and Will had just shared.

"Well," Sarah said, when Margaret had finished, "I'm really happy for you. You deserve someone special. You've put your own needs on the backburner for far too long. It's time you looked after yourself first."

Margaret swallowed back the guilt that came hard on the heels of her friend's words. It wasn't fair to deceive her like this—to deceive anyone, for that matter—but to save Jason's job she had to keep the truth very firmly locked deep inside.

"Thanks, Sarah. So, anyway, that's enough about me. Tell me, how's your grandmother doing?"

Sarah laughed. "You know Grandma Kat. She's great. She's already roped me in to helping plan her birthday party in a couple of months' time. Like she even needs the help!"

Margaret let Sarah's conversation wash over her and breathed a sigh of relief that she had been diverted from Margaret's engagement being the topic "du jour." It was a few minutes before she realized that Sarah was waiting for her to answer something.

"I'm sorry, what did you say?" Margaret asked apologetically.

"Apology accepted," Sarah said with an exasperated smile. "Too busy reliving that weekend of yours, I suppose. Can't say I blame you. Anyway, I just noticed that guy over there.

Does he look familiar to you? I feel like I should know him from somewhere."

Margaret looked across the gardens at the tall cowboy walking along the path toward the main building. In amongst all the suits he stood out, and not in a bad way. She looked a little harder. There was definitely something familiar about the way he looked, even the way he moved, but she couldn't pin him down.

"I know what you mean." Margaret shrugged. "I can't place him, though. Maybe he has a double out there. They say we all do."

"Hmm, yeah," Sarah said before looking at her wristwatch. "Oh, my, look at the time. I really have to go. I have an early start to my shift this evening and a ton of stuff to do before then. It's been great to see you again. Don't leave it so long next time, okay?"

Margaret embraced her friend and took solace in the warmth of Sarah's unabashed hug. She ached to tell her the truth. To share it with the one person who'd probably understand better than most just why she was doing what she was doing. But she knew she couldn't.

"I won't. And you take care."

"Always do." Sarah stood and started to gather up their trash.

"Leave that. You brought it, the least I can do is clean up. Thanks again for lunch."

"No problem. Your turn next time." Sarah grinned back at her. "See you soon, yeah?"

"Definitely."

Margaret gave a small wave as Sarah headed off toward the car park. For a minute she sat back on the bench and closed her eyes against the brightness of the sun burning high in the clear blue sky. Being with Sarah had been a breath of fresh air. But now she had to get back to business—and back to the business of continuing to be the best counterfeit fiancée Will Tanner could ever want.

Margaret was exhausted by the time she let herself into the front door at home. It had been a busy day and, to her chagrin, she'd missed Will's presence in the office far more than she'd anticipated. It both irritated and surprised her. It wasn't as if they really were engaged, or as if they actually meant anything to one another.

"Not out with the boss man tonight?"

Jason's voice made her start.

"No," she replied carefully. "How was your day?"

"As good as it gets when you have a hundred sets of eyes watching your every move," he said bitterly.

Margaret sighed. So it was going to be like that. She'd hoped that maybe they could have a nice quiet evening together. Catch a movie on cable and just enjoy one another's company like they used to. Like before this whole business with Will Tanner.

"At least you still have your job. It could be worse, you know."

Jason snorted a laugh that totally lacked a spark of humor. "Sure, although not by much."

"Hey, why don't we put Cameron Enterprises behind us for a night," Margaret suggested. "Sit down, order in some dinner and watch some movies together."

"Can't," Jason said, tugging on his jacket which he'd snagged from the couch in front of him.

"How come?"

"Overtime."

"Overtime? Really? I would have thou—"

"Thought what? That because I'm under supervision that they don't want me there any more than I need to be?"

"Jason, that's not—"

"I don't care what you think, Maggie. Right now I just don't want to be around you."

Her gasp of hurt split the air between them. She watched, stunned with the emotional pain that reverberated through her, as Jason closed his eyes for a couple of seconds and heaved a sigh that seemed to come from Methuselah himself.

"Ah, hell, Maggie. I'm sorry. I don't want to hurt you. I mean, I know it's ridiculous to feel this way. You're my sister and you've looked after me better than anyone else ever could. Given me opportunities that Mom and Dad always wanted me to have. You've even kept the house exactly the way they left it. Sometimes it feels like a freaking shrine to our old life before they died—and most of the time that's okay, it's something solid that we have in common. But sometimes it's suffocating and right now, looking at you—seeing the way you've changed for *him,* seeing how happy you are—it's just more than I can stand."

She crossed the room and put her hand on his arm. "It doesn't have to be like this, Jason. He's a good man. I've seen a side of him that's different from what everyone else sees—you should see how much he has contributed personally to Hannah's Hope. He wrote a check today that was huge. Sure, he's intense and driven, but he's just and loyal, too."

"Just? You can still say that after what he's done to me?"

"Jason, I saw the reports."

"Oh, sure, that figures. You'd believe a bunch of words and numbers before you'd believe me."

"I hardly have any cause for blind loyalty, Jason," she protested. "I don't even know if I got this job on my own merits or because he wanted to keep an eye on me because of what he believed *you'd* done!"

"Oh, so now that's my fault, too. Well, sis, I don't see you protesting very hard. After all, look at you. Look at yourself.

Look at what you wear now. You'd never have been seen dead in that stuff before. You don't even drive your own car."

"So you're mad at me for wanting to look nice? For needing a vehicle that's more reliable?"

"You always looked nice—if anyone ever bothered to go beneath the surface of what you hid behind. I'm not stupid. I know you did it deliberately. And I know you haven't upgraded your car because we've been paying off my loans. But seriously, Maggie, you're so dolled up now I don't even recognize my sister inside you anymore." He snatched his arm away from her hold. "You know, I can take the changes, I can even take that you're working for that arrogant SOB, but what hurts the most is that you believe him over me. Your own brother."

Before her very eyes Jason appeared to age, looking every one of his twenty-four years, and more.

"Jason, I know it must have been tempting, but you've been given another chance."

"When will you understand, Maggie? I. Didn't. Do. It."

He turned sharply away from her and headed straight for the front door.

"Wait, please!" she cried, moving to block him. Anything to make him stay. Make him understand. "I love you, Jason. You're my brother. I've always been there for you, you know that."

"Not anymore," he said bitterly, grief stark on his face. "But when I prove that I'm right and your precious Mr. Tanner is wrong, maybe you'll believe me again."

The door slammed resoundingly behind him. Margaret stood there for some time, hoping against hope that he'd be straight back, but through the thick slab of wood she heard him start up his motorbike and head out onto the street.

On unsteady legs she made her way to her bedroom and sank onto her neatly made bed. Was Jason right? Was she struggling so hard to hold on to everything they had before their parents died that she was stifling him? She'd fought so hard to hold on to him, to prevent him from being taken into foster care.

Margaret looked up at the bedroom wall, at the map of the world covered with red pins marking all the countries she wanted to visit one day, and with a single yellow pin marking where she'd been. Here. Vista Del Mar, California.

She'd sacrificed her own dreams of education and travel to ensure that Jason had the most stable upbringing he possibly could with both their parents gone. She'd given it up without so much as a thought or regret for what might have been. She'd done it because she had to, needed to. Because it was what their parents would have expected of her. Because she loved her brother.

Slowly she got up from the bed and crossed to the wall, then slowly, painstakingly, began to remove the pins from the map. Once they were all gone and tucked back in the box from which they'd come, she took the poster off her wall and systematically tore it in two, then in two again. Then and only then did she let go of the grief that now built with steady pressure in her chest.

Nothing mattered. Not a single thing she'd done. Ever. She'd failed her brother and now she was in a relationship with a man who thought only in terms of profit and loss. Hell, it wasn't even a real relationship. It was a farce perpetuated so he could trick his father into signing over ownership of something that should, by right, have been his all along.

Margaret knew she would continue to do whatever it took for Will to have what was his. She'd given her word and that word was gold. And, in the past week, she'd seen a different side to the man they'd all said was unflinchingly ruthless. A side that spoke to her on a level she'd never anticipated.

She'd shared intimacies with him this weekend she'd never

shared with another man. Been lifted to heights of pleasure that were as addictive as they were seductive. She'd felt special and cherished—as if she were half of a pair that belonged together—and, damn it, she wanted it all again.

Margaret fisted the torn poster between her hands and threw the balled-up mass to one corner of the room, before collapsing on her bed—sobbing now as if her heart would break. A heart that she now knew belonged irrevocably to a man who didn't return her feelings. A man whose world was so far removed from her own reality that she felt like a fairy-tale princess when she moved within it.

But the clock was ticking fast toward midnight. Once Will had what he needed she'd be redundant to him, in more ways than one. As redundant as it now appeared she was to Jason as well. Suddenly, her life yawned before her like a gaping dark hole. Without the things she'd anchored herself to, where would she go, who would she be?

Everything she'd done until now had a purpose. She'd had a brief to follow. She'd been needed. But when all this business with William Tanner and Cameron Enterprises was over, where would that leave her? She knew for herself, from the celebrity gossip magazines and articles, that men like him changed their mistresses as often as they changed their designer shirts. Even in the past week she'd seen conjecture in the *Seaside Gazette's* gossip column about who William Tanner would adorn his arm with next. The photos they'd shown of him with various other girlfriends, some of them supermodels, just made her heart ache even more.

Given what he was used to, was it even worth hoping that he could fall in love with someone like her—as she'd fallen in love with him?

Eight

William sat at his desk in his office and leaned back in his chair. Tired and irritable after a difficult night, he'd given up on trying to sleep and had come into the office early. A lack of sleep was one thing. Something he was used to on occasion and something that he usually took in stride. The cause of last night's lack of sleep was quite another.

Margaret Cole had gotten to him.

Somehow she'd inveigled her way under his thick skin and settled like a burr. Now that he'd had her, he wanted more of her. He'd never felt a need such as that which now consumed him. He tried to rationalize it—to put it down to the exceptionally long period of time he'd waited from their first meeting back in February, to actually being able to be with her. Anticipation had a way of sweetening things, of increasing the expectations and pleasures to be discovered.

Yet, now that he'd been intimate with Margaret, rather than be assuaged, the anticipation had only built to greater heights.

Their intense physical connection had come as quite a surprise to him. A welcome one, nonetheless. There was no denying they lit up the sheets together. Margaret was an unexpectedly passionate and generous lover. Her lush feminine curves drove him crazy—whether she was clothed, or not.

Completely without guile or artifice, she'd simply been herself. That was a refreshing breath of air in a life that had become increasingly superficial in recent years. Or at least that was how he'd aimed to keep his relationships to the fairer sex. Light and commitment-free.

Which brought him to the question—could anyone really be that giving without an ulterior motive? His dealings with people in recent years would suggest not. Not even his father was above a bit of manipulation to get what he wanted. So where did that leave Will with Margaret?

He'd coerced her into their arrangement, a fact that hadn't bothered him in the least when he'd done it. But now, he wanted her to be with him because she wanted to be there. Not out of any misplaced loyalty to her younger sibling. Was she the kind of woman who would go so far as to sleep with a man to keep her brother out of jail? He'd told her she had to be convincing in her role as his fiancée. Did that extend to convincing him, too? If so, she was a damn good actress.

Any other man would probably tell him to simply accept his good fortune. Not only did he have someone prepared to act as his fiancée—without the usual pressure to make the situation genuine, to soothe his parents' ruffled feathers—at the same time she was willingly warming his sheets.

He was getting exactly what he wanted—more, even—and yet he still wasn't satisfied. Deep inside of him guilt festered over having forced Margaret's hand in this. Would she have come to him without the coercion of protecting Jason? He'd never know.

It was beginning to give him a headache. No matter

which way he looked at things, he kept coming back to the same point. She was fiercely loyal. A quality he held in the highest respect. Yet he'd used that loyalty against her and that knowledge left a bitter taste in his mouth.

William sighed deeply and shook his head. He knew, deep down, that he wasn't man enough to willingly let Margaret go. Now that he'd had a taste of her, there was no way he'd be so stupid as to give all that up. And, he reconciled himself, it wasn't as if she was getting nothing from their liaison. She carried herself with a newfound confidence since her makeover. He'd given her that. He'd allowed her to discover the real woman she was capable of being.

But no matter how much he tried to convince himself that the end justified the means, his attempts lay shallow on his conscience.

His cell phone chirped discreetly in his pocket and he reached for it, sliding it open without checking the caller ID—a fact he regretted the minute he heard his mother's voice on the other end.

"William? Would you care to explain how you came to be engaged and yet you neglected to tell your family of this event?"

"Mum, great to hear from you. How's Dad doing, and you, of course?"

"Don't think you can hedge with me, young man."

"I haven't been a young man for some years now." William smiled at his mother's tone. No matter how old he was, she still spoke to him as if he'd just come in from the garden with muddied clothes and all manner of scrapes and bumps on his body. "And my engagement is still new to me, by the way. I haven't had a chance to share the news with you before now. How did you hear about it, anyway?"

His mother mentioned the name of one of the tabloids she perused over her morning coffee each day. The news painted a grim smile on his face. So, the reporter who'd caught them coming out of the theater on Friday evening had followed them to the restaurant and seen Will give Margaret her ring. His story had obviously sold to a syndicated outlet. The news would be nationwide by now. It was what he'd wanted, wasn't it? And yet, there was a side of him that wished he could have kept it quiet just a little longer. Spared Margaret some of the notoriety that would be associated with their "engagement."

"Wow, that didn't take long."

"No matter how long it took, William, your father and I are disappointed you didn't see fit to include us in your news. I would have thought that given the circumstances we would have been the first to know."

Olivia Tanner's displeasure radiated through the phone lines from her New York brownstone, making William feel as if he was about eight years old all over again. Except her underlying threat now was far, far more powerful than any threat of withdrawal of privileges when he was a child.

"If the rug hadn't been pulled out from under me by the tabloid, you would have been receiving my call in the next few hours," he said smoothly. "Would it help any if I bring Margaret home to meet you and Dad at the end of this week?"

"This week? You can come that soon? Of course we'd love to meet her."

The sudden change in his mother's tone of voice should have made him laugh out loud, but he knew that her concern came from her deep-seated love for all her children.

"Sure, I have some business that's come up in New Jersey and I need to make the trip anyway. There's no reason why Margaret can't accompany me. Why don't you organize one of your famous dinners for Saturday night and invite the whole family over?"

"I hope everyone will be free at such short notice," she

mused out loud. "Never mind, I'll make sure it happens. Pre-dinner drinks at seven, then."

"Sounds good to me," Will agreed.

"Will you be staying in your apartment or would you like me to make up the guest room at home?"

Will's lips curled in a sardonic smile. Oh, he'd give his mother points for trying but she wasn't going to get her claws into Margaret that easily.

"I thought we'd stay in a hotel this time around. It's only a short visit. Hardly worth putting anyone out over it."

Despite the fact the concierge of his apartment building would happily see to stocking his refrigerator for a quick weekend visit home, Will didn't like the idea of taking Margaret there to stay. He'd had other women there and, for some reason, the very thought of associating Margaret with those others sat uncomfortably with him.

"So what's she like, this Margaret? I have to say I'm surprised at the speed with which you two have become engaged. I didn't even know you were seeing anyone."

Will chose his words carefully. "She's not like anyone I've ever dated before, that's for certain."

"Well, that's a relief. Those other girls were very shallow, Will. It was clear to both your father and me that you had no intention of settling down with any one of them. What drew you to this girl?"

"I couldn't help myself." He gave a rueful laugh. "I know it sounds clichéd, but I saw her across a crowded room and I just…"

Will's voice trailed off as he recalled what it had been like to see Margaret for the very first time. Even with her upper face masked, she'd caught his eye with her poise and the hints of beauty he saw beneath the costume she'd worn. It hit him again, square in the solar plexus—that sense of shock and yearning. The need to take, to possess. That need hadn't lessened. If anything, it had only grown stronger.

His mother's voice had softened considerably when she spoke again. "I can't wait to meet her, Will. She looks lovely in the picture in the paper."

"You'll like her even more in person."

"Well, you should let me go so I can start organizing things for Saturday. You haven't left me much time."

"Mum," he warned. "Just family for Saturday night. I don't want you to scare her off."

"Oh, of course I won't do any such thing. How could you even suggest it?"

He heard the humor behind Olivia Tanner's words and felt his lips tug into an answering smile.

"Gee, I really don't know. Maybe past experience?"

"Really, I have no idea what you're talking about. Now look at the time, I must go. Take care, Will. I love you, son."

"Love you, too, Mum. See you Saturday."

He disconnected the call with a wistful smile on his face. They really only wanted the best for him, he knew that. But it was endlessly frustrating to be continually treated like an infant. And therein lay the crux of most of his conflict with his parents. Being their youngest child, he supposed they'd found it harder to let go of him than his older brothers. A fact which had only made him rebel harder and push more firmly to be independent from a very young age. Even when his father had been offered a position with one of New York's leading financial institutions, and the family had transferred to the United States from their home in New Zealand, Will had insisted on remaining behind to finish his degree in accounting and finance at the University of Auckland.

As much as he loved his family, that time alone, without their well-meaning interference, had been a Godsend for him. And it had helped him make decisions about himself and the kind of future he wanted—one not unduly influenced by his parents' dreams for him or his older brothers' accomplishments. Decisions that had led him to work for Rafe Cameron and had ultimately led him here.

He was happy with his life, satisfied with where he'd worked his way. The work here in Vista del Mar, checking into the financial complexities of Rafe's latest acquisition, was the kind of challenge he loved to get his teeth into. And as for Margaret Cole, well, she was an enjoyable segue into the next stage of his life. A transitional relationship that was bringing him surprising delight and would ultimately bring him exactly what he wanted from his father.

"We're going to New York?" Margaret asked, surprise pitching her voice high.

"Yes, is that a problem?"

"To meet your family?" She paled and plunked herself down hard in the seat opposite Will's desk.

"It was always in the cards that they'd want to meet you when our relationship went into the public domain."

Margaret swallowed against the lump of fear in her throat. It was one thing pretending their engagement was real to her work colleagues, friends and Jason, but quite another to do so in front of his parents.

"But they know you. Surely they'll see right through us. What if I mess up?"

"Not if you keep on doing the stellar job you've been doing."

Will rose from his chair and walked around his desk. He bent and tipped Margaret's face up to his, giving her a short hard kiss that sent her scrambled senses totally haywire.

"Don't worry. You'll be fine. Just be you."

Just be you, he said. But the person Will Tanner knew was

not the person she'd been for so very long. The fight with Jason last night had been proof of that.

"Margaret?"

She blinked and realized he'd been talking to her. "Sorry, what did you say?"

"You can do this, you know. All you have to do is smile, be friendly and convince my parents you love me."

Margaret's stomach clenched into a painfully tight knot of tension. *Convince his parents she loved him?* After last night's torturous admission to herself that she was totally and utterly in love with him she'd hoped that she could somehow keep that monumental truth to herself. It would go at least some way toward protecting her when he walked away and returned to his life in New York and she was left here to pick up the pieces of her own.

Pretending she loved him would be the least of her worries this weekend. Of a far more pressing concern was what she'd do if he realized the truth of her emotional state.

Firming her resolve, Margaret gave a short nod.

"Of course I can do this. After all, you're paying me well to do the job you hired me to do. You can count on me."

The words were like ashes in her mouth but they gave her strength at the same time.

"They're not ogres, you know, my parents," Will said with a wry look on his face. "There's no need to be frightened. I will be with you."

"I know. It just kind of threw me. We've been so busy here that I hadn't stopped to think about meeting your family, especially with them all the way in New York."

"The opportunity presented itself. I thought it better to make the most of it. Have you been to New York before?"

"Never. Seriously, I haven't been anywhere farther than Anaheim when I was a kid to visit Disneyland."

Fleetingly, Margaret thought of the map she'd destroyed

in her bedroom last night. New York had been one of her markers. One of the first she'd carefully placed when travel had been one of her big dreams. Well, if she had nothing else after all this, she'd at least have this journey to look back on.

"We'll have to make it worthwhile for you, then," Will said decisively. "I'll show you around."

"I'd like that," she said with a smile, making a solid decision to grasp every minute of the unexpected bonus of the trip to New York.

The next couple of days at work went quickly for Margaret. Will spent a great deal of time in meetings with Rafe Cameron—meetings that extended into the evenings, leaving her to her own devices. She was puzzled when those meetings didn't generate a great deal of work coming back her way. She would have thought that she'd be hard at work typing up summaries, projections and reports as a result, but maybe this was a temporary lull. She took advantage of the respite to ensure all her work was completely up-to-date so she could head away knowing she was coming back to a clear desk.

As he had with their foray into San Diego, Will had taken care of all their arrangements for the visit to New York. He'd suggested they leave early on Friday morning. With the time differences between the West and East coasts they'd be arriving at JFK in the late afternoon. Time, hopefully, to see a little of the city before sunset.

Will picked her up from her home before sunrise and Margaret felt an air of excitement as she wheeled her case out and locked the front door behind her. She would be traveling on a plane for the first time in her life and, despite the obscenely early hour, she felt as energized as a sugar addict locked in a candy shop.

"Got everything you need?" Will asked as he met her at the door and took her case from her.

"I think so," she said.

"There's something you've forgotten."

"No, I think I have everything," Margaret said, mentally running through her list of things she'd packed.

"This," Will said succinctly as he bent to kiss her.

As ever, Margaret's entire body rushed to aching, pulsing life. He tasted of a pleasant combination of mint and fresh coffee and she kissed him back with all the fervor and abandon she'd been holding back since their weekend in San Diego. She'd missed seeing him, being with him in every sense of the word, and their all too brief times together in the office had only sharpened her hunger for him—for this.

Will broke free with a groan and rested his forehead against hers. His breathing was uneven, his heart pounding in his chest beneath the flat of her hand.

"I think I should have requested the company jet for this trip. At least then we might have had a little privacy on the flight," he said, his breathing now slowly returning to normal.

"I missed you this week," she answered simply.

"I'll make it up to you, I promise," he said and gave her another quick kiss before lifting her bag and carrying it to the waiting car in the driveway.

The driver alighted from the car as they approached and stowed her case in the trunk while Will held the door open for her. She slid into her seat and he moved in alongside her. In the climate-controlled interior of the car she welcomed the warmth of his body against hers but she held her posture straight and erect. As much as she wished she could snuggle into his side, she wasn't sure enough of her position with him to do so. Even after last weekend, while they'd conquered some of the physical distance between them in their make-believe relationship, she still didn't feel comfortable breaching the invisible boundaries he had erected between them.

Traffic had yet to build up on the freeway and the trip to the San Diego airport went smoothly, as did check-in. Margaret's eyes widened in surprise as they were greeted by name by the cabin crew and shown to their seats in first class. Will ushered her into the window seat before stowing his briefcase in the overhead compartment.

As he settled into his seat beside her, she turned to look at him.

"First class?" she hissed under her breath.

"Why not?" he replied smoothly. "It's your first flight, isn't it? May as well be memorable."

Margaret shook her head in wonder as she looked again at the man who'd given her so much in such a short period of time. He would never understand how much this meant to her. For him, traveling this way was commonplace. But for her, it was something she'd never have achieved in her wildest dreams. She sat back and gazed out the side window, a sudden glaze of tears hazing her vision.

What would he be like with the woman he loved? she wondered. He'd give her the world on a gilded platter. Whoever she was, she would be the luckiest woman on the planet. How Margaret wished it could be her.

Nine

A discreetly uniformed driver stood with a card bearing William's name as they exited the baggage claim area at JFK. Before Margaret realized it, they were being shown into a shining limousine and the car was pulling into traffic leading onto the Van Wyck Expressway.

Will was an excellent guide, noting points of interest as they drove along the expressway. All in all, the trip only took about half an hour and Margaret was totally enchanted as they pulled up outside their stately looking hotel on East 55th Street.

As Will helped her from the car she said, "You have a thing for classic architecture, don't you? First the hotel in San Diego, and now this?"

"Blame it on my good old Kiwi upbringing." He smiled in return. "My parents were very much into ensuring we had the necessities as kids, but not luxuries, at least not until we were older and could be relied upon not to break anything. Staying in places like this is one of my indulgences."

"But don't you have a home here in New York?"

"An apartment, yes, but since we're only here for a few nights I didn't see the point in having it aired and stocked with perishables when we could stay here."

Margaret nodded. She could see the point in that, but she was curious to see what his residence was like. He let so little of himself out in the course of a day at work, exhibiting only the kind of concentrated control that had sent his reputation ahead of him during the Worth Industries takeover.

Even in bed she'd felt as if he held something back. Not completely surprising, she supposed, when their attraction, on his part at least, was purely physical.

She was distracted from her thoughts as they checked into the hotel and were shown to their suite. Named for one of the original owners of the hotel, the suite was plushly appointed and Margaret could barely stop oohing and ahhing over the furnishings and accoutrements. Will watched her with an indulgent look on his face that made her feel quite naive and inexperienced but, when she thought about it, it would be a sad day for her when such delights became commonplace. As if that was likely to ever happen, she reminded herself as she checked her reflection in the mirror of the opulent marble bathroom. No, she had to make the most of every second of this. Every second with him.

Once she'd freshened up, she and Will rode the elevator back down to the street. There were people everywhere, it seemed—office workers at the end of their day, tourists looking about with the same wide-eyed wonder Margaret knew was on her face.

"How's your head for heights?" Will asked as he pulled her hand through the crook of his elbow and led her around the corner and onto 5th Avenue.

"I'm okay, why?"

"I thought we'd start your introduction to New York with an overview of the city, from the Empire State Building."

"Seriously? Is it like they show in the movies?"

"Depends on the movie, I suppose, but yeah. Come on and I'll show you. What would you prefer, walk or cab?"

"Oh, walk, please."

"Walk it is, then."

Margaret was surprised that it took them less than half an hour to reach their destination. All along 5th Avenue her attention had been captured by the amazing storefronts and buildings. After they'd gone through security screening, Will bought their tickets and they followed a group of people to the elevators that would take them up to the 80th floor. Margaret had to hold on to her stomach as the elevator car traveled upward.

"Wow," she laughed, a little shakily. "That makes the elevators at work seem positively snail-like."

"There's one more ride up, to the 86th floor. Unless you'd rather take the stairs?"

"No, I'll be fine."

Will smiled back and took her hand as they joined the queue waiting to be shown into the cars that would take them up the tower to the observatory level.

"Oh, my," she breathed as she and Will left the car and walked out into the viewing area. "I knew it would be something else, but this...this really is something else." As far as she could see, the city stretched out like a three-dimensional patchwork of color, texture and light interspersed by water and bridges. "It's so huge."

"Never fails to take my breath away," Will commented as he stood close behind her, wrapping his arms around her waist.

The warmth of his body against her back was most welcome, almost grounding for her. Just feeling him there behind her gave her a sense of security. Even though they were surrounded by other tourists, all clamoring and pointing as they took in the cityscape spread before them, they could have been completely alone. She leaned back against his solid strength, relishing the moment and tucking it away in a corner of her mind. This experience was something she would never forget in all her days.

In the end, they spent nearly an hour on the viewing deck, looking at the city from all aspects. She'd shuddered as they looked below at the streets teeming with traffic. From up on the observation deck it didn't seem real, it was as if what happened beneath them was another world completely, one devoid of sound, yet she knew it was completely the opposite.

The sun had begun to set, casting long shadows over the city. Will teased her about wanting to stay until full dark so she could see the city lights spread out like a pirate's sparkling treasure chest, but the long shadow of the Empire State Building stretching out like a dark finger over the buildings beneath them reminded her that their time together was fleeting and there was still so very much she wanted to experience with Will in his adopted home city.

Will found Margaret's open enjoyment in New York utterly refreshing. Aside from one moment, shortly before they left the observation deck of the Empire State Building, where she'd suddenly appeared pensive and quiet, she'd displayed an unabashed joy in everything she experienced. Even now she clutched a souvenir pewter replica of the building in her hand, pointing out where they'd stood and watched the city bustle beneath them.

Seeing her like this, so different from the cool composed assistant who worked for him in the office, made him realize just how far he'd pushed her out of her comfort zone with this trip, and it made him want to see more of this side of her. He wanted to be the one to show her more of everything—starting with New York and leading who knew where.

He wondered what she'd think of his parents' place in Manhattan. His mother was inordinately proud of the brownstone where they lived. She'd always loved being in a busy city, even back home in New Zealand. Suburbia had never really been her thing, but she'd tolerated it so he and his brothers could have a big backyard to play in. Once his brothers had graduated high school, and while he was still attending, they'd moved into a luxury apartment building in Auckland. The eventual move to New York had seen his mother find her spiritual home and she hadn't been homesick, ever.

Beneath his arm he felt Margaret shiver a little. The evening temperature had dropped, reminding him that while he was quite used to New York's climate, his West Coast companion was not. The coat she wore did little to cut the chill, so he hailed a cab to take them to their next destination. If she enjoyed the Empire State Building so much, he had no doubt she'd enjoy what he had planned next.

Times Square at night had to be seen to be believed, and if the look of awe on Margaret's face was any indicator, she was having trouble believing anything anymore.

"What on earth do they do in a power outage?" she asked as she looked from one brilliant display to the next.

Will just shrugged before changing the subject. "Hungry? I know your body clock is probably still on California time, but we missed lunch somewhere along the way and I'm starving."

"Sure, but nothing fancy, okay?" she insisted.

He knew just the place that would appeal to her. The intimately lit Greek restaurant he frequented in the theater district was the perfect solution to both her tourist instinct and the grumbling hole in his belly. It was inexpensive and casual, and he knew she'd enjoy its atmosphere, not to mention the highly-rated food. But by the time they'd been seated and enjoyed their entrées he could see she was beginning to droop.

"Don't tell me you're getting tired already?" he cajoled.

"It's all just so much to take in today. So many firsts. Really, you have no idea."

No, he didn't. There was so much about Margaret he didn't know and so much she didn't know about him, either. Things that might be necessary for them to carry off the dinner at his parents' tomorrow night. The reminder was sobering.

"Are you up to a little conversation?" he coaxed.

"Sure, what did you want to talk about?"

"Tomorrow evening."

"Oh, yes. That." She shifted uncomfortably in her chair. "I know you said I should just be 'me.' But do you honestly think I'll be okay? I'm sure I'm nothing like your other wo—"

"You'll be fine," he interrupted, not wanting to even think about other women when he was with her. "It won't be any different than at work. If we stick as close to the truth as possible—meeting at the ball in February, keeping things quiet but that our feelings just overtook us—then they'll take it hook, line and sinker. Dad might work in finance but he's an incurable romantic. He'll be only too happy just to see me engaged."

"What about your past? You know, school, hobbies, things I should probably know about you."

"Given that we haven't known each other that long, I think they'll be satisfied with what you already know about me. After all, we supposedly have the rest of our lives to get to know one another's secrets."

Margaret turned her glass on its coaster, a small frown

on her face. "Doesn't it bother you at all, that we're lying to them?"

Will stiffened. "It bothers me that I have to," he said coldly.

Margaret reached out a hand and placed it on his thigh under their table. "I'm sorry. I didn't mean to make you mad."

He placed his hand over hers before speaking. "I'm not mad at you. Just angry with the situation. You're helping me here, and I appreciate it." He sighed—the sound a short huff of air. "Look, I know we didn't exactly embark on this in the most friendly or pleasant way, but you're not unhappy, are you?"

"No, I'm fine. Really. I appreciate that you gave Jason a second chance. I'm just sorry it had to come to that. But as to how things have developed with us, well, I'd prefer to think that's something separate from what brought us together." She looked sad for a moment, but then she flicked her gaze up to his—her dark brown eyes glowing warm in her face. "Can we head back to the hotel now?"

Will felt an answering heat spread through his body as he interpreted the look in her eyes. They could continue their talk later. Much later.

In the short cab ride back to their hotel Margaret struggled with her thoughts. All day, Will had been attentive and kind, and she'd allowed herself to once again sink into the fantasy that they were a couple—a real couple. She needed to retrain herself. To stop hoping for what couldn't be. Talking with him about tomorrow night had forced her to take a reality check. She might not be able to be with him the way she wanted, but she'd take what she could get.

Will tossed the key card onto the side table in the entrance to their suite and closed the door behind her.

"Would you like a drink?" he asked, crossing to the mini-bar.

"No, actually. There's only one thing I really want right now."

She closed the distance between them, shrugging off her coat along the way and letting it drop on one of the chairs in the sitting room.

Will smiled at her, a smile that did funny things to her insides and heightened the tightly coiled tension in the pit of her belly.

"Is that right?" he asked, his voice suddenly thick with desire.

"Oh, yes, and I think I know just the man who will give it to me," she teased as she ran her hands up over his chest.

Beneath the thickness of his sweater she could feel the lean muscle she knew corded his body. She skimmed her hands up to his shoulders before linking her fingers at the back of his head and drawing his face down to hers. Her boldness surprised her, all along in their orchestrated union she'd been the one acted upon. Now it was her turn to take control.

She traced the outline of his lips with the tip of her tongue before pressing her lips to his. His arms banded tight around her, drawing her against his strength, letting her know in no uncertain terms that he wanted her. The knowledge gave her license to do what she wanted and it was a power she relished.

Her entire body vibrated with need for him and she could barely wait to be skin to skin. Reluctantly breaking their embrace, she took his hand and led him to the bedroom where she pushed him, none too gently, onto the luxurious covers. She followed him into the enveloping softness and kissed him again, this time sucking his lower lip into her mouth and laving it with her tongue. He groaned into her mouth, his hands shoving aside her blouse and caressing her back before he skimmed his hands down to palm her buttocks and press her lower body tight against his.

An electric current of sensation shot from her core as she flexed against him, against the hard ridge of his desire for her. Eager to repeat the sensation, Margaret let her legs fall to either side of his and pushed herself upright, leaving only the apex of her thighs connecting with his groin. She looked down at him and smiled.

Will gripped her hips and tilted her against him and she flexed again.

"You're killing me here," he growled.

"I know, isn't it great?" she teased.

Her fingers flew to the buttons of her blouse and one by one she slid them free, before shrugging the garment off her shoulders. She was wearing one of her new bras, one she'd chosen herself with a boldness she'd never indulged in before. She'd never been comfortable with her body, but when she'd tried this bra on she'd felt incredible. The café au lait-colored lace, appliquéd over black satin, appealed to a decadent side of her she'd never really known existed, and the cut was something else—exposing the soft globes of her breasts while barely concealing her nipples.

"Do you like it?" she asked.

Will trailed his fingers across the smooth rounds, his touch sending tiny shocks sizzling through her. When he traced the outside edge of the scalloped lace, his fingertip almost brushed against her nipple and she shivered in delight.

"I like it very much," Will said, his voice a low rumble. "But I like what's inside it more."

Before she could stop him, his hand snaked around to her back and he'd flicked open the clasps. He pulled the confection of satin and lace away from her, exposing her to his ravenous gaze.

"Yes, that's much better," he said.

Will jackknifed up from beneath her, cupping her breasts in his hands and burying his face in their fullness. She felt the heat of his breath against her skin and let her head drop back, arching her back so nothing restricted him. He traced the outline of one nipple with his tongue, while gently squeezing the other between one finger and a thumb. Sensation spiraled through her, increasing in intensity as it arrowed to her center. Gone were all feelings of self-consciousness or embarrassment about her body. Instead, all she felt was the overwhelming sense that this was so very right.

And she wanted more of it.

Somehow, through the sensual assault on her senses, she found the capability to reach for the bottom edge of Will's sweater and began to tug it up over his torso. He reluctantly relinquished her to help her denude him of both his sweater and the shirt he'd worn beneath it. She felt him shudder as she lightly scratched her fingernails across his shoulders and down over his chest.

He pulled her to him and Margaret gasped at the warm shock of his skin against hers. At the delicious pressure of his chest against her breasts. He nipped lightly at the sensitive skin of her neck and she clutched his upper arms in response, her nails digging into him as a sharp, involuntary pull from deep inside her swelled and threatened to consume her.

Will peppered her neck and shoulders with fleeting kisses, his hands once again at her breasts. She loved the feel of his strong fingers on her body, loved the way he made her feel.

Loved him.

She might never be able to tell him the truth of her feelings, she realized, but she could show him with every caress, every gesture, exactly how much he meant to her. She put her hands to his shoulders and pushed him backward, tumbling forward onto him as he allowed himself to drop back onto the bed again. Her lips found his and meshed with them, tongues dueling in a sacred dance of mutual worship.

She forced herself to break the kiss, to drag herself upright and to reach for his belt and the fastenings on his jeans. His fingers tangled with hers.

"No, let me," she bid softly.

His eyes clouded and became heavy-lidded as she undid his jeans, exposing his boxer briefs and the prominent erection that strained against the stretched cotton. She stroked him through the fabric and felt him strain against her fingers. With as much grace as she could muster, she slipped off the bed to her feet and dragged off his boots and socks, then pulled his jeans down and off his long legs before easing his briefs away from his body and tossing them behind her.

He was magnificent. For a moment she just drank in the sight of him lying there on the bed. Hers for the taking. But then need overtook her and she quickly kicked off her shoes and yanked off her socks before shimmying out of her trousers and panties.

Even though it had been only a week since his eyes had feasted upon her naked form, the sheer beauty of her took his breath away again. From the fall of glossy black hair to her creamy shoulders, to the mouthwatering fullness of her breasts. From the smallness of her waist to the very feminine flair of her hips. She was all woman—every delectable inch of her. Would it be like this every time they made love? he wondered fleetingly. This awe and amazement in the perfection of her body?

He sucked in a breath as she straddled his legs—the smooth skin of her inner thighs like silk against him. The heat of her core, calling to him. When her fingers closed around his aching shaft he caught hold of the bedcovers, his hands twisting in the finely woven fabric as tight as they could in an effort to resist the urge to thrust within the gentle sheath of her fist.

She was driving him out of his mind with her touch and as she bent forward, her hair drifted over him, as gossamer soft and fine as a breath. He could have lost it right there and then, her effect upon him was so intense. But instant gratification had never been his thing. No, far, far better to prolong the ecstasy. To draw pleasure out for as long as humanly possible before giving in to the inevitable.

Will had cause to question his resolve as in the next breath he felt her lush mouth close over his tip. Felt the swirl of her tongue over the ultra-sensitive surface. Again and again. She took him deeper in the heated cavern of her mouth, her hand working firmly on his shaft and he knew without a shadow of a doubt that he'd lost all semblance of being in charge of himself. He'd never submitted as completely as this to anyone. He'd always held back a level of control, choosing when he'd let go. But this was completely different. Margaret held his pleasure in her power. It was thrilling and daunting at the same time.

As she increased the pressure of her hand and her mouth, he felt his climax build inside him, out of control, banishing thought and replacing it with the sure knowledge that what would come next would be bigger, brighter and better than anything he'd ever known before. Every nerve in his body was poised for the intensity of the pleasure escalating through his body. Pleasure she gave him.

And then it burst through him, pulse after pulse of rapture, each one stronger than the one before. A raw cry of completion ripped from his throat as bliss invaded his every cell, suffusing him with a boneless sense of well-being. He reached for Margaret and drew her into his arms, her body aligning with his, her hair a swath of black-velvet softness across his chest and shoulders.

Words couldn't adequately describe how she'd made him feel or the depth of his confusion when it related to her. Outside of the bedroom she was Miss Prim. Carrying herself with poise and an air of quiet efficiency, as if she moved in a sea of calm. Yet, in the bedroom she was something else altogether. And that lingerie. He was tempted to ask her to put it back on, just so he could peel it off her all over again.

He stroked a hand down her long smooth spine, over the curve of her rounded buttocks. Despite the intensity of his climax, he could feel his body begin to stir to life again, and this time he relished the fact that he'd be the one bringing her pleasure.

He rolled them both onto their sides and continued his slow lazy exploration of her body.

"You have the softest skin," he murmured. "Makes me want to kiss you all over."

"So what's stopping you?" she answered, a slow smile curving her mouth.

"Absolutely nothing," he answered and leaned forward to capture that smile with his lips before he nuzzled her neck, inhaling the sweet, intoxicating scent of her skin.

Nothing else in the world came close to it, he decided. Once you got past the "touch me not" signals that she sent out, you discovered the many layers that made her who she was and the treats she had in store for a man like him. A man who was prepared to bring her the world of delight. Who could worship her as she deserved to be worshipped.

He traced the cord of her neck with his tongue, smiling to himself as she let out a soft moan, and committing the erogenous zone to memory. Next he followed the line of her collarbone, from just below her shoulder until he found the hollow at the base of her throat. A tiny kiss there to punctuate his journey and he continued across her collarbone to the other side. Beneath him, Margaret squirmed and pressed her shoulders back hard into the bedcovers, thrusting her breasts proudly forward. Never a man to waste an opportunity, Will trailed his tongue over one creamy swell—working in an ever-decreasing spiral that led to her tightly budded nipple.

Her breath came in shallow gasps as he drew closer to his ultimate goal, and halted for several excruciatingly long seconds as his mouth hovered over the distended tip.

"Please?" she begged, her voice no more than a tortured whisper.

"Your wish is my command," he answered.

He blew a cool breath over the taut bead, then outlined it carefully with the firm tip of his tongue. She arched even more, thrusting upward in complete supplication and he finally gave her what she wanted. He closed his lips around her, drawing the peak into his mouth and suckling hard.

She cried out his name, her fingers suddenly tunneling through his hair and holding his head to her. Her extreme sensitivity drove his body to even greater demands but he held himself in check. This time, it was all about her.

He eased off the pressure of his tongue, his lips, then built them once more before transferring his attention to her other breast. Again he followed the painstaking path of the decreasing spiral. Again he felt her body grow taut, her back arch, until he at last gave in and lavished his mouth upon her.

She was on the edge of orgasm, he realized with a sense of wonder. Purely from his ministrations to her nipples. He'd heard of it, but never before experienced it with a lover. Her very responsiveness and abandon made his control stretch tight, but he renewed his attention to her, his hands gently molding the shape of her breasts with a reverence he'd never experienced before.

Her release, when it came, sent her entire body rigid, before she collapsed back onto the bed. Will rested his head a moment on her breasts, feeling her rapid breathing as it slowly returned to normal.

"I've never done that before," she said from beneath him, her voice filled with wonder.

Her hands came to rest on his shoulders, her fingertips drawing tiny circles on his skin. Even the lightest touch from her drove him crazy. He shifted, pulling himself higher over her body so they were face to face. Her hands coasted down his back, past his waist to his buttocks. The feather-light touch had him totally wired on top of having just brought her to orgasm.

"You okay with it?" he asked.

She seemed to think about it for a few seconds before a beatific smile spread across her face. "Oh, yes. Most definitely."

"Good, then let's not stop there."

Will reached for the box of condoms he'd shoved under his pillow before they went sightseeing and ripped it open, scattering the foil packets on the covers beside them.

"So many?" Margaret commented.

"So few," he laughed in return.

He grabbed one of the condoms and ripped away the foil before sheathing himself and returning to the warmth of Margaret's embrace. Positioning himself with his knees spread wide on the bed, he dragged her hips toward him, and pulled her legs over his thighs.

His blunt head probed at the moist entrance to her body. He tore his gaze away from the compelling view of their bodies joining together and watched her face instead as he eased his length inside her. Her inner muscles clenched tight around him, and he hesitated a moment, allowing her to ease and accept him. The control he had to employ made sweat break out on his back. A trickle of moisture ran down his spine to the cleft of his buttocks, the sensation it evoked driving his hips forward until he was buried within her.

A flush of color spread over her chest and she moved beneath him, silently encouraging him to continue. Her lips parted on an indrawn breath as he withdrew then drove into her again slowly.

"More," she whispered. "Don't stop."

Determined to give her pleasure before he lost all semblance of command, he began to thrust deep within her—at first slow and then with increasing pressure until he felt as if he was going to shatter. Margaret's hands gripped his forearms, her fingernails digging into his skin as he increased momentum, her breath coming in short, sharp cries of pleasure until her entire body spasmed and she let go with a gut-deep groan of satisfaction. The sound of her, the feel of her, the pulsating strength of her orgasm, drove him over the edge and beyond. His hips jerked against her as ecstasy flooded through him and he gave himself over to the sensation.

Over to her.

Ten

They were on the ferry coming back from the Statue of Liberty and Margaret still felt as if she was lost in the haze of the rapture they'd explored together. If Will had suggested they forego her continued introduction to his home city and stay in their suite for the rest of the day she would have happily agreed.

Sleep had been snatched in small increments during the night and through part of this morning, and in between they'd indulged in one another virtually every way she could have imagined. She would have thought that her desire for him would have diminished, but she only wanted him more. Even now, tucked against his side, his arm around her shoulders, her body hummed with suppressed energy. Energy she knew exactly how to expend.

Her wonder in the incredible monument she'd just visited paled in comparison to the wonder she felt every time he touched her. Whether it was as intimate as his caress across her clitoris as a precursor to bringing her to yet another amazing peak of pleasure, or whether it was something as simple as brushing a strand of hair from her cheek, when Will touched her she was instantly and irrevocably on fire for him.

Will bent his head and pressed a kiss against her temple. "Enjoying today?"

"Very much," she said with a smile.

"I have something else planned for you."

"Oh, something that involves you, too, I hope."

"Later tonight, yes. But when we get back to the hotel I need to leave you for a couple of hours."

"Could I come with you?" Margaret asked, sensing his response in the way he pulled away from her.

"Not this time. It's just some business. It shouldn't take more than a couple of hours."

"Business? On a Saturday."

"It can't be avoided."

She studied his face. It was as if he'd become someone else. The corporate Will Tanner, not the lover who'd painstakingly brought her to a state of frenzy so many times last night.

"If it's business, why can't I come with you?" she pressed.

"Because of the special treat I've arranged for you. Besides, I don't want you to be bored and I do want you looking your best for tonight. Don't worry about anything except for being the perfect fiancée," he said, lifting her left hand to his mouth and pressing his lips to her ring finger.

By looking her best, he obviously meant looking polished within an inch of her life, she decided when he left her in the entrance of the beauty spa at the hotel with four hours to spare before they were due to leave for his parents' apartment. Did he not trust her to be able to present herself well to his family?

The thought tarnished the cloud of joy she'd been enveloped in for the past day and a half.

The irrefutable reminder that their entire relationship was a sham, despite their physical affinity, was a much needed wake-up call. She was playing a part and would do well to hold on to that truth. Already she risked far more hurt than she'd ever counted on by falling in love with him.

Well, if he wanted polished and perfect, that's exactly what he'd get. Margaret tried to tuck away her disappointment but it was easier said than done. By the time she'd been waxed, massaged, tinted and made up she felt even more tense, if that was possible.

Despite Will's assurances last night that they'd be able to carry off their elaborate web of deception in front of his family, she was feeling almost sick to her stomach. Even the exceptional glass of French champagne she'd been given during her pedicure failed to quell the nerves that held her muscles hostage.

What if his family hated her on sight? He'd be no nearer to a resolution to his quest. Worse, what if his family adored her? Would she and Will then be expected to maintain their deception even longer? Already her heart was fully engaged. She knew she wasn't going to be able to walk away from this, from him, without pain. But she knew without fail that staying with him for very much longer would be equally, if not more, damaging. And yet, even at her most pragmatic, she had to admit that there'd always be a part of her that clung to the distant hope that they could make this real. That the fairy tale could come true.

By the time Will rushed into their suite a bare ten minutes before they were due to leave, she still felt no more confident about her ability to carry this off tonight. While he grabbed a quick shower she set out the clothes he'd told her he wanted to wear. He came through from the en-suite bathroom, followed by a cloud of steam and the inimitable scent that she would forever associate with him.

As she sat on the bed and watched him finish getting ready it struck her as ironic that he'd given her four hours to prepare for tonight while only leaving himself ten minutes.

"What's so funny?" he asked, catching her eye in the mirror while he adjusted his tie.

"Oh, just that you seemed to think I needed so much time to be ready for tonight."

"Didn't you enjoy your time in the spa? I thought all women loved to be pampered."

"Oh, I enjoyed the pampering but I did start to wonder just how much work you thought I'd need."

He reached out and caught her arm, pulling her up to him. "You're really worried about that?"

"Not worried, exactly. Not about that, anyway."

"As far as I'm concerned, you don't need all that primping, ever. You're beautiful. I knew you were anxious about tonight and I thought it would be a nice relaxing way for you to spend the rest of the afternoon."

"I'd rather have been with you," Margaret said.

"You'd have been crazy with boredom. Believe me. Now," he flicked a look at his watch, "we'd better get going or my mother will skin me alive."

"You're afraid of your mother?" she asked, one perfectly shaped brow raised in disbelief.

"Let's just say I respect her and her expectation of punctuality."

Despite her nervousness, Margaret soon relaxed once she was behind the doors of the Tanners' brownstone in the Upper East Side. Will's mother, Olivia, refused to stand on ceremony and enveloped Margaret in a giant hug the moment she'd shed her coat.

"Welcome to the family, Margaret. We've all been dying to see you," Olivia said warmly. "Come through and meet everyone. Better to get it over with quickly, that way you can relax and just enjoy yourself for the rest of the evening."

Margaret instantly warmed to the older woman, who tucked a hand in the crook of Margaret's elbow and led her away from Will and through the immaculately furnished apartment to the main sitting room. Tastefully furnished in shades of green and cream, accented with black and white animal prints here and there, the room could have graced the cover of any of the glossy home magazines Margaret occasionally daydreamed over. The hardwood floors were polished to a mirror finish, yet still retained the well-used and homey feel of a home that was lived in and enjoyed, not just used as a showcase of wealth and position.

"This is Michael, he's Will's eldest brother, and this is his wife, Jane."

Margaret was immediately struck by the likeness between Michael and Will. It was in the eyes, and the intensity in their gaze. She felt as if she was being analyzed on multiple levels before he smiled and thrust out his hand.

"Call me Mike," he insisted, his fingers enveloping hers and shaking her hand.

"Mike, pleased to meet you." Margaret smiled back. She turned to the petite blonde at his side, "And, Jane, lovely to meet you, too."

"Welcome to the clan," Jane said with a quick smile. "Are you sure you know what you're letting yourself in for?"

"Not at all." Margaret laughed.

"Probably for the best," said another man who joined them. "I'm Paul. Middle son, best-looking and by far the most popular family member."

"Oh, you are not," interrupted the elegantly coiffed brunette who rose from the sofa where she'd been sitting.

As the woman's flowing outfit settled around her body, Margaret couldn't help but notice she was heavily pregnant. It drove home to her what a close unit this family was—and what an imposter she was.

The brunette sidled up next to her husband. "You'll have to excuse Paul's delusions of grandeur. I'm Kelly, and this," she patted her belly proudly, "will be Quin."

"Congratulations to you both," Margaret said, painting a smile on her face. "You must be very excited."

"Excited, scared, all the above," Kelly responded with a laugh.

"Who's this, then? Why haven't we been introduced yet?"

An older man, tall and lean and with gray receding hair and wire-rimmed glasses, materialized through an arched doorway.

"This is Margaret, Will's fiancée," Olivia said, drawing Margaret forward. "Margaret, this is Albert, Will's dad and, for his sins, my husband."

Despite her words, it was obvious there was a deep love and respect between the two.

"So this is the miracle woman who is going to take my boy down the aisle, hmm?"

Albert Tanner scrutinized Margaret from behind the lenses of his glasses. As with his eldest son, Mike, Margaret felt as if she were under a microscope but she held his gaze, not backing down for a second.

"I don't know about miracle woman," she said softly, "but yes, I'm Margaret Cole, and I'm pleased to meet you, Mr. Tanner."

The man's face wreathed in a wide smile. "Call me Al, we don't stand on ceremony here. Besides, if I'm to be your father-in-law, you can hardly spend the rest of your days calling me Mr. Tanner, now, can you? So, what can I get you to drink?"

Half an hour later, Margaret could feel herself begin to relax in increments. From across the room she saw Will, deep in conversation with Paul and Mike, while she sat talking to Jane and Kelly. Will chose that exact moment to look up, his eyes meeting hers. He gave her a small smile and lifted his glass toward her in a silent toast. The last vestiges of tension in her shoulders eased away. It was okay. She was doing okay.

When Olivia called everyone through to the dining room, Margaret was surprised when Albert came and took her arm.

"Since you're the guest of honor tonight, you get to sit near me," he said with a wink. "Besides, those women can't monopolize you all night. I want to get to know you better, too."

He seated Margaret to his right at the long table before taking his position at the head of the table. He was an amusing dinner companion, disclosing stories about Will when he was younger that brought the whole table roaring to laughter on several occasions. Will accepted the attention with good grace, however, he wasn't above sharing a few stories of his own about his brothers and his father.

It didn't take a rocket scientist to see the family was very close-knit. Even Jane and Kelly were an integral part of the special weave that drew them all together. Margaret continued to play her part, smiling and laughing along with the rest of them, but deep down inside she ached to belong.

Later, when they retired to the sitting room for coffee and liqueurs, Will made a point of sitting on the arm of the chair she settled in. His arm lay lightly across the back of her shoulders and she allowed herself to lean into him. She told herself it was just for show, she was merely keeping up her end of the bargain and helping him to achieve the goal he sought so avidly. But she knew she was grasping at straws. Happy to get what she could, while she could, because in a few more weeks this would no doubt be nothing more than a fond and distant memory.

By the time they left, it was well past midnight and there was a great deal of noise, hugs and promises to organize another night together as soon as Will and Margaret could get back to New York. Her ears were almost ringing with the friendly farewells as she and Will got into the back of the limousine he'd ordered.

In the darkened compartment she let her head drop back against the leather headrest and let go a deep sigh.

"Tired?" Will asked, his fingers lacing through hers.

"No, not exactly."

"You did brilliantly tonight. They adored you."

"Thank you. The feeling was mutual. Which is why it bothers me that…" Her voice trailed off into the shadows.

"Bothers you?" he prompted, giving her hand a gentle squeeze.

"That it was all such a lie."

"Don't worry, Margaret. By the time I tell them we've gone our separate ways we'll have achieved what we set out to do. As for Mum and Dad, well, they'll be disappointed but they'll get over it."

Sure they would, she thought. But would she? The question rattled through her mind over and over but she knew she was helpless to escape the truth of its answer. Instead, she sought surcease in the only thing she knew would distract her. The minute they set foot back in their suite, Margaret turned to Will and kissed him with the pent-up longing she'd been building all night long.

He didn't disappoint her—returning her passion with equal fervor, peeling away the layers of her clothing one by one until she was naked, all except for her hold-up stockings and her high-heeled pumps. They didn't even make it to the bedroom the first time. Instead, Will began to make love to her right there in the sitting room of their suite, paying homage to her breasts as only he could until her entire body quivered in anticipation. When he turned her around and placed her hands on the back of the large sofa that faced the main windows looking out onto 5th Avenue, she found herself clutching at the upholstery fabric as he positioned himself behind her.

She didn't have to wait long. A telltale sound of foil tearing, the slick of a condom onto his erection and he was there—the blunt head of his penis probing her wet folds, in, out. Only just so far and no farther. Teasing, driving her insane with wanting him. Wanting his possession of her.

His hands slid around her, to her belly, then up to her ribs until he cupped her breasts, his forefingers and thumbs squeezing her nipples. Sharp jolts of pleasure shot from the tips of her breasts to her core, making her inner muscles clench tight, then release. As if he knew how her body ached for him, he pushed himself deeper within her. Margaret shifted her feet slightly and tilted her hips forward. The knowledge that all he saw of her now was the length of her back and the roundness of her buttocks sent an illicit thrill through her body. A thrill that was rapidly eclipsed by the sensation of him thrusting within her, his hips cushioned by her backside as he drove himself deeper.

She braced her arms, meeting his thrusts with a need that threatened to overwhelm her. Close, she was so close. He squeezed her nipples again, simultaneously penetrating deep into her body, touching some magical spot within her that sent her screaming over the edge into a blinding orgasm. Will's sharp cry of satisfaction signaled his simultaneous release and he collapsed over her back, both their bodies now slippery with sweat.

Tremors still rocked her body. Diminishing aftershocks of pleasure that made her clench against him, holding him tight within the sheath of her body as if she never wanted to let him go. She moaned in protest as he began to withdraw from her and he pressed his lips to her back, just between her shoulder blades, sending a shiver down her spine.

"Let's take this into the bedroom," he whispered against her skin.

"I don't think I can move," she said, her voice still thick with the aftermath of their desire.

She heard Will laugh softly before he swept her into his arms, holding her tightly against him.

"Don't worry, I'll take care of you," he promised.

And, just like that, she let herself believe that it was true—that he'd take care of her. Forever.

Eleven

Margaret lay sprawled across William's chest, her body lax and warm in the afterglow of their lovemaking. Will brushed a strand of hair from her face and pressed a kiss to her forehead. He was more grateful to her than she'd probably ever know. Before they'd left his parents' apartment tonight, his dad had taken him aside and told him he was going to start the necessary paperwork to transfer ownership of the farm to Will.

Will had been ecstatic. Finally, he would get his due. And it was all due to the beautiful woman in his arms.

"Thank you," he said softly.

"Mmm? What for, specifically?"

He could feel her smile against his chest and it made him smile even more in return.

"Tonight. For being you."

"Anytime. I enjoyed meeting your family. They're wonderful people."

"They obviously enjoyed meeting you."

She snuggled against him, tracing tiny whorls on his chest. "Being around a family like that again, it reminded me of the good times we used to share with my mom and dad before they died. It reminded me of how much we're missing now that they're gone."

"You were all pretty close, then?"

"Very. Mom and Dad were everything. Our rock, our foundation, our moral compass. They worked really hard so we never went without but they didn't mind teaching us the value of a dollar as well," she said. "Anyway, it was really nice to be a part of a family gathering again, especially one where I wasn't responsible for everything."

Will lay there, at a loss for words. While he loved and appreciated his family, there were times when he begrudged the attention they demanded. Looking at it from Margaret's perspective was a sobering reminder that they wouldn't all be around together forever.

"I like your dad. He seems to be a very upright kind of guy."

"Oh, he is. Upright, opinionated, but always there in our corner when we need someone."

"You're so lucky to still have them in your life, Will. Don't take them for granted."

Will wrapped his arms around Margaret's naked form and gathered her even closer. She sounded so alone and he had no idea how to change that.

"I won't. Not anymore, okay?"

She nodded, her hair tickling his skin as she moved. "At least you've had them supporting you through your formative years. Poor Jason, he only had me and I seem to have made a total mess of him. I wonder how he would have turned out if he'd had a strong male role model in his life. Would he still have gotten into so much trouble?"

"Hey, don't knock it. You did your best." Will tried to comfort her.

"But it wasn't enough, was it? I failed him somewhere."

"Look, the choices he makes as an adult are his own, Margaret. Seriously. You can't be responsible for him and his every move for the rest of his life. At some stage he has to stand up and be a man."

She didn't answer but he could tell she was still thinking about it.

"Margaret, you've done the right thing by him. Don't ever doubt that."

He stroked her silken, soft skin until she fell asleep, her breathing settling into a deep and even pattern. But even as she lay in his arms, he couldn't find the relief of sleep for himself. Her words turned over in his mind. Her fears for her brother—the responsibilities she'd borne for the past ten years. All of it on her own.

Suddenly, he really didn't like what he'd done to her by forcing her to act as his fiancée. He'd taken her weakness, her love for her brother—her sole remaining family—and he'd abused it. He thought about tonight, about how genuinely happy his family had been to see him there with Margaret. To, apparently, be settling in for a long and happy future together.

He'd betrayed them all. From Margaret through to his parents. Even his brothers and their wives, and his unborn nephew. His whole family had embraced Margaret with open arms. Their very generous spirit showing them for the truly loving and supportive family they were. And showing him for the bastard he was to have lied to them the way he had.

Seeing everyone together tonight, knowing the pressure to marry was finally off him, he'd been able to genuinely relax and enjoy the evening. So much so that he could now appreciate what it was that his family strived for him to learn and accept—that all they wanted for him was a share of the love and security that came from relationships such as theirs.

When had he lost sight of what was so important? When had being so darned determined to be the best in the business completely eclipsed the decency with which he was raised?

He looked at himself through new eyes and he didn't like what he saw. Not at all.

As the hours of darkness ticked slowly toward dawn, Will thought long and hard about the type of man he'd become and what he could do to rectify things. It had to start with Margaret. He had to do the gentlemanly thing and let her go— release her from the draconian arrangement he'd browbeaten her into.

Everything inside him told him it was the right thing to do. The only thing to do. And yet, his arms closed even more firmly around the woman in his arms. She made a small sound in her sleep and he eased his hold ever so slightly.

Yes, he'd let her go. But not yet, he decided as he allowed his eyes to slide shut and sleep to overtake his exhausted mind. Not just yet.

When they woke late the next morning, Will wanted to make the most of Margaret's first trip to New York. They didn't have to be at the airport until midafternoon for their flight back to San Diego, so he treated her to a lazy brunch at the Russian Tea Room. As they dined over scrambled eggs and Scottish smoked salmon they talked little, although their casual touches and long gazes said pretty much all they needed to say to one another.

After brunch, they took a short stroll to Central Park where he negotiated an hour-long carriage ride through the park. Having Margaret nestled against him during the ride was a bittersweet joy. They hadn't known each other long, yet he felt so very right with her. When the ride finished and they reluctantly returned to their hotel to collect their luggage and take a car back to the airport, he had the overwhelming sensation that a door was closing on what had possibly been one of the brightest highlights of his life.

Will had a lot of time to think that night, alone in his bed at the Tennis Club. Margaret had insisted on being dropped back home, saying her brother was expecting her. He'd suggested she give Jason a call and let him know she was staying with him, but she'd been adamant.

He thought about Jason Cole. How old was he now? Twenty-four? And still he appeared to be quite dependent upon his sister. Will could understand sibling support, but that went both ways. It seemed that the relationship between Margaret and her brother was very much a one-way affair. Will had no doubt the younger man had been spoiled by his sister, as much as she was able. It wasn't right that Jason should still be molly-coddled at his age. He should be striking out on his own now, at this stage of his life. Being responsible for his own costs and allowing his sister to make her own life, her own way in the world.

Margaret's enjoyment of the trip to New York was the perfect example. She clearly loved to travel and enjoyed seeing new places. Will thought about how he could expand her horizons—show her other, even more exciting places in the world, then reminded himself of his decision to let her go her way.

As he thumped his pillow into shape for the umpteenth time, he reached a decision. It certainly wasn't in his plans to accompany Margaret on the travel he now knew she longed for, but he could swing something to make it easier for her—to free her and allow her to do all those things she'd always wanted to do.

He could indulge in a little man-to-man chat with her

punk brother and give the guy a few pointers in growing up. Satisfied with his plan of action, Will finally drifted off to sleep.

Monday morning he sent a message to Jason Cole, requesting his presence in his office at the end of the workday. Will didn't want to take the risk of brother and sister crossing paths, especially not with what he had to say. Margaret had begged off having dinner with him tonight, saying she had a whole lot of housework to catch up on at home, so he didn't feel guilty when he suggested she leave early for the day. He knew she got a hard time from some of the other staff over early finishes since their engagement had become public knowledge, but he was feeling snarly enough right now that if he overhead anyone say a thing about her, their job would be in jeopardy.

Will was mulling over the report he had to put together about his trip to New Jersey when he heard a knock on his office door.

"Come in," he called, throwing down his pen and closing the file he'd been analyzing.

Jason Cole came through his door and closed it behind him. It was only the second time Will had come face-to-face with Margaret's brother and he was struck by the similarities between them. Although Margaret's features were softer, more rounded, there was no denying the family resemblance between them in coloring and their eyes. Except while Margaret's eyes looked at him softly and with a combination of desire and admiration, Jason Cole's expression left little doubt about his antipathy toward Will.

"Take a seat," Will instructed, getting up from his chair and coming around to the front of his desk. He leaned against the edge of the desk and looked down at Jason who stared straight back at him, not giving so much as an inch. "How's it going, Jason?"

The younger man crossed his arms. "You should know—my supervisor answers to you on a daily basis, doesn't she?"

Will tamped down the anger that instinctively flared at Jason's open disregard for his authority.

"Yes, she does. So far, so good, apparently."

Will's slight hesitation over the last word seemed to act as a catalyst for Jason's anger.

"What the hell do you mean—*apparently?*" he asked belligerently.

"Hey, calm down. Your supervisor has noted your attention to detail and the fact that for the past couple of weeks you've rigidly maintained company operating procedures. I'm pleased to see you've taken this chance to clean up your act."

"I didn't have an act to clean up. I've told you before, and I'll keep saying it until someone believes me. I haven't been defrauding Cameron Enterprises."

Will put up a hand. "Whatever. I'm glad to see that you're shaping up. There's one other area, though, where you're still sadly remiss."

Jason rolled his eyes. "Look, if you're looking for an excuse to fire me—"

"No, this isn't work related."

Ah, he definitely had Jason's attention now.

"What is it, then?"

"It's about Margaret."

"Maggie? What do you mean? I hardly see her anymore, no thanks to you."

"Yet she still feels she needs to be there for you, Jason."

"Of course she does. She's my big sister. Don't you have older siblings who always try to tell you what to do? Do they let you make your own decisions all the time?"

Jason's words fell painfully close to the mark, enough to put Will on the attack again.

"Tell me, exactly when are you going to take responsibility for your own actions? Stand on your own two feet without your sister either bailing you out or protecting you from harm? She's put her entire life on hold for you. Given up opportunities that might never come her way again, for you."

"Do you think I don't know that? Why do you think I'm working so hard here to help her financially?"

"I don't know what to think when it comes to you, Jason. From here you look and act like a spoiled brat. You need to let her go, let her be herself."

"Oh, that's rich, coming from you."

Jason got up from his chair and started to pace the office.

Will's back stiffened. "I beg your pardon," he said, his voice clinically cold.

"What I mean is that at least I'm not actively using her in a lie, like you are. I love my sister. I'd do anything for her, which is a heck of a lot more than you can say. Oh, sure, you have your money and you can give her nice things and take her to exciting places, but at the end of the day, where does she come? Home, that's where. Because despite everything we've been through, she loves me and she knows I love her."

A solid lump choked in Will's throat. There was no way he could refute what Jason had said. In fact, his words spoke volumes as to the relationship brother and sister shared.

"And because I love her," Jason continued, "I would never deliberately do anything to hurt her—like cheat my employer. I think I have evidence as to who actually did cheat Cameron Enterprises, though. *If* you're interested in the truth, that is."

The challenge lay between the two men. A gauntlet hovering on the air.

"What kind of proof?" Will asked.

He didn't believe Jason for a minute, no matter how

impassioned his speech about his love for Margaret. He knew for a fact that when there was smoke, there was generally fire.

Jason reached into the back pocket of his pants and took out a folded sheet of paper.

"It's all there."

He handed the paper to Will and explained his neat notations on the printout. Will's inner sense of order sprang to the fore. Jason's notes did show that he appeared to be onto something. Even so, if he was clever enough to present the information this way, he was probably creative enough to have generated a false trail, as well. Still, it was enough to send up a flag in Will's mind. A flag that sent the analytical side of his brain into overdrive.

"What do you think?" Jason asked.

"I think this is definitely worth investigating further," Will said carefully. "Thank you for bringing it to my attention. Can I ask whether you were actually going to do that any time soon, or did our meeting precipitate it?"

"I wanted to be certain first. When you summoned for me today I thought now was as good a time as any."

"Have you told anyone else about your findings?"

"No, I needed to be sure."

"Good man. Give me your cell number. I might need to call you outside work for more information."

Jason gave Will his number. Will entered it into his phone and then told Jason he could go. He was surprised when the younger man stayed in the same position.

"Problem?" he asked.

"No, not exactly. Just something I need to say."

"Well, then, spit it out."

"Don't hurt my sister."

The words sounded simple enough, but there was sufficient

fire in Jason's eyes for Will to know without a shadow of a doubt that Margaret's brother meant every syllable.

"I won't," he answered.

After Jason left, Will sat for several hours at his desk, his fingers flying over the keys of his laptop or alternately tracing rows of figures. By the time he was finished, he knew the truth. A truth that should have made him rejoice, yet only served to underline what a complete and utter bastard he'd been. He'd seen only what he'd wanted to see. Seen what he could use to his own advantage. But now his blinders had been ripped off. The information he had now gathered was irrefutable.

Jason Cole was innocent.

Twelve

Things had been hectic in the office since their return from New York. Margaret had begun to sense a distance in Will that she couldn't quite put her finger on. In the office he was still the same focused and detail-oriented boss she'd come to expect. Even if they hadn't become lovers she would have enjoyed working with him. He challenged her on many levels, lifting her own abilities so that she could now approach several different tasks with a confidence she'd never known before.

And yet when it came to their personal time together, things were different. They didn't go out as much in the evenings as they had in the beginning. Will seemed content to cook for her in the compact kitchen of his beachfront suite or to order in from one of the Tennis Club's restaurants. In many ways she felt as if he was just marking time, and it bothered her.

She forced the niggling thoughts to the back of her mind and concentrated on the incoming courier package that had arrived from Will's New York office a few minutes ago. As she logged and prioritized each missive, her attention was drawn to a bound report. The date on the cover coincided with the weekend she and Will had spent in New York. Was this related to the hours he'd left her alone at the hotel? Curious, she thumbed through the pages.

Her curiosity didn't last long. Instead, she became filled with a deep sense of dread. The report was a clinical account of a facility in New Jersey, which in itself wasn't so unusual. What was unusual though, was the comparative statement on productivity and costings—comparative with the Vista del Mar branch of Cameron Enterprises. Margaret's eyes scanned the figures, every line making her stomach twist with fear, but the written testimony from Will was what horrified her the most.

For all intents and purposes, the report read like a recommendation to close down the Vista del Mar facility and to relocate the factory work to New Jersey. Margaret closed the report with shaking hands. No wonder Will hadn't wanted her to come along for the trip to New Jersey. He'd had another agenda all along.

Without a second thought, Margaret got up from her chair and took the report into Will's office, entering without even knocking on the door.

"Could you explain this to me?" she asked as she slammed his office door behind her.

The beginnings of a fury like nothing she'd ever known permeated every cell in her body.

"Ah, it's arrived," Will commented.

"Yes, it's arrived. How could you do this?"

"Margaret, it's just a report. Calm down."

"Calm down? No, I won't calm down. Do you have any idea of what this will do to the people here when you recommend to Mr. Cameron that he shut the factory down? This won't just destroy the lives of everyone who works here, it will destroy Vista del Mar altogether."

Will got up from his desk and walked over to Margaret, taking the report from her and throwing it on the desk behind him before taking her hands in his.

"You're overreacting."

"No, I'm not. I thought you were better than this, Will. I thought you had begun to really have an interest in protecting the people who've worked here—some of them for generations! If you do this you will not only break the hearts of hundreds of people, you'll destroy any sense of hope for the young people who live here. Cameron Enterprises is *the* major employer for miles around here. If we close down, communities will be ripped apart when everyone has to leave the area to find work."

"People move away from home all the time," Will said, his voice unnaturally calm given her temper.

"Not here. Not in Vista del Mar. We're old-fashioned. We look after our own. We believe in the core of family and giving kids grandparents and extended family to grow up with. Not everyone and everything is about the mighty dollar."

"Worth Industries has been bleeding money for years. Why else would Cameron Enterprises have even bought them out— have you asked yourself that?"

"Then there must be another way. A better way. You're the brainiac in these matters. Find a solution," she implored.

"This is the simplest solution to offer. The simplest and the most cost effective. It's there in black and white."

Margaret shook her head. "I know what's in the report, Will. I've read it and, more importantly, I understand it. But there has to be another way."

When he didn't respond, she yanked her hands from his.

"I can't believe I misjudged you so badly," she said bitterly.

"You're not the man I thought you were. I thought you prized loyalty."

"I do."

"Then why this?"

"Emotions are not a part of the equation."

"Emotions are everything in the equation. Emotions equate to people. Real people, not numbers. If you go ahead with this recommendation you're nothing better than a cold-blooded, heartless corporate raider like Rafe Cameron. You came here, you saw nothing about the heart of Vista del Mar, and now you'll just head on back to your structured world in New York. Where's your compassion? Did you *ever* have any?"

Margaret stared at the man she loved and realized she didn't know him at all. He stood there in front of her. Every inch of him familiar to her yet she still had no idea who William Tanner, the man, was.

She watched as he pushed a hand through his hair and sighed.

"Look, I know you're upset about this, but you have to understand that I was brought here to do an in-depth analysis of Worth Industries' financial position and make recommendations based on those findings. To do anything less would mean I'm not doing my job to the best of my ability."

"Damn your ability," she said softly, tears now burning in the backs of her eyes.

Will was shocked by how much it hurt to know he'd angered and upset Margaret so profoundly. Even worse was knowing how much he'd dropped in her estimation. He hadn't understood just how much her opinion of him mattered, or how important it was to him deep down.

He knew the results of the report wouldn't be met with any level of joy from the Board of Directors. No one liked the prospect of making so many workers jobless, no matter the economic climate, but the bottom line was as clear as the distress on Margaret's face.

"It's a preliminary report, Margaret. There's no guarantee that Rafe will go ahead with it."

"But it's more than likely, isn't it?"

He nodded. He couldn't lie to her. Not about this. Not when it affected her so completely. She was shaking her head as if she couldn't quite believe it. Will reached out to touch her again but she stepped just out of his reach.

"Don't, please," she said, her voice trembling.

"Don't? I'm simply doing my job."

"I just don't think I can be around you right now."

"Right now, or ever?"

Her eyes flew up to meet his, surprise on her face. "I…I don't know. I need to think about it. I need to go."

He watched in silence as she turned and left his office. For the balance of the day she remained aloof. Answering his questions when he posed them, yet not offering anything but the bare minimum in response.

By the end of their working day he knew what he needed to do. It was something he'd known needed to be done since New York, yet he'd been unable to bring himself to do it—to break that link between them and give her back her life. Now, with Margaret's opinion of him shattered, it would be so much easier to follow through. To do what was best for her. Granted, if the decision to close down the Vista del Mar location became a reality, then she'd be out of a job along with all the rest of them, including her brother. But they were both bright and intelligent individuals. He'd see to it that they were offered work elsewhere through his contacts. It was the least he could do for them both, long-term.

Short-term, however, it was time to release Margaret from

their agreement, but first he needed to make a very important call. To his dad.

Margaret had left the office for the day by the time Will finished his call to his father. He felt completely hollow inside. While his dad had been angry with him for his deliberate deception, he'd appeared to be even more disappointed about the fact that his relationship with Margaret had not been real. Will grabbed an antacid from his top drawer and chewed it down to try and relieve the burning in his gut. He'd damaged and hurt so many people—and for what? A piece of land he personally had no intention of living on or farming? His father was probably already giving the green light to list the property to the realtor he'd kept hanging for the past year. The very idea made him feel as if his heart were being cut out. But he couldn't have continued with the lie.

All those generations of Tanners he'd wanted to revere and remember—the hard-working men and women whose ethics had been as strong as their dream for their land—he'd disrespected them all with his single-minded behavior.

It would be a while before he could mend the fences with his family. Already his cell was buzzing with messages from his brothers, demanding to know if it was true. He'd sunk to his lowest ebb. There was one more thing to do and the sooner he faced it, the better.

The drive to the quaint home where Margaret and Jason lived was short and when he pulled up outside, he waited inside his car for a few minutes. Even though he knew he had to do this, every part of him railed at having to go through with it. He couldn't understand it. They'd had an agreement. Margaret had honored every letter of it. He was the one who had been in the wrong. Letting her go should be easy.

With renewed resolve, Will got out of the car and crossed the pavement to the narrow path leading to her front door. He knocked firmly and waited. Inside, he heard footsteps approaching and his heart rate increased incrementally. Margaret couldn't hide the surprise in her eyes when she opened the door and saw him standing there.

"Will? What are you doing here?"

"There's something I need to tell you."

"Do you want to come inside?"

Even though she'd made the invitation, her voice lacked the warmth he'd come to associate with her.

"No, it's all right. I can say what I have to say here as well as anywhere."

She waited patiently, one hand still holding the door, the other wrapped across her stomach as if bracing for something bad. Will took a deep breath.

"In light of your reaction this afternoon, I'm releasing you from our agreement. You no longer have to pretend to be my fiancée. I don't think it fair or reasonable for you to have to continue with something, or someone, that you obviously find so abhorrent."

She paled, but remained silent. He could see the steady throb of her pulse in the smooth pale column of her throat and had to push down the urge to lean forward and kiss her right there. That was no longer his right. Finally she spoke.

"I see. But what about the farm?"

"I've spoken to my father and told him the truth. He's not happy, but we'll work through it."

"I'm sorry to hear that." Her voice was stilted, unsure. She took a deep breath. "So, us, everything. It was all a complete waste of time. You've just given it all away."

It wasn't like that, he wanted to tell her, but he simply nodded. "For the duration of my work here at Vista del Mar I'd like you to stay on as my assistant, if you're okay with that."

Hell, why had he said that? Back in the office he'd already decided that continuing to work with her, seeing her up close every single day would be torture. He'd already written a letter of recommendation that she take on an EA role elsewhere in the firm. For as long as there remained a firm, that is. But, he faced the daunting truth, he couldn't let her go—not entirely—no matter how good his intentions.

"Of course. Why wouldn't I be?" Margaret responded coolly. "And Jason, is his job still safe, too?"

Of course she'd think of her brother before anything else.

"For now. By the way, I've reopened the investigation into Jason's case at work."

Margaret's lips parted on a gasp and her hand fisted at her chest. "Really?"

"He presented a very convincing argument to me and I've done a little more work on it. It looks as though your brother was telling the truth," Will admitted.

"So he's innocent?"

"It's not proven yet, but it's looking that way."

"That's fantastic. How long have you known?"

"A few days. We'll have the true culprit identified soon, I hope."

"A few days? And neither of you thought to tell me?"

"What difference would it have made?"

Will looked at her, watching the emotions that flew across her beautiful face, clouding her dark brown eyes. Would she have been the one to renege on their agreement first, if she'd known?

"Difference? All the difference in the world. I don't know how you could even ask me that. You have no idea the toll this has taken on me, thinking my brother was a thief."

And the toll sleeping with him had taken on her? What about that? Had every moment been purely for her brother's sake? He'd never know now. Feeling unaccountably empty inside, Will took a step away from the front door. "Well, I'll head off."

"Wait."

Will felt a small kernel of something bloom ever so briefly in his chest until he saw her working the engagement ring he'd given her off her finger.

"Here." She handed it to him. "I won't need this any-more."

He looked at the ring in the palm of his hand and felt a cold lump expand and solidify somewhere in the region of his chest.

"You can keep it if you like."

"No, I don't want it. Really."

Her voice was so detached. Where was the warm and deeply affectionate woman he'd come to know? Had she lost all respect for him over that stupid report?

He shoved the ring into his pocket, not wanting to look at it for another second and certainly not wanting to examine why he felt so suddenly bereft over her returning it. It wasn't as if they had truly been engaged or as if his emotions had been involved.

"I'll see you in the office on Monday, then," he said before turning to walk back to his car.

Behind him the front door slammed closed, the echo of it resounding in his ears—the finality of the sound altogether too real.

The second she shut the door behind him Margaret sank to her knees—her entire body shaking, wretched sobs ripping free from her chest. How she'd held it together while they'd talked she'd never know. It was only once the cold tile floor began to make her knees ache that she struggled upright again.

Thank goodness Jason hadn't been home to witness her breakdown, she thought as she headed to her bathroom to repair the damage to her makeup before he arrived in from the overtime he was so involved with.

She looked at her reflection in the mirror. Outwardly, she looked no different, yet inside she hurt so very much.

Margaret closed her eyes. She'd hoped against hope that Will could have really heard what she'd said to him this afternoon. That he'd have been able to look into his heart and really think about how he presented that report. But it looked as if her heartfelt plea had been in vain. As had been her ridiculous love for him.

Pain rent her anew, and her eyes burned bright with a fresh wash of tears. She had to gather some semblance of control. She'd done it before, in the awful dark days after her parents had died. She could do it again. Bit by bit, piece by piece, put herself back together again and learn to function as if nothing had happened. Grief was something you kept deep inside because if you didn't, it would consume you whole.

She'd known all along that she and Will were not a forever thing. No matter that he'd touched her heart in such a way that she knew she'd never love another the same again. No matter that she'd shared her mind and her body with him in ways she'd always dreamed of. There'd been no foundation to their pretense. They'd been two adults who had come together with no illusions or promises between them.

That she was stupid enough not to be able to keep her mind separate from her heart was her own cross to bear. He, it seemed, had no such difficulty. She doubted she'd even touched his emotions. The way he'd ended their arrangement just now was a perfect example of that. And the way he'd just walked away from the very thing he said he'd wanted most left her head reeling.

The fact that he'd given up his rightful inheritance so easily didn't augur well for the factory. She'd thought he was a better man than that. She'd believed longevity and loyalty had really counted in his world. How wrong she'd been.

She forced her eyes open and looked herself square in the eye. She'd known from the start that it was all make-believe, just as she'd known that when it was over, her heart would be irreparably broken. Now she needed to call on past reserves of strength to find some way to get on with it and to keep working with Will as if breaking off their fake engagement hadn't been the worst thing that had happened to her since her parents died.

In the house she heard the sound of a key turning in the lock at the front door. She rapidly washed her face and threw on a light application of makeup, just enough to create a mask of normality for when she faced her brother. She was the grand master at putting on a brave face. Ten years of hard work at it couldn't have been all for nothing.

She should have known her efforts were in vain.

"What happened?" Jason asked the instant he saw her.

"It's nothing," she said, shaking her head and hoping against hope that he'd leave it at that.

"It doesn't look like nothing. Tell me, Maggie. What is it?"

"Oh, just that I've gone and done the stupidest thing in my entire life," she said, her voice breaking.

Jason looked ill at ease in the face of her raw emotion.

"Don't worry, I'll get over it," she hastened to add. "You know me. Tough as nails."

Jason shook his head. "Get over *him,* you mean."

Margaret swallowed against the lump in her throat. Under Jason's inquiring eyes she could only nod.

"Ah, Maggie. Why did you have to go and fall in love with him?"

Jason held his arms open and Margaret walked into them,

taking comfort in the strength of his hug. It felt strange to have their roles reversed.

"I couldn't help it, Jason. I just did."

They stood there for ages, just holding one another, giving and receiving comfort. Eventually Margaret pulled free from her brother's caring embrace.

"Thank you."

"For what?"

"Not saying, 'I told you so,' about him using me."

Jason just shook his head. "You're a big girl now, Maggie. But it's about time you started to make your own mistakes instead of constantly picking up after mine."

"What do you mean?"

"You need a life of your own. You've been so devoted to me and to making sure that our lives have gone on as close to normal as possible to before that you've completely forgotten to take time out for you. Maggie Cole got lost somewhere along the line."

"I love you, Jason. I couldn't let Mom and Dad down. I had to step up to the plate for you with them gone."

"I know you did, and I appreciate everything you've done for me. Especially for giving up your own college dreams for me to go instead. But…" He grimaced. "I stopped *needing* you a long time ago. I'm twenty-four, Maggie. I have to stand on my own two feet and you have to let me."

Fresh tears sprang to her eyes, but she valiantly blinked them back. He was right. She'd put her life on hold to support him and she hadn't known when to stop. As a result she'd risked suffocating him. It was a miracle she hadn't already.

"Okay, I understand. It might take me a while." She smiled. "But I'll do it. By the way, Will tells me that you might be cleared of wrongdoing in the fraud investigation. Why didn't you tell me?"

Her voice rose a little, showing some of her frustration at

being kept in the dark. After all the subterfuge from Will, was it too much to have expected her brother to have included her in what was happening? After all, it had directly affected her, too.

"He asked me to keep it to myself until we could identify the real culprit."

"I'm so sorry I doubted you. I just—"

"I know," Jason interrupted. "I programmed you to distrust me. But now maybe we can both take a new step forward."

"Definitely," she answered, pasting on a smile for her younger brother's benefit.

Because no matter how many new steps forward she took with her brother, she'd still be without the one person who meant more to her than she'd ever believed possible. Will Tanner.

Thirteen

Telling her their arrangement was over had nothing on the past few days, Will thought to himself as he watched the sway of Margaret's hips as she left his office with the work he'd just given her. He shifted slightly in his seat to ease the discomfort in his groin. The discomfort that despite every command known to man, paid no attention to him and ridiculously leaped to attention every time she was within a few feet of him.

She seemed to suffer under no such difficulty, he noted with a degree of irritation. Each day she serenely sat at her desk, turning out work of an exemplary level without so much as an error or transposition of characters anywhere. It was as if they'd never happened. As if the passion between them had never existed.

He should have been relieved. After all, he'd extricated himself from enough relationships to know that her response to this was indeed a blessing—especially as they continued to work together. But there was a part of him that had begun to sorely regret releasing her from their agreement. He knew it had been the right thing to do, but for the first time in his life the right thing had never felt so utterly wrong.

He missed her. There, he'd admitted it. He missed her in his bed—in his life. Sure, they shared office space, but it was as if she operated inside a protective bubble—immune to all around her. The elements that he'd grown to enjoy most about her—her humor, her wonder in things that were new, her ability to give and give—were now extinguished. .

The office had become a somber place to be. The report he'd put in to Rafe and the Board had been met with some serious discussion. The general consensus, though, had been to accept his recommendations, and as if they'd sensed the writing on the wall, there had been a distinct rise in the ill feeling directed toward him by the staff since then. It was a good thing he had broad shoulders, he thought to himself.

It was just before lunchtime that Margaret came marching into his office. Her face more animated than he'd seen it in days—albeit the animation was, once again, anger. Anger directed squarely at him.

She threw a sheaf of papers onto the desk in front of him.

"What kind of game are you playing?" she demanded.

Will put down his pen and leaned back in his chair. "Care to explain your question?"

"This." She gestured to the scattered papers. "You're recommending the complete opposite of the last report. Are you trying to commit career suicide? Don't you know that you probably risk totally alienating your boss with this? From what I understand, Rafe Cameron is determined to dismantle what's left of Worth Industries no matter what—even if a more profitable solution for us can be found. He certainly seemed keen enough to adopt your last report. Why are you even bothering with this one?"

He shrugged. "The report is what it is. I've compiled my most recent findings and presented them here." He tapped the papers. "Are you telling me you disagree with my recommendation again?"

"Of course I'm not, but why didn't you say this the first time around?"

Will leaned back in his chair and tucked his hands behind his head. "I didn't have all the information at my disposal. Now I do. The other report was a preliminary finding. Obviously, since then, I've gleaned further information. I'm meeting with Rafe tonight to discuss it. I really think the factory is viable if, and that's a big if, they make product changes and convert the factory for a more specialized high-tech use.

"Sure, it's going to cost Cameron Enterprises a few cool million in updating the factory and continuing education for the staff, but long-term the gains will be huge. I'm hoping that'll be the carrot that secures Rafe's interest, besides the fact that doing this will ensure the community remains economically healthy with, hopefully, an even higher level of employment than Vista del Mar currently enjoys."

Margaret just stood there looking at him as if he'd grown two heads. Eventually, she spoke.

"So you're seriously going to pursue this avenue? It'll mean everything to the staff here if it can go ahead. Lately everyone's just been walking around as if they're waiting for a guillotine to fall. Morale has been terrible," Margaret commented. "Do you really think he'll go for it?"

"No, probably not. But I couldn't let this pass without bringing it to his attention." He leaned forward and gathered up the papers. "Much as I appreciate the speed with which you've transcribed this, I don't think I can give it to Rafe looking like this. I don't want him to have any excuse to trash it before he's even read the contents."

She reached forward and snatched them from him. "Don't worry," she said. "They will be perfectly bound and back on your desk in ten minutes."

Margaret went home later that day completely unsure of how she should be feeling. She was afraid to hope that Rafe Cameron would accept Will's current proposal. Sure, on paper it all made sense and the forward projections were almost embarrassingly promising. But would Cameron go for it? It was pretty clear now that he'd had some agenda against Worth Industries long before he'd come back. Gillian's acerbic editorials in the *Gazette* had probed his every decision for all to see. You couldn't even go to the grocery store without overhearing people questioning his motives. No matter how much effort he was seen putting into Hannah's Hope, everyone still suspected it was a smoke screen for whatever it was that he really planned to accomplish. And right now that seemed to be the total decimation of the only business that had kept the town alive. She doubted he'd even give Will's new proposal the time of day, no matter how prudent the recommendations.

The thing that struck her most about today was Will's total apparent commitment to this new course of action for the company. He was prepared to go head-to-head with Rafe Cameron over the whole thing, even knowing that his proposal was unlikely to be adopted. Maybe she'd made a terrible mistake in judgment about him after all. She'd been so quick to accuse him of being a corporate raider just like his boss. Wondering whether she'd gotten the completely wrong idea about him didn't sit well with her. Nor did the awareness that he'd let her go on thinking that way.

Would she have listened to him? Let him persuade her

thinking back his way? Or had he just been looking for a reason to end their arrangement—perhaps had wearied of her? She still didn't understand his about-face on the farmland he'd talked about with such enthusiasm. It had meant so much to him on so many levels, and yet he'd let it go, just like that. It just didn't make any sense.

Margaret went through the motions of preparing dinner for herself and Jason even though she'd had no appetite for anything lately. She was just about to remove the chicken cacciatore from the oven when she heard the roar of Jason's motorbike coming up the driveway. She straightened as she heard the front door bang open on its hinges and the sound of Jason's feet swiftly moving through the house.

"What's wrong?" she asked as he came into the kitchen.

In response, he wrapped his arms around her and swung her in a circle until she was dizzy.

"Nothing's wrong," he shouted happily. "Everything couldn't be more right!"

Margaret laughed as Jason set her back on her feet and she put a hand out on a nearby chair back to steady herself.

"Wow, what brought that on?"

She looked at her brother's face. He hadn't been this animated since he'd graduated college. For a second her heart squeezed. Right now he looked so much like their father with his big happy smile and dancing eyes.

"Good news. No, *great* news."

"So tell me already," she coaxed, still laughing.

"I've been cleared. Exonerated. Acquitted and, most important, vindicated, from all wrongdoing."

"Jason, that's wonderful news! I'm so happy for you. I should never, ever have doubted you."

Unexpected tears filled her eyes and started to spill down her cheeks.

"Ah, Maggie," he said gruffly, pulling her into his arms

for a massive bear hug. "It's okay. I know I wasn't always an angel, but I meant it outside the courthouse the last time, when I said I would never let you down like that again. I guess from now on you'll believe me, huh?"

She nodded and sniffed, pulling from his arms and searching out a paper towel to wipe her face dry.

"I didn't mean to get all blubbery on you. I'm sorry. This is great news, so that makes these happy tears, okay?"

"Sure, whatever you say." Jason grinned back.

"So tell me what happened," Margaret said, reaching for her oven mitts. She took the chicken dish from the oven and ladled it onto plates.

"It was awesome," Jason enthused. "She didn't know it, but we had her neck in a noose."

"She? Your supervisor?"

"Yep. She's being grilled by Tanner now. From what we can tell, there's a whole lot more that she's been dipping her fingers into than what she tried to pin on me."

"That's terrible. And to think she was ready to let you take the blame for all that."

Margaret added steamed green beans to their plates and took them to the table. Jason readily sat down and picked up his fork.

"And that's not all," he said, gesticulating with his fork. "Tanner commended me for my forensic accounting skills in uncovering the clues that led to the real culprit. You know, he might come across tough as nails, but deep down he does seem to care about people, doesn't he? I mean, he was all staunch and tough on me when he thought I was in the wrong, but he was still man enough to shake my hand and apologize when he knew I wasn't."

The bite of chicken she'd just swallowed stuck in her throat and Margaret reached for her water glass to help swallow it. Now Jason was in the Will Tanner fan club? The irony would have been funny if it wasn't so unbearably painful. The way Jason had described Will was spot-on.

When she didn't speak, Jason continued, "You know, I was wrong about Tanner's motives. He really does have our best interests at heart. I'm sorry I was so down on the two of you and you helping him out the way you did."

"Don't worry about it," Margaret managed to say. "That's all over now, anyway, except for the EA role."

Jason shot her a sharp glance, but she was relieved when he didn't press for more.

"He's gone the full distance for me in this, Maggie. He's recommended to the head of my division that I be offered a company scholarship to go back to school and specialize in forensic accounting, since I seem to have a knack for it. Natural aptitude is what he said. Reckons I'll be an asset to the company in the long term."

Margaret could barely believe her ears. Somehow she must have said the right words and Jason, thank goodness, carried most of the rest of the conversation in his excitement at the new opportunities opening up for him. But had she heard him right? Was this the same William Tanner who'd manipulated the situation with Jason to coerce her into his arms and into his bed?

She had to admit that sleeping with Will was a choice she'd made on her own, but she was completely overwhelmed by what the day had brought. First the new proposal, and now this? It was almost too much to take in. As much as she was thrilled for Jason and his future prospects, what would happen to them if the factory was forced to close their doors and cease operations?

Either way, William Tanner would eventually head back to New York or whatever role Rafe Cameron had lined up for him next. And no matter how much she wished otherwise, he'd be taking her fractured heart with him.

When Jason offered to clean up after their meal she didn't argue, which earned her a concerned look from her brother. And when she said she was heading off to bed for an early night he looked even more worried. But she couldn't find the energy to tell him she was okay. Not when she faced another night lying in her bed, alone, staring at the ceiling and wondering how on earth she was going to get through the next day.

Will stepped out onto his terrace facing the ocean and sank into one of the chairs, nursing a shot of whiskey in a tumbler between his hands. He stared out over the darkened ocean as exhaustion dragged at his body. What a day.

Normally a day like today would have seen him pumped to the max, exhilaration oozing from every pore, and yet he felt flat. The meeting with Rafe had been short and sweet and to the point but Rafe had kept his cards close to his chest, refusing to make a decision at this stage of the game. And in many ways it was a game to him. The guy literally was a rags-to-riches story of success. Which made his fixation on Worth Industries all the more intriguing.

Not for the first time, Will wondered what drove a man like Rafe. The guy had lost his mom at a fairly young age and his dad had later remarried. For a couple of minutes Will tried to dwell on what it would have been like to lose either of his parents while he was still a kid. There was no doubting it would have a monumental effect on anyone.

Rafe was currently living in a spectacular property overlooking the beach. The condo had cost a pretty penny and Rafe had commented on it being a far cry from what he'd grown up in. And yet, he was probably on his own at this very moment. Alone like Will was himself.

In fact, he'd never felt more alone.

Deep inside there was a hollow emptiness that he couldn't

ignore. Outwardly, he had everything he'd ever wanted. He had his apartment in Manhattan, a job he loved. Challenges every day that tested his mental acuity and ability to its fullest extent.

He should be on top of his game right now. He'd done a bloody good job on the Worth Industries takeover and proposals and, with Jason Cole's assistance, uncovered who had been acting outside of company procedure for pecuniary gain. So why then did he lack the sense of satisfaction that usually accompanied a job well done? The "rightness" about his work. Something was very definitely missing.

Will took a sip of the whiskey and swallowed it slowly, feeling the burn all the way down to his stomach. Who was he kidding? Of course he was missing something. Margaret. Just thinking her name was enough to sharpen the ache he felt deep inside. Not having her with him, not seeing her smile or hearing the sound of her voice, not feeling the softness of her welcoming body beneath him.

Will put his drink down on the table in front of him and stared at the glass. He'd never felt this way about a woman before. Somehow, Margaret had become as integral to his every day as breathing. She was his first thought on waking, his last on going to sleep and she infiltrated his dreams with recurring frequency. He'd royally screwed up.

They'd shared a powerful attraction back in February and he'd acted on it as he acted on everything—with determination to achieve his ultimate goal. So what was his ultimate goal now? He'd told himself he needed to use Margaret to get his dad to sign over the family farm, but even he hadn't been able to stand himself any longer when he'd analyzed how horribly he'd used her and deceived his family. The end had never justified the means.

He was left with less than nothing. His brothers had left curt messages on his cell phone and his mother hadn't even been in contact with him since Will's discussion with his father. He'd hurt them all so badly, but, he suspected, none as badly as he'd hurt Margaret. He'd lowered her importance in his world to nothing less than a pawn in an intricate game of chess. A vital piece on the playing board, yet sacrificial at the same time.

He'd been a prize fool. He'd sabotaged what had the potential to be the best thing he'd ever had, and he'd done it all himself. Finally he could begin to understand where his family was coming from. What they wanted for him. He'd been on the verge of having that with Margaret, and he'd ruined everything.

Now he could understand why he'd been so reluctant to end their affair. She'd begun to mean more to him than anyone or anything he'd ever loved before.

Will sat up straight in his chair.

Loved? He loved Margaret Cole. The words turned around in his mind, over and over, as if he couldn't quite believe them. He said it out loud.

"I love Margaret Cole."

The hollowness in his chest began to ease, so he said it again, even louder, and then again, in a shout that attracted the attention of a couple strolling on the darkened shoreline in front of the hotel.

He loved Margaret Cole with the kind of love that came from deep inside him. So deep even he had not wanted to reach that far to examine how she made him feel. How much he wanted, no, *needed* her at his side, in his life, forever. In his pigheadedness he'd done a huge amount of damage but he hadn't gotten where he was today by giving up at the first, or even the highest, hurdle.

Forgetting all about the almost untouched whiskey he'd left on the patio table, he went back into his suite, grabbed a jacket and his car keys from his bedroom and went out through the door at a run. He couldn't waste another moment. He had to try to mend things between them now.

As he drove to Margaret's home, he thought about the things his family had wanted for him and yet he'd been too stubborn and too darn focused on work to ever believe that kind of love could have a place in his life. Now he knew his life was all the more empty, that he was only half a man, without it.

He turned onto her street and felt the first seeds of doubt. The sensation was foreign to him. Usually he could bank on the outcome of any situation he instigated but this wasn't something he could define with numbers. It wasn't assets or liabilities, or profit or loss. It was a fearful thing he couldn't quantify in any shape or form.

Will pulled up at the curbside and turned off his engine, staying seated in the darkened interior of his car. This was crazy. He'd come without warning, without even knowing if she reciprocated his feelings. Logically, sure, he knew she had to have some feelings for him. A woman like Margaret wasn't the type who'd embark on a sexual affair at the drop of a hat with a man she barely knew. He replayed some of their time together through his mind—the moments where she'd seemed at her happiest. The moment, in particular, when he'd given her the ruby and diamond ring. Happy, and yet pensive at the same time. She'd had so many moments like that, and if he thought about it properly, there'd been a yearning in her eyes. Maybe he was only grasping at straws but the idea gave him a glimpse of hope. Hope he probably wasn't entitled to feel given his behavior in forcing her to be with him. Could he honestly expect Margaret to believe him when he told her he loved her? Could he even dream to hear the same in return?

There was only one way to find out. Will got out of the car and strode to the front door of the modest home. There was no porch light on and he hesitated before knocking. It was late, maybe she was asleep already. Well, she'd have to wake up. This was far too important to wait until tomorrow.

He knocked sharply on the door and waited. Footsteps on the other side signaled that someone at least was home and awake. The door opened, revealing Jason on the other side.

"Mr. Tanner. What—?" he started.

"Is Margaret home?"

"Yes, she is. She went to bed early, though."

"Jason? Who is it?" Margaret's voice echoed down the hallway.

Will stiffened at the sound of her voice and looked at Jason, who was studying him with a strange expression on his face.

"Maybe I should head out for a bit," Jason said.

"Good idea," Will said, tossing Jason the keys to his car and pushing the key card to his suite into Jason's hand. "Feel free to stay out all night."

He closed the door behind the now smiling younger man at the same moment Margaret came out from a side room—her bedroom, he surmised. The instant she saw him she wrapped her robe tightly around her body, revealing far more of her than she probably hoped to conceal.

Will started to walk toward her.

"We need to talk," he said in a tone that brooked no argument.

Margaret couldn't believe her eyes. Will Tanner, here in her house at this time of night? Even if she'd dreamed it she wouldn't have believed it.

She led him through to the kitchen where she gestured for him to sit down.

"Coffee?" she asked, realizing it was the first thing she'd said to him since his shocking arrival.

"Leave that," he answered as he reached for her hand and tugged her down into the seat next to his.

For a man who'd seemed so intent on a discussion he was being surprisingly quiet. Margaret clutched at straws for something to talk about.

"How did the meeting with Mr. Cameron go?"

Will shrugged. "He said he'll take the recommendations on board but he didn't make any promises."

Margaret sighed, but started as he spoke again.

"I'm not here to talk about work."

"So why, then? That's all we have in common, right?"

"No. That's not all we have in common." He huffed a sigh of frustration. "At least, I hope that's not all we have in common."

She waited patiently, silently, hardly daring to move a muscle as he appeared to pull his thoughts together, his eyes cast down as if he was examining the very grain of the wooden tabletop.

"I'm here because I don't want to be away from you tonight. In fact, I don't want to spend another night without you in my arms—ever."

He looked at her then and she could see it in his eyes. He meant every single word of it. But she wanted more than that. It wasn't enough that he wanted her body. He had to want *her*—mind, body and soul.

"What exactly do you mean by that, Will? Are you asking me to resume the arrangement we had?" she asked cautiously, not even daring to hope for her heart's desire.

"I'm not talking about some half-assed arrangement. I was a complete idiot to even dream that up. I never gave us a chance to be a proper couple. To court you. To show you how much I've grown to love you and to hope that one day you'll also love me in return. I want that opportunity now. I love you, Margaret. I want us to start again."

Margaret's breath caught sharply in her throat. He loved her? Was she dreaming? No, he was definitely here in her kitchen, looking as gorgeous as ever, the scent of his cologne subtly teasing her senses. She looked at him, unsure of what to do or say.

"Margaret, please give me another chance. I don't expect you to return my love straight away. I know I've gone about this all the wrong way but I'm hoping you'll find it in your heart to forgive me for that start and grant me a new one."

"Shh." Margaret laid a finger on Will's lips. "You don't need to say any more. Will, I've loved you pretty much from the moment I first saw you at the ball. I know it sounds stupid and horribly romantic, but I'd never felt such a connection with another person before. When you kissed me, it was as if I was being transported into another world. A world I'd craved ever since I was a little girl. I was afraid to admit that I could feel so much so soon, but when we started our fake engagement I knew I was fighting against the tide. I could never have been with you in San Diego, the way I was, if I didn't love you. I can't believe you love me in return."

"Believe it," Will said gruffly.

He stood and pulled her to her feet, gathering her gently into his arms and tilting her chin up so she looked straight into his face.

"I love you, Margaret Cole. More than I ever thought possible."

When he kissed her, Margaret was instantly assailed with the familiar surge of desire that always accompanied his touch, yet at the same time it was permeated with a sense of rightness, a belonging that had been missing from their liaison before. And when she took his hands and led him down the hall toward her bedroom, she knew she'd be able to finally show him, with all the love within her, exactly how she felt about him—using both words and her touch.

In the darkness of her childhood bedroom, their lips met and melded together again. Margaret's hands deftly slid Will's jacket from his shoulders, before flying to the buttons of his shirt and sliding each one free. As soon as his chest was bare she smoothed her hands over his skin, her hands tingling at the touch, her entire body warming in response. Beneath her palms she felt his nipples grow taut and she relinquished his lips only long enough to press a kiss to each one, swirling the tip of her tongue around each hard male disk, loving the way his body shuddered in response.

He wasted no time disrobing her, her robe soon a jumbled mass of cotton on her bedroom floor. The satin three-quarter pants she wore soon followed, as did the short-sleeved satin shirt. Once she was naked, he pushed her gently onto the bed before shucking his shoes and socks and finally, his jeans and briefs, which he slid off in one smooth rush.

She sighed in contentment as he covered her body with his own, relishing the heat of his skin, the deftness of his touch. And when he brought her to orgasm with his skillful fingers before donning a condom and sliding his length inside her, Margaret felt tears of joy spring to her eyes. Nothing before had ever been like this. Not with him, not with anybody.

They belonged together. In love as in all things.

As Will started to move within her, she met and welcomed each thrust—sensation spiraling tighter and tighter until she let go on a burst of joy so complete she thought she'd lose consciousness. His own climax came simultaneously and as she held him in her arms, feeling his body shake with the strength of his pleasure, she'd never felt so right with her world in all her life.

They lay together, joined, she supporting the weight of his body with her own, for some minutes. Their breaths mingling, the rhythm of their lungs in perfect synchronization. Their heartbeats slowing to a more natural tempo as their skin cooled.

Will shifted, withdrawing from her, and supporting his weight on his elbows. In the shadowed light of her room, Margaret looked up into eyes that gleamed with intent.

"I want you to wear my ring again," he said, his voice a little unsteady but growing stronger with each carefully chosen word. "And one day, when you're ready, I want you to be my wife. Except this time, we'll do everything the right way. In our own time. So, how about it? Will you marry me?"

Marry him? Margaret searched his face, almost too afraid to believe what she was hearing. But it was clear in his eyes, in the expression on his handsome features. He meant every word. She felt the final remnants of the sorrow around her heart begin to melt.

"Yes," she whispered against his lips. "Yes, I will marry you."

As their lips met and as they began to make love again, she knew she'd done the right thing. For today and for all her tomorrows.

The sun caught the gleam of brilliance residing on Margaret's ring finger as they exited Paige Adams's office the next morning. Although she was snowed under with work for the upcoming gala for Hannah's Hope, she'd gleefully agreed to arrange their wedding for the same weekend so all their friends, and Will's family, who'd be in town for the gala, could attend.

Will had scarcely been able to believe that Paige could organize a wedding at such short notice, yet he had to admit, as he looked at the woman on his arm, she'd already proven she had the touch of a fairy godmother about her.

Margaret's fingers squeezed his forearm and he watched as a supremely happy smile spread across her face.

"Happy?" he asked, knowing he already knew her answer.

"I couldn't be happier," she said. "Everything is right with my world. Jason is well and truly on the straight and narrow and I have the one thing I've always wanted my whole life."

"And that is?"

"The love of a very good man. You."

* * * * *

A WIN-WIN
PROPOSITION
CAT SCHIELD

Cat Schield has been reading and writing romance since school. Although she graduated from college with a BA in business, her idea of a perfect career was writing books. And now, after winning the Romance Writers of America 2010 Golden Heart Award for series contemporary romance, that dream has come true. Cat lives in Minnesota with her daughter, Emily, and their Burmese cat. When she's not writing sexy, romantic stories for Desire, she can be found sailing with friends on the St. Croix River, or in more exotic locales, like the Caribbean and Europe. She loves to hear from readers. Find her at www.catschield.com. Follow her on Twitter, @catschield.

One

Multi-colored lights winked at Sebastian Case, enticing him to come try his luck. He ignored the electronic clatter of slot machines as they chimed, beeped and sang of fortunes won and lost. Gambling didn't appeal to him. He believed in hard work and perseverance, not chance.

A couple in their sixties halted in front of him, forcing Sebastian to slow. The wife insisted the buffet was to their left. The husband assured her they'd missed the turn near the keno area. Both were wrong.

Before he could circle past, the woman spied him.

"There's someone who can help us." Her bright-red lips parted in a cheerful smile. "Hello…" She scrutinized his chest, where a name tag might be. "Young man. We love your hotel, but it's very confusing. Can you direct us to the buffet?"

She'd mistaken him for a hotel employee. Not surprising. He was probably the only person in the casino wearing a business suit who didn't work there.

"If you angle to the right, you'll see it." He pointed in the direction they needed to go.

"I told you." The woman shot her husband a smug look, dead wrong but taking credit anyway. "Thank you."

With a nod, Sebastian resumed walking toward the bank of elevators that would sweep him to his fifteenth-floor suite. Missy better be there. While he'd been on a conference call with their lawyers, going over last-minute changes to the contract for the purchase of Smythe Industries, she'd pulled a vanishing act. That had been almost six hours ago.

Concern buzzed. He'd left three messages on her voice mail and sent her four or five emails. Not a single response. Assistants didn't come any more efficient or reliable than Missy. Should he be worried that she'd gotten into trouble?

Noisy, crowded, chaotic Las Vegas lured tourists with over-the-top promises of adventure and spit them out with blurry memories and empty pockets. Had Missy fallen prey? Her small-town upbringing in west Texas couldn't have prepared her for such dangers. Was she somewhere in the maze of slot machines, pouring her paycheck into one? Or perhaps she'd left the hotel and been accosted on the street.

A cheer went up from the craps tables on his right. If his BlackBerry hadn't been set to vibrate, he never would have known he'd received an email. Slowing his pace, he pulled the handheld out of his coat pocket. Missy had finally responded. The two-word subject line stopped him cold.

My resignation.

He stared at the concise note in disbelief. Missy was quitting? Impossible.

His executive assistant had been with him for four years. They were a team. If she were unhappy, he'd know it.

Sebastian dialed Missy. After four rings he was directed to her voice mail.

"Call me."

Without waiting to see if she would, he shot her a terse text message demanding her location. Thirty seconds later, he received a response.

The bar.

Which bar?

He gnashed his teeth during an even longer pause.

Zador.

He pulled up a mental image of the casino's layout and turned to his left. A five-minute hike brought him to the bar. Red walls, black-lacquer accents and Asian-inspired art gave Sebastian the feeling he'd been transported halfway around the world. Enormous fish tanks lined the wall and provided most of the room's light. Twelve-inch koi drifted through the clear water as Sebastian strode into the room, scanning the occupied tables for his assistant. A redhead at the bar derailed his search.

She faced the bartender, gesturing as they conversed. With her back to him, Sebastian couldn't hear her laugh but suspected it would be husky and intimate, a siren sound that lured men into her sensual web. She sat with her long legs hitched to one side, her modest hemline offering a view of slender calves and delicate ankles.

Even without seeing her face, he was hooked.

Her allure was so potent he'd taken half a dozen steps in her direction before he recalled why he'd come here. A quick survey of the room assured him that Missy didn't occupy any of the small round tables. He would deal with her later.

First, he needed to meet the redhead at the bar.

"No, no. Really. He did that?"

Sebastian was close enough to recognize the redhead's voice. Shock vibrated through him. "Missy?"

His assistant turned her head and peered up at him through a screen of long, dark lashes. If it had been another woman, he would have described the action as flirtatious. But this was Missy.

"Hello, Sebastian." Her voice rasped along his nerves like nails dragged over bare skin. She pivoted the stool a quarter turn and gestured at the empty seat beside her. "Joe, get my boss a shot of Patrón."

Sebastian sank onto the stool, unable to believe what he was seeing.

Where were her glasses? Her eyes, the rich hazel of a mossy grotto, watched him with open curiosity, waiting for him to say or do something.

"What's with your email?" he demanded, struggling to pull free of the whirlpool of attraction he'd been sucked into. "You picked a hell of a time to quit."

She nudged the shot glass toward him. "There's never going to be a good time."

He swallowed the tequila without tasting it. The alcohol's burn was a mild discomfort compared to the inferno raging elsewhere in his body.

At some point in the six hours since they'd gotten off the plane, she'd freed her lush, auburn hair from its long thick braid and cut off twelve inches. The shorter style waved and cascaded over her shoulders like Chinese silk. Had it always been that vibrant and alive? His fingers itched to comb through the cinnamon ripples and wrap the long strands around his hands. He could almost feel the sensual caress against his skin.

His gaze traveled downward. She'd traded her amorphous pantsuits for a figure-hugging dress that framed and flaunted the creamy curves of her breasts. Had her skin always been this pale, this flawless? Or did it just appear that way in contrast to the black of the dress?

And speaking of skin. Had he ever seen her bare this much?

The Missy he knew was modest and reserved. The woman occupying the stool beside him reveled in her sensuality.

Sebastian shook his head. "What did you say?"

"I said it's your turn."

His turn. His turn to what?

The valley between her breasts called to him. He imagined plunging forward and burying his face in her cleavage. To arouse her with lips and tongue. To suck one nipple after another into his mouth until she wept for joy.

The intensity of the urge shocked him. He hauled a steadying breath into his lungs. Her seductive scent infiltrated his senses and fogged his brain.

"Sebastian?"

"What?" He wrenched his gaze from her stunning cleavage and blinked to refocus his thoughts.

"Is something wrong?" Her lips curved in a way both mysterious and feminine. As if she knew exactly what he was thinking. And liked it.

What had happened to the levelheaded, professional girl he'd come to rely on these last four years? Maybe bringing her to Las Vegas hadn't been such a good idea.

"No. I'm fine." What the hell was wrong with him? He couldn't seem to think straight. He peered at the empty shot glass. Had he been drugged? "What were we talking about?"

"My resignation."

Her words slapped him out of the sensual daze. His brain cleared. Heat receded. Or perhaps retreated was a better word.

"What do you want? More money. Or are you after a better title?"

"I want to get married. Have babies."

More shocking revelations. She'd always struck him as a career girl. His entire image of her consisted of the efficiency and dedication she exhibited within the walls of Case Consolidated Holdings' offices. Sure, it made sense that she'd have a personal life that involved friends and lovers, but it had never occurred to him that she did.

"You don't need to quit your job to do that."

"Oh, but I do."

"Are you trying to tell me I'm keeping you from getting married and having kids?"

"Yes." Her long lashes fell over whatever she didn't want him to read in her eyes.

"How?"

Sebastian signaled the bartender for another tequila, shaking his head when the man glanced at Missy's drink. How much alcohol had she consumed? Her clear gaze didn't suggest intoxication. But what else could explain her rash decision to resign?

"You keep me working late most nights," she began. "You call me at all hours to make changes in your travel arrangements or to pull together conference calls. How many times have I worked through the weekend making last-minute changes to whatever presentation I'd spent the entire week creating for you?"

Was she trying to say he expected too much? Maybe he'd come to rely on her more and more the longer they worked together, but he liked knowing he could call on her whenever and wherever he needed her help.

"You never take a break," she complained, finishing the last of her pink-tinged drink. "And you never give me one."

"I promise not to interfere with your weekends anymore."

"It's not just my weekends. It's making your doctor appointments and getting your car serviced. It's dealing with the contractors remodeling your house and choosing the tile, color scheme, fixtures. It's your house. You should be making those decisions."

They'd had this discussion before. "I respect your taste."

"I know, but decorating a house is something your wife should do."

"I don't have a wife."

"Not yet." She regarded him in obvious frustration. "Your mother said things are heating up between you and Kaitlyn Murray."

"I wouldn't say heating up."

Although it annoyed him that she and his mother had discussed his personal life, he had no right to complain. He'd been the first to step across the line when he'd made requests of Missy outside her duties as his executive assistant. It was just easier to have her take care of his needs both professionally and personally.

"You've been seeing her for six months," Missy continued. "Your mother said that's the longest you've dated anyone since…"

She trailed off.

Since his divorce six years earlier.

Sebastian wasn't opposed to remarrying. He might have done so years ago if his ex-wife hadn't trampled his ability to trust. Chandra's antics hadn't just dented his domestic side. She'd turned him into a remote bastard with no interest in developing romantic entanglements.

Unfortunately for the women in his life, he'd tended to focus his attention on something he could control—making money. Growing Case Consolidated Holdings.

"Okay. I won't ask you to do any more personal stuff." He would eliminate one excuse after another until she ran out of reasons to leave him. "Does that about cover it?"

Her hazel eyes became polished jasper. "Nothing you can say or do is going to change my mind, Sebastian. I'm quitting. Effective as soon as this week is over."

"You gave me a two-week notice."

"You can have four for all I care. I have at least that much vacation banked." She caught the bartender's eye and pointed to her drink.

"Don't you think you've had enough?"

He clasped her hand and lowered it. Contact with her skin had caused a startling revelation. He wanted her in ways that were primitive and defied rational thought. What was wrong with him? This was Missy. They'd worked side by side for four years with no sizzle, no fireworks. No craving to spend hours lost in sensual exploration.

She was his employee and as such, he was responsible for her. Only he wasn't thinking responsibly. He wasn't thinking at all. He was feeling. Hot. Intense. Sexual.

"You aren't my father," she said, sliding her hand free. "Stop telling me what to do."

He rubbed his thumb over his fingertips but couldn't eradicate the way her softness lingered on his senses. "This isn't like you."

"It isn't like the old me." She chugged half the drink the bartender set in front of her before continuing. "Do you know what today is?"

"April fifth. The leadership summit starts tomorrow evening." The annual week-long event brought together the executives of the dozen companies Case Consolidated Holdings owned. It was a chance to talk strategy for the future and facilitate a cohesive, global outlook among what were individually run companies.

"It's my birthday."

Sebastian winced. He'd forgotten again. Usually a card got passed around the office that he'd sign and there would be crepe paper and balloons decorating her desk to remind him to wish her a happy birthday. But he'd been preoccupied with the summit and the last-minute details for his motivational opening speech. What a poor leader he was if he couldn't even remember the birthday of the second most important woman in his life.

"Did I get you something nice?"

She threw her arms wide and gestured down her body. "A day of pampering in the spa and a total makeover."

"I have excellent taste," he said, his smile rueful. "You're the most beautiful woman in the bar." It probably wasn't the best comparison in the world because men occupied most of the chairs. The few women he noted were older and downright frumpy.

Her eyes narrowed. "Gee, thanks. Knowing that I'm hotter

than a bunch of grandmothers is a huge boost to my confidence."

Regret pinched him. He could do better than that. She deserved better from him. It was her birthday, after all. But the only way he could think of to show her how gorgeous she was involved taking her upstairs to his suite and peeling off her very sexy dress.

He took another kick to the groin. The residual ache made him frown. He was speeding down a dangerous path. Whatever had awakened a latent fire inside her, turning her into a seductress capable of ripping out a man's heart, was having a detrimental effect on his self-control.

"No, really," he assured her. "You look incredible."

"Incredible, incredible?" she demanded, seeking clarity as she often had to do with him. "Or incredible for thirty?"

Ah, a milestone number. No wonder she'd freaked out. She was facing another decade. That was especially difficult for a woman with a ticking clock.

"Incredible."

She pulled a face at him. "You probably think I'm overreacting to the whole turning-thirty thing." She paused so he could inject a comment, but Sebastian held his peace. "It's just that I always figured I'd get married at twenty-eight. Seemed perfect, you know? I'd have enough time for a career. Travel the world. Sow some wild oats. Make some mistakes."

He couldn't picture Missy doing any of those things. She liked going to movies. Knitted prayer shawls for her church. Rescued cats and fostered them out. If any woman seemed doomed to stay close to home and live a quiet life, it would be Missy.

But that was before she turned up tonight looking like sin, smelling like heaven, and tasting like…?

He leaned forward and brushed his lips across her cheek.

Tasting like perfection.

She put her hand against her skin where he'd kissed her and regarded him warily. "What was that for?"

"Happy birthday."

Her eyes narrowed. "I hope you're still feeling warm and fuzzy when you see what I spent on my birthday present."

He shrugged. "You're worth it."

Missy's lips opened into a perfect O. How had he never noticed how sexy her mouth was before? With a thin, arched upper lip and a plump, delectable lower one, her cupid bow mouth practically demanded he smear her perfectly applied brick-red lipstick.

Without warning, her fist shot out and hit him hard on his arm. "Damn you, Sebastian Case. You can be such a jerk."

With that, she slipped off the stool and as soon as her shoes hit the patterned carpet, she was off. Rubbing the spot where she'd struck him, Sebastian stared after her in surprise. She had a hell of a punch for one so feminine. He launched himself off the stool as she neared the exit and tossed some bills on the bar before he raced after her.

She wasn't used to walking in four-inch heels so he caught up with her easily. Sliding his arm around her waist to offer her support as she stumbled, he murmured, "Where to?"

"I'm off to celebrate." She pushed his hand away from her hip.

Sebastian's palm tingled as he strode after her. He rubbed his hands together, trying to eliminate the uncomfortable buzzing sensation, and watched the way Missy's determined stride gave her curves a little bounce and jiggle.

His ex-wife had been model thin and forever on a diet. She'd lacked the one thing he'd always adored in a woman, generous handfuls of breasts. That might account for why he'd lost interest in sex with her. Or perhaps he'd grown tired of her neediness. Her lies about being pregnant every time he talked about leaving her.

Missy veered to the right as Sebastian was cataloging all

the things that had gone wrong in his marriage. A beat later, he changed direction, stalking her down the row of gaming tables. She moved with purpose, seeming to know exactly where she was heading. He caught up to her at the roulette wheel.

"Do you have any idea what you're doing?" he demanded, certain he already knew the answer.

"I know exactly what I'm doing." She pulled out a wad of cash. "I came here to blow this and I'm not leaving until I do."

Missy had fallen in love with Las Vegas the second she'd stepped into the hotel lobby this afternoon. The ringing slot machines reminded her of the final bell before summer vacation. Flashing lights and the prospect of a big win around every corner unleashed her long-repressed wild child. She'd barely resisted the urge to dash into the casino and plunk down twenty dollars on the first blackjack table she came to. In a heartbeat, fifteen years of sensible living went out the window.

Sebastian set his hand on her arm and used his body to block her view of the roulette table. "You don't want to play this. It's one of the worst games for winning. Let's go play blackjack. The odds are better."

His touch awakened a shiver despite the warmth of his skin. He restrained her with gentleness, but Missy knew he could call on steel if he ran out of patience.

Rich. Powerful. Used to getting his way. Intimidating when he didn't. A man in control of every aspect of his life. He never relaxed. Rarely smiled. Demanded excellence from everybody.

If she'd known what she was getting into before she'd accepted the position as his assistant, she probably would have run screaming from his office. Instead, she'd been drawn to the mystique of Sebastian Case, the elusive, gorgeous, exasperating millionaire businessman.

She shook off his grip. "I don't care."

"You've gone completely mad. How much do you have there?" He plucked the bills from her hand and riffled through them. His lips puckered in a silent whistle.

Afraid he might hold on to the money in some misguided attempt to save her from herself, she snatched the cash back. "It's enough to buy the wedding dress of my dreams."

If her use for the money surprised Sebastian, he didn't show it. "And how much is that?"

"Five thousand dollars."

"That's a lot of money to bring to Las Vegas." Concern deepened his voice into a dusky rumble.

Missy dodged eye contact, refusing to let his censure keep her from throwing caution to the wind. "It sure is. Took me two years to save it. I ate tuna sandwiches three days a week. I never bought any clothes unless they were on clearance. I limited myself to one movie and one dinner out per pay period."

"Those are significant sacrifices," he said with a straight face, but mockery hovered in the back of his eyes.

Missy tossed her head. What did he know about making sacrifices? He'd paid eight hundred thousand dollars for a home because he liked the neighborhood, then tore down the house so that he could spend another two million building something to his exacting taste. A mansion he barely lived in because he spent so much time at the office.

"They were," she retorted, frustrated with everything in her life at the moment and taking it out on Sebastian because it was easier to blame him than face where she'd gone wrong. "Aren't you curious why I've decided to blow the money rather than buy the wedding dress of my dreams?"

"I'd love to know." Calm and measured, he sounded like a firefighter talking a crazy lady off the ledge. "Let's go somewhere quiet so you can tell me the whole story."

"I don't want to go somewhere quiet. My entire life has been quiet. I'm looking for a little excitement."

A chance to run wild.

Sebastian's disapproving frown would not steer her off course. She was tired of behaving like a mouse when what she wanted to do was roar like a tiger.

Daughter of a small-town pastor, she'd been a free-spirited kid, breaking rules and flaunting authority. True to herself but a disappointment to her father and mother, Missy's carefree days had come to an end in high school when her mother suffered a stroke. Bound to a wheelchair, needing help with the simplest of tasks, she'd needed Missy to grow up fast. Missy had shouldered a lot of her mother's daily caretaking until her death after Missy's twenty-fifth birthday.

"Haven't you had enough excitement for one day?" Sebastian asked. "You had a makeover. You've had too much to drink. Let me take you back to your hotel room. We have a big day tomorrow."

"I haven't even gotten started." She turned to the roulette table and plunked down her wad of cash. "Five thousand in chips, please."

Sebastian put a hand over the cash before the dealer could move. "Think about what you're doing here. That's a lot of money. Two years of saving and sacrificing."

She tugged at his wrist but might as well have been an ant trying to move a mountain. Her efforts brought her in close to his body. His heat surrounded her, seeped into far corners of her soul where wild impulses waited to be set free. His masculine aftershave invaded her nostrils and sped along her already overstimulated nerve endings. She was teetering on the edge of something reckless.

"I know what I'm doing." That was the furthest thing from the truth. She had no step-by-step plan. No clue if she was making good decisions. And she didn't care. For the first time in fifteen years, she was following her instincts wherever they led. Whatever the cost.

And it felt amazing.

"Miss?"

The dealer interrupted their argument and Missy shoved an elbow into Sebastian's ribs. With an oomph, he released her money.

"Five thousand in chips, please," she repeated, turning her shoulder away from her boss's frustrated frown.

His disapproval made her uncomfortable. As she had done with her father, she'd grown accustomed to doing things the way Sebastian wanted them done. How many times had she let his opinion dominate hers? Too many to count.

And old habits were hard to break.

The wheel spun before she placed her bet. Annoyed that she'd second-guessed herself, Missy drummed her fingers and waited for the ball to drop.

"Don't throw your money away like this," Sebastian said.

"Why not?" What good was being in Las Vegas if she couldn't do something that she'd regret even a little? "I was supposed to spend it on my wedding dress. That's not going to happen now."

"You'll find someone," Sebastian argued. "You'll get married."

"I had someone." He knew absolutely nothing about her, did he? "He dumped me." Yesterday. The day before her birthday. Two years after she thought she'd be getting married, she was back to square one. No. Worse than that, she was two years older with fewer single men to choose from.

"I'm sorry."

"You should be. It's your fault."

"My fault?" Usually he gazed at her in a neutral way as if he never truly saw her. At the moment he was assessing her with something other than his normal cool. "I don't see how."

What was going on here? Sebastian regarded her as if she were a luscious chocolate truffle he wanted to devour. Unsettled, she stammered her first word. "H-he broke up with me because I wouldn't quit working for you."

"Why would he care that you worked for me?"

Because he thinks I'm in love with you.

And, of course, she wasn't. Well, maybe she had been a little in the beginning. For the first year or so. But after Tim came along, she'd gotten over her feelings for her boss. Unrequited feelings. Feelings with no hope of ever being reciprocated.

She wasn't in Sebastian's league. He dated women with money and prestigious social status. She knew the type. For a time in high school, she'd dated a boy from the wealthiest family in town. She'd been as infatuated with his promises to take her out of west Texas as she'd been with the guy. But in the end, it was the sting of why he'd broken up with her and how he'd handled it that remained branded on her psyche.

"Tim hated how I went running whenever you called," Missy continued. "Every one of our fights was over you. I should've quit a long time ago."

"Why didn't you?"

In true Sebastian fashion, he arrowed straight to the heart of her dilemma. Her boss grasped underlying problems faster than anyone she'd ever known, including her father, who had an uncanny ability to read people. People, but not his daughter.

She couldn't answer his question. To do so would force her to admit that leaving his employ would be akin to chopping off her arm. She needed him in her life. Needed to be around him to feel alive.

How pathetic was that?

"I just did." Only not soon enough because yesterday Tim had told her he'd met the girl of his dreams, and they were getting married. Her hands shook. "I waited for two years for him to propose." Her throat tightened, blocking the next few words.

And he decided to marry someone else after only knowing her a month.

Tears dampened her eyes, but Missy blinked rapidly to make them go away. Facing her undesirability hurt too much. If she wasn't good enough for Tim, an unmotivated pharmaceutical salesman, who was she good enough for?

"Place your bets," the dealer called as people began setting chips all over the table.

Missy pushed all her chips onto red. "Five thousand dollars on red."

"Don't do this." Sebastian spoke softly but it was a command.

"Why not?" She didn't attempt to keep defiance out of her voice. He needed to realize she wasn't his to boss around anymore. "It isn't as if I have anything left to lose. Not really."

"Take the money and spend it on something of value. A new car. A down payment on a house. Something that will last longer than twenty seconds."

Solid advice, but she could never look at the thing she'd bought with the money and not see her wedding dress. The gorgeous flowing gown of satin and lace with the gathered skirt and beaded bodice. She'd cut the picture out of a bridal magazine two years ago when she and Tim had had their first conversation about the future.

"Tell you what," she began, feeling audacious and desirable beneath Sebastian's keen appraisal. Mad impulses had been driving her all day. Maybe turning thirty wasn't the worst thing that could have happened to her. Start a new decade with a new attitude. "I'll make you a bet."

Sebastian set his hands on his hips and looked resigned. "What sort of a bet?"

"Last call," the dealer announced.

Missy heard the wheel begin to spin and the ball start its journey around and around. From reading up on roulette, she knew she had a forty-seven percent chance of winning. Those weren't such bad odds.

"If the ball lands on black and I lose, I'll keep working for you." She gave a rueful smile. "I'll have to, won't I, because I'll be five thousand dollars poorer."

Sebastian's eyes locked with hers. The winds of change had begun to blow. Storm clouds loomed. Dangerous for the unwary.

"And if the ball lands on red?"

She licked her lips and his attention shifted to her mouth, lingering as if something fascinated him. Fever consumed the last of her hesitation. Every one of her senses came to life and soaked up the sights, smells and sounds of the man towering over her.

Hunger thrummed, longing to be sated. Only one man had the passion, sensuality and persistence to do just that.

She moved her left leg forward, bringing her thigh into contact with his. The effect on him was instantaneous. His nostrils flared. His entire body went perfectly still. His fist clenched where it rested against the table.

Intrigued, she shifted a few inches more. Her skirt rode up her thigh, baring more of her leg. She wore thigh-high stockings, the sort with a backing beneath the lace band at the top that allowed them to stay up on their own. Standing before the mirror in stockings and her brand-new black silk underwear earlier tonight, she'd been flushed with confidence in her sex appeal.

How many times had she watched his steely muscles flex beneath his tailored suits and wondered what it would be like to get her hands on all that unadulterated male beauty? To experience the immense power contained in his body.

Suddenly, she knew exactly how she wanted to celebrate her birthday.

His chiseled mouth flattened as she leaned into the space that separated them. Thick lashes hid his gaze from her, but a slight hitch in his breath told her he wasn't undisturbed by her nearness.

"I want a night with you." The proposition tasted like warm

honey against her lips. She had no idea where she'd found the boldness to voice it, but now that she had, she wouldn't take it back for a million dollars.

"I'm not going to take advantage of you like that."

A chuckle broke from her. Was he kidding? She was the one doing the advantage-taking here.

"One night," she coaxed, silencing the sensible voice in her head that howled in protest. One night to rediscover what made her happy. "That's all I want."

"This is ridiculous." Despite his words to the contrary, he didn't pull back.

Did he desire her? Was she brave enough to find out?

"Black, you get me," she said, hearing the ball slow. Only seconds now. Seconds that would change her life forever. "Red, I get you."

She slipped her fingers beneath the lapel of his suit coat and rested on the expensive cotton covering his broad chest. He grabbed her hand with his as her fingers grazed his nipple. His harsh exhalation thrilled her.

If something as mundane as standing close to him and touching his chest made her feel this incredible, what would happen when they were naked together? Her knees wobbled as his hand slipped around her waist.

His eyes burned into her. "Why are you doing this?"

"Because it's my birthday." *Because I've wanted you for four years but never dreamed that you'd want me in return.* "Because it's Vegas, baby," she crooned.

"Very well," he growled, arm tightening to draw her body against his. "It's a bet."

Two

The ball dropped into the slot.

It landed on red. Missy didn't need to look for herself or hear the dealer announce it. She just knew deep down that it was so.

And she knew because Sebastian stiffened.

In all sorts of interesting ways.

"Red thirty," the dealer said, confirming Missy's win.

She felt like cheering, but one look at Sebastian's tight expression told her he wouldn't appreciate her victory dance.

He loosened his grip, releasing her by slow increments. His fingertips grazed across her lower back just above the swell of her butt. Had he meant the caress? His remote expression offered no answer.

"I guess this means I won." She spoke quietly to hide the tremor in her voice.

"Five thousand dollars," Sebastian said, scooping up her winnings and depositing it in her hands.

"And you," she reminded him, clutching the chips to her suddenly tight chest.

Winning a man at the roulette table. If her family could

see her now. The thought made her shudder. She pushed aside her concerns. This was Vegas and everyone knew that what happened in Vegas, stayed in Vegas.

One night. One night she'd never forget. But only one night.

Her knees wobbled.

Sebastian scrutinized her expression. One eyebrow rose. "Let's cash it in and get out of here."

"Eager to start paying up?" Her weak attempt at teasing got lost in the cries of dismay around them as the ball dropped into place.

Sebastian caught her by the elbow and pulled her away from the roulette table. Was he afraid she was going to gamble away her winnings, or was he in a hurry to start their time together? The significance of the debt she was about to collect prompted an unexpected bout of vertigo.

Sebastian steadied her. "What's wrong?"

She, Missy Ward, unassuming girl from Crusade, west Texas, was about to sleep with the gorgeous and oh-so-elusive Sebastian Case.

If the girls in the office could see her now.

"My heels are a little higher than I'm used to and your legs are longer than mine." Missy tipped her head back so she could stare into his gray eyes. "However, I'm delighted you're so eager to get me alone."

His mouth tightened, but his gaze remained as impenetrable as reinforced steel. "That's not why I want to get out of here."

Four-inch heels couldn't begin to eliminate his height advantage, but she doubted even if they stood eye to eye that his presence would be any less intimidating. A born leader, he took charge in every circumstance. The perfect head of a family owned-and-run business where his brothers were strong-willed and opinionated.

Missy admired how he kept tension from erupting between his brothers Max and Nathan.

Cool. Calm. Collected. Always one hundred percent in control no matter what the situation.

The exact opposite of how she felt at the moment.

"Really?" She slipped on a half smile. "Because I was hoping you were planning on giving me my money's worth."

"Let's cash you out." Sebastian collected her winnings from her cupped hands and jerked his head toward the cashier. "Then we'll go upstairs and discuss this crazy wager of yours."

Not fair, damn it. She'd won him fair and square.

"We wouldn't be discussing it if you won," she grumbled as he turned away. She trailed after him. His powerful stride covered ground faster than she could in her heels. By the time she arrived at the cashier, she was out of breath. "You won't talk me out of it. In fact, the only topic up for discussion is what time you get to put your clothes back on tomorrow morning."

The woman behind the bars stopped counting out bills. She stared from Sebastian to Missy and back again before starting over.

"Keep your voice down."

"Why? No one cares." No one except him. "Unless, of course, you're ashamed of being seen with me."

"Don't be ridiculous."

"Then what's the problem?"

The look he leveled on her would have reduced every vice president at Case Consolidated Holdings to quivering idiots. Missy had seen it before. She straightened her spine and braced herself against his annoyance.

As the cashier placed ten thousand dollars in front of them, Missy counted along. By the time the woman had lined up the bills on the counter, Missy's lightheadedness had returned.

She'd won five thousand dollars. And a big hunky millionaire. She wasn't sure which one shocked her more.

Stuffing the bills into her purse, she tugged at Sebastian's sleeve. "Let's go."

She was glad to have him at her side as they found the elevators that would take them to the suite of rooms they shared. Besides having gotten lost twice today already, the wad of cash in her purse made her feel as if she had a target painted on her back. Knowing security was a scream away reassured her somewhat, but Sebastian's tall form guarding her body made her feel completely safe.

As the elevator rose to the fifteenth floor, Missy wasn't sure if it was Sebastian's ongoing disapproval that caused the panicky flutters in her stomach or the thought that within the next ten minutes she was going to be naked in his arms.

"You look nervous," he remarked smoothly as he slid the keycard out of his pocket.

"Nervous?" She released a wild cackle, loosening the death grip on her beaded clutch. Letting him believe she wasn't one hundred percent ready to make love would give him ammunition to shoot holes in her decision to collect on the bet. She cleared her throat. "Do I have a reason to be?"

A long-suffering sigh spilled from Sebastian. "You are obviously not the sort of girl who sleeps with a man once and walks away. Why don't I escort you back to your room and we can call it a night?"

"Because if you'd won, you'd collect, and that's what I'm going to do." She plucked the keycard from his hand and unlocked the door.

Sebastian's suite was three times the size of her onebedroom condo back home and way better decorated. Lattecolored walls, carpet and furniture, espresso drapes and accents gave the room a sophisticated feel. Bold, modern paintings added slashes of color during the day. At night the Vegas strip glittered through the large west-facing windows.

The suite boasted three separate conversation areas and a conference room that seated ten.

While Sebastian strode around the room turning on lights as he went, she crossed to the wet bar. "I had them put a bottle of champagne in your fridge."

"Did you plan for us to drink it together?"

She jumped as he appeared beside her without warning. The carpet had muffled his steps. Eyes hard, he awaited her answer.

"It's my thirtieth birthday." Two champagne flutes sat beside the ice bucket on the bar. "I wanted to celebrate. I thought that maybe you'd have a drink with me. I don't know anyone else in Las Vegas."

"Did you order the champagne before or after you decided to resign?"

"Before." She'd been feeling blue this morning. Tim's reason for dumping her had opened a deep wound in her psyche. Stepping on to the plane, she'd felt like an ugly frumpy mess. Sebastian had treated her like a dictation machine the whole flight. She was invisible. Unremarkable. So when they'd arrived at the hotel, she'd bought a new dress, gotten her hair cut and styled, and realized she wasn't dull after all. "Can you open this?"

He took the champagne bottle and set it aside. "If you need liquid courage to go through with this, maybe we should forget the whole wager."

"No." She cursed her breathless tone. "It's my birthday. I want to celebrate."

She reached past him for the bottle, determined to open it herself. Shock waves buffeted her as he threaded his fingers through her hair.

His heat pounded against her like a rogue wave, catching her off balance. She grabbed at his forearms and hard muscle flexed beneath her touch.

He lowered his lips to the very corner of her mouth. Skin

tingling at the grazing contact, she shifted her head, but his lips were already gone. She sighed in dismay as he drifted kisses along her cheek.

"You smell like sweetness and sin," he murmured, dragging his thumb across her lower lip. "How do you manage it?"

Relieved to know he wasn't completely immune to her, she said. "New perfume. It's called Sweetness and Sin."

"Remind me to buy you a case for Christmas."

His hands cupped her head, holding her poised between close-enough-to-kiss and his-lips-weren't-going-anywhere-near-hers. Despite the anticipation humming through her body like a high-voltage power line, anxiety was beginning to seep in.

Why was he stalling?

Had she imagined the interest in his eyes? What if he didn't find her attractive after all?

Maybe if she gave him a little reminder why they were here, he'd remember his manners and make love to her.

"Sebastian," she began, her tone a low warning.

"Yes, Missy?"

In one long caress, he eased his hands down her spine to her hips and back up again. Her muscles melted against his hard body. As nice as it was being this close to him, proximity to so much raw male power was causing a dramatic spike in her sexual frustration.

"We had a deal."

"Deals are made to be broken."

"I won you fair and square," she said, determination punctuating each word. "So, quit stalling and pay up."

Frustrating woman.

Yet amusement dominated annoyance at his assistant's command. How had he never noticed her bossy streak before? "Where would you like me to start?"

"I'd like a kiss."

His attention zeroed in on her gorgeous mouth. At the moment, it was pursed like a disapproving librarian's. Far from kissable.

"Then what?"

His question launched her eyebrows toward her hairline. When her lips popped open to utter whatever brazen retort brimmed in her eyes, he lowered his head and took control of her mouth.

Warm. Sweet. Pliant. Her lips came alive beneath his. She opened to him and surrendered. He'd never dreamed it would be like this with her. No hesitation. No games. Just pure joy. Delicious perfection.

Right now, he wanted Missy like no other woman he'd ever known. His need gave her power and that infuriated him. But he couldn't stop the onslaught of longing to take everything she offered him.

Her tongue danced with his. Already he knew how she liked to be kissed and what to do with his lips and teeth that made her writhe against him in wild abandon. Desire swept over him, an enormous, overwhelming rush unlike anything he'd ever experienced. He swallowed her curves in his hands, pulling her tighter against his body.

Seconds before he lost himself, Sebastian tore his mouth from hers and twirled her around. Chest heaving, he trapped her in his arms.

"Why'd you stop?" she demanded.

Because taking advantage of this situation would come back to haunt him later. She wove her hips from side to side in a way that drove him half out of his mind. He groaned.

"What are you doing to me?" Fanning the fingers of one hand on her pelvis, he pulled her snug against his erection.

"If you don't know, maybe I'm not doing it right."

He set his mouth against her neck and sucked gently, marking her. "You're doing just fine."

"Do you need me to tell you what to do next?"

Damn her for making him smile. "No, I think I've got that covered."

He gathered her dress in his hands, bunching the material in slow increments. The hem crept up her thighs as she gulped in air. When her legs were exposed to the top of the stockings, Sebastian stopped what he was doing and grazed his fingertips along the very edge of the nylon a hairbreadth from her bare skin.

What was his ordinary assistant doing in clothing this provocative? "Sexy, sexy woman. You're driving me mad."

Missy murmured something unintelligible.

He didn't ask her to repeat it. Instead, he let his hands wander upward. Contact between his caressing fingertips and her bare skin threatened the semblance of control he'd recaptured.

"Sebastian."

Frustration filled every syllable of his name as it slipped from her lips. He sympathized. He ached for her in ways he'd never imagined. He drifted a light caress upward over the triangle of silk that covered her mound. Scarce inches below, her heat called.

"Are you sure about this, sweetheart?" He traced her panty's edge. His heart thundered against his ribs. "Because if I go any further, I won't be able to stop."

Truer words had never been spoken.

"Touch me," she begged, a catch in her voice.

Sebastian slid his fingers lower, aiming for the soft, wet center of her. Despite the throbbing in his groin, he stopped short of his goal. His muscles shook with effort while he forced himself to consider the consequences of what he was about to do. This was Missy. They'd worked together as professionals for four years. What if there was no going back from this? Where did that leave him? Leave them?

"Sebastian, please."

She squirmed in his grasp. His control wavered. He tried to hold on while rational thought melted as fast as an ice cube in hell.

Her palms came to rest against his thighs. The bite of her fingers against his legs sparked stars in his vision. Her frank sensuality excited him. So did her wanton gyrations.

"Sebastian." She seized his hand and pressed it against her hot flesh.

With a jubilant roar his carnal side broke free. Surrendering to instinct, Sebastian slipped his fingers between her thighs, applying the perfect amount of pressure to make her cry out. Satisfaction detonated inside him. He intended to make her come. He needed to take back the power she'd stolen with her sexy transformation.

She ascended fast. Faster than he'd anticipated. Great breaths turned her lungs into bellows as she neared the top. Her orgasm hit her so hard she almost took him with her. He'd never experienced anything as incredible as the feel of her as she abandoned all control to him and came apart in his arms.

To his dismay, Sebastian's knees lost strength. He knelt and supported Missy as she sagged, easing her to the floor. Once she was flat on her back, he followed her to the carpet, pressing her breasts beneath his chest. Linking their fingers, he set their joined hands beside her head and surveyed her flushed cheeks and unfocused gaze.

Mission accomplished. She looked as shell-shocked as a well-satisfied woman should.

Time to stop before either one of them did something they couldn't take back. He'd agreed to a night with her. No reason that night had to involve either of them naked and rolling around on Egyptian cotton sheets.

They could spend the time working.

That's what he should do. It's what logic told him to do. She might be disappointed, but she wouldn't be surprised. He always based actions on reason, not emotion.

Sebastian dipped his head and stroked his lips against hers. His heart rocked in his chest. What was he doing? This was madness.

He released her hands and framed her face with his fingers. She caressed his shoulders and gathered handfuls of his hair, tugging him closer. He obliged her with a second sweeping pass. This time, finding her lips parted, he lingered, tangling their breath, coasting his tongue along the inside of her lower lip.

She tasted delicious. Tart and sweet like lemons and cherries. Savoring her low hum of encouragement, Sebastian explored her teeth, noting a slight roughness on one in front. Her tongue flicked against his, and the insistent ache in his groin grew. He ignored it. This wasn't going any further.

Missy had other ideas.

He sank deeper into the kiss, losing himself in the heady wonder of it.

His world narrowed to her soft mouth and the passionate undulation of her body. Intoxicating noises erupted from her throat, their crescendo warning him she was on a fast track to another orgasm.

He might as well help.

Breaking off the kiss, he slid down her body. Her skirt had ridden up and exposed two inches of skin above her black stockings. He shoved the hem even higher, giving him a glimpse of black underwear. Silk. Tiny. And if that wasn't enough to enthrall him, the musky scent of her arousal invaded his nostrils. There was no turning back.

Sebastian placed a kiss on her skin just above the black material. She gasped. Intrigued, he drew his tongue from hipbone to hipbone and her body began to tremble. His mouth played over the fabric of her thong, teasing her with lips and teeth, down between her thighs to where moisture soaked the silk.

He smiled as he hooked his fingers around her panties and

tugged them downward. As she was slowly exposed to his gaze, he was forced to take a series of deep, steadying breaths.

She was a true redhead, he noted absently as he peeled the underwear over her thigh highs and heels and cast them aside. Then, settling back between her thighs, he leaned forward and with the tip of his tongue licked the seam where her inner leg and body came together. Her hips bucked.

Her wild, unrestrained movements made him want to forget the preliminaries and take her. But he held his own needs in check. He was the one setting the tone here. The one in charge.

By the end of the night she would learn what happened when she provoked him.

It was a mistake she would never make again.

He set his mouth against her. His first taste made him groan. Blood surged into his groin, drained from every other part of his body. He sucked hard and her hips jerked and twitched in helpless yearning. Using his tongue to tease and his teeth to tantalize, he brought her to the edge of orgasm twice, backing off each time until a low, keening sound emitted from her throat.

Then she did something unexpected.

Her hands had been busy in his hair, against his shoulders. Now, as he eased the pressure of his mouth and let her body quiet, she tugged her dress off her shoulders, exposing her black bra.

She snagged his hand and brought it to her neckline. Understanding what she wanted, he skimmed his fingertips against the rough lace before hooking them beneath the fabric. Her skin might look like cool porcelain, but heat raged below the surface of her breast, scorching his knuckles.

"Sebastian." The plea broke from her throat.

With ruthless urgency, he yanked the fabric downward, freeing her breasts. Large and round with erect rosy nipples. Every bit as perfect as he'd imagined they would be. He filled his hands with them, a savage groan rumbling in his throat as he settled his mouth against her once more.

Her every cry drove his desire higher. He threw finesse out the window and stormed her with everything he had. She shuddered against his mouth, her body taking her places he doubted she even knew existed.

She released a half-strangled shout. Sebastian pushed her still more and watched her climax unfold. Watched her unravel. It was a thing of beauty.

And he needed to be a part of it.

Fumbling his belt free with one hand while his other continued the movement that would extend her orgasm, he succeeded in getting his pants and boxers down far enough to free his erection. Harder than he ever remembered being in his entire life, he slid up her body and placed his tip at her entrance. Braced above her, he paused for a fraction of a second to ask himself what he was doing. Before the answer came, her hips lifted off the carpet, taking him in an inch. The silken caress smothered the voice of reason. He thrust forward. She was both tight and slick. The last pulses of her orgasm sucked him in.

The wonder that settled over her features matched the sensation expanding in his chest.

"Missy?" His fingertips grazed her cheek.

Her eyes flashed open, unfocused and dazed.

"Don't stop now," she whispered, depositing a clumsy kiss on his chin. "It was just getting good."

She wrapped arms and legs around his body, binding him to her as began to move. A low growl of satisfaction rumbled out of him at the incredible slide of their bodies. They fit together as if she'd been fashioned for him alone. The sensation was beyond anything he'd ever felt before.

Pressure built in his groin no matter how he tried to hold it off. He wanted to savor the moment as long as possible. But her movements beneath him were impossible to resist and he drove furiously to his own finish. As with her, the orgasm hit him hard and without warning. Stars exploded behind his eyes as he emptied himself into her.

And collapsed, breathing hard, too spent to consider the consequences of what he'd just done.

Three

So that's what all the fuss was about.

Too exhausted to hold on any longer, Missy let her arms fall away from Sebastian's shoulders. He lay with his face buried in her neck. His chest pumped against hers as if he'd finished a mile-long sprint. She marveled at the feel of him buried inside her.

He filled her unlike any man she'd ever known. Of course, there'd only been two. Tim and her high school boyfriend, so she didn't have much to compare him to, but deep down where it counted, she knew that only one in ten million men could have done the things to her that he just had.

"Well, that was something," she said into the silence, her heart clenching in a manner that had nothing to do with her winded state. Repercussions swarmed her mind. She shoved the irksome thoughts away. She didn't want this moment to be tainted by regrets. What she did want was much less clear.

Sebastian had always been able to jumble her emotions. He could make her hungry for his approval and curse his pig-headedness in the space of one conversation. She craved his full attention but feared the effect it had on her hormones.

So, what did she want? An honest answer eluded her. Since she was fifteen, she'd let her family's expectations subjugate her heart's desires. Liberating her wants was as uncomfortable as standing from a crouch held for hours. Just as muscles and joints protested being used again after a long period of inactivity, so did her spirit.

Fear drove a spike of doubt into her chest. She closed her eyes until the pain eased. In her mind, she summoned every fantasy about Sebastian that she'd stockpiled during her four years of working for him. Was it reckless to want to explore a couple dozen?

Absolutely.

But if she couldn't check her inhibitions at the door in Vegas, where could she?

Her fingers itched to wander over Sebastian's back, shoulders, face, but he'd shuttered emotion and passion behind his granite features, and her earlier boldness was in short supply.

Glancing down his body, she stared, dumbfounded, at the erotic picture that greeted her. Her splayed legs cradled her oh-so-formal boss. The sight of him so intimately arrayed between her thighs, still mostly dressed, flooded her with satisfaction and possessiveness. He was hers. At least for tonight.

It thrilled her to have driven the impassive Sebastian Case to make love to her on the floor. He hadn't even gotten his pants all the way down. Or his coat off. She bet his tie was still perfectly knotted. The image of them with clothes askew in such a compromising position struck her funny bone. If her friends in the office could see them now. Few would believe that the decisive, controlled Sebastian Case could have gotten swept away by the moment. And not one would believe he would have done it with her.

He lifted his head, eyebrows hammering together as he stared at her mouth and the grin she couldn't control. "Did you plan this?"

"No."

Her wager had been desperate and mad. She'd never dreamed she'd win. Or that he'd actually honor the bet.

If she'd had any inkling, she would have stood at that roulette table, tongue-tied and as trapped by her family's expectations as ever. Even now, if she opened the door to her rational side even a crack, she'd start to hyperventilate at the stark reality of her and Sebastian together like this.

She waited for him to move, but nothing happened. Was he intending on staying like this all night? Not that she was complaining. Just thinking about it caused an immediate spike in her hormones. Tiny ripples of delight, aftershocks of that last incredible orgasm, tugged in her loins.

Chaos muddled her emotions. She cleared her throat. "So, what do we do now?"

For a long moment he stared down at her in that unfathomable way of his. Then, he seemed to arrive at some sort of decision. Tension seeped out of him. "What would you like to do?"

Her mouth opened, but nothing came out.

"You appear stumped." He eyed her. "Would you like me to offer some suggestions? I am at your disposal for the night."

Irony rode his tone. Missy chomped on her lower lip. Was that true? Did he intend to let her have her way with him? As if she could. He could snap her like a twig. Not that he would.

"You're frowning." He dusted his lips between her brows. "What's on your mind?"

His kiss relaxed her and increased her tension at the same time. Soothed her soul and awakened her desires.

"I don't have much experience with men like you," she admitted. "I'm not sure of my options."

"I see."

Was he laughing at her? Missy surveyed his expression. Neutral. No amusement crinkled the skin around his eyes or curved his lips.

She began again. "I mean, we've already done a couple

things…" She ran out of words about the same time she ran out of bravado.

"So we have."

"What would you suggest?"

Grabbing her by the hips, he rolled until she sat on him. "We have lots of things we could do next."

Where a second earlier she'd been exhausted, being on top inspired a rush of exhilaration. "Such as?"

His eyes burned with scarcely banked desire as he watched her. "There's quite a list."

"Starting with?"

"I could tell you." A second later he'd rolled her beneath him once again.

Breathless and lightheaded, she clutched at his shoulders while he dusted her chin, her eyes, her nose with his lips. The light kisses frustrated and aroused.

"Or?" She groaned as he framed her face with his hands and continued to ply her skin with gentle sweeps of his soft lips.

"Or." He drew the word out, nipping her neck, making her shudder. "I could show you."

His offer liberated her breath. It whooshed out of her. "Perfect. I love demonstrations."

Sebastian rested his forearm against the shower wall and his forehead on his arm. The effort it took to stand upright spoke to the rousing night of lovemaking he and Missy had shared. Cold water poured over his shoulders and back, deflating his morning erection. Waking with an ache below the belt wasn't unusual. The curvaceous Missy slumbering beside him was a different story.

The bedside clock had warned him it was eight in the morning. After the night he'd had, he was a little surprised he'd regained consciousness before noon.

To his intense dismay, he'd spooned Missy at some point

during the wee hours after they'd surrendered to exhaustion. Arm wrapped around her ridiculously tiny waist, face buried in her neck, he'd aligned them head to toe.

He'd never spooned a woman in his life.

Hell, aside from his ex-wife, he hadn't spent the night with more than a handful of women, and none since his divorce. He'd didn't like being touched while he slept.

Yet there he'd been, cuddled up against Missy as if he was afraid she'd steal away in the night. With a heavy, thick erection that poked at her backside. He'd kissed the side of her neck, his fingers gliding along her petal-soft skin. She'd stirred. Murmured. Stretched.

He'd jerked his hands away. The night was over. His debt paid. Awakening her with slow, sweet loving would imply that he intended to keep the affair going.

He'd been shocked by how hard it was to leave the bed. What was the matter with him? Sure, the sex had been incredible. Her enthusiastic, uninhibited responses to his lovemaking had blown his mind and unraveled his control. She'd denied him nothing. And he'd given her a night she'd never forget.

A night he'd never forget.

Sebastian shoved his head beneath the cold water to banish his steamy thoughts. Not being the sort of man who did things then lived to regret them later, he didn't like the sensation churning in his gut. He shouldn't have let himself agree to Missy's wager. If he hadn't been so damned certain he would win, he might have considered what would happen if he didn't.

What the hell had happened to his sanity? She was his assistant for heaven's sake.

Not anymore.

Losing the bet last night meant he would need to split his attention between the all-important leadership summit and convincing Missy to stay.

Everyone had a price. He just needed to figure out hers.

He slammed his fist against the tile. The sting restored his calm. He switched from cold to hot and soaped down.

The bed was empty when he left the bathroom to dress. His gaze slid over the rumpled covers. Images of last night's lovemaking flashed through his head. His body's predictable reaction infuriated him.

Convincing Missy they could go back to being boss and employee would be impossible if he let lust rule every time he thought about her.

Sebastian yanked a pair of boxers from the drawer and hauled them over his erection. Sliding into a shirt, he fastened the buttons and glared at his reflection, willing his body to behave as if he, and not it, was in control. At least Missy had made herself scarce. One glimpse of her sexy curves beneath the sheet and he'd have tossed his towel into the corner and his better judgment to the wind.

He found his watch on the nightstand and fastened it around his wrist before donning his suit coat. Sebastian closed his eyes briefly. Had he really been in such a hurry with Missy that he hadn't taken the time to do more than shove his pants to his knees? Obviously he needed to devote more time to his sex life.

Since divorcing Chandra, he'd grown way too suspicious of the women he dated. He treated every one as if they intended to get pregnant in an attempt to compel him to marry them. He and Kaitlyn had been seeing each other for several months and hadn't yet become intimate. So what had prompted him to throw caution to the wind with Missy?

Sebastian left the disturbing question unanswered and strode into the living room to retrieve his cell phone. The sight of Missy, wearing nothing more than a happy smile and the shirt she'd stripped off him last night, stopped him cold.

His shirt bared her long slender legs and tormented his imagination. With her moss-green eyes obscured by her glasses once again and her hair pulled into a ponytail, she looked like a cross between a pinup and the girl next door. What had happened to the conservative, somewhat frumpy assistant he knew and relied on?

"I ordered breakfast," she said, retrieving their clothes and shoes from the floor. "It should be here any second."

To keep from ogling her, he stared at the mixture of garments draped over her arm. "Have you seen my BlackBerry?"

"It was in your pocket." As she held it out to him, her neckline gaped.

She'd left the top two buttons undone, offering him a tantalizing glimpse of the voluptuous curve of her breast. His fingers twitched, muscles yearning to swallow that perfect roundness in his palm.

One night. That's all she'd demanded and all he'd intended to let her have. He needed to get them back on professional footing.

"Thanks." He watched her carry his suit into the bedroom, unable to tear his gaze away. When she disappeared from view, he shook his head to rearrange his thoughts.

He keyed up his emails to see what sort of trouble the morning had brought with it. Dueling emails from Nathan and Max told him it was business as usual with Case Consolidated Holdings.

A troublemaker from the moment he could crawl, middle-brother Max raced cars on the weekend and partied too much during the week. But as reckless as he could be in his personal life, he was conservative in business.

That made for some interesting battles with youngest brother, Nathan, who had made his money taking risks in the stock market and venture capital. The charm Nathan used to get what he wanted was in short supply whenever Max was around.

Max was in Germany trying to save one of their key suppliers from declaring bankruptcy while Nathan looked for a replacement supplier closer to home in Ohio. Max didn't believe Nathan's claim that the new company could produce their one-of-a-kind part at a seventeen percent reduction in cost and still maintain the quality.

"I have reports to go over from Nathan about this new supplier he found. I could use your help right after breakfast."

"I was planning on doing a little sightseeing this morning." Her voice emerged from the bedroom, tinged with impatience. "I've never been to Las Vegas before."

"There's not much to see. Just a bunch of casinos."

"That may be the case." She reappeared as a knock sounded on the suite's front door. "But I intend to win money in every single one."

The words on his handheld screen stopped making sense as she strolled past him. His gaze locked on her bare legs.

With an effort, he refocused on his emails. She would not distract him all week. Playtime was over.

A familiar voice greeted Missy at the door. Sebastian's head shot up. Framed in the doorway was not a room service waiter, but a tall man in his late sixties dressed casually in a golf shirt and khakis.

For about a millisecond Sebastian's father looked startled to be greeted by a half-naked woman, then a broad grin bloomed. The man standing just behind him, however, dressed like Sebastian in an expensive gray suit, appeared positively shocked.

The very air in the room stilled as if everyone had stopped breathing.

Missy was the first to move. "Hello, Brandon. Good to see you." She held out her hand to the former CEO and looked startled when Brandon not only took her hand, but also leaned forward to kiss her cheek. While Sebastian watched, she wrapped herself in professionalism as if she wore a business suit instead of a man's shirt. She then extended her hand to the second man. "I'm Missy Ward, Sebastian's assistant."

"Lucas Smythe."

Lucas might be seventy and happily married, but that didn't stop his gaze from roving downward over Missy's gaping neckline and bare legs.

"We've spoken on the phone." Missy's only sign of discomfort was the hot color in her cheeks as she stepped back from the door. "Won't you gentlemen come in?"

"Hello, Sebastian," Brandon called, noticing his son for the first time. "Look who I found in the lobby."

"Dad, what an unexpected surprise." And unwelcome. "Good to see you, Lucas."

Even more than getting caught with a half-naked Missy in his suite, the appearance of his father knocked Sebastian off balance. What the hell was he doing here? And with Lucas Smythe? Brandon had been against the purchase of Smythe Industries from the start. Not that he had a say in the way Case Consolidated Holdings was run since his retirement nine months ago. Still, this hadn't stopped him from popping into the office to say hello and lingering to voice his opinion of how his sons were running things.

Sebastian advanced past his assistant to shake hands with Lucas, making sure his body blocked Missy, giving her a chance to fade backward.

"Glad you could join us this week."

"Glad to be here," Lucas replied, his attention edging past Sebastian. "I'll admit I've been a bit curious how you run things. Want to make sure my company's going to be in good hands before I sign her over to you."

Strong in his opinions about professionalism in the workplace, Sebastian now looked like a hypocrite. The fact that Missy had quit before they'd had sex didn't make the situation any easier to stomach. Debaucher of female employees was not the image Sebastian wanted to portray.

"Have you eaten?" Sebastian asked as a waiter arrived,

pushing a cart loaded with covered dishes into the room. "Looks like there's plenty of food."

"I've already eaten," said Lucas, his gaze following Missy as she disappeared into a room Sebastian hadn't noticed yesterday.

They were sharing the suite?

Giving the appearance of being oblivious to the undercurrents in the room, Brandon followed the waiter. "I'll take a cup of coffee."

"Of course." Frustration engulfed Sebastian.

Uncharacteristically, he wanted to offer an explanation for Missy's presence in his suite and her attire, but his father's smirk and Lucas's frown told Sebastian they'd already formed opinions.

With ruthless determination, he banned Missy from his mind, slamming the door on his personal life so he could concentrate on the business at hand.

"Too bad you didn't bring your appetite." He began uncovering trays. "Looks like Missy ordered everything on the menu."

Brandon glanced toward the door she'd departed through. His lips formed a sly grin. "Have we caught you at a bad time?"

"Not at all."

Filling his plate with eggs, bacon, pancakes and toast, Sebastian sipped coffee and fixed his gaze on Lucas. Seeing the speculation in the man's eyes, Sebastian ground his teeth. He refused to feel guilty about what had happened in this suite last night, and he sure as hell wasn't going to make excuses for his behavior.

"I think you'll be impressed with the division executives you'll meet this week," Sebastian said. "We believe our employees are our most important assets."

"I'm sure he can tell that you appreciate your employees'

assets," Brandon said, stirring the pot with a heavy dose of irony.

Sebastian ignored the dig. His father had no business judging. Brandon had indulged in his own indiscretions in years past.

He turned to his father and decided to be blunt. "What are you doing here?"

"I told you. I came by to see if you could tear yourself away long enough for a round of golf."

"Not here in the suite," Sebastian countered, working hard to keep his tone even while nettles drove into his gut. "I mean in Las Vegas."

"This is your first time in charge of the leadership summit. With both your brothers putting out fires elsewhere, I thought you could use my help."

More likely he'd thought to take over the leadership summit and undermine Sebastian's authority as the current CEO of Case Consolidated Holdings. Brandon hadn't wanted to resign after his heart surgery nine months ago. He'd only agreed to step down to appease his wife of forty years.

"I appreciate the offer," Sebastian lied, regarding his father over the rim of his coffee cup. "But I have everything under control."

Missy closed the door between her room and Sebastian's suite and leaned back against it, heart pounding. Dismay tightened around her chest like a vise. She'd never seen Sebastian that angry before. Usually when irritated he froze someone in place. For the first six months she worked for him, she had heard one horror story after another of how he'd terrified her predecessors, and she waited for him to turn his icy disapproval on her. But he never had. Maybe because she made sure everything was done to his exacting specifications, giving him no reason to be annoyed with her.

But was that any way to live?

She deserved a job where she was appreciated for her talents.

Sebastian appreciates your talents.

At least she thought he did. He wasn't the most effusive boss she'd ever had. But he did give her a big raise every year.

But it wasn't enough.

She'd wanted more from a job than a paycheck.

She wanted more from Sebastian than employment.

Her nerves stretched taut as she closed her eyes and skimmed her hands over her body, sliding her fingertips along her naked thighs, cupping her breasts in her palms while she relived the highlights of the previous evening. How could she still ache for him after he'd satisfied her with hours and hours of the most creative lovemaking ever? She should be wrung out and exhausted—not revved up for more.

Missy pushed off the door and headed for the bathroom. Catching a glimpse of herself in the mirror, she regarded her reflection in bemusement. Her lips looked fuller than usual and felt more tender. She gently ran her tongue over her lower lip. Passion-bruised. Not surprising. The man could kiss. She'd been happy to let him demonstrate his prowess over and over.

Her red hair was a tangled mess. Her cheek color high. The neckline of Sebastian's shirt gaped, baring more than a little cleavage. She leaned forward to investigate the faint bruise on her neck put there by her boss. Branded. She stepped back and examined the full picture. Bare legs, mussed hair, well-kissed mouth. Son of a gun, she looked like she'd been up having sex all night.

No wonder Brandon had shot his son a knowing grin.

No wonder Lucas Smythe had scanned her up and down.

No wonder Sebastian appeared as if he'd very much like to throttle her.

He'd been in negotiations with the conservative business owner for four months over the purchase of Smythe Industries. Would Lucas Smythe reconsider selling his family-owned business after finding her almost naked in Sebastian's suite? Missy prayed that wouldn't happen. If her actions last night had blown the deal, Sebastian would never forgive her.

Caught in the undertow of repercussions, she doubled over, unable to breathe. What had she done?

Nothing any other red-blooded American girl wouldn't have.

Slowly, her lungs began to work again.

And really, what had she done? She'd slept with a man she'd known for four years. Big deal. She'd already quit working for him. No line had been crossed. It had been one night. Casual, maybe not forgettable, but certainly not life-changing. Sebastian wasn't interested in pursuing a relationship with her. And she didn't want to set herself up for heartbreak thinking she could fit into his world of money and social status.

For her, it had been rebound sex, pure and simple. After Tim's rejection, she'd needed a man to demonstrate that she was an attractive, desirable woman. Sebastian had done an admirable job. Her memories would keep her smiling for a long time to come.

Straightening, she stepped into the shower, taking her time beneath the spray. The idea of returning to the suite to face Sebastian's wrath lacked appeal. He needed some time to cool down. About a week might do it.

She'd go shopping. After her win last night, she had five thousand dollars burning a hole in her purse. The black dress had been her only new purchase yesterday. Sebastian and her father would counsel her to squirrel the money away. The pre-Las Vegas part of her agreed with their logic. Especially now that she'd quit her job. But her new future required a new attitude, and nothing boosted a woman's confidence like looking fabulous.

She stepped out of the shower, dried her hair, and then set about taming the natural wave with a straight iron. Humming her mother's favorite gospel song, Missy sorted through her luggage for something to wear. She'd packed nothing but boring business wear. Pantsuits in black and navy. Dress pants and sweater sets for sightseeing and business dinners.

Nothing sexy or eye-catching for her.

Tim wouldn't have approved of last night's dress. He was as conservative as her father. But Tim wasn't in her life anymore. He'd lost any right to an opinion on her wardrobe the second he'd met his "soul mate" and decided to marry her instead of Missy.

Piece by piece, she consigned her wardrobe to the wastebasket beneath the desk. The act of emptying her suitcase was no less cathartic than quitting her job or wagering five thousand dollars on one spin of the roulette wheel. She'd become too complacent in her life. No wonder Tim had found somebody new.

A firm knock sounded on the door that connected her room to the suite. Startled by the sudden noise, Missy answered it without considering her attire. Sebastian stood before her, holding her purse.

"Are your father and Lucas Smythe gone?" she asked.

"Were you hoping to offer them an encore?" His gaze burned hot enough to torch the towel she'd wrapped around her body.

An encore? As if she'd planned for his father and business associate to catch her half-dressed. Whatever had transpired after she'd left had turned his mood from bad to foul.

She glared at him. "Of course not. What is your dad doing in Las Vegas?"

"He didn't say."

"Did you ask?"

Sebastian communicated more with one raised eyebrow than most men could with a ten-minute rant. "He claims he's here to help with the leadership summit."

"But you don't believe him?"

"Let's just say I wasn't happy to see him in Lucas Smythe's company."

Few employees at Case Consolidated Holdings would know the vast chasm that existed between Sebastian and his father when it came to business strategy. Brandon liked to take risks and chase profits, often losing huge amounts of money in the process. Sebastian and Max preferred to use more structured methods when it came to growing Case Consolidated Holdings. Acquiring Lucas Smythe's company was a perfect example of where they differed.

The two brothers liked the conservatively run company and the way the acquisition would help diversify their mix of product offerings. Brandon wanted to spend their investment capital on something that might offer more growth potential, and he had an ally in his youngest son, Nathan. Problem was, to get to the big gains, it was often necessary to risk big losses.

"Do you think he wants to sabotage the deal with Smythe?"

"He hasn't had one good thing to say about the purchase. His showing up here means I have to keep an eye on him."

"What did you tell them about us?"

"Us?" he echoed softly, the warning hiss of a cobra. "I didn't tell them anything."

"Why not?"

"It's none of their business."

"But they're bound to wonder. The contracts aren't yet signed. What if Lucas decides not to sell you his company? You have to make some excuse why I was in your suite, wearing just your shirt."

"Like what?"

"You could have told him I'd gotten something on my dress and needed to rinse it out."

"That might have worked if you didn't look like a woman who's been thoroughly made love to."

She tingled all over, reacting not to his sarcastic tone, but to his choice of words. And his sizzling gaze. Her argument went numb.

"And the fact that we're sharing the suite." He crossed his arms over his chest. "Why are we sharing the suite, by the way?"

"We're not sharing the suite. My room adjoins yours. The door between us has a lock." That last bit sounded somewhat foolish. As if she didn't trust him. As if he couldn't persuade her to let him in. "You could have told them that I got drunk and quit. That I came on to you because I've had a thing for you for years."

His gaze rested heavily on her, weakening her knees.

"No."

"Don't be a…" She bit her lip before the rest of that sentence came out. Had she almost called the imposing Sebastian Case a fool? "What about the deal? Are you still going forward with the purchase of his company?"

"I don't know."

Her breath caught. She scrutinized Sebastian's impassive features, searching for anger, frustration, disappointment, but she saw nothing.

"What do you mean, you don't know?"

"Just that." His lashes lowered, giving him a sleepy look until you noticed the intensity of his watchful gray eyes.

"Yesterday, he was ready to sign the contract once one or two points were ironed out."

"Some things have come up since then."

"Like him thinking you make a habit out of seducing your employees?" Missy couldn't believe how angry she was at the moment. Angry with herself for lingering in Sebastian's suite because of some silly romantic hope that maybe last night had been the start of something. Angry with his father for showing up this morning with Lucas Smythe. But most of all, angry with Sebastian for his stubborn refusal to make explanations. "You need to tell him the truth. And if you don't, I will."

His fingers wrapped around her upper arms and bit deep. "Stay out of it."

Eyes blazing, he pulled her onto her toes and bent down until inches separated his mouth from hers. Memories of their night together swamped her. Her fingers loosened their grip on the towel, ready to discard it if he showed the slightest hint of wanting to pick up where they'd left off in the wee hours of the morning.

He must have read her thoughts because he lowered his head still farther. Missy closed her eyes in anticipation of his kiss. When it didn't come, she blinked in surprise. Sebastian had his own eyes closed. Tension pulled at his features, drawing his mouth into a grim line.

His chest lifted as he sucked in air. A second later she was free. Her heels hit the floor with a jarring thud that loosened her grip on the towel. It slipped off one breast before she caught it.

Snarling a curse through clenched teeth, Sebastian shifted his gaze to the pile of clothes spilling out of the trash. When his attention resettled on her, the only emotion he let her see was cool curiosity.

He used his chin to gesture toward her former wardrobe. "What's going on with you?"

"Nothing."

"You've thrown away your clothes."

"I don't need them anymore."

Iron-gray eyes swept down her body once again. "Planning on spending the entire week naked?"

"No."

He'd buried his mood beneath a neutral tone and an impassive expression, but her stomach muscles tightened. Getting caught half-dressed in Sebastian's suite meant their encounter was no longer a complete secret. Were they to be boss and assistant or secret lovers? She tingled in anticipation of the latter.

"I thought I would buy some new things," she continued.

He shook his head. "You don't have time to shop. I need you to go over the arrangements for tonight's cocktail party."

Missy's mood deflated. As far as Sebastian was concerned the night was over. He'd paid his debt. Time to get back to work.

"There's no need," she said. "I double-checked everything yesterday. We're good to go. Let's go down to the casino and have some fun."

"This is a business trip."

"And you can't mix business with pleasure?" She cocked her head.

"I've already done that," he retorted, biting off each word. The way he stared at her mouth, she could almost feel the firm pressure of his lips against hers. She swayed into the gap between them, brought up short by his next words. "Get dressed and let's go over the arrangements."

"I quit, remember?"

"You gave me your two-week notice," he said. "Time to get back to work."

He pivoted and left her staring at his retreating form. With a huff, she shut the door. She kicked at the pile of business attire that lay on the floor. At the thought of wearing any of it, a frustrated shriek built in her chest.

The phone on her nightstand rang. Summoned already? It had only been a minute since he'd left. She glanced at the door to Sebastian's suite and imagined him pacing. She understood his impatience. This was his first time leading the summit. In past years, his father had been the CEO of Case Consolidated Holdings. Since taking over, Sebastian had made numerous changes to the business that involved selling off two companies that hadn't fit their new business model and looking for new investments that were a better fit. He was growing into the CEO role and had a lot riding on this week in Vegas.

In the month leading up to the annual event, months of

planning had gone into every presentation, every speech. Months of hard work and not just by Sebastian. When he worked hard, so did she. Sixty-hour work weeks meant late nights and weekends.

No wonder her boyfriend had strayed. She was never around when Tim wanted to get together. A part of her didn't blame him for dumping her. She just wished he hadn't done it the day before her birthday and that it hadn't taken him less than a month to decide to marry someone else.

When the phone refused to stop ringing, Missy snatched up the handset.

"Missy? It's Susan." Sebastian's mother sounded unfazed by Missy's cranky greeting.

Over the years, Missy had grown close to Susan. And Brandon for that matter. They practically treated her like one of the family instead of Sebastian's employee.

"Because my husband insists on golfing today," Susan continued, "I wondered if you had any plans."

"Sebastian expects me to work."

Susan made a dismissive sound. "Tell him I need you to keep me company by the pool. I'm sure he'll give you some time off."

Missy ran that conversation in her head and didn't arrive at Susan's conclusion. "He really wants to make sure the conference goes smoothly."

"And with you behind the scenes, it will. Now, you've done enough. Grab your sunscreen and meet me by the pool. I'm not going to take no for an answer."

The people who thought the Case brothers got their determination from Brandon had never met Susan. "Sure. Give me ten minutes."

"Wonderful."

Feeling squashed between a rock and a hard place, Missy replaced the phone and scooped up her bathing suit. If she told Sebastian about his mom's request, she would be in for another argument. She dropped the towel and stepped into the suit. Sebastian was already accustomed to her flaky behavior on this trip. And it wasn't as if she hadn't already decided that she wanted to go have some fun. Susan had just given her the nudge she needed to act.

She slid the straps onto her shoulders and shot a last glance at the door to Sebastian's suite. Deserting her boss was going to make him even more irate than he already was.

Too bad.

Since starting as Sebastian's assistant, the only time she'd taken off was to visit her family. And there's no way anyone would consider that relaxing. Sebastian owed her four weeks of vacation. The least he could do is give her the morning to have some fun.

Grabbing her cover-up and a hat, she slipped out of her hotel room.

And when he caught her?

She'd cross that bridge when she came to it.

Besides, what's the worst he could do?

Fire her?

Four

Location?

Sebastian hit the send button on the text to Missy as the elevator doors opened. It had taken half an hour for him to figure out she'd pulled a vanishing act on him again. He'd intended to spend the morning going over his opening speech for the summit, catching up on emails and checking in with Max and Nathan. Instead, he was cruising through the casino, once again, in search of his wayward assistant.

His phone vibrated.

Pool.

Tucked into a protected hollow created by the hotel's tall towers, the pool area, with its waterfalls, swim-up bar and assorted potted palms, looked more like tropical paradise than a desert oasis. Two-thirds of the lounge chairs were occupied, but as it had the night before, his gaze went straight to Missy.

She wore a cerulean blue one-piece with a wide white band around the waist that drew attention to her hourglass shape. Barely a hint of cleavage showed above the suit's straight, unadorned neckline. In color and style, the suit was unremarkable. Sebastian doubted that anyone would give her a second look with so much skin being bared by the less modest women in her vicinity.

But she was all he was interested in.

His mother waved to him from the pool as he neared Missy's lounge chair. Missy looked up as his shadow fell across her.

"Are you sure you should be sitting in the sun with your skin?"

"Don't worry." She pointed to the sunscreen label. "It's SPF 75."

The morning sun poured over his head and shoulders, warming the charcoal wool suit he wore and raising his temperature. He tugged his tie loose and unfastened his shirt's top button. "Maybe you should move into the shade."

"I'm fine."

"With skin like yours you should be careful." His gaze trailed down her legs, following the movement of her hand as she smoothed lotion over her creamy skin.

His fingers balled into fists as memories of the night before intruded. The taste of her kisses. The way she'd moaned his name. How her breath caught as he slid deep inside her. The fact that her hunger for him had matched his need for her.

"Sebastian?"

He wrenched his attention back to her face. "Yes?"

"I said, if you've come to drag me back to work, I'm not going without a fight."

For a second, the notion of tossing her over his shoulder and carrying her back to his suite blocked every sane thought in his head. "I'm not paying you to sit by the pool."

"Then consider this a vacation day. I have plenty to burn."

"You picked a hell of a time to go AWOL."

She sighed. "Everything is organized. The summit doesn't start until the cocktail party tonight. There's plenty of time for me to have a little fun. You should, too."

"I'm not here to have fun," he reminded her.

She wrinkled her nose. "Yes, I know. But you're so pre-pared you could probably do the entire summit in your sleep. Why don't you relax a little today?"

"How do you suggest I do that?"

She stopped in the act of spreading lotion on her arm and brought gaze to bear on him. The unbridled hope in her eyes twisted his gut. Was he that much of a tyrant?

"You could start by buying me a drink."

"It's ten o'clock in the morning."

She snapped the lid of the suntan lotion closed and picked up a beige sun hat, adorned with blue forget-me-nots. Once she set it on her head, the wide brim hid her expression from him.

"Make it an orange juice."

Sebastian held his hand out to Missy and braced him-self for the contact with her skin. She wiped lotion from her palms before giving Sebastian her hand. As expected, a pulse of fire sped up his arm and struck below his belt. He released her before the temptation to pull her close gave him away. Instead, he set his palm at the small of her back and nudged her toward the tiki-style bar.

From beneath her ruddy lashes, she peered his way. "I'm sorry I ran off without telling you this morning."

"I'm sorry you felt you had to."

"Am I hearing things or did the never-wrong Sebastian Case just apologize to his lowly assistant?" Laughter bright-ened the green in her eyes.

"I'm wrong on occasion and am not such an ass that I can't admit it." Driven by compulsions too strong to fight, he grazed his fingertips upward until he encountered bare skin. "And you are far from lowly."

A faint tremor beneath his hand told him she found the skin-to-skin contact as disturbing as he did. This attraction between them was a distraction he couldn't afford.

He directed her on top of the only empty stool and stood

behind her. Her sun-warmed shoulder brushed his chest as he leaned forward to order her a drink, increasing his temperature even further. With a dismayed sound, she scooted away.

"You're going to ruin your suit if you get suntan lotion on it."

"I don't care."

"How can you not care?" she countered. "You spend a fortune on your clothes."

He lifted a shoulder. He'd ruin a hundred suits if it meant being close to her. The scent of suntan lotion rising off her skin aroused the craving to strip that boring bathing suit off her body and determine if the sun had marked her gorgeous pale flesh.

She gasped as he hooked a finger beneath her bathing suit strap and tugged it out of place. "What are you doing?"

"Making sure you aren't getting too much sun."

"When you touch me, I have trouble thinking straight," she whispered.

Her admission awakened a rumble of pleasure. "You shouldn't say things like that."

"I don't understand what's going on between us."

Nor did he. "Nothing is going on."

"We made love last night."

It took a great deal of effort, but he locked away his erotic musings. "It should never have happened."

"But it did." She met his gaze, her eyes soft with curiosity.

She wanted to know why he'd made love to her when he'd been so determined it was the wrong thing to do. He hadn't quite answered that question for himself. He could blame it on intense sexual chemistry, but that wouldn't be the whole truth. Grasping the whole truth might just lead him into uncharted territory where his assistant was concerned.

A familiar figure emerged from the pool and reminded Sebastian that he had more problems at hand than his wayward assistant. "Did my mother give you any hint of what my father is really doing here?"

Reeling from what she'd glimpsed in Sebastian's somber gray eyes, Missy scrambled to reorient her thoughts. "She said your dad went golfing this morning. I assumed they came here on vacation."

"He took Lucas Smythe golfing. Probably intends to talk him out of selling Smythe Industries to us."

Missy's chest tightened. Sebastian's relationship with his father was uneasy. During the years she worked for the eldest Case son, she'd had a front-row seat to Sebastian's battle with his father over business strategies and the direction the company should move in the future.

When Brandon's health problems had surfaced and he'd announced his plans to retire, Missy had assumed Sebastian and Max would at last have the chance to run things their way. Then the surprise announcement—Brandon had convinced Nathan to return to Houston and join the family business.

Although everyone at the company knew Nathan was a half brother to Max and Sebastian, Missy suspected she was the only one outside the family who knew that Nathan was a love child produced by Brandon's long-time mistress who died when Nathan was twelve.

Because Missy had gotten to know Sebastian's mother fairly well, Susan had discussed those early days when her husband first insisted that Nathan move in with them. Missy wasn't sure she could have put aside her hurt and anger at a husband's betrayal the way Susan had. In fact, she'd treated Nathan no differently than if he'd been her own son.

Nor had her biological sons made things any easier. Susan had described a house in turmoil. Sebastian and Max were old enough to understand how deeply their father had hurt their mother and resented the appearance of a half brother that didn't belong. Bitterness led to bad behavior. It was no surprise when Nathan took off after college. And from what Missy had gathered, he might have stayed away if Brandon's heart problems hadn't grown serious. Too bad having Nathan work for Case Consolidated Holdings was just the first of many times Brandon had interfered since his retirement.

"My father's planning on attending the summit," Sebastian continued.

"Are you going to be okay?" She put her hand on his arm, sympathy spilling into her voice.

"Fine." His terse reply was typical of how Sebastian coped with any emotion having to do with his father. Shut it down and pretend nothing's wrong.

She offered up an inaudible sigh to St. Monica, the patron saint her mother often prayed to for patience. "This is your summit, Sebastian. He won't interfere."

"He's here, isn't he?" His gaze shifted from her to his mother. "He's already interfering."

"Maybe he won't."

"Stop being so damned positive."

Rarely, in all the years that they'd worked together had she dared physical contact. Sebastian wasn't the sort of person who invited anyone to enter his space.

But last night, a shift had happened. A connection, however tenuous, had formed between them. Before she considered her actions, she dropped her hand from his arm to his thigh. His focus swung toward her. A quick squeeze and she had his complete attention.

"Missy." Her name sighed out of him, a weary, reluctant sound that spoke of weakening resistance.

Delight found its way around her guards and set up camp inside her heart. If she was smart, she'd shut it down. No good would come of flirting with Sebastian. This thing between them had nowhere to go. She should be content with their one night together. But her willpower was a fickle thing where he was concerned.

"Yes, Sebastian?"

"I can't focus with your hand on my thigh."

"Seems to me you're focusing just fine." The long muscle beneath her fingers tensed.

He trapped her hand beneath his. His touch heated her as hot as the Nevada desert in July and baked her mouth dry. The crowd gathered around the pool vanished as she lost herself in the pull of his charismatic allure.

"What I mean is I can't focus on the problems at hand."

"I thought I was your problem at hand." She tried a smile.

His shoulders relaxed. "Only one of them."

"Stop worrying so much," she coaxed. "Enjoy the moment."

"That's not the way I work and you know it."

"Maybe you should try something different and see how it goes."

"I'd love for it to be that easy, but it's not." He carried her hand back to her side and patted it. "I'm not going to take advantage of the situation."

No, he was too damned honorable to take advantage no matter how much she pleaded for him to do so. Why had she picked such an upright guy to get worked up about? Because his principles contributed to his appeal. She'd be proud to bring Sebastian home to meet her father. He would see the same admirable qualities she did and approve.

Too bad Sebastian was out of her league.

"Your mother spotted us," she said, waving back at Susan. Sebastian nodded. "Grab your drink. Let's go."

The air cooled dramatically without Sebastian's warmth beside her. She trailed after him, her untouched orange juice clutched in her hand.

"Hello, darling." Dressed in a black one-piece that showed off her athletic figure, Susan Case offered her cheek for Sebastian's kiss. "Never expected to see you by the pool. Of course, you're not really dressed for it, now, are you?"

"Not exactly."

The easy affection between mother and son made Missy smile. Sebastian treated his mother with relentless charm. He was at his most unguarded around Susan. The first time Missy had ever seen them together had been the moment her hopeless crush on Sebastian had begun. Her brothers had been that way with their mother, reverent and affectionate. The same behavior spilled over into how they treated their wives.

She knew Sebastian would treat his wife with similar adoration if he ever married again. The thought hammered her confidence flat. No use wishing she could be the woman who captured Sebastian's heart. He would probably choose someone like his mother. Sophisticated, elegant, gracious, and well connected. A nobody like her wouldn't have a chance in hell of surviving in his circles.

"Sebastian, it was good of you to let Missy have some time off for a little fun. You work her too hard."

"I didn't give her time off," Sebastian growled. "She took it."

Susan's brows rose. "Well, then good for her. You should follow her example. I'm getting tense just looking at you."

No one but his mother could speak to Sebastian like that and get away with it. Missy bit the inside of her cheeks to contain a grin.

"Then perhaps I should return to work and leave you two to enjoy the sunshine."

"You're letting me stay?" Missy asked.

He shot his mother a severe look. "It seems I don't have much choice."

Susan watched the exchange with interest. When her son was out of earshot, she turned to Missy. "I thought he'd never go. Let's order some cocktails. Then perhaps you'll tell me what's going on between you two."

Sebastian had just finished up a conference call with Max and their financially troubled overseas supplier when his mother sauntered into the suite. She'd come straight from the pool and smelled of sunshine and chlorine. She loved the water and kept in shape by swimming two miles each day.

"Can you break long enough to take your mother to lunch?"

Sebastian checked behind her, half expecting to see Missy using his mother as a protective shield. "Just you?"

Sebastian cursed as speculation lit up his mother's eyes. Sometimes her romantic nature went on overdrive. That was fine for Nathan, who was happily married. Or Max, who'd vowed loudly and often that he had no intention of ever tying the knot. But Sebastian had no issues with finding the right woman and settling down to raise a few kids. He just didn't want his mother pushing available females at him while he searched.

"Just me." His mother offered him an off-center grin. "I had a few things I wanted to discuss with you."

Sebastian raised his eyebrows. "Such as?"

"Missy told me what happened last night."

Annoyance tightened his gut into stone, but Sebastian decided to play dumb and see just how much she'd told his mother. "She told you she quit?"

"She told me she had too much to drink while celebrating her birthday and threw herself at you but that you were too professional to take advantage of her." Susan's eyes narrowed. "That's a lot of bull, isn't it?"

"I'm not going to discuss it."

"Is that why she's quitting?"

"No."

"Sebastian, I don't know what to say." And yet she continued talking. "This isn't like you."

On that they both agreed. "I'm still not discussing this with you."

His mother kept going as if he'd never spoken. "She has a boyfriend. Did you think for one minute how much trouble this will create between them?"

"They broke up."

"So, she was on the rebound." His mother tried for stern, but something sparkled in her eyes. "Oh, Sebastian. How could you take advantage of her in such a vulnerable state?"

He could clear his name by revealing that Missy had been the one to proposition him, but he refused to defend himself at the risk of her reputation.

Before he could answer, his mother changed her line of questioning. "What are you going to do about Kaitlyn?"

There was nothing to do about Kaitlyn. His mother had it in her head that he was involved with her. That couldn't be further from the truth. They were casually involved, emphasis on casual.

Sure, marriage to Kaitlyn made sense in a lot of ways. They attended the same charity galas and came from similar backgrounds. She would fit seamlessly into his life. But most important, he needed someone that soothed his spirit, not aggravated it. And Kaitlyn possessed a tranquil quality, rare among women. She'd make an ideal wife.

That made him question why, when he pictured a woman living in his home and sharing his bed, he imagined her with red hair.

"Kaitlyn and I are friends, Mother. Nothing more." Tired of being on the defensive, Sebastian changed topics. "Why are you and Dad here?"

His mother held his gaze for a long moment before answering. "He regrets retiring and wants to return to work."

Annoyance kicked Sebastian in the temple. A sharp pulse began in his head. "As CEO?"

"He said no. He claims he wants to return part time so he has something to occupy him besides golf."

And once he came back to the company, Brandon would undermine Sebastian at every turn until he got fed up and stepped down. Bile rose in his throat. He should have known his father would pull something like this.

"You need to talk him out of it." His mother put her hand on his arm. Her blue eyes widened with concern. "I almost lost him a year ago. He promised me we'd travel and make up for all the years he wasn't around."

Brandon's twelve-year affair with Nathan's mother had taken a severe toll on his wife. Sebastian had often wondered what bargain his parents had made that had kept them together and had convinced his mother to raise her husband's illegitimate son.

"As much as it benefits both of us for Dad to stay far away from Case Consolidated Holdings," Sebastian said, "I'm not sure how I'm supposed to stop him from returning to work."

"Talk to him. Make him understand that you're doing a wonderful job running the company."

His mother's optimism made Sebastian shake his head. Her husband rarely thought about anyone's needs besides his own unless forced to do so.

"He showed up for the leadership summit, and I'm sure he intends for it to appear as if he's still in charge. He took Lucas Smythe golfing and probably spent the entire round badmouthing my leadership abilities. You don't seriously believe anything I say will sway him, do you?"

Sebastian refused to battle his father this week in front of all the executives.

"Do what you can."

With those words, his mother left to shower and change for their lunch. Sebastian was staring at the Vegas strip when Missy emerged from her room.

Her expression shifted from cheerful to uncertain when she spotted his frown. "What's wrong?"

"Did you have a fun morning with my mother?"

"As a matter of fact I did." Missy crossed to the table he'd been working at all morning. "Are you mad because I had fun or because it was with your mother?"

She set her cell phone down and used her finger to spin it.

Today's outfit of jeans and a snug white T-shirt had about the same effect on his libido as the sexy black dress she'd worn last night. Russet waves, still damp from her shower, rested on her shoulders, turning the cotton fabric transparent.

Sebastian spied the straps from her simple white bra. It frustrated him that everything about her turned him on. How was he supposed to maintain a professional relationship with her when all he could think about was lifting her onto the conference table and checking her for tan lines?

"She's been lecturing me on taking advantage of you," he muttered, stepping near enough to touch her. Keeping his hands to himself tested his control, but he triumphed. "I thought I told you to leave it alone."

"You told me not to say anything to your father or Lucas Smythe."

He barely heard her. She'd interpreted his words literally to defy him. His annoyance with her behavior had yet to run its course.

"Only you didn't set things straight. You spun a story. An outrageous story."

"Not so outrageous," she said, her full lips drawn tight. With her impudent chin cocked at a belligerent angle, she concluded, "I'd just broken up with my boyfriend. It's not so hard to believe I got tipsy celebrating my birthday and hit on you, but you were the perfect gentleman and turned me down."

"And if I turned you down, how exactly did you explain why you were in my suite wearing my shirt?"

"Because I was naked when I climbed into bed with you."

Vivid images of exactly that leapt into his thoughts. Even without his eyes closed the evocative memories tormented him.

"I told you not to interfere." He gripped the back of a chair to keep from throttling her.

"If I hadn't, Lucas Smythe wouldn't know that you'd never take advantage of any employee, drunk or sober." For good measure, she added, "Your mother promised to help me straighten out the misunderstanding."

"There was no misunderstanding." Sebastian knew Lucas Smythe would never believe such a ridiculous story. Who in their right mind could resist a naked Missy? "But now it looks like I'm making excuses for my behavior."

His sharp tone eviscerated her composure. She set her hands on her hips. Her brow puckered. "Can't you trust me to handle this?"

"No."

"This is just typical of you."

She'd never had the nerve to criticize him before. Apparently an abundance of sexy curves wasn't the only thing his assistant had been keeping from him.

"What do you mean?"

"If you're not the one in control of a situation, you don't think it's being handled correctly."

Her accusation fell on deaf ears. If she'd hoped to stir his temper, she'd taken the wrong tack. He'd heard it all before. Being the one in control had led Case Consolidated Holdings to higher profitability and kept his personal life calm and peaceful. He wasn't going to surrender the power without a down and dirty fight.

"That's what makes me successful."

"In business maybe."

He smirked at her. "What else is there?"

"There's your personal life," she retorted, her color high. "Maybe if you didn't have to be in charge all the time, something wonderful might happen."

"Are you referring to last night when I let you set the terms for that ridiculous bet?"

Head held high, she blew out air with a disparaging noise, but her hunched shoulders told a different story. "I'll bet the only reason you agreed to the wager in the first place is because you thought I'd lose."

"Haven't you learned that bets between us don't work out?"

"Maybe not for you," she said, her voice losing much of its vigor. "But I don't regret what happened between us."

"I can't say the same."

"So, if you had to do it all over again?" She spoke slowly as if the weight of the words made the question hard to ask.

"I'd have left you home." Why deny it? If she hadn't come, he never would have been sucked into her rebellion. Never would have made love to her. And he certainly wouldn't feel like a poker player down to his last dollar.

"I'm sorry you feel that way," she said, her brisk tone almost masking the throb in her voice. "For what it's worth, I'm glad I came. I'm glad we spent the night together. It made me realize that Tim was right. I have been preoccupied with you ever since we started working together. Without these past two days I would be questioning my decision to quit. Now, I'm confident I made the right decision."

"You didn't. We're a good team." Sebastian barely recognized himself reflected in her eyes. She was right about him needing to control everything. He liked his life neat and without distractions. Until yesterday, she'd understood. "I'm not giving up on persuading you to stay."

She looked surprised. "We've done nothing but fight."

"We're not fighting. We're on opposite sides of an issue we both feel strongly about."

"How is that not fighting?"

He lowered his voice. "I don't want to fight with you." No indeed. He wanted her in his arms, surrendering to his kisses. The realization infuriated him. He shoved his hands in his pockets to stop himself from reaching for her.

Her body lost its stiffness. "I don't want to fight with you, either."

"How can we come to an understanding?"

"You could let me get on with my career and give me a glowing recommendation."

"Or?" he prompted.

"There is no or." Her lips formed the saddest smile he'd ever seen. "I think we both know there's no going back from what happened."

While Sebastian grappled for words to change her mind, Missy exited the suite, successfully ending the conversation with the last word.

The cell phone she'd left on the table buzzed. Sebastian pulled the phone toward him and checked the display. Instead of it being someone from the office or a member of the hotel staff about the arrangements, the incoming number belonged to someone named Tim. The boyfriend. Wasn't he out of the picture?

The call went to voice mail. Sebastian didn't hesitate before hitting speed dial to listen to the message.

"Hey, babe."

Babe?

Sebastian couldn't picture anyone calling Missy by that pet name.

"I just realized I missed your birthday. I know you must be pretty pissed at me, but I want you to know that I still care about you."

That wasn't the speech of a man who was done with his ex-girlfriend but one who was covering his bases in case things didn't work out with the new squeeze. Sebastian deleted the message. An ex-boyfriend unable to make a clean break was only going to distract her. He needed her focused on the leadership summit this week—and on him.

Five

At seven, Sebastian surveyed the transformed suite. Two fully stocked bars awaited guests. Wait staff flanked tables loaded with mouthwatering finger food. The atmosphere was relaxed and elegant.

Missy had come through again. He'd never really doubted that she would.

Even if the scent of her perfume hadn't reached his nose, the way his nerves began to buzz told him she was close by. Sweetness and sin. An intoxicating blend that made him crazy.

"Everything is exactly as we discussed," she said from behind him, her crisp tones reassuring Sebastian that his efficient assistant had returned to the fold.

"Good."

He glanced over his shoulder and saw a goddess. Missy wore a strapless dress with alternating bands of black and white sequins that hugged all her curves and emphasized the fiery brilliance of her hair. She'd pinned it up. The sleek updo emphasized her long, elegant neck and the delicate hollows below her collarbones.

Cool and composed, she regarded him through eyes more brown than hazel tonight. Hard to believe this tranquil beauty was the same spitfire that propositioned him last night. His senses crowed in appreciation of every luscious inch of her while his thoughts grumbled about unnecessary distractions.

Where had his practical assistant gone? The old Missy had taken his orders without question. She'd never distracted him from working with her intoxicating perfume or her provocative curves.

"Is this what you're planning on wearing tonight?" Frustration with her allure jolted the blunt question out of him.

"Yes." Her curt reply told him she had not appreciated his tone. "Why?"

"It's not exactly appropriate for a business meeting."

Picking a fight with her was simple self-preservation. He needed her as annoyed with him as he was attracted to her. Otherwise, the door that separated his suite from her hotel room wouldn't be much of an obstacle for him later.

"This is a cocktail party." She inclined her head, her tone vibrating with restraint.

"And you're my employee, not my date."

Her eyes widened at his severe tone. "I'm aware of that."

"Are you?"

"Of course." She looked piqued that he'd even ask. "You don't think I got the message loud and clear earlier?"

"What message?"

"That I'm not your type and this attraction between us has nowhere to go."

"What makes you say that?"

She rolled her eyes. "Come on, look at the women you date when you take the time for a social life. They're all sophisticated, beautiful, wealthy, and half-starved to fit into all those gorgeous designer clothes."

Yet not one of them stirred his blood the way Missy did.

"It's okay," she continued. "I'm not in your league. I never

thought I was." When he didn't deny her claim, the corners
of her lips wobbled before achieving a brave smile. "I never
expected anything beyond last night."

And that's exactly how it should be. So, why did his mood
sour at her admission?

"Forgive me if I find that difficult to believe when you
were wandering around here in my shirt and nothing else this
morning. Were you hoping I'd spend the day in bed with you?
Our deal was for one night."

Her eyes widened in dismay, but her clenched fists told Sebastian she wasn't going to be cowed by his bad mood. "And
one night is all you're going to get."

"All *I'm* going to get?" He leaned forward, feeling her
sharp inhalation like a punch to his solar plexus. Her parted
lips drove him mad with longing. He wanted to taste her
again. Cherries and lemons. The memory of her kisses was
carved into his brain. "The bet and the terms were your decision, not mine."

"You went along with it happily enough," she shot back.

Why were they fighting when all he wanted was to haul
her tight against him and claim her mouth? "I didn't think I
was going to lose."

"But you did."

"And I honored my part of the bargain."

Her eyes almost popped out of her head. Her mouth opened
and closed like a fish on land. Her hands formed tight fists at
her sides.

"Well, excuse me for forcing you to have sex with me."

Seeing that she was completely exasperated with him, Sebastian pulled her phone out of his pocket and extended it.
"You left this behind earlier." She took the phone, but he
didn't let go. Fighting with her hadn't eased his suffering. In
fact, he wanted her more than ever. The urge to sweep her into
his bedroom and find out what she was wearing under that

black and white dress was close to driving him mad. "Some-one named Tim called you."

"Tim called?" Obviously that gave her hope that their relationship wasn't over. Her lashes lowered to her cheeks but not fast enough for Sebastian to miss the delight shining in her eyes.

Annoyance growled like a cornered badger. "I suppose he wants you back."

She reined in her emotions until nothing showed in her expression. "I doubt that. He broke up with me because he found his soul mate online." She checked her phone's display. "There's no voice mail. I'll bet he called because he wants his anime collection back."

"Maybe he forgot to wish you a belated birthday."

"Maybe." Missy's gaze sliced to Sebastian. "Did you listen to my messages? You did." She speed dialed and put the phone to her ear. "And deleted one from Tim."

He stared at her impassively.

She shook the cell phone at him. "Why?"

"You deserve better."

"Did it ever occur to you that I can't do better?"

Is that what she thought? From her downturned lips, Sebastian gathered that's exactly what she believed. Foolish girl. She was better than a hundred Tims put together.

"Any man would be proud to call you his girlfriend."

"Any man but you." The slight lilt at the end of her statement made it sound more as if she asked a question.

Sebastian ignored the desire to assure her that he had not excluded himself. To tell her that would create possibilities, and he couldn't do that to her. He needed an executive assistant—not a lover or a girlfriend.

"I'd like you to change," he said.

"And I'd like world peace. Seems neither one of us is going to get what they want tonight." A smile curved her lips, but her eyes resembled granite. "Excuse me. I'd better make sure everything's perfect."

Once again her cheeky attitude left him without a comeback. She slipped past him and headed toward the buffet table. He stared after her, the delectable sway of her hips turning his mouth into a sand trap. He remembered trailing his fingertips from her nape to the small of her back. She'd shivered. Her body's reactions had been exquisite, delicate perfection.

With an impatient snort, Sebastian headed for the bar and ordered a scotch.

An hour later, he stood on the opposite side of the suite's living room from Missy and made small talk with the president of their hydro division and his wife. His assistant hadn't glanced his way once since walking away from their conversation. She'd drifted through the crowd, exchanging pleasantries with everyone, laughing and charming each guest and acting as if Sebastian was no more to her than a piece of furniture.

Her snub battered his pride. He regretted inferring that he'd felt obligated to sleep with her last night, but she had to believe that nothing like that was going to happen again.

A cleared throat brought Sebastian back to his companions. He swiveled his head and found two pairs of curious eyes on him. "I'm sorry. Did you say something?"

Owen Darby shot his wife a wry look. "I was just saying that I didn't recognize Missy when I first saw her. She looks wonderful."

"She did something different with her hair," Sebastian said.

"And she got rid of her glasses," Owen added.

"Her dress is fabulous," Alicia Darby said. "She has terrific taste."

Sebastian's attention slid toward the source of his frustration. "Yes, I suppose she does."

"I hear you're going to be an uncle," Alicia said. "Your mother is excited about the new addition to your family."

Nathan's wife, Emma, was pregnant. Sebastian smiled to cover his wince. His future niece or nephew wasn't related to his mother by blood, but that didn't stop her from being thrilled. Susan Case had been looking forward to grandchildren for a long time. She'd hidden her upset, but Sebastian had seen the shadow in his mom's eyes each time Chandra had enacted her pregnancy dramas when he brought up the topic of divorce.

After two years, he'd ended his marriage almost as much for his mother's sanity as for his own. He couldn't put her through any more disappointment. She longed to be a grandmother. That's why she was so excited about Nathan's child. She would love it the way she'd loved Nathan when he came to live with them.

Sebastian pushed aside old bitterness. Resenting his mother for being a loving, generous person was wrong on so many levels. "She's already setting up a nursery so she can babysit."

Alicia gave a wistful sigh. "Do they know if it's a boy or a girl?"

"Not yet." Talking about the baby was no more comfortable for Sebastian than discussing Missy's makeover. Every time his mother mentioned the things she was planning once the baby came, he calculated how old his own son or daughter would have been if Chandra had actually been pregnant when he married her as she'd claimed. Or if she'd gotten pregnant at any time during their two-year marriage. "I think my mother's hoping for a girl. She complains all the time about how she missed out on the fun girly things by having all boys."

"I know all about that," Alicia said. "I have two boys of my own who love to hunt, fish, golf and do all the same things their father enjoys." She smiled up at her husband to take the sting out of her words. "But they are my pride and joy. I just wish they'd get married and start giving me some granddaughters."

Sebastian's attention wandered in Missy's direction once

more. She'd cornered Lucas Smythe. From the expression on the old man's face, Sebastian guessed Missy was feeding him the same improbable tale she'd told his mother. Why couldn't she just do as he'd asked and leave the matter alone?

He excused himself from the Darbys, but was intercepted by the president of the chemical division. By the time he extricated himself from that conversation, Missy had disappeared. Nor did she return to the party. As the wait staff cleaned up and then left, he half hoped that with the guests gone she'd reappear and they could continue...

What? Fighting? Making love?

Sebastian tugged his tie askew with a growl.

Wearing her favorite pair of pajamas, with her hair scraped back into a ponytail and her black framed glasses perched on her nose, Missy stared at the door connecting to Sebastian's suite and wondered if she could ignore her boss's summons.

"Missy, open the door. I need to speak to you."

With Sebastian, it was always about him. What about what she needed?

She kicked her legs free of the covers and stalked across the room. "What about?" She called through the door. He'd been a jerk all evening and she wasn't exactly dressed to receive visitors.

"You left the party early. Are you all right?"

The steel in her spine bowed a little. "I'm fine. Just tired." She rested her cheek against the door. "I didn't get a lot of sleep last night."

She didn't mean to make the remark flirtatious, yet a cascade of sparks trickled along her nerves.

"Please open the door." Less demanding, more like a request.

"I'm not sure that's a good idea."

"Why not?"

"Because I'm in my pajamas."

The silence on the other side of the door lasted so long Missy wondered if he'd left. Disappointment stormed her defenses. How was she supposed to act as if the night before meant nothing to her when she hung on his every word and look?

"Show me."

At first she thought she'd misheard him. "What?"

"Show me."

What was his game? "You don't believe I'm dressed for bed?"

"I believe you. I'm just curious what you wear."

She was hot and bothered before he uttered his last syllable. Damn him. She hadn't done any flirting since high school. Her relationship with Tim had been straightforward and uneventful. He'd never given her heart palpitations or made her wet with a single glance.

Missy unbolted and threw open the door. "Here I am."

Sebastian slouched, his shoulder against the wall. With his tie pulled off center and his dark hair falling forward to obscure his eyes, he looked as tired as she felt. Her caretaker gene kicked in. He had a full week ahead of him and should be in bed instead of standing outside her door. But she quashed the urge to tell him to go get some sleep. She was not his girlfriend or his mother.

"Somehow I knew you'd be wearing red." His weary tone was at odds with the simmer in his gray eyes as he trailed his gaze from her chin to her toes. "Are those palm trees?"

"And surf boards. My brother brought them back from Hawaii."

Despite the conservative nature of her sleepwear, Missy felt edgy and vulnerable. She had no doubts that if he touched her she was a goner. But why would he? Sebastian had emphasized that he was done with her. So, why was he standing at her door so late?

"Is there something else?" she prompted, eager for him to

leave. Her muscles shivered with restrained impulses. The longer he stayed, the harder to resist the urge to grab his tie and haul him to her bed. "Because I'm really, really tired."

Earlier, he'd been right when he'd accused her of wanting to spend the day with him. Four years of suppressed longing hadn't been assuaged by a mere ten hours of lovemaking. In fact, the night with Sebastian had fueled her appetite for more.

"Missy—"

She cut him off. "Don't you dare." Something about the way he said her name spurred her to action. The urge to hit him came out of nowhere. Her fist connected with his chest.

"What the hell was that for?" His eyes flared to life, but he looked more surprised than angry.

"I don't know."

She'd sensed whatever he'd been about to say would persuade her to get naked. That couldn't happen. One night with him was about fulfilling dozens upon dozens of erotic fantasies. A week would mean she'd fallen prey to the same unrealistic pipe dream that had gotten her heart broken in high school.

She didn't fit into Sebastian's world any more than she'd fit into Chip's. Repeating the pattern would be idiotic. She liked to think she'd gotten wiser since age sixteen. This morning with Sebastian, she'd discovered how close she'd come to making the same mistake all over again.

He fingered the spot where she'd struck him. "I was going to compliment you on how well the cocktail party went. I couldn't have pulled this week off without you."

Confusion reigned. Is that really what he'd intended to say? If so, she'd just made a fool of herself again. If not...

No. She couldn't think about the alternative. Sebastian had made his need for her clear. She was his assistant. That's the only role he wanted her to play.

"Thank you."

"What will it take for you to stay on? More money? A company car? An extra week of vacation? I'll give you anything you want."

She wanted him to make her feel like a desirable woman, not a valuable commodity because she was organized and detail oriented.

"Anything?" It intrigued her to see the uncompromising Sebastian offer her a blank check.

"Anything." His low voice slid over her skin like warm silk. She recalled its effect on her the night before. He'd coaxed her to do things that even now roused goose bumps.

She kept her tone level so he wouldn't see how he disturbed her. "Good thing Nathan's in charge of acquisitions because you suck at negotiating."

"Not usually, but something about you brings out the worst in me."

"I never used to," she complained softly.

"You also never used to come to work dressed like you were tonight, either." Hard as iron, his eyes held hers. "What is it going to take to keep you on as my assistant?"

She pondered the long hours at her desk and the price she'd paid in her personal life. She'd made the decision to quit before she'd slept with Sebastian. Nothing had changed. In fact, moving on was more essential than ever.

"It's no use. You might promise me the same thing won't happen again, but I know it will. You just can't help yourself."

His eyebrows arched. "You think I can't keep my hands off you?"

At his misunderstanding, her body flushed asphalt-in-August hot. "I'm not talking about sex, I'm talking about your promise not to bother me evenings and weekends. You'd start regressing. I want to work for someone who understands that an employee's off-hours are sacred." She tossed her head. "In fact, someone already made me an offer. Someone who knows the value of a personal life."

"Who?"

"Nothing's finalized yet. But when it is, you'll be the first to know."

Donning a plum-colored dress, Missy slipped out of her hotel room at six-thirty to make sure she missed Sebastian. After yesterday, she needed a cup or two of coffee before she faced him.

Missy reached the ballroom where most of the summit meetings would take place. After checking on the food arrangements and making sure all the audiovisual equipment was working, she assured herself that Sebastian's opening speech awaited him at the podium. Everything had to be perfect.

"I see my son has you burning the candle at both ends." Brandon stood at the back of the room, dressed for a round of golf rather than a business meeting. "Have you given any more thought to my suggestion that you take over for Dean as director of communications? Max liked the idea and wants to discuss it with you after the summit."

"I'm not sure I have the experience required," Missy hedged, wondering if she should even be discussing a job change without talking to Sebastian first. The opportunity tempted her, but she'd be happier about it if the idea had come from Sebastian.

Working for a family business, regardless of size, offered challenges. As Sebastian's executive assistant, Missy had often found herself trapped in the middle of a power play between her boss and the head of the company. Since Brandon had stepped down as CEO, her job had grown less complicated politically, but he still owned a large share of the company and of late had begun to insinuate himself back into the business with frequent visits to the office and happily offered opinions.

He'd escalated his interference by taking Lucas Smythe

golfing yesterday. Not that Missy believed he'd come right out and tell Smythe not to sell his company to Case Consolidated Holdings. But involving himself by talking with Max about the communications director position was a pretty overt act. Was Sebastian right? Did his father want to be in charge once more?

Brandon dismissed her concerns with a wave. "Don't sell yourself short. I've watched you these past four years. Your talents are wasted on my son."

"I'm not sure Sebastian would agree." But the truth was she had no idea if her boss appreciated her or just took her for granted.

"You let Max and me worry about Sebastian." Brandon held the door so she could exit the ballroom. "You'd make an outstanding director of communications."

Missy was flattered that someone had recognized her skills. She'd graduated two years ago with a degree in business and a minor in journalism. Her background made the position a dream job.

Too bad Sebastian liked her right where she was.

"I appreciate your faith in me," she said as they strolled down the hallway that led to the hotel's atrium and casino.

"You should have been promoted years ago. I know you'll do a great job."

And she would. Much better than the guy who'd held the position for the past three years. But staying at Case Consolidated Holdings meant seeing Sebastian all the time. How was she supposed to get over her feelings for him and move on in her personal life with daily reminders of how amazing they'd been together?

Missy lifted her hand to hide a yawn. Sleep had eluded her for a long time last night. Sebastian's visit had left her keyed up and wide awake. Damn the man for being so aggravating and attractive. Her seesawing emotions were a source of utter frustration.

"Are you playing golf again this morning?"

"No. I thought I'd stick around and listen to Sebastian give the opening speech."

Wincing in sympathy for her boss, Missy forced a bright smile. "It's a good one. You'll be impressed."

"I'm sure it's wonderful. Did you help him write it?"

"I offered a couple suggestions." In fact, she'd created the first draft and Sebastian had revised it to suit his style.

"I'm sure you did." Brandon put his arm around her shoulders and squeezed. "Have fun with the ladies today."

In addition to making sure the conference arrangements were hitch-free, she had the job of playing social director for the executives' wives. Today's schedule called for a sightseeing trip to the Hoover Dam. Then lunch followed by the Haunted Vegas tour.

Brandon winked. "Don't let them get you into too much trouble."

With that cryptic remark ringing in her ears, Missy watched Sebastian's father head toward the casino. She had almost an hour before she was to meet the wives for breakfast. Yesterday she'd won another two thousand dollars. The windfall was burning a hole in her purse. A little gambling would go a long way toward distracting her from what had just happened with Sebastian.

Lucky at cards, unlucky at love.

Missy had become a walking, talking example of that idiom. Fetching a twenty from her wallet, she cruised the slot machines, looking for a likely candidate. The first machine swallowed her money like a party girl guzzling imported champagne. Thirty minutes later, she was down five hundred. Sighing over her change of luck, Missy checked her watch. She had fifteen minutes before she was supposed to meet the wives. Time enough to feed one last crisp twenty into a slot machine.

At the center of the casino, a couple dozen machines

surrounded a bright-blue, convertible Ford Mustang. Picking one at random, Missy fed in her twenty. Four spins later,
she had resigned herself to walking away when five gold coins
lined up in a row and her machine began whooping like a
pack of crazed football fans with their team poised to score
the game-winning touchdown.

"You won a car." Gloria Smythe stood next to her, wearing a big smile.

Missy had met her last night at the cocktail party and liked
her immediately. The vivacious blonde was twenty years
younger than her imposing husband and smiled as much as
he frowned.

"I did?"

"Sure looks that way to me."

And the way the bells were sounding and the lights pulsed
with frantic enthusiasm, Missy was starting to agree. She'd
just won a car. Why wasn't she jumping up and down in delirious excitement?

Because nothing compared to the thrill she'd felt in Sebastian's arms.

Missy shook herself out of her mooning. Pining over a man
she couldn't have was idiotic. "What do I do now?"

"I think that nice young man coming this way will have
you fill out some paperwork."

"I don't have time." Missy spotted a skinny guy with a
shaved head in his twenties heading her way. "I'm supposed
to meet everyone in ten minutes."

"Don't worry about that." Gloria smiled.

"But the tour is scheduled to leave no later than nine, and
I'm supposed to be on the bus to make sure all of you have a
great time."

"Don't you worry about that. Fill out the paperwork and
come find us in the restaurant over there. We're sitting on the
patio."

Missy stared at Gloria's back as she sauntered away. That wasn't where they were supposed to meet. What was going on?

Thirty minutes later, with her paperwork done, Missy wound between the tables of the most expensive of the three restaurants open for breakfast. Bordered on two sides by French doors that offered access to the outside dining, the rattan furnishings, potted palms and soothing green and white color scheme gave the space a comfortable, relaxed feel.

Missy spotted two tables of women on the patio just as Gloria had said. The day promised to be in the upper seventies, but at eight in the morning, the cooler temperature required sweaters and light jackets. Missy shivered in her sleeveless dress.

All conversation ceased as a couple of the women spotted her. Heads turned in her direction.

"We heard you won a car!" Susan Case said. "Congratulations."

"Thanks. Are you ready to go on the Hoover Dam tour?" Missy gazed at each of the women. A few wouldn't meet her eyes. Most grinned at her. Three frowned.

"We've decided to pass," said a woman with teased black hair and enormous sunglasses.

"In fact, we're not going to do any of the tours," Alicia Darby added. "But don't let us stop you from going."

Missy shook her head. "I don't understand. A lot of planning went into your itinerary."

"And we appreciate it," Gloria said. "But for most of us, our lives are busy and hectic."

Alicia nodded. "The last thing we want to do is go on vacation and have to do a bunch of sightseeing."

Missy imagined Sebastian's annoyance with this turn of events. He'd given her the task of making sure the wives were happy. "What do you want to do instead?"

"Go shopping."

"Spend a day at the spa."

"Lie around the pool."

"Drink."

"Gamble."

The answers came at her like bullets from a machine gun.

Missy didn't blame the women for wanting to relax and have fun. Isn't that what she'd ditched work to do yesterday? "Can I make arrangements for spa treatments or arrange transportation for shopping?"

Susan shook her head. "We're all set. Why don't you join us?"

The offer tempted her, but this morning she'd reminded herself that she wasn't on vacation. She really needed to stop acting like it. "I'm supposed to be working."

"You're supposed to be in charge of keeping us entertained," Gloria countered. "No reason you can't have a little fun at the same time."

True. Sebastian was already going to be unhappy when he found out they'd skipped the tours. So what did Missy have to lose?

She grinned. "Sure. That sounds like a lot of fun. But are you up for a little adventure?"

Several of the wives eyed her with interest.

Sebastian's mother, apparent spokeswoman for the group, spoke up. "We might be. What'd you have in mind?"

Six

When Sebastian returned to the suite at the end of that day's leadership summit, he poured himself a large scotch and stood at the window staring out at the Las Vegas strip. At five in the afternoon, the view lacked glitter.

His opening speech had gone well, despite the distraction of his father texting in the front row through the entire thing. But by the time Sebastian had finished speaking, he'd felt exactly like someone who'd barely snatched three hours of sleep two nights in a row.

During lunch he'd made the rounds and caught up to the executives he'd missed at the cocktail party the night before. Everyone commented on how well the summit was organized. Setting the schedule had been Missy's doing. Had he given her the credit she deserved?

Or had he simply taken for granted her superior organizational skills, her ability to anticipate his needs, her nonstop encouragement? She managed his calendar, kept track of mundane details and acted as his first line of defense so he could focus on the big picture. He'd given her access to every aspect of the business and control over some major aspects of his private life, like the decisions on the home he'd built. In doing so, he'd demonstrated his faith in her. But he wasn't sure he'd ever voiced his appreciation.

No wonder she'd quit.

"Sebastian?"

Missy's soft voice crossed twenty feet of hotel suite and tugged him back to the present. He glanced in her direction.

She'd poked her head through a narrow opening in the door that connected their rooms. A white towel was wrapped turban-like around her head. Did that mean she was fresh from a shower and that on the other side of the door she wore little more than a towel? Last time she'd appeared dressed like that, his lust for her had been fully sated. After thirty-six hours of celibacy, he wasn't convinced she'd be safe from him this time.

Grim and not the least amused by how fast his body tightened in reaction to his speculation, he swallowed the last of the scotch. It seared a path down his throat and straight into his belly.

"Were you expecting someone else?"

Her eyes widened. "I was hoping for nice-twin Sebastian instead of evil-twin Sebastian. Give me a ring when he shows up, won't you?"

To his surprise and amusement, she shut the door and he heard the decisive click of the lock as it engaged. "Damn her," he muttered, unable to fight a grin. In a matter of seconds she'd transformed his dark mood into something so much better. How did she do that with such minute effort?

He rapped on the closed door. As he waited for her to answer, he considered whether he would kiss her first or rip the towel from her body and then kiss her.

"Who is it?" she called.

"The big bad wolf," he called back.

"The three little pigs aren't in at the moment. Can I take a message?"

"Tell them I'm going to huff and puff and blow their house down unless you open this door."

"No can do. I'm afraid you'll eat me up."

"If you had any idea how true that was, you'd stay locked in there forever," he muttered, resting his forehead on the wood panel separating them.

The long silence that followed left Sebastian wondering if she'd heard him. Heart thumping, he waited, his muscles bunched in anticipation. When he heard the lock turn, he pushed back and waited for her to open the door.

To his intense disappointment, she wore a sophisticated cocktail dress of dark gold that bared her arms, showcased her tiny waist, and emphasized the flare of her hips. The color enticed gold highlights from the cinnamon locks tossed about her creamy shoulders.

"You look beautiful."

"I'm having a hard time reading you," she said. "One second you're my grumpy boss with high moral fiber, the next you're flirting with me. What's going on?"

He tugged her through the doorway and backed her up against the wall.

"You're driving me crazy, that's what."

"I'm driving you crazy?" She gazed up at him, eyes widened by his forceful handling. "How exactly?"

Gentling his touch, he coasted his palm up the generous slope of her hip to the valley of her waist, his caress aided by the silky material she wore. For all its sensual decadence, it couldn't compare to the hot, luxurious texture of her skin.

"You've changed since arriving in Las Vegas, both in looks and attitude," he said.

"And that's a bad thing?"

"It is when you wager five thousand dollars and a night with me on the turn of a roulette wheel."

"You could have said no."

"I'm not the sort who backs down from a challenge." He

grazed her collarbone with his fingers. "But you know that, don't you? In fact, you'd probably counted on it."

"Are you accusing me of something?"

He followed her neckline to the start of her cleavage. There, he picked up the gold locket he'd seen her wear many times. The piece of jewelry had never fascinated him when it had rested against fabric. Against her skin…that was another thing entirely.

"You played me."

"Hardly."

"You knew the instant I walked into the bar that I wanted you and you took advantage."

"Wait. Are you trying to tell me that I took advantage of you?" Her husky laugh made him mad with wanting. "Is that even possible?"

"It's possible."

Comprehension dawned in her eyes. "You want me."

He reached between them and cupped her breast, kneading the round contours. "I think we've established that." He eased his hips forward, letting her feel how much.

Her lashes fluttered and her breath hitched. He knew what would happen if he kissed her. They'd never make it to dinner, and he had two-dozen people converging on the restaurant at that very moment. This was his leadership summit. He was supposed to be playing host.

"And in your mind that's bad because what keeps your world all nice and tidy is me, working as your assistant." Her voice gained strength as she ferreted out all his secrets. "But you think I'm sexy."

"Missy."

She ignored his warning growl. "And you want to make love to me again."

"We have dinner reservations."

"The fact that you won't let yourself must be what's driving you crazy." She fanned her hands across his abdomen, nails digging into his muscles. "I'm not driving you crazy. You're driving yourself crazy." Raising on tiptoe, she breathed in his ear. "Let yourself go, Sebastian."

Yesterday at the pool she'd made it clear she wanted him. He sure as hell wanted her. Telling himself he was keeping his distance to restore their relationship to a professional level had kept him from acting on his desire for her. But she'd hinted last night that she was close to accepting a job offer.

Once she was gone out of his life, how long before he would no longer be tortured by the longing to skim her curves and spend hours drifting kisses over her skin?

"I can't." He pulled her hands away and pinned them to the wall. "People are waiting for us."

"Typical."

"What does that mean?"

"You always do the right thing. The thing everyone expects."

"What's wrong with that?"

"It gets old pretty quick. I offered you a free pass for one night of uninhibited sex—sex without expectations of anything more—and it's as if the whole thing made your world a bad place to be. You need to loosen up and learn to have fun or you're going to miss out on all the wonderful things life has to offer." She drew a deep breath and kept going. "Everybody at Case Consolidated Holdings lives in terror of not being completely perfect. Have you ever wondered why we've had so much staff turnover in the last year? It's because working for you makes people crack up."

Had she just called him a tyrant? "You've survived for four years. It can't be that bad."

"Survived?" She stared down her nose at him, a monumental feat, considering he towered over her by at least eight inches. "Do you think surviving a job is something I should be grateful for?"

Perhaps not. "What do you suggest I do?"

"Well, for starters, you could lighten up. Have some fun. Stop trying to manage every single thing around you."

"I don't manage *everything.*"

"You've scheduled the summit down to the minute."

"We have a lot to get through."

"Not at night, you don't."

"Part of what makes this summit work is that all the executives spend time together."

Missy rolled her eyes. "Right, but they're together all day."

Sebastian had worked with Missy long enough to know when she had a point to make. "What do you have in mind?"

"Cancel the group dinners and let everyone go their own way."

"It's too late for tonight's dinner."

"True." She nodded, her eyes shining. "But it would be a simple thing to cancel the rest of them. I know you'd make the wives very happy if you gave them more time alone with their husbands. With the amount of traveling you have got everyone doing, your executives don't get to see much of their wives or their families." Her gaze lifted no higher than his chin. "And about the tours…"

Raw impatience burned in his gut. "What about the tours?"

"No one wanted to go to the Hoover Dam."

"You didn't go?" Sebastian couldn't believe what he was hearing. This summit was coming apart. Not one thing had gone according to plan since he and Missy had stepped off the plane. "Dare I ask what you did instead?"

"We hit a couple casinos then I suggested they might like to try skydiving."

"Skydiving?"

"Oh, don't worry. It was indoor skydiving," she said in a breezy tone. "I wasn't out to get anyone killed. They found it fun rather than terrifying."

"Fun," Sebastian muttered. "Your idea?"

She looked surprised that he'd even asked. "Of course."

"Is there anything else I need to know?"

"Like what?"

"Oh, I don't know. Did you rearrange tomorrow's summit schedule without telling me?"

"Now that you mention it—" She broke off when he growled. Her laughter filled the suite and took the sting out of everything he'd just heard. "I'm kidding. I wouldn't dream of messing with your precious summit."

"Because, I'm assuming, you've already promised my agreement on the change of plans," he said. "Fine, I'll go along with it."

"That was too easy." For the first time she sounded concerned. "What did I miss?"

"The fact that from now until the end of the summit, you have seen to it that my nights are free."

"And?"

"So are yours."

"She almost started to cry today while we were shopping." Alicia Darby's voice lifted over the laughter bouncing off the glass walls separating their private dining room from the rest of the Eiffel Tower Restaurant.

"How can you call what you do shopping?" Missy protested.

"So, we found a nice quiet bar." Susan's eyes were dancing with mirth.

"We're calling her the one-drink wonder," Alicia said. "She's a lightweight."

Maggie Hambly jumped in. "No stamina."

"You have no idea how hard it is to keep these ladies happy," Missy protested, fluttering her hand in the direction of the wives.

"Oh, we know." Owen Darby looked to the other husbands. They were all nodding.

Missy sat back with a defeated sigh as the waiter cleared

her plate. Dinner had been a boisterous affair, driven by the wives' enthusiasm over the day's activities. She'd joined in when prompted, but for the most part she'd eaten in silence, her nerves on high alert.

Driven by a compulsion too strong to resist, her gaze sped down the table toward her boss. The sparks in his eyes reminded her of muzzle fire. He'd watched her all night, his intense scrutiny disturbing her equilibrium as effectively as if his hands were gliding along her skin.

Missy dropped her gaze to the elegant dessert the waiter placed before her. The dish was beautiful, but her stomach could no more handle the rich chocolate soufflé than the delicious sea bass in champagne brown butter broth she'd ordered.

Had he meant what she hoped when he'd pointed out that she'd freed up his nights and hers also? He'd gone all mysterious when she'd asked him to explain. She wasn't sure where they stood anymore.

Did he mean to spend the nights with her? In what capacity? As boss and employee? As lovers?

Anticipation shivered through her.

For two days she'd been longing to be in his arms again. Teasing Sebastian had been like playing with fire, but she wasn't worried about getting burned. Her boss had made it clear that while he might find her attractive, he intended to keep their relationship professional. Had that changed?

She had no idea how long she'd been lost in thought when the couples around her began to get up from the table. A warm hand grazed her shoulder. From the way her nerve endings perked up, she knew Sebastian stood behind her.

The room was clearing fast. Everyone was excited about the Cirque du Soleil show they were attending. Before she knew it, only she, Sebastian and his parents remained.

"Dad, you and Mom use our tickets for the show tonight."

Our tickets? Missy tipped her head back and stared at him in confusion. What did he mean?

"Are you sure?" his mother asked, her gaze bouncing from Sebastian to Missy.

"Absolutely." Sebastian slid his thumb along her nape. "I have some unfinished business I need to attend to."

Missy's stomach dipped and rolled at the subtext beneath his statement. Did his unfinished business involve her?

"Come, Missy. Let's get back to that matter we were discussing earlier."

Heat bloomed in her cheeks as she pushed back from the table. What had she gotten herself into? Did he really intend to work or was his mind occupied with the same carnal thoughts that had plagued her throughout dinner?

"What matter?" she muttered as they followed his parents out of the restaurant.

"The matter of your free time."

Well, that didn't tell her a darned thing. Dazed by the knowing glint in his eye, she gnawed her lower lip and joined his parents in the elevator.

While Susan exclaimed over the show they were about to see, Missy cast surreptitious glances at Sebastian's profile. The third time she looked his way, his eyes snagged hers. One dark eyebrow twitched, telling her he knew his ambiguous response was driving her crazy.

Missy shifted her attention to the wall beside him until the elevator doors opened. The heat of his hand on the small of her back further knotted her emotions and her pulse skittered like a nervous mouse as they bid the group of executives and wives goodbye and settled into a taxi for the ride back to the hotel.

She stared out the window at the millions of lights that set the strip ablaze and wondered what was going through his mind.

As the cab drew up to the hotel, she summoned the nerve to find out. "Do you really intend to work?"

The shadows inside the cab masked his expression. "No."

"Then what are we going to do?"

The taxi stopped beneath the hotel's canopy. Sebastian paid the driver and slid out. Missy took the hand he extended and let him pull her from the cab.

"I thought I'd leave that up to you."

She trembled at the husky rumble of his voice. Putting the ball in her court gave her control over what happened in the next few hours. She knew what she wanted. Another night of heaven in Sebastian's arms. Isn't it what she'd been lobbying for? He probably expected her to suggest they run up to the suite and hop into bed.

Not a bad idea, really.

"Why let me decide?"

"You said I'm too hung up on being in control so I'm handing you the power." He let go of her hand and slid his hands into his pockets. His watchful gaze sent shivers up her spine. "So, what's it going to be, Missy?"

Sebastian tensed as he awaited her answer. Around them, bellhops and hotel guests faded from his awareness. His entire being was focused on Missy and the parade of emotions across her beautiful face.

Eyelashes casting shadows on her cheeks, she nibbled on her lower lip while a smile played with the corners of her mouth. Thousands of lights blazed above them, highlighting the bright spots of color in her cheeks. Her body language spoke of indecision. Now that he'd taken a step down that path, she was hesitating?

"Feel like taking my new car for a spin?"

From her tiny clutch she'd produced a set of keys. Sebastian stared at them without comprehension. While he'd been pondering the joys of taking her naked body for a spin, she'd had another sort of ride in mind.

"What new car?"

"The one I won earlier today."

Humor dimmed the roar of his libido. "You won a car?" He shook his head. "Of course, you did. It seems you've come to Vegas to break the bank."

"Where else can a girl get lucky?" she quizzed, peering at him from beneath her lashes.

Sebastian let the double entendre pass by without comment. "Lead the way."

Half an hour later, they'd cleared the lights of Las Vegas and headed north and west into the mountains. Missy drove. She'd been surprised that he'd insisted she get behind the wheel and seeing his broad grin, she was pleased he had.

She'd hiked the hem of her snug dress to mid thigh. Given that she'd bared more at the pool yesterday, he shouldn't be enjoying the view as much as he was. A couple of hair clips, scrounged from her purse, kept her fiery locks from whipping in the wind, but a few tendrils had escaped her top knot and blew about her cheeks.

"You're looking pretty relaxed over there," she remarked.

"Any reason why I shouldn't be?"

"I'm doing a hundred and ten miles an hour."

He was unfazed by the dangerous speed. His only anxiety involved how much of the night this wild ride would eat up. He wanted to get her alone and naked as soon as possible to take advantage of the exhilaration that gripped her.

"Do you want me to slow down?"

"You're in charge tonight, remember? I'm at your mercy."

The wind snatched away the disparaging sound she made, but he had little trouble reading her skepticism in the fading light.

The sky had lost any tinge of red as they'd reached the outskirts of Las Vegas. Stars appeared as cobalt then became navy. Sebastian let his head fall backward and stared at the vast space that surrounded them. Leaving behind the frantic energy of Vegas was like stepping into a rain forest. Peace filled him.

A reduction in the car's vibration told him she'd eased off the accelerator. The world continued to streak by, but he could pick out a few more details in the shadowy landscape.

"Are you sure you don't want to drive?"

"Positive." He turned his head in her direction. "Being your passenger lets me enjoy the view."

Her gaze left the road and darted his direction. "Except you're not looking at the scenery. You're staring at me."

"Exactly."

She returned her attention to the empty two-lane road. "I don't get it." Her lopsided smile told a different story. She liked his attention.

"Don't get what?"

"Why'd you leave your dad in charge of entertaining the executives tonight?"

"Rather odd for a control freak like me, isn't it?"

"Are you planning on throwing that in my face all night?"

"I don't know. Are we going to spend the night together?"

"I hadn't given it much thought." Missy's breathless tone gave her away.

Sebastian grinned. "I have no plans in case you're wondering." He noted the time on the dashboard clock. Nine-thirty. They'd been driving an hour. "We can drive all night if that's what you want."

"But what do you want to do?"

"I'm not the one in charge of tonight's entertainment. You are."

The car slowed still more. "I don't like being in charge."

"Really? I'm enjoying it immensely."

The car stopped. Missy made a U-turn and began to head back to town. Sebastian hid his relief.

"Why?"

"Because role reversal is a good way to broaden your understanding of someone else."

"And that's what we're doing?" she prompted, her tone wry. "Broadening our understanding of each other?"

"You tell me. How does it feel to be in charge of all the decisions?"

"Exhausting. How do you do it all the time?"

He laughed. "It's not so bad once you get used to it. And I don't make all the decisions all the time. Why do you think I gave you my house to decorate?"

"When did you become so enlightened?"

"Around the time you called me a tyrant, I think."

She shook her head. "I never called you a tyrant."

"You told me my demanding ways were responsible for the company's employee turnover. If that's true, I'm not acting like a good leader, am I? And that's what this week is all about—improving leadership skills."

"I forgot to ask you how it went today. Is your father behaving himself?"

Sebastian entertained Missy with stories of his father's preoccupation with his cell phone as they drove back to the hotel.

"I'm surprised," she said as the lights of Las Vegas drew closer. "He seemed very interested in your speech."

"When did you talk to him about that?"

"This morning as I was checking to make sure everything was ready to go."

Sebastian drummed his fingers on the car door. "What else did you talk about?"

She must have heard the tension in his voice because she grimaced. "Nothing about what he saw in your suite yesterday morning, if that's what you're worried about."

"I wasn't," he lied.

Conversation drifted into less complicated topics as she

negotiated the strip and parked the car back at the hotel. He set his hand on the small of her back as he guided her across the concrete to the elevator that would return them to the hotel's lobby. From there they could head into the casino or back to his suite. He wondered which she'd choose.

"Winning the car was fun," Missy said as they stepped off the elevator and were met by the activity of a casino in full swing. "Problem is, I don't know how to get it home."

Sebastian followed her as they headed toward the elevators that serviced the hotel's rooms. Tension leaked out of his body with each step. She was obviously not interested in gambling away the night. But was she up for anything else?

"Max ships cars all the time," he said. "I'll give him a call in the morning and see if he has a carrier he can recommend."

"I never thought about shipping it home. I figured I'd either have to drive it back to Texas or sell it before I left."

The elevator deposited them on their floor. Sebastian kept his hands to himself as they walked down the hall. He didn't trust himself to touch her. Plus, he'd put her in charge of tonight's entertainment. She was in control.

"Why would you sell it?"

"I've never owned anything so impractical before."

"Maybe it's time that changed."

They stopped beside the door to her hotel room. Missy regarded him with open curiosity, waiting to see what he'd do. Sebastian surveyed the pliant curves of her mouth.

"Good night, Missy," he said, squashing his satisfaction at her disappointed expression. Whether they spent the night together was her decision to make. He bent down and brushed his lips across her cheek, lingering to enjoy her tantalizing fragrance. "Sweet dreams."

With her disappointment in Sebastian's chaste kiss thundering through her body, Missy watched him disappear into his hotel suite, leaving her abandoned in the empty hall. Heat blasted her cheeks. Her hands trembled so badly she had trouble fitting the keycard into the slot. She stumbled through the door when it opened, scarcely supported by knees turned to warm jelly. The bed looked like a safe place to rest until the whirling in her head slowed. Instead, she walked to the door that connected her room to Sebastian's.

When she pulled it open, she found him waiting for her. Before she completed her sigh of relief, he'd caught her up in his arms and strode toward the bedroom.

"Hey," she protested. "I thought I was in charge of tonight's activities."

"As soon as I get you naked I'm at your command."

Sebastian dispatched her dress with more urgency than finesse. She wasn't wearing stockings, but he made quick work of her bra and panties.

"Beautiful," he murmured, his lips drifting down her neck. He lowered her to the bed, ignoring his earlier promise to let her be in charge.

Missy didn't care. She tugged his coat off his broad shoulders and somehow worked all his shirt buttons free.

"Help me," she demanded as her fingers fumbled with his belt.

Brushing her hands aside, he rolled off the bed and shed the rest of his clothes. Gloriously naked and aroused, he returned to her.

"Fast or slow?" he queried, his tongue dipping into her navel.

Missy's hips bucked off the mattress as his fingers glided up her thigh. "Yes."

He chuckled. "It can't be both. That was an either-or question."

"Shut up and kiss me."

"That I can do."

And to her delight he did.

Long, slow and deep. Tender and adoring. By the time

Sebastian settled between her thighs, his kisses and caresses had touched every inch of her skin.

"I could get used to this," she sighed as his erection nudged her entrance. She clutched his shoulders as he flexed his hips and drove home.

He framed her face with his hands and smiled. "Get used to what?"

As he began to move, Missy arched her back to take him deeper, the sense of fulfillment touching every cell in her body. She belonged to him. And he to her. They were a match. No wonder she'd lasted longer than any other assistant he'd had. She understood him like no one ever had before.

She could get used to having his arms around her every day. Get used to arguing with him as often as they made love. Get used to being the woman he came home to every day.

"I could get used to telling you what to do."

Seven

A good three feet separated Missy from the floor-to-ceiling windows in Sebastian's suite and the fifteen-story drop to the bright lights of the Vegas strip. The view enthralled her, but the height made her head spin. Seemed like a lot of things made her head spin since she'd come to this glitzy city. The man sleeping in the bed behind her was the leading cause.

"What are you doing?" A large hand cupped her upper arm while his other one brushed aside her hair so he could place a warm, compelling kiss on the spot where her neck and shoulder came together.

She leaned back against his warm muscles and sighed. "Looking at the view. It's beautiful."

"Why so far from the windows?"

"It's silly but I'm a little nervous about heights ever since my brother Matt scared me into thinking he was going to push me from the bell tower of our church."

Those sexy, persuasive lips coasted along her bare shoulder. "Why would he do that?"

"Because he was twelve and thought it was funny."

"How old were you?" His fingertips slipped along the edge

of her bra and ghosted around her nipple. It peaked against the fabric as a bolt of sensation shot to her core.

"Six."

"I remember being mischievous at that age, but I don't recall tormenting little girls half my age."

"You didn't have sisters," she reminded him, losing herself in the sensual fog that filled her mind whenever his hands were on her.

"Why are you wearing this?"

The straps of her bra slipped down her arms as he unhooked it. Missy pressed her hands to her chest, catching the flimsy material to preserve her wits.

"I was heading back to my room."

"But the night is still young."

He coaxed her to give up the bra and palmed her breasts, kneading the tender flesh and rolling her nipples between his fingers until she gasped and closed her eyes. The rest of her senses sprang to life.

Before she knew it, her underwear had pooled at her feet. He raised her arms above her head, arching her back against his torso. He stroked his hands over her breasts, across her stomach and down toward the triangle of hair at the apex of her thighs. She buried her fingers in his hair and parted for him, a moan escaping her lips as he pressed the heel of his hand against her mound.

He found her ultra-sensitive bud and circled it with his index finger. "That's it, let it happen."

Missy shuddered as he fondled her, breathing Sebastian's name as she surrendered to his mastery. Her lips parted as meaningless words of encouragement poured out of her, and she felt herself start to unravel as he slid his finger up inside of her. He dragged kisses down the side of her neck, teeth nipping at the cord of her throat. Her body jerked in response, cueing the explosion that erupted like a series of deep shock waves through her.

Limp as a noodle in the aftermath, she appreciated the support of Sebastian, solid and steady against her back. In that second, she knew she could face her worst fears with his arms around her.

Spinning out of his arms, she caught him by the hand and backed toward the windows.

"What are you doing?" he asked, his free hand cupping her cheek.

"Facing my fear." Her peripheral vision filled with bright lights and empty space. A familiar anxiety tightened like a band around her chest. She shoved the panic down and ran her hand along Sebastian's bicep. The muscles in his chest flexed as her fingers traced his powerful contours. Appreciation purred through her. "Feel like helping me?"

"What did you have in mind?"

"I was hoping you could replace my negative memory of heights with a positive one." She continued to move backward until there was nowhere to go. A gasp escaped her as she realized nothing stood between her and a fifteen-story drop but inch-thick glass.

The arms Sebastian slid around her tensed as if he was ready to pull her to safety at the first sign of trouble.

She concentrated on Sebastian's strength and concern, refusing to be ruled by fear. The sensation of chilly glass against her back and hot male against her breasts and stomach was far more powerful than any phobia.

"Are you sure this is a good idea?"

"It will be if you make the memory sensational."

The lips that grazed hers wore a smile. "I can do that."

She felt the urgent bite of his hands on her hips and butt as he trailed his tongue across her lower lip. She grabbed fistfuls of his hair and pushed up on tiptoe as his mouth seized hers, stealing the air from her lungs before sharing his breath with her.

Urgent, wordless moans erupted from her throat as he

lifted her off her feet. She clutched his shoulders, legs parting wide, and wrapped her thighs around his hips as he settled her onto his engorged shaft. They both growled in appreciation at the snug fit of their bodies.

Sebastian rocked against her powerfully, driving her pleasure higher. Missy held on to him for dear life and wondered at the strength of the passion between them. How could he make her so wild with so little effort?

Astonished to feel another surging orgasm ripping through her, Missy called his name and heard Sebastian groan in masculine appreciation. He drove deep into her, his hips pulsing frantically as he neared his own completion. While wave after wave of sensation rolled through her, Sebastian's fingers bit down hard on her hips as he came.

He sagged against her, pinning her to the window. The drop that had terrified her moments before now filled her with delight. She might not be ready to go bungee jumping or skydiving, but she'd make love with Sebastian in a skyscraper anytime.

He stroked the hair from her face and bussed her cheek. "How was that?"

"Fabulous," she retorted weakly, leaning her head back against the glass. "Thanks to you, I'm now a fan of heights."

"Glad I could help." His voice soft with amusement, he kissed her temple. "Give me a second and I'll put you down."

"Don't hurry on my account. I'm quite comfortable." She tightened her inner muscles around him and he shuddered. If she'd been able to see his expression, Missy knew for certain it would make her grin.

Her heartbeat had almost returned to normal by the time he eased free of her body and set her back on her feet.

"Come back to bed." He towered over her.

"I really have to go," she began. Her proclamation ended in a sharp cry as he hoisted her off her feet and carried her back to bed fireman style.

"Stay a while longer. I'll make it worth your while."

"Worth my while?" Missy rolled onto her stomach, a mild but satisfying ache in every muscle, and buried her face in the mattress. "I don't think I can take much more."

"Oh, you might be surprised," he said, joining her on the bed. "We'll rest a while and then see how you're feeling."

He sounded so pleased with himself she picked up her head to scold. "You are completely insatiable."

"I'm insatiable?" He settled on his back beside her, hands behind his head, and smirked. "Who's been having orgasms at the drop of a hat?"

Kicking her feet in the air, she threaded the sheets between her fingers. "So you're a great lover. Quit bragging."

"I don't think it has anything to do with my skills." He leaned over for a quick kiss. "I think we have great chemistry."

"For another four days," she reminded him. "Then, it's back to Houston and what happened in Vegas…"

"Stays in Vegas." Suddenly serious, he took her hand and kissed her palm. "What if I don't want it to end?"

She froze. Her entire body flushed hot, then cold. Goose bumps broke out on her skin. "It has to."

"Does it? Until two days ago, you've had a knack of keeping me on track and calm."

"And now?"

"You drive me crazy. And I don't care." One side of Sebastian's mouth kicked up. "I'm not ready to lose you."

The predatory glint in his gray eyes warned her some shift in their dynamic had happened.

"I'm not sure I understand what you mean."

"Then let me be clear." A soft light entered his eyes. "One night was not enough. A week is not enough. I want more."

Her heart stopped beating. She'd had no expectations when she'd wagered one night with Sebastian. But a connection had been made. Hearing him reveal that he, too, felt it made her heart sing.

"More?" A second week? A month? "How much more?"

"Do we have to define it?"

Anxious buzzing began in the back of her mind. "I'd like some idea what you have in mind."

"Let's start slow and see where it goes."

Start slow and soon she'd be making plans. She wouldn't mean to. It was just something that happened in her psyche. She'd been saving for two years to buy a wedding dress. She wanted to get married. And deep down, where she knew better than to look, she suspected she wanted to marry Sebastian.

Missy shook her head. This thing between them was about passion. Like her high school boyfriend, Sebastian had just seen something he wanted and taken it when the opportunity arose. And as with her high school boyfriend, eventually their differences would drive them apart.

"Where do you want it to go?" Despite every sensible thought in her head, hope made her heart dance. She squashed the emotion. Sebastian didn't want to date her. This went against everything she'd been telling herself to expect from him.

"I have no expectations," he said. "No need to control the outcome. Let's see where it takes us."

"And my job as your assistant?"

"Can I convince you to stay on?"

"No."

He nodded as if he'd expected that answer. "You've been a part of my life for years. I'm not ready to let you go quite yet."

Sebastian's desire for her might be real, but she knew it wasn't something that would last once they returned home. Unfortunately, she was already half in love with him. Any more time in his arms was going to make it impossible to walk away.

"And when you're done with me? What then?"

"Aren't you being a bit dramatic?" His lips tightened. "I should probably warn you that Chandra overplayed her hand all too often. I don't like it."

He rarely talked about his ex-wife, but from his mother, Missy knew Chandra had been a handful. "I'm not being dramatic—just trying to figure out what's in it for me."

"After tonight, I would think that would be obvious."

If he'd offered her something besides fabulous sex, she'd have melted like butter on a hot skillet. Annoyed by his unromantic pitch, she scowled. "I suppose you think that's the sort of offer I'd jump at."

"What do you want?"

His question startled her. Sebastian had fulfilled all her fantasies and introduced a few new ones.

"I don't want anything."

"That's not true. Everyone wants something."

"Not me." Nothing she was willing to admit to him, anyway.

"You have me in the palm of your hand." Turning her hand palm up, he rubbed his thumb along her lifeline until her entire body began to tingle. "This would be a great time to tell me what would make you happy."

She shook her head, her heart in her throat. "You really do suck at negotiating."

"I like to think of myself as direct."

"I don't want anything more than what I have right here and now." To expect anything more would only lead to heartbreak. "The rest of the week together and then we go our separate ways."

"Unacceptable."

Before she could protest, her purse began to ring. Like

Pavlov's dog, she was conditioned to react to a familiar sound, only instead of drooling, she sat up.

"Leave it," Sebastian commanded, tugging her back down.

She squirmed out of his grasp. "It's not you calling so it must be important."

"Very funny." He rolled onto his side and watched her cross the room to the dresser.

The phone had stopped ringing by the time she fished it out of her purse. "Whoever it was, I missed the call."

"Come back to bed."

"Just a second, let me check my messages." Something about the late-night call gnawed at her nerves. No one except Sebastian would call her at such an hour. That meant something was wrong. When her brother's voice sounded in her ear, she knew she was right.

"Missy, when you get this, call me. Dad's been hurt. We're heading to the hospital now." Heart twisting in fear, she ended the message and turned to face Sebastian.

He came off the bed in time to catch her as she swayed. "What's wrong?"

"Sam left me a message. He said my dad's been hurt. They're heading to the hospital."

"Call him back and see what happened."

Her hands shook so badly, it took her three tries before she keyed up her address book and found her brother's cell phone number. Not until the phone started ringing did it occur to her that she could have just found his missed call and hit send. Sebastian wrapped her in a robe and rubbed her arms while she waited for her brother to pick up.

"Missy, it's bad," Sam said.

"What happened?"

"He was stabbed."

"Stabbed?" Her gaze found Sebastian's. She caught concern reflected there. His fingers tightened. "How did that happen?"

"I don't have a lot of details. There'll probably be more once we get to the hospital and talk to the cops."

"Is he going to be okay?"

"He's a tough old bird."

She squeezed her eyes shut and counted to five. "I'm going to catch the first plane out of here."

"Aren't you in Vegas at that thing for your company?"

"Yes, but Sebastian will understand that I have to leave."

He leaned forward and kissed her on the temple. The tender caress brought a lump to her throat. She sank into his strength, letting him absorb some of her trembling.

"I'll keep you informed as we get news."

The hand holding the phone dropped to her side. "My dad's been hurt. I have to go home."

"Let me take care of everything. You go pack."

Numb, she got to her feet and stumbled out of the bedroom. She tossed clothes and toiletries into her suitcase and dressed in jeans and a T-shirt. Zipping her bag, she slid her feet into sandals.

Sebastian entered her room. He wore slacks and a dress shirt. "I have a plane waiting to take us back to Texas."

"Us?" She couldn't be processing his words properly.

"You don't seriously think I'm going to let you go by yourself, do you?" He took charge of her suitcase and wrapped strong fingers around her elbow to escort her into the hall.

"But what about the summit? And your meeting with Smythe tomorrow? You can't disappear at such a crucial time."

"I guess it's good that my dad showed up, isn't it?"

They stepped onto the elevator and Sebastian pushed the button for the lobby. Missy shivered as reaction settled in. Sebastian pulled her into his arms and shared his heat with her.

"You're chilled. Do you have a coat?"

She shook her head. "I tossed everything out. Remember?"

He bought her a sweatshirt at the hotel gift shop and

dressed her in it as if she were a small child. Caught in a
dark place, Missy let him lead her across the lobby and get
them into a cab. Tucked into the crook of his arm, she hud-
dled against his side as she watched the Las Vegas strip slide
by the car window.

They boarded a private plane and were taxiing down the
runway as the sky began to lighten over Las Vegas. As the
city lights fell behind them, Missy began to disengage from
the fantasy of the last few days.

Sleeping with Sebastian a couple times might not be a mistake, but letting herself fall for a man who never intended to
marry her went against her solemn vow to never again let herself reach too high. If she hadn't let her heart lead, she never
would have begun a game she could never hope to survive,
much less win.

Missy put her hands between her thighs, all too conscious
of Sebastian's shoulder a few tempting inches away. It was
more than wonderful of him to worry about her comfort. To
arrange for a plane to take her to Crusade. To sit beside her
the whole way there. This sort of behavior made a girl want
to rely on him. To lose herself in his strong arms and let him
soothe her fears.

And then what?

When they returned to Houston, she wouldn't be his employee or his lover. She wouldn't be anything.

It was better to disengage now. Before she became too dependent on a dream.

His hand covered her forearm, the firm pressure bringing
a lump to her throat. She told herself the sympathetic gesture
was one anyone would make. She'd seen her mother offer support in a similar manner.

Her heart squeezed. What did she expect? That he'd fall
madly in love with her in the space of a few days? She pressed
her lips together and shot a tight smile his way.

"Your father's going to be fine."

"I hope so." Worrying about her love life while her father's life hung in the balance demonstrated what a selfish idiot she was. "Thank you for everything."

"You don't need to thank me."

But she did. He'd left Las Vegas in the middle of his leadership summit to be there for her. He'd gone above and beyond the call of duty. And she wanted to make more of his motives than was wise.

"Sebastian." She struggled with how best to frame what she needed to say next. "I'd prefer it if my family didn't know anything about what happened between us in Las Vegas. I haven't told them that I broke up with Tim yet and…"

"You'd rather not further complicate an already complicated day."

"Yes." Although she was glad he understood, she couldn't help but wonder if he was relieved she wouldn't expect anything more from him.

An hour later, the plane landed at a small airstrip outside her hometown. She'd called Sam from the air and let him know what time they'd be landing. David was waiting as the sky began to lighten in the east. She hugged the youngest of her big brothers, clinging to him without asking how their father was doing, afraid the news had changed for the worse in the past two hours.

"Sebastian, this is my brother David."

The two men shook hands. David assessed Sebastian through narrowed eyes. Missy had spoken of her boss often, some of it not particularly flattering. She'd never expected him to meet anyone in her family.

"Thanks for bringing my sister. Dad's out of surgery, but he's still listed as critical."

They followed David to his truck. He tossed Missy's suitcase in the back. She sat between the men, staring out the windshield.

"What happened?" she demanded.

"We're not exactly sure. We think he got a call from Angela Ramirez's son. Her ex-boyfriend showed up drunk and half out of his mind. Dad went over there and tried to calm the guy down. He got stabbed."

"Why didn't he call the police?" she asked, ticking off familiar landmarks as they slid by in pre-dawn light.

"I think Angela Ramirez is here illegally."

"And Dad thought nothing of his own safety," Missy grumbled. "He was only worried that a member of his congregation was in trouble."

Beside her, Sebastian tensed. "Congregation?"

She'd never told her boss about her family or her upbringing and he'd never inquired about her past. Hopefully that wasn't about to blow up in her face.

"Didn't Missy tell you?" David piped up. "Our dad's a pastor."

Eight

Rarely was Sebastian struck dumb.

Missy was a preacher's daughter? How had she worked for him for four years and not shared that bit of news? Did he know her at all?

Unbidden, doubts rushed in. He'd known very little about Chandra before letting his passion get the better of him, and look how that had turned out. Her supposedly pregnant. Them married. Him discovering her lies and manipulation.

Now history was repeating itself with Missy. With her sexy curves and knack for shattering his restraint, she'd ignited his desire, made him lose control, and once again, he'd moved too fast.

Sebastian rubbed his cheek, hearing the rasp of stubble. He'd left without packing a bag, figuring he'd accompany Missy to the hospital, find out how her father was doing and then leave her in her family's care. Now he wished he'd never gotten on the plane in Las Vegas and never found out this tidbit about her origins.

"No," he said, rediscovering his voice. "She never mentioned that."

From the way she stared straight ahead, her eyes fixed on the road before them, he figured she had a pretty good idea how frustrated he was at the moment. He couldn't wait to get her alone so he could hear her reasons for keeping him in the dark.

Or did the blame lie at his feet?

How come he'd never asked about her family? Pressed her for details about growing up in west Texas. He'd taken and taken. Her free time. Her loyalty. Her expertise. And he couldn't even remember her birthday. Missy deserved better.

He glanced her way. Her fixed gaze and frozen expression confirmed that she wasn't happy. He rubbed his forehead.

"I'm not surprised," David said, appearing unaware of the tension that filled the pickup's cab. "She never acted like one growing up."

"I can't wait to hear all about it," Sebastian said.

"Wild." David slapped the steering wheel. "That's the best way to describe my sister."

"That's just not true," Missy protested. "I didn't act any different than any of my classmates."

"Oh, I don't know. You pushed things pretty far."

"That surprises me," Sebastian said. "She certainly doesn't give the appearance of someone with a checkered past."

"Checkered?" Missy shot him a warning look. "I'd hardly call staying out past curfew and drinking with my friends worthy of being called a checkered past. It was all the regular stuff teenagers get into."

"No stealing cars to go joyriding?"

"No."

"There was that time you and Jimmy McCray got stopped coming back from the lake."

"That was his mom's car. He didn't steal it. Just took it without mentioning it to her and she thought it had been stolen."

"That's probably because he was grounded and so were

you. Neither one of you was supposed to be out at three in the morning. And you sure weren't supposed to be doing whatever it was you two did down by the lake." David wore a wicked grin. "But you can't really stop young love, can you? Hey!" David exhaled air on a protest as his sister jabbed her elbow into his ribs.

"Shut up, David. You weren't exactly the poster child for upright behavior, either, when you were young. Chet's going to be eleven in five months. Maybe I should tell him about the time you stuck fireworks in a dead squirrel and blew it up on the back porch. I don't think you could sit down for a week after Dad found out." Missy paused for only a second before continuing. "Or, how about the time you and our trusty brother Matt—"

David's voice rose over hers. "Okay, I get your point, I'll shut up."

"Thank you." She smirked, but her pleased expression didn't last long.

Sebastian spoke softly in her ear. "I see we'll have lots to discuss when you get back to Houston."

She eyed him without turning her head. "It was a long time ago."

"But it's part of who you are so I'm interested in hearing all about it."

Like all small towns at five in the morning, Main Street looked buttoned up tight. David blew past five blocks of storefronts before Sebastian had a chance to blink. What had it been like for Missy to grow up in such a place? He'd guessed her hometown was small, but he had no idea how isolated. He'd assumed as a preacher's daughter, she wouldn't have had a lot of chances to learn how the world worked. Now, however, Sebastian recognized signs of the teenage rebel lurking beneath the sensible, efficient exterior of the woman who'd been his assistant for the past four years.

The truck passed a sign pointing the way to the hospital

and David took a right at the stoplight. Conversation suspended as David turned into the front driveway that would take them to the entrance.

"I'll drop you off here and park. Dad's probably still in recovery so everyone should be in the waiting room."

Sebastian slid out of the pickup and reached for Missy's hand to help her down. Despite the warm night and the sweatshirt she still wore, her hands were like ice. Shock. He recognized the signs. His mother had been like this when Brandon had collapsed. Sebastian knew what to do, offer a strong shoulder to lean on and keep the Kleenex coming. His mother had gone through an entire box before her husband had come out of triple bypass surgery.

Pulling Missy's arm through his, he tucked her hands between his arm and his body to warm her. She moved like a zombie at his side, her steps jerky as if her muscles had stopped functioning properly.

"It's going to be okay," he murmured as the hospital doors swung open before them.

They stepped over the threshold. Missy straightened her shoulders and pulled away. As hard as it was to let her go, Sebastian held back as Missy reunited with her family. Three tall men, mirror images of David, gathered her into tight hugs that left her teary and out of breath. Four women hovered behind the men, then took their turns, each returning to offer support to one of Missy's brothers.

With the greetings complete, Missy cast about for him. Sebastian's heart bumped against his ribs as her shell-shocked gaze found him. He came to her side, needing to wrap her in his arms, but she sensed his intention and shook her head, eyes pleading.

Turning to the group, she said, "Everyone. This is my boss, Sebastian Case."

As he shook hands with Missy's brothers, he couldn't help but contrast this tight group of brothers and wives with his own family. He and Max were close in age and the best of friends growing up, but as adults they'd gone out of state to different universities and taken different career paths. Eventually those paths had converged at Case Consolidated Holdings, but the years of separation had taken their toll. They'd become less like family and more like coworkers.

From what he gathered, Missy's family all lived within a couple miles of each other. In a few short minutes, he learned each brother was married and had between one and five kids ranging in ages from four months to fourteen years. He visualized boisterous family dinners every week with tons of children running around, and he understood why hitting thirty had heightened Missy's longing for marriage and children.

Two hours after they arrived, Reverend Ward was released to the ICU where he would be watched and monitored. Each of his children got to visit him one at a time. Missy went first, then sat beside Sebastian on a molded plastic chair, hands in her lap, distanced from him by her need to keep her family in the dark about their altered relationship.

He wasn't accustomed to seeing his ultra-efficient assistant so down and out. The sight unnerved him. Being unable to offer her support frustrated him. As she'd pointed out often these past couple days, he wasn't the sort to sit idle. He needed to help.

But he also needed to be in Las Vegas at the summit. Leaving his father in charge for more than a day could spell trouble.

At eight o'clock, he could wait no longer to check in. Not wanting to disturb Missy's family, he stood. Missy had closed her eyes and let her head fall back against the wall behind her. When he moved, she straightened and blinked in blurry disorientation. Rubbing her eyes, she looked around. The sisters-in-law had gone home to check on their children. All who remained were Missy's brothers.

"I'm going to step out and see how the summit is going," he told her, giving her hand a squeeze.

The cellular reception at the hospital had prevented him from receiving any calls. However, two messages awaited him. The first one made him curse.

Damn it. What the hell was going on?

He dialed Max's cell and heard the frustration in his brother's voice when he answered.

"Sebastian, I've been trying you for hours. Where've you been?"

"In Crusade with Missy. Her father was in an accident." No need to explain more. "Lucas Smythe said he's leaving the summit. What's going on?"

"He's not selling us his company." Despite the fact that this was an overseas call, Max's tension came through loud and clear.

Curses reverberated through Sebastian's head. "Why not?"

"Said he's having second thoughts."

"He was completely on board a week ago." What had their father said during a round of golf to convince Lucas that selling to them was a bad idea—or was getting caught with a half-naked Missy in his suite to blame? "Did he say what he's going to do instead?"

"No. He's heading home this morning. You have to convince him to change his mind. I'm in Amsterdam at the moment. My flight won't get in for another twelve hours."

"Send Nathan."

"Nathan isn't on board with this deal."

"He's on board," Sebastian said.

"I'm not sure I trust him to convince Smythe to sell to us."

Max still had a chip on his shoulder where their half brother was concerned. Sebastian suspected it had more to do with being unable to forgive their father for his infidelity than any animosity he felt toward Nathan.

Sebastian sighed. Early on, he'd had his doubts about being

able to work with Nathan; but lately their half brother had demonstrated that even though he might not be keen on the current business strategy for Case Consolidated Holdings, he was open to working with it.

"I won't make it back to Vegas before he leaves." Sebastian's gaze traveled across the waiting room to where Missy sat beside her brother.

"Fly to Raleigh and talk to him there."

An ache formed in Sebastian's chest as Missy rested her head on David's shoulder. She hadn't been willing to take comfort from him.

"Fine. I'll go." Sebastian ended the call without waiting for his brother's response.

He banked his fury at this unwelcome turn of events and headed toward Missy.

She'd been watching him the whole time and offered a weak smile as he neared. "Usually that would be me looking for you." She checked her watch. "It's almost eight in the morning. What's the crisis?"

"I have to fly to Raleigh. Lucas is backing out of our deal."

"Go," she said, nodding. "That's important."

More important than her. He read her loud and clear.

"I don't want to leave you."

She offered him a grateful smile. "I'll be okay. Dad's not out of danger, but the doctors think he'll make a full recovery. Smythe Industries is important." She got to her feet and tugged at his arm. "Come on. David can drive you back to the plane."

He was startled by how reluctant he was to leave her. For the first time in his life, he had no desire to return to work. Someone else should be able to take care of business, leaving him free to be with Missy a while longer. But that's not the way Case Consolidated Holdings was structured. His need to control all aspects of the business had made it so that he was the one who stepped in when things weren't working.

"You're sure you don't need me to stay?"

She shook off the scared, lost girl she'd been for the last few hours. Her spine straightened. She firmed her lips and enfolded herself in the brisk professionalism she usually demonstrated.

The transformation caught him off guard.

How often had she hidden hurt, fear or sadness from him? He'd taken her efficiency for granted, he saw now. She wasn't made of granite. Far from it.

He cupped her face in his hands. "Tell me you need me and I won't go."

Tears brightened her eyes. Her breath caught. She blinked a few times and swallowed hard. "That's not necessary. I have all my family here. I'll be fine."

"I don't doubt that. You're all wonderful support for each other. I just feel funny leaving you behind."

In truth, he'd gotten used to having her around all the time. Except for a half-dozen business trips that had lasted a week, he realized that he hadn't gone without seeing her for more than three days.

"You feel funny?" she echoed, a grin ghosting through her eyes.

And that was all it took. He leaned down and kissed her, not caring one single bit who saw.

Sebastian registered her utter shock before the compelling warmth of her soft lips made him forget everything but the way she made him feel. He wrapped his arms around her. With her fingers threaded through his hair, he savored the texture of her lips and the sweetness of her soft body.

A throat cleared behind him. "We should probably get going," David said.

Releasing her took longer than it should have. How long until he held her again? He knew she needed to be here for her dad and family. But he'd been a selfish bastard for so long and couldn't resist hoping that she was back in Houston within a couple weeks.

With her cheeks a bright pink she peered at him from beneath her lashes. "If it's okay with you, I'm going to stick around for a while."

His instincts screamed that leaving her here was a bad idea, but what could he do? Her family needed her. His company needed him.

"Take as much time as you need."

Just come back to me.

"I'm doing fine," Malcolm Ward said, pushing away Missy's attempt at dinner. "Don't you think it's time you went back to Houston? It's been three weeks."

Missy stopped dragging her fork through the lumpy mashed potatoes and met her father's gaze. She hadn't told him she'd quit her job. He needed to focus on his recovery. If he had any idea she had no pressing reason to return to Houston, he'd start worrying about her instead of getting better. Not that her dad was any good at thinking about himself. Always, his congregation came first. Then his family. Then the rest of the world. Then himself.

Having a saint for a father had never been easy.

"I have over a month of vacation saved up. Sebastian doesn't have any problem with me using it to take care of you."

"How much time do you have left?"

Three days.

"Plenty."

She carried her plate to the sink and dumped the burnt meatloaf and overcooked green beans into the garbage disposal. Normally her father protested any waste, but not even he would wish that dinner on anyone.

"Who's filling in for you while you're gone?"

"They hired a temp. It's done all the time. Don't worry.

There'll be a job for me when I go back." Someone would hire her. Or she could stay at Case Consolidated Holdings as the director of communications. If the position was still available.

"Your brothers like him."

"Who?" She transferred a large slice of chocolate cake to a plate and set it before her father. Chocolate was one thing he let himself indulge in.

"Your boss."

"Sebastian is terrific." Thinking about him sent a sweet pain shooting through her body. During the three days her father had spent in the hospital, struggling to heal and overcome the infection that had kept him delirious, Missy hadn't had time to dwell on what had happened in Las Vegas or fuss over what the future might bring.

"Cares about you, does he?"

Missy sat down with her own wedge of triple chocolate delight. She couldn't cook, but she knew how to bake.

"I've worked for him a long time."

"From what I hear, there's more to it than that."

Her cheeks burned beneath her father's all-knowing stare. Who'd told him? David? She'd sworn him to secrecy. He wouldn't spill the beans for fear that she would tell his wife how much he paid for that new revolver.

"I have no idea what you mean."

"He's called here every day, sometimes twice a day."

"That's about work." She found little breathing room in the barrage of her father's questioning. "They've recently bought a new company." In her absence, Sebastian had saved the deal with Smythe Industries. "There are a lot of details involved in integrating their employees into Case Consolidated Holdings, and he's calling me to help the temp with contact information and such."

"And the kiss he gave you at the hospital?" her dad

quizzed, his tone conversational. "How were you planning on explaining that? Improved employer-employee relations?"

"Who told you?" Missy clapped her hands over her hot cheeks. She hadn't felt this embarrassed since her father had caught her and Wayne Stodemeyer necking in the tool shed when she was fifteen. "If it was David, I'll…" She let her threat trail off, unwilling to voice her intention to break one of the Ten Commandments to her dad the minister.

"Don't worry, your brother didn't rat you out. It was one of the nurses."

"Great. Just great."

"Is that why Tim broke up with you?" her father quizzed, revealing that his ability to know everything that went on around him wasn't quelled by the fact that he'd almost died three weeks ago.

Missy shoved aside that horrifying thought so she could deal with setting her father straight.

"No. Tim broke up with me because I worked too many hours and he was lonely. He found someone new. Sebastian had nothing to do with it."

Nothing directly. Although in the past few weeks she'd analyzed her relationship with Tim and come to see that her crush on Sebastian hadn't been as over as she'd assumed. It had interfered with her priorities.

"I see. Are you two a couple then?"

"Sebastian and me?" The words exploded out of her on an incredulous laugh. "Of course not. I'm not his type. If he ever gets married again, he's going to choose someone gorgeous, wealthy and sophisticated. Three things I'm not and never will be."

"Maybe you have it wrong."

Not possible. She'd seen the way he'd looked at her small town. He'd been polite to her family, but he'd also been sizing everyone up. She wouldn't trade a single brother, sister-in-law, niece or nephew for anyone from Sebastian's well-connected

circle; but that didn't mean she was blind to their flaws or
shortcomings.

None of her brothers had the sort of ambition that kept
them working sixty hours a week at their jobs. The second
oldest, Jacob, had taken until he was in his mid-thirties to
figure out what he wanted to be when he grew up. They were
college educated and had successful careers, but they bal-
anced work with family.

Sebastian wouldn't recognize the value in balance. He'd
chosen business over family.

"Do you have feelings for him?" her dad persisted, breaking into her thoughts.

"Of course. And he has feelings for me. Just not the same
sort of feelings."

Or that's what she told herself. She really didn't have a
clue what Sebastian wanted beyond her returning as his assistant—or her spending an indefinite amount of time in his
bed. Back in Las Vegas, she'd doubted there was a future for
them past Las Vegas. Now that he'd seen where she'd grown
up, she doubted it even more.

If only she could get that goodbye kiss out of her head. The
hungry strength in the arms around her. The way it seemed
to take a long time for him to let go. She told herself not to
read too much into his daily phone calls or the smooth caress
of his tone as he asked her how she was doing.

She rubbed her arms as goose bumps appeared. Beneath
her father's keen regard she finished her chocolate cake and
went to start the dishes.

"Thanks for dinner," he said, his arms sliding around her
from behind. He kissed her cheek. "I think you should go
back to Houston. You can't hide out here forever."

Missy whirled on her father, a protest cocked and ready, but
he was already out the door, moving better than he had since
coming home from the hospital. He'd done that on purpose,

hit her with a blunt opinion and then fled before she could defend herself.

Was she hiding?

Damn right she was hiding.

Almost four weeks ago she'd quit her job and slept with her boss. Returning to Houston meant having to cope with both things. She wasn't ready to decide on anything more taxing than whether to bake another chocolate cake or to shake things up and try lemon.

"I'm going to the store," she called, grabbing her purse and the keys to the truck.

"Can you pick up a prescription for me while you're out?" her father asked from the living room.

Missy made the drugstore her first stop. She could use a tube of toothpaste. All she'd packed before going to Las Vegas was travel-sized toiletries. A week ago she'd run out of her brand and started using her dad's and didn't like it at all. Another sign that she needed to go home.

Browsing the aisles, she added shampoo, lotion and dental floss to her basket. It wasn't until she passed the feminine products that she stopped cold. She'd been in town almost four weeks and in Las Vegas three days before that without having her period. Whipping out her phone, she keyed up her calendar and tracked backward.

She should have started two weeks ago. Either she'd skipped her period because she was stressed, or she was pregnant. How was that possible? She and Sebastian had been careful.

A wave of dizziness struck her. Except for that first time. They'd been so caught up in the moment neither one of them had thought about protection. But to get pregnant after one mistake? That just wasn't realistic.

She needed to find out for sure, and she needed to know tonight. But she couldn't buy the test here. Everyone would know. Her father would find out. She'd head over a couple towns and hit a pharmacy where no one would recognize her.

In a fog, Missy paid for her purchases and headed to the truck. Forty-five minutes later she sat in the bathroom of a roadside diner and checked her watch for the fifteenth time in thirty seconds.

She was waiting for a blue bar, but she didn't really need it. She'd convinced herself she was carrying Sebastian's child. Time rushed at her like a charging bull. Regret squeezed her eyes shut. It was like high school all over again. Except she hadn't been pregnant then, just the victim of a vicious rumor. Not that it had stopped her boyfriend from dumping her when word got out.

And if she could count on one thing, it was that Sebastian would not react well to her being pregnant. He would think she'd done it on purpose. All her talk of getting married and babies. He would believe she'd tricked him, and who could blame him? It's what his ex-wife had done.

But he'd marry her. And spend the rest of his life resenting her the way he resented his first wife. Missy couldn't bear that. She loved him too much to put him through it. So, she wouldn't tell him.

Her phone rang. It was a Houston number, but not Sebastian's.

"Missy," Max Case boomed. "I hope your father is doing better."

"Yes, much. Thank you." She stared at the stick and watched the blue bar coalesce.

Positive. Pregnant.

"Glad to hear it. Do you still want the director of communications position?"

She couldn't be pregnant. She didn't have a husband. No job meant no income, no health coverage. What was she going to do?

"I'm sorry, Max, you broke up." What had he said? "Could you say that again?"

"I asked if you're still interested in Dean's job."

This answered the problem of her job situation, but what about Sebastian? A second ago she'd decided that she wouldn't tell Sebastian he was going to be a father. Could she have his baby and stay working around him at the same time?

"Missy?" Max prompted. "Are you still there?"

"Yes."

"So, what do you say?"

What could she say? "I'm still interested in the job. I'm just worried about Sebastian's reaction."

"Don't let it stop you from what will be a wonderful career move."

"You're right. I'll take the job. And thank you."

"When are you coming back?"

She scrubbed her cheeks free of tears and shook her shoulders like a dog shedding water. With her spine as stiff as she could make it, she exited the bathroom and headed for the truck.

"I'll head home Wednesday," she said, wishing she could linger in Crusade and hide from her troubles a little longer.

"I'll see you in the office on Thursday."

"Max, can you let me tell Sebastian about the job?"

"If that's what you want."

"It is."

Missy sighed as she ended the call. Sebastian would be unhappy that she hadn't talked to him about staying on at Case Consolidated Holdings before accepting the job.

Hopefully he would be glad she was sticking around. From the start, he'd made it clear that his need for her started and stopped at the office. Besides, no matter how amazing the sex between them had been, they'd both known it was only a matter of time before Sebastian came to his senses and relegated what had happened between them in Vegas to a massive mistake.

Or perhaps he'd figured it out already. Although she heard from him almost every day, their conversations were strictly business. She couldn't help but wonder if Sebastian had been going out with Kaitlyn. His mother wanted him to marry the wealthy socialite. Missy understood why. They were a perfect social and economic match. Sebastian was practical. Was it only a matter of time until he saw the advantages?

Could she work at Case Consolidated Holdings and watch him marry someone else while she raised his child on her own? Missy grimaced. It would be hell. And she'd spent enough years pining after a man she couldn't have.

Lightning arced across the sky overhead. A storm had blown in while she'd awaited the results of the pregnancy test. By the time she got a mile down the road, rain hammered the truck roof like angry fists. Visibility diminished to ten feet in front of her. Driving in these conditions was beyond reckless. But she couldn't shake an urgent need to get home.

The windshield wipers flew back and forth at top speed, but as quickly as they cleared water from the windshield, more replaced it. A pair of lights appeared before her, too close for her to stop. She swerved toward the shoulder and hit the brakes. The tires caught in the soft gravel, turned to thick mud by the downpour and pulled the truck even farther from the road. Coming to a full stop, she gripped the wheel hard. A jackhammer pounded away in her chest.

The near miss had brought crystalline clarity. No matter what happened between her and Sebastian, this wasn't just about them anymore. She was going to be a mother. Maybe sooner than she'd expected and without hope that the father would ever believe she'd had no ulterior motive when she slept with him. But she had a new focus for her life. Going forward, every decision she made would be with her child's best interest as her priority.

And if that meant working as the director of communications for Case Consolidated Holdings and letting the love of her life never know he was the father of her child, that's what she'd do.

Nine

Sebastian raced home, hoping to beat Missy there. Her plane had landed an hour ago, but the heavy rush-hour traffic from the airport would probably double her half-hour commute. He checked his cell, expecting an irate phone call when she discovered the car he'd sent to fetch her wasn't taking her to her house but to his.

Being separated from her for a month had taken its toll on him both professionally and personally. He'd gone through three temps, the longest one lasting nine business days before dissolving into tears.

"Impossible to find good help," he muttered, turning into his driveway, his fingers tapping an impatient rhythm on the armrest as the wrought iron gates swung open.

The neighborhood where he'd built was an eclectic mix—mid-century ranches and twenty-first-century mansions. Close to downtown Houston and boasting a highly desirable school system, many people, himself included, had bought an older home on a large lot with mature trees and torn down the house to make way for a mini estate.

A black town car idled near the front door. He parked

behind the vehicle and got out. As he approached the car, the driver met him by the rear passenger door.

"Good afternoon, Mr. Case."

"Hello, Burt." Sebastian used this driver often when he traveled. "Did Miss Ward go inside?"

"No, sir," the driver said, hand on the door handle. "She wanted to wait until you got home."

"How long have you been here?"

"Ten minutes." He opened the door.

Sebastian peered in, expecting to catch the brunt of Missy's annoyance and found her curled sideways on the seat, cheek cradled on her hand, asleep. The sight dismantled all the walls he'd erected around his emotions. In an instant he was transported back to their first night together when he'd spent an hour watching her sleep.

Crouching beside the car, he skimmed a russet strand of her hair behind her ear. When she didn't stir, he scooped her into his arms. "Bring her bag," he told the driver as he strode up his front steps.

His housekeeper must have been watching from the window because the door opened as he neared it. Without pausing, he carried Missy up the wide marble stairs and down the hallway to his bedroom.

How taxing had her time away from him been that she'd fallen asleep in ten short minutes? Hadn't her brothers and their wives pitched in? Or had everyone taken advantage of her generous nature and let Missy shoulder all the nursing duty?

She woke as he eased her down onto the mattress. "Sebastian?" She reached up and touched his cheek, her eyes soft and barely focused.

"I missed you," he admitted, stretching out beside her.

She rolled onto her side and snuggled against him. "Missed you, too," she murmured into his neck, her warm breath puffing against him. Her fingers tunneled beneath his tie and between his shirt buttons, finding skin.

Instantly aroused, he cupped the side of her face in his palm and brought his mouth to hers. Desire blindsided him. Going without her in his arms for a month had turned him into a ravenous bear. He feasted off her soft sighs and the press of her lithe body against his. Rolling with her across his king-size bed, he stripped her down to her underwear and settled between her thighs, his jacket, tie and shoes gone, his shirt ripped open by her impatience.

Breathing in her delicious scent, he drifted his lips down her throat and between her breasts to the lacy edge of her bra. Drawing his tongue along the edge of the lace, he savored the rapid rise and fall of her chest as his fingers tickled up her thigh.

"Make love to me," she gasped, her fingers coasting down his sides and burrowing between their bodies in search of his belt. "I need to feel you inside me."

Her words inflamed his already overstimulated body. "Don't rush me. I intend to get reacquainted with every inch of you before that happens."

"I can't wait that long." She rotated her hips, bringing his erection into better contact with her core.

Even through the layers that separated them, he could feel how she burned for him. That knowledge pushed him over the edge. In seconds he'd shed the rest of his clothes and come back to find her naked and waiting for him.

Driving into her tight sheath, he groaned as she closed around him, drawing him deeper inside. He buried his face in her neck. Her fingernails sank into his back as they moved together, as connected in soul as they were joined in body.

He struggled to hold off his climax, but her impassioned cries and urgent movements slashed the tethers binding his willpower. Reaching between their bodies, he touched her, setting off the chain reaction of her orgasm. With a final thrust he let out a triumphant cry.

"That wasn't the homecoming I pictured," he muttered, rolling over so her limp body draped across his chest like an erotic daydream.

She nuzzled his neck. "Really? It's all I thought about."

Her round backside called to his hand. He followed the curve with his fingers, measuring the perfect rise from the small of her back to her thigh. Every inch of her fascinated him. Contentment settled over him as he stroked her hip with his thumb.

She raised her head and braced her forearm against his chest. Her voice may have been light and airy a second ago, but she wore a serious expression now.

"Something on your mind?" he prompted as the silence stretched.

"I'm just going to come right out and say this."

But still she struggled with whatever she needed to tell him. Making love to her had pacified his earlier impatience. He kept silent and let her work out whatever was bothering her.

"I think it would be better if we got dressed first."

She shimmied off his body, her long hair falling forward to conceal her expression as she retrieved her clothes and slid into jeans and shirt. Jerky movements and her lack of playfulness warned him something serious was up with her. He ignored the agitation that flared in his gut. The month-long separation had been harder on him than expected. Now that she was within his grasp once more he wanted nothing disagreeable to distract him from the pleasure of watching her.

She tossed his boxers at him. As he slipped them over his hips, the words erupted from her.

"Tomorrow I'm starting as the new director of communications."

* * *

If the situation were reversed, and Sebastian had kept something this big from her, Missy would have stormed hard enough to level a house.

But Missy never knew him to thunder and rage like a summer squall. No, Sebastian had a calm, icy way of being furious that was ten times worse.

"When did this happen?" There was enough frost in his voice to ruin an entire orange crop.

"Your father mentioned the idea to me in Las Vegas." She searched his rigid expression, assessing just how angry he was. "Then Max called me a few days ago and I said yes."

"I see."

What did he see? That she was perfect for the job? That discussing a job with his father and brother made her feel disloyal and low? That she loved him so much she'd rather spend every day thirty feet down the hall than never see him again?

"Are you okay with it?"

"We can't keep seeing each other if you work for Case Consolidated Holdings."

"I considered that." Was it wrong of her to choose something sensible like a fabulous job instead of a risky venture like dating Sebastian for as long as he wanted her? The old her, the impulsive girl who'd made a brief appearance in Las Vegas, would have chosen an uncertain future with Sebastian. Unfortunately, she'd spent more than a decade making decisions with her head, not her heart. "But we'd already agreed that once we left Las Vegas it was over between us."

"That's what you wanted. I had something different in mind."

She refused to feel guilty for disappointing him. It was ridiculous to think she could keep his interest long-term. "I'm perfect for this job."

"Then if the job is what you want, you should take it."

Throat too tight for words to escape, Missy nodded. Sebastian's impassive acceptance of her decision left her stomach in knots. But what had she expected? An impassioned plea for her to choose him over her career? Eventually he'd be glad she'd given him the perfect out.

Wrung out and miserable, she let Sebastian take on the bulk of the conversational duties as he drove her home. He asked her about her family and updated her on what had happened with the business since she'd been gone. By unspoken consent, they avoided discussing the elephants crowded in the backseat: her new job, how everyone at the office would react to her promotion and what had happened between them an hour earlier.

"Thank you for sending the car to pick me up," she said as he carried her suitcase into the condo she rented. Feeling awkward for the first time ever around him, she fiddled with her purse strap and wondered if she should offer him something to drink.

"You're welcome." He bent down and grazed his lips against hers.

Although the touch of Sebastian's kisses would forever cause her to melt like snow in the tropics, Missy's stomach clenched in despair. The brief kiss was goodbye.

"I'll see you tomorrow morning," she said.

"I have a breakfast meeting. I'll stop by your new office when I get in."

He left her standing in the middle of her living room, nodding after him like a bobble-head doll. He'd changed from ardent lover to supportive ex-boss so fast she had whiplash. She was glad she'd decided against telling him about the baby.

Once her pregnancy became public knowledge, she'd let everyone believe Tim was the father. No reason to let what had happened between her and Sebastian in Vegas create life-long consequences for him. So what if her instincts told her what she was doing was wrong? She'd ignored her gut feelings for fifteen years and let her head lead. She'd grown accustomed to weighing options. Logic dictated her actions.

Back when she'd been a teenager, she'd learned what happened if she let her heart run amuck.

Pity she hadn't remembered those lessons in Vegas.

Sebastian let himself into his parents' house. He was furious with his father for interfering in the running of the business again and angry with himself for not thinking of putting Missy into the communications director position himself.

"Sebastian," his mother said, getting up from the computer in her office. "What are you doing here?"

"I came to talk to Dad."

She surveyed his expression. "What did he do now?"

"He offered Missy a job without telling me."

"I'm sure he had good intentions."

"You give him the benefit of the doubt too often." Sebastian tempered his tone. After all, he wasn't angry with his mother. "Where is he?"

Following his mother's directions, Sebastian found his father in the library. "You offered Missy the communications director job?"

"Hello, Sebastian." Brandon pulled off his reading glasses. "I did."

"Why did you do that?"

"Because she belongs with us. And she can do the job. You should've promoted her years ago. If you had, maybe she wouldn't have quit."

Sebastian bit back a growl. As much as he hated to admit it, his father was right. Missy was overqualified to be his assistant. He'd been a selfish bastard to keep her as long as he had.

"You should have talked to me first."

"I spoke with Max. She'd be working for him. He liked the idea."

How could Sebastian argue? His father's logic was flawless. It was his methods that set Sebastian to grinding his teeth. Nor would he stop Missy from taking a job she so obviously wanted more than she wanted to keep seeing him.

He wasn't about to admit he'd realized he was glad she'd resigned. That he was glad she'd be sleeping in his bed instead of working for his company. Letting passion dominate reason went against everything he believed in. So, why did he want to hit something?

"Why didn't anyone talk to me about it?"

"Missy wanted to be the one to break the news."

"I wish you'd come to me before speaking to Missy. I would have liked the opportunity to offer her the position."

"Sorry we left you out of the loop." Brandon didn't look one bit sorry that he'd bypassed Sebastian and asserted his authority once again. "After I found out she'd quit, the decision happened pretty fast. I spoke to her about it in Las Vegas, but because of what happened to her dad, she didn't give us her answer until a couple days ago."

She'd kept this from him for a month.

"You've been busy with Smythe Industries," her father continued. "I don't see why you're so annoyed. We're keeping a valuable employee."

And Sebastian had lost the ability to pursue a personal relationship with her.

The temptation to ask his father to back off held Sebastian mute. He'd never felt less like a leader in his life. Leaders were the ones with all the answers. The ones in control. He was neither.

"Missy will make a terrific communications director," his father said. "You'll see."

Sebastian offered his father a tight smile. "I don't doubt that for a second."

"Then this isn't about me interfering?"

"Do you want to be CEO again?" Sebastian wasn't sure

where the question came from. He only knew he was ready to walk away from the job he was born to do. Maybe he'd go work for a Fortune 500 corporation. Or start his own company. Do something that wouldn't involve family. "Say the word and I'm gone."

From the surprise on his father's face, Sebastian could see he was finally getting through.

"I don't want to run the company. Retirement…"

"Is boring as hell. I get it. Mom wanted me to convince you to stay retired. She's enjoying having you around. Heaven knows why when all you do is golf." Sebastian set his hands on his hips. "I think she's scared if you go back to work it will aggravate your heart problems. But maybe she's wrong to keep you from something you love so much."

"Sebastian?" His mother entered the room. How much had she heard? "Can you stay for dinner?"

"No. I'm heading back to the office. Without Missy's help these past few weeks, I'm behind." He shot his father one last look. "You were right to want her to stay with the company. I just hope you did it for the right reasons."

Sebastian eased his car toward the curb in front of the downtown Houston hotel. As he put it into Park, a valet stepped up to the passenger door. Missy smoothed her hands down the front of her cornflower-blue cocktail dress. The gown's silky material grazed her curves with elegant style. The cool color contrasted wonderfully with her red hair.

"I don't see why you needed me to come here with you," she complained, questioning his motives for about the tenth time. Her tension was palpable in the confined space. She'd been clenching her evening bag hard the entire drive from her house.

"Because you're our director of communications and there are a lot of people attending that you should meet." For the past two weeks, he'd been keeping discreet tabs on her.

She stepped into a position without anyone to show her the ropes. That couldn't have been easy. Sebastian knew no one who could have handled the transition as well as Missy had. "Relax." He took her hand, compelled by a strong need to reassure her.

"Easy for you to say—you do this all the time."

"There's nothing to it." He stepped out of the car and circled the vehicle. "Just picture them all in their underwear."

For a second his suggestion flustered her. She stared at him in astonishment before a wry grin curved her lips. "I thought that only worked for public speaking," she said, tucking her purse into the crook of her arm and letting him guide her into the elegant lobby.

"It works anytime you need it."

The organizers of the fundraising event—which was geared toward supporting a local food shelf—had decided a casino night was a fun and profitable way to raise funds. Sebastian experienced a moment of déjà vu as they entered the ballroom.

Missy rubbed her hands together gleefully, her earlier nerves forgotten. "Time to take a little cash home."

"This is a charity event," Sebastian murmured, amused by the frankness of her avarice. "I think the idea is to leave your cash on the table."

"How about I try not to win as much as you lose?"

Sebastian gripped her elbow and steered her toward the roulette table. "What makes you think you're going to win?"

"You're my good luck charm, aren't you?" A flirtatious glance slipped from beneath her eyelashes.

"Is that all I am to you?"

Before she could answer, a man stepped into their path. With a drink in his left hand and an ingratiating smile plastered on his face, he swung his palm toward Sebastian. An executive in name only at one of Houston's larger banks, Bob Stokes attended these functions because his wealthy wife liked being seen with her attractive younger husband as much as she enjoyed flaunting her family's money.

"Good to see you again, Sebastian."

"Bob." He gave a curt nod as he crushed the man's hand in a firm handshake. "This is Missy Ward," he added. "Bob Stokes."

Missy murmured a polite greeting that was scarcely acknowledged by the man. Her gaze shifted past the interruption toward the roulette table. Sebastian felt her sigh as Bob launched into a detailed description of his new driver and how it had improved his golf game.

"Sorry, I don't golf," Sebastian said, turning down an invitation to join the man at his club. "If you want to talk about drivers, catch up with my father. He's the enthusiast."

"You don't golf?"

Sebastian was too busy running a multimillion-dollar corporation to putter around on the links like so many of his colleagues. He'd always believed that the boss should work harder than any of his employees. His father had never shared that opinion. Brandon had only worked as hard as he had to. That partially explained why the company's profits had been so erratic during his father's stewardship.

Steering Missy around Bob, they resumed their trek toward the roulette wheel. Five steps later, he was waylaid again.

"You came," the petite brunette exclaimed. Ignoring Missy completely, she rose on tiptoe and kissed Sebastian on both cheeks. "Wait until I tell Gina that Sebastian Case came to my fundraiser. Stay here while I fetch her."

"We're heading for the roulette table," Sebastian told her.

"We?" The brunette blinked her bright-blue eyes in confusion.

Sebastian turned to Missy. "Missy Ward. Communications director for Case Consolidated Holdings. Tanya Hart."

The brunette frowned at Missy as if trying to place her.

"Nice to meet you." Suddenly she began waving to someone across the room. "Don't move," she commanded.

As Tanya sped off into the crowd, Missy said, "Remind me again why I'm here."

"You need to meet the movers and shakers in this town."

"Well, apparently, they're not terribly interested in meeting me."

From her mild tone, she sounded unaffected by the brush-offs she'd received, but the corners of her lips tightened, betraying her misery.

"They will be." He gave the words a fierce punch. "Let's go lose some money."

A bright smile emerged. "You mean win some money, don't you?"

Sebastian avoided eye contact with everyone as they approached the tables set up for gambling and focused his entire attention on Missy. How had he not anticipated this evening might be uncomfortable for her? Maybe because he'd seized the opportunity to spend some time away from the office with her. Maybe because he'd never seen these people through someone else's eyes.

He bought five thousand dollars' worth of chips and nudged the stack directly in front of Missy. "Time to see if your luck is still holding," he told her.

As eager as she'd been to play five minutes earlier, she now backed away from the table.

"That's a lot of money," she said, her gaze fixed on the pile of chips.

"It's no more than you gambled in Vegas on a single turn of the wheel."

"That was different."

"How exactly?" He leaned his hand on the table so he could peer at her expression.

"That was my money."

"Think of it as a donation to charity." He pushed five one

hundred dollar chips onto black. "Care to make a side bet
with me?"

She nudged a single chip onto the red, her gaze flicking
toward him with interest. "What did you have in mind?"

"If I win, you spend the night at my house."

The ball began its circuit of the wheel. Missy didn't seem
to breathe as the circling silver blur slowed.

"We can't do that. I'm your employee, remember?"

Sebastian lowered his lips within an inch of her ear. "I miss
you."

Even though they weren't touching, he felt tension exit her
muscles.

"I miss you, too," she whispered. "But if it lands on red,
you don't ask me again."

"Double zero," the dealer called.

They'd both lost.

Missy began to laugh. "Maybe that's fate's way of telling
us we should leave well enough alone."

Sebastian didn't care for the sound of that. Not one bit.

Ten

Between Missy's good luck and Sebastian's bad, the height of the chip pile remained constant until a man in his mid-fifties approached, keen on getting Sebastian's opinion on the current political climate in Austin. The conversation held no interest for Missy so she excused herself and headed for the ladies' room.

When she emerged from the bathroom stall, a brunette with long silky hair stood at the sinks, reapplying her lipstick. Missy felt the woman's gaze on her as she washed her hands.

"Are you Sebastian's date?" the woman asked.

"No. Heavens, no." Missy's laugh sounded hysterical to her ears. "I'm the director of communications for Case Consolidated Holdings."

"Oh." The woman's sunny smile could have cut through the thickest fog. "I'm Kaitlyn Murray."

The woman Sebastian had been seeing casually for six months before the Vegas trip. The one his mother thought Sebastian should propose to.

"Nice to meet you. We've spoken on the phone. I'm Missy Ward, Sebastian's former assistant."

"You've been out for a while. Sebastian said your father had been in an accident."

Okay, so Kaitlyn was genuinely nice, a delightful change from the other people she'd met that evening. And she and Sebastian had been in contact since he'd returned from Las Vegas. Missy wasn't surprised.

"If you call being stabbed an accident, then yes."

"Stabbed?" Kaitlyn looked shocked. Undoubtedly she couldn't fathom that sort of violence entering her gilded world. "How awful. What happened?"

"My father's a minister. He went to the aid of one of his parishioners and got between her and the boyfriend who was trying to hurt her. He's fine now," Missy assured her, seeing that her bald summary of the facts had shaken the woman. "The guy's in jail."

"I should hope so." Kaitlyn dropped her lipstick into her clutch. "Are you enjoying yourself tonight?"

"I'm afraid I'm a little out of my element."

"Oh? Why is that?"

"I'm from a small town in west Texas. Events like this are so intimidating. Half the time I have no idea what people are talking about."

A mischievous smile broke out on Kaitlyn's beautiful face. "I'll give you a little insider's tip. Most of the time they don't know what they're talking about, either."

As Missy laughed, some of her insecurities faded. She really liked Kaitlyn. No wonder Susan hoped her son would ask the socialite to marry him. "How long have you and Sebastian known each other?"

"Oh, forever. My daddy and his went to college together and remain the best of friends. I practically grew up with Sebastian, Max and Nathan. Of course, I'm a lot younger than them. They treated me like a pesky little sister."

"I know that feeling exactly," she said, liking the woman more and more even as her heart grew heavy at how perfectly

Kaitlyn fit into Sebastian's world. Same background. Same lifestyle. "I have four older brothers that I used to tag after like a lost puppy."

"Exactly." Kaitlyn's laugh rolled from her throat in a melodious ripple. "I thought one day they might see me as something else." She shrugged. "But all any of us will ever be is friends. It was nice to meet you."

"Nice meeting you," Missy echoed.

She lingered in the bathroom, powdering her nose and applying lipstick. Meeting Kaitlyn had put her in a thoughtful mood. Ever since high school, she'd envied the girls like her. They all navigated this world of wealth and sophistication with such ease. She felt gauche and awkward beside them. If she and Kaitlyn stood on either side of Sebastian, onlookers would always assume he and Kaitlyn were the couple. They both exuded a confidence that Missy couldn't match.

All the more reason to stick to her plan and keep things strictly professional between them. With a grimace, Missy exited the restroom and searched for Sebastian.

"I've gambled away all the money," he said as she approached. "Let's get out of here."

"But we've only been here an hour." Was he already embarrassed that she didn't fit in with his crowd?

He looked displeased with her answer. "I suppose you want the chance to win the money back." He slid his fingers over the small of her back and applied the perfect pressure to coax her closer. "I've made an appearance and done my duty by the food shelf. Now, I want to take you home."

That's what she was afraid of. "Sure. Tomorrow's a workday after all. I suppose we should make it an early night."

"You misunderstand me," Sebastian said, his eyes alight. Her pulse skyrocketed as the compelling warmth of his hand penetrated her silk dress. "Will you be angry if I tell you tonight was merely an excuse to spend time with you?"

Her mouth dropped open as his meaning penetrated, but

already her longing for him was threatening her common sense. "You're making a huge mistake."

"I don't follow."

She gestured at her hair and clothes. "This isn't me. Las Vegas was nothing but a fantasy."

"I think this is you."

"No. I'm the girl who works long hours at a job she's over-qualified for and spends her free time knitting prayer shawls and volunteering at women-at-risk shelters. I don't drink. I don't club. I'm not glamorous or interesting." She kept her face turned away so he couldn't see the hot tears brimming in her eyes.

"Have you looked in the mirror? You're beautiful. And the most fascinating woman in the world." His compliments might be a complete lie, but they weakened her knees all the same. "Now, let's get out of here."

After that speech, how could she be anything but putty in his hands? Fortunately, their exit was delayed by a half-dozen more people who asked about business, or mentioned his father or tried to corral him for lunch. She recognized a majority of the men. Many she'd spoken with on the phone during her four years working for Sebastian.

They, in turn, seemed surprised to see her at Sebastian's side during a nonwork event. She could almost hear them wonder why Sebastian brought his former executive assistant to the fundraiser. Despite being introduced as the new director of communications, she couldn't stop feeling like an outsider.

If it were only Sebastian and her, she wouldn't have a care in the world. His kisses banished every worry from her mind like magic. Every time they came together it was a roller-coaster ride of desire. But real relationships existed in public as well as private. She couldn't picture herself ever fitting into his world.

On the way back to her condo, Sebastian drove in silence.

His fingers tapped the steering wheel, keeping time to a rhythm only he heard. Almost as if he was anxious. Unaccustomed to anything but utter calm from him, she eyed Sebastian from beneath her lashes.

"I met Kaitlyn Murray at the party," she said. "She seems very nice."

"Kaitlyn is a great girl."

"She said your families are very close."

"I guess that's true." Sebastian shot her a questioning look.

"Your mom's right. She's the perfect choice for you. She knows all the same people you do. Attends the same events. I'm sure she went to all the right schools."

"And I feel nothing but friendship toward her."

"You could build on that."

"It might have been enough once." Sebastian let his gaze slide over her. "Before I got to know you in Las Vegas."

Her heart felt lighter than air. For a second it was hard to breathe. Before she floated away, Missy got herself back under control. Nothing about their situation had changed. "What happened between us there was just passion."

"Then why can't I stop thinking about you?"

His words awakened a tremor. "It just didn't get a chance to burn out."

"That's your explanation?" Sebastian nodded. "If we'd been together for a couple months, maybe a year I'd have gotten tired of you. Is that what you think?"

"Something like that. Only it might not have taken longer than a couple weeks. I don't fit in your world. Tonight proved it."

"Proved it how? Do you seriously think a bunch of blowhards are my world? Or those two-dimensional women whose lives revolve around parties and spending money?" Sebastian's voice softened. "What the hell made you such a cynic?"

Missy hesitated. It wasn't her proudest moment, but if he

knew the truth, he might realize why they'd never work outside the bedroom.

"When I was a sophomore in high school I dated a guy from the wealthiest family in the county. He was a senior and heading to college on a football scholarship. We'd talk for hours about the future. He couldn't wait to get out of Crusade. His daddy owned the bank. Chip was supposed to get a business degree and come back."

"Chip?" Sebastian repeated the name.

"Robert. His daddy called him a chip off the old block and the name stuck." She always smiled when she remembered those months before her world crumbled. "But Chip's dreams were bigger than Crusade and that's what I loved about him. Not his fancy car like my family thought or his money. He was going to reach for the stars and I wanted to be right beside him, living my own dreams."

Her voice faded. Funny how fifteen years later her dreams consisted of spending two years saving for a fairytale wedding gown, only to have her boyfriend dump her in favor of a woman he scarcely knew.

"So, you dated a rich kid with big dreams. What happened?"

"His friends never liked that I was dating him. They thought being with me lowered his status. One of them started a rumor that I'd gotten pregnant on purpose hoping that he'd marry me."

Why even now did her mouth go dry when she remembered how he'd screamed at her, calling her a stupid slut who'd ruined his life? It was fifteen years in the past, yet as vivid as if it had happened yesterday.

"Maybe I believed myself in love with him. And, sure, I considered what being married to him would be like—but I wasn't trying to get pregnant. I was on the pill and I made him use protection. But he freaked out. Dumped me. Ruined my reputation." She eased her death grip on her clutch. Forced her shoulders to relax. "Told everyone I'd done lots of things." The rest of the explanation wouldn't come. Sebastian would just have to use his imagination. "Needless to say, my family was horrified. My mom had suffered a stroke a couple months before. Dad grounded me for about a year. Which was okay. My social life was over."

"I'm sorry you had to go through that. But the party tonight wasn't high school."

"No. But the concept is the same. Chip dumped me because his friends believed I wasn't good enough for him and made him believe terrible things about me. Those were your friends in there tonight."

"Not my friends. Business associates and acquaintances."

"But they're your social circle. They didn't welcome me with open arms."

"You're comparing me to some weak-minded boy. Do you really imagine I would turn on you like that?"

"I never said you would." But it wasn't only about the two of them. She was pregnant. What if he wanted to marry her? She'd eventually disappoint him. Or worse, he'd be too furious to ever want to see her again. "But you can't blame a girl for wanting to protect herself from getting hurt."

After leaving Missy at her front door with a kiss designed to get him inside her apartment—a kiss that failed—Sebastian swung by Nathan and Emma's. His new sister-in-law crafted jewelry. Dazzling one-of-a-kind pieces that had garnered her some great publicity and made demand for her work soar.

That's why, with a minor difficulty with her pregnancy slowing her down and the demand for her work increasing, Sebastian had to wait three weeks for the special piece he'd commissioned.

Nathan answered Sebastian's knock, looking none too pleased at his brother's late appearance. Already dressed for bed, he blocked Sebastian's entrance with his hand on the door. "You're the mystery client she's been working night and day for?"

"Hardly night and day," Emma said, ducking under her husband's arm. She smiled at Sebastian. "He worries too much."

"You heard the doctor. You're supposed to take it easy."

"It's a little high blood pressure."

"It's preeclampsia." Nathan's tone made it sound like a death sentence.

"Forgive my husband," Emma said. "Come in. Your order is ready."

"Order?" Nathan echoed, stepping back as his wife applied an elbow to his ribs. He trailed her as far as the living room. When she headed into her workroom, he rounded on Sebastian. "What sort of order did you place with my wife that has kept her up late working?"

Sebastian observed the changes in his sibling with interest. Nathan had such a casual, freewheeling style at work. Nothing much seemed to bother him. He handled successes and setbacks with the same cool confidence.

His pregnant wife, however, brought out a keen, possessive side.

"It's nothing I feel like talking about at the moment."

"You're keeping her from getting the rest she needs. I think I have the right to know why."

"I'm sorry if I've caused problems. It wasn't my intention to put her health at risk."

"You didn't." Emma returned and nudged her husband with her hip.

Nathan's hand settled on her round belly. "You've barely rested all week."

"I'm pregnant," she said, covering his hand with hers. "Not an invalid."

"What did you make for him?"

"Sebastian asked me not to say anything to anyone." She

handed Sebastian a box and wrapped her arms around her husband's waist.

Nathan visibly relaxed in his wife's embrace. "I'm your husband. You should be able to tell me everything."

"Nice try." She reached up on tiptoe and kissed his chin. "Would you make me a snack while I walk Sebastian out? I bought some fresh strawberries today."

"We're out of whipped cream."

"But there's chocolate sauce." Her eyes took on a particular softness as she gazed up at her husband.

"Fine." Grumbling, Nathan headed deeper into the condo.

Watching Nathan and Emma awakened Sebastian to envy. After his disastrous first marriage, he'd refused to let emotion lead him back to the altar. He'd approached his personal relationships more like business deals, analyzing, weighing the pros and cons of each potential merger.

Until that night in Las Vegas with Missy.

Missy was real and endlessly fascinating. He adored her ability to sit back and observe and then arrow straight to the heart of someone's character. How many times had he brought her into his office and wrestled an opinion out of her when a problem came up in one of their divisions?

She dismantled his restraint with her audacious opinions of him and her enthusiasm for adventure. His desire for her astonished him, but he could no more fight it than stop an avalanche.

Tonight, what he'd learned of her past left him with concerns. She'd obviously suffered at the hands of a teenage idiot with no thought of anyone but himself, but how badly damaged was her ability to trust? She claimed she didn't view him in the same light as her high school boyfriend, but Sebastian wondered if she intended to hold his wealth and position against him.

He'd thought a lot about Missy during the four weeks she'd been gone. And that had led to missing her. He'd invented

excuses to call her once, even twice, a day, just so he could
hear her voice.

The behavior struck him as unnecessary, yet he couldn'
stop himself from dialing. He hated that she was on his
mind all day long. He wasn't in control of his actions or his
thoughts, and fighting the need to connect with her a dozen
times a day warned him he might be on the path to even more
disastrous tendencies like skipping work to spend the day in
bed with her or clearing his schedule so he could enjoy her
company over a long lunch.

Her new job might have created a wall between them, but
it was a flimsy barrier to Sebastian's desires. A more formi-
dable impediment was convincing her to trust him to keep
her safe in his social circles.

It was a task he was up to. Tonight had demonstrated how
much he wanted her in his life.

"Sorry about my husband," Emma said with an apologetic
shrug. "He's become a little unreasonable since our last doctor
visit."

Sebastian was on the verge of telling his sister-in-law that
her husband had a knack for being unreasonable when he realized that a certain woman had accused him of the exact same
failing. Maybe all the Case men were cursed with a gene that
made them more of a handful than the average man.

While Emma walked him to the front door, Sebastian
cracked the lid on the box and stared at the contents. Diamonds shot sparks at him from their nest of black velvet.

"This is incredible," he told her. "The sketches don't do
your work justice."

Emma sagged into her smile. "Thank you. With all the
success I've had you'd think I'd get used to people liking my
work. But this piece is special. It's going to sound silly but
working on it felt magical."

"Not silly at all. You are a true artist." He leaned down and kissed his sister-in-law on the cheek. "Thanks, Emma. I hope my brother knows how lucky he is to have you."

"I know." Nathan stood just inside the foyer, arms crossed, eyes flashing with annoyance. "And as soon as you get the hell out of here, I'm going to give her a demonstration she won't soon forget."

Her new office as the director of communications gave Missy less square footage than the cubicle she'd had outside Sebastian's executive suite. But it had a door. And a window.

At the moment, she was enjoying both.

Sipping the tea she'd picked up on the way in, Missy watched as the building next door turned to gold in the dawn light. Why was she at work at six-thirty in the morning? Because yesterday she'd left early to go to a doctor's appointment and because she was worried about doing a good job in her new position.

A firm knock on her door warned her she had company. Only one man got to the office this early.

"Good morning, Missy." Sebastian surveyed her with a toe-curling grin. "You're in awfully early."

For the past three days, he'd made an effort to pop by and say hello. In all the years she'd worked for him, she'd never seen him so chipper. It was unnerving.

"I had some things to catch up on."

Shoulder propped against her doorframe, he eyed her cup. "You're drinking tea?" Commenting on her daily caffeine jumpstart was a typical morning conversation opener for him. "That's a change."

"I haven't been sleeping well so I'm cutting out caffeine." Her eyes burned.

She hadn't slept well since discovering she was pregnant. Too many worries crowded her. During the day she mastered anxiety by throwing herself into learning the ins and outs of her new job.

"What you need is some exercise before bedtime." He'd also taken to flirting with her. "I could help you with that."

"No." Heavens. That was the last thing she needed. "It's the new position. I have a lot to learn."

"You were always a perfectionist." He took a step into her office. "Max is very happy with what you're doing. So relax."

Some of her tension eased, but her dizziness remained. "Thanks, that's good to know."

"It's my mother's birthday on Friday. There's a family get-together at their house. Will you come?"

It wasn't an unusual request. She'd celebrated occasions with his family before. Nothing had changed except she no longer worked directly for him. Yet, her instincts told her to refuse.

"I'd like to, but it's Memorial Day weekend and I'm heading home to check on my father."

Not a complete fabrication. She'd told her family she'd try to make the annual Ward barbecue.

"She specifically asked me to invite you. She'll be very disappointed if you aren't there. My father has some big surprise planned. She's worried it could end up being a disaster."

Missy felt herself weakening. She really loved Susan. And Brandon had gone out of his way to make certain she took this job. "I guess it would be okay if I took off for Crusade early Saturday morning."

"Excellent. I'll pick you up around six. Dinner's at seven."

Dinner with his family might not be out of the ordinary, but having Sebastian pick her up was. "I can drive myself."

"No need." His tone told her she'd be wasting her breath by arguing. "See you Friday."

"Friday," she echoed, wondering what the hell she'd just gotten herself into.

About a dozen times in the two days that followed, Missy started an email to Sebastian or picked up the phone to tell him she'd changed her mind. Since she'd slept with him in Las Vegas, she was no longer his overworked executive assistant. Now she was an ex-lover. The dynamic between them had altered, trapping her between craving his affection and dreading disappointment.

As Friday night rolled around, nerves unsettled her stomach so she used chocolate ice cream to settle both. Maybe not the best choice for a queasy pregnant woman, but she'd taken the last of the crackers to nibble on at work.

When the doorbell rang, she set the unfinished ice cream on her nightstand and went to answer it. She smoothed her hands down her dress and told herself to calm down. It was just a routine dinner at the Cases'.

But instead of Sebastian, Tim stood outside her door, a large cardboard box in his hands. He seemed shorter than she remembered. His blond hair thinner. And that crooked front tooth she'd always thought gave him character made her long for Sebastian's perfect smile.

"Wow." His eyes widened. "You look incredible."

"Thanks." She'd put on one of the new outfits she'd bought in Las Vegas, hoping to see Sebastian's eyes light up with that special glow that told her he appreciated what she was wearing if only so he could have the pleasure of taking it off. "What are you doing here?"

"I mean it." Tim stared at her as if he'd never really seen her before. "You look hot."

She glanced at the clock. It was five minutes to six. She had to make Tim leave and fast. "It's just a dress."

"It's more than the dress. You look completely different. Like wow."

The old her would have been thrilled by his enthusiasm. Tim wasn't much for compliments. Most of the time, he'd given her the impression he could do better. And since she'd worried that he was right, she'd never complained.

"Why weren't you like this when we were together?"

She refused to give him credit for her transformation, although she'd still be plain old Missy if he hadn't dumped her. "What's in there?" She gestured at the box he held.

"It's some of the stuff you left at my place. One of those shawls you knit. One of those books you read."

"It's a biography on John Adams. I left it for you. It was very good. I thought you would like it."

"That's okay. You know I don't read much." He used the box like a battering ram as he made his way into her condo. "Can I come in?"

"This isn't a great time." Knowing she'd never win a shoving match with Tim, Missy reluctantly gave ground. Anxiety hummed as he moved to the center of the living room and looked around. "You really need to go."

He shot her an exasperated look. "It'll just take a second for me to grab my anime DVDs."

"They're where you left them."

They'd never spent much time at Tim's house. He had a black Lab with no manners that Missy couldn't stand being around. Being unable to spend the night meant their sex life was sporadic. In fact, she couldn't remember the last time they'd been together. Unlike with Sebastian, where she felt each second without him as if an eternity had passed.

Had she seriously considered marrying Tim?

He dropped the box on her couch and turned toward her. "I broke up with Candy."

That explained his visit. He'd come by because he was alone once more, and if there was anything Tim hated, it was flying solo.

"That's too bad. You two seemed perfect for each other." A trace of bitterness entered her voice. Being dumped still stung even if her heart was no longer vulnerable to him.

"So did I until she left me." Tim looked ready to lay the whole sob story on her.

Missy edged toward Tim's anime collection. Sebastian was

due to arrive any second. The sooner she got rid of Tim, the better.

"It was then I realized I should never have broken up with you." He'd gotten that right at least. Too bad for him it was too little and way too late.

"That's sweet of you to say, but now you really have to go. I'm expecting someone…"

"I was hoping we could get back together."

He'd crushed her dreams without mercy, and now he wanted her to take him back? She almost laughed.

"I can't."

"Why not?" He really thought she'd still be pining over him.

And maybe he was right to. She'd let him treat her as if she wasn't good enough for him.

"Because I'm not the girl you dumped. More has happened to me in the last six weeks than new clothes and a better haircut." For one thing she was pregnant. For another, she'd fallen in love with the baby's father. Missy gathered a shaky breath as the hopelessness of her situation battered her. "I'm in love with someone else."

"In six weeks?" Tim scoffed, his eyes and mouth hardening. "That's not like you. It took a dozen dates before you'd let me kiss you. Is this your way of getting back at me?"

"No. It's true."

"Who is it?"

Missy hesitated. Tim had no right to any answer. It was none of his business.

"You're making this up," Tim cried, misinterpreting her pause. He grabbed her arms and pulled her close to his body. "You still love me. How could you not? We were together for three years. We talked about getting married."

Alarmed by her sudden predicament, she braced her hands on Tim's chest and pushed. Yes, they'd talked about it, but that's all they'd done. He hadn't proposed. Three years she waited for him, and he'd fallen in love with someone else and left her.

"Am I interrupting something?" A voice spoke from the front door.

Tim looked toward Sebastian and his expression darkened. He let her go. Missy stumbled back and caught herself on the rocking chair her grandfather had carved for her grandmother.

"I see the score now," Tim snarled. "He's what you want. He's all you ever wanted." Grabbing the videos he'd come for, Tim headed for the front door. He tried to muscle Sebastian out of the way and ended up bouncing off him like a pinball. "She's all yours. Not that it was ever in doubt."

Missy watched him go, her heart hammering at the expression on Sebastian's face. He didn't look overjoyed to find her in Tim's arms. Not that she'd been participating in the embrace.

"Was that your boyfriend?" His tone was neither conversational nor friendly.

"My ex-boyfriend."

"He didn't look very ex to me."

"He left me for his soul mate." She tried to keep the hurt from her voice. She didn't succeed. "I guess it didn't work out between them."

"And now he wants you back." Not a question, a statement. Sebastian's flat expression gave away none of his thoughts on the subject, but in his gray eyes, storm clouds gathered.

"He doesn't know what he wants."

"What about what you want?"

She was completely sure that she wanted Sebastian. He stirred her like no other man. The thought of waking up every morning to his handsome face made her blissful beyond words. But none of that changed the fact that she didn't fit into his world and never would.

When she didn't answer his question, Sebastian prowled toward her. "What do you want, Missy?"

"Nothing." She couldn't tell him the truth.

Sebastian captured her face in his hands, compelling her to meet his gaze. "Do you want him back? Because if you do, I'll chase him down."

"You would?" Missy regarded him in confusion. "Really?"

"No." His voice smiled, but his expression remained tense and watchful. "Maybe you need me to give you some help."

Her knees wobbled. "What sort of help?"

"I could tell you what I want."

"You've been pretty clear about that," she retorted dryly, but her banter didn't rouse a smile.

"No, I don't think I have. I want you. In my life. For as long as you'll have me."

Her breath caught.

She marveled at how his eyes glowed in the seconds before he captured her lips in the softest kiss imaginable. She remembered how his lovemaking had helped her overcome her fear of heights. Maybe it could help her overcome her fear of not fitting into his world.

"I'd like that, too," she breathed when he let her come up for air.

And between one exhalation and a gasp, he'd swung her off her feet and moved toward her bedroom.

"Wait. What about your mother's birthday party?"

"We'll be late."

He set her on her feet beside her bed, reached around her and grasped her zipper. His lips coasted along her neck as the dress came undone. Missy smiled, dazzled by the realization that she'd admitted her feelings to Sebastian and the sky hadn't fallen.

She was getting ready to shimmy out of her dress when Sebastian stilled all movement.

"How long after you two broke up did we make love?"

Every cell in her body froze solid. "A day." Lightheaded

with dismay, she nevertheless forced herself to ask, "Where are you going with this?"

He grabbed her upper arms and turned her toward her nightstand. Her throat trapped a small cry as she spied the pregnancy book she'd been reading before bed the previous night.

"Are you pregnant?"

"Yes."

"Were you planning on telling me?"

Misery engulfed her. "Yes." But she'd hesitated too long before answering.

His body vibrated with suppressed fury. "You set me up from the beginning, didn't you?"

"What?" She flinched away from the suspicion in his eyes. "No."

But he didn't hear her denial. Or if he had, he didn't believe her. His fingers bit into her flesh, keeping her pinned beneath his merciless stare.

"You found out you were pregnant. Your boyfriend dumped you. You seduced me so I'd believe the baby was mine."

His accusation came at her like a tire iron. Missy was too stunned to protect herself. Reeling from the impact, she struggled to breathe.

She wasn't surprised he'd jumped to that conclusion. His first wife had used a pregnancy lie to first get and then stay married to Sebastian. Why would he trust any woman after what he'd been through?

But that he believed it of her aligned all her defensives against him. She stiffened her muscles and straightened her spine. Digging the heel of her palms into his chest, she gave him back glare for glare.

But beneath her outrage, her heart had been gutted. The pain made trying to be strong so much harder. She thought she'd be better prepared for this moment. Hadn't she seen it coming the first morning after they'd made love? But knowing he'd eventually reject her and the reality of the experience were vastly different.

And deep down, she'd wanted to trust him. She'd even started to. After the casino night fundraiser, a seed of hope had sprouted. She'd fought to keep it from taking root, but with every fiber of her being she'd wanted things to work out between them. He'd sure done a good job convincing her she'd fit into his world. That he'd be by her side, protecting her.

Look how long that had lasted.

"Answer me, damn you," he ground out, looking ready to shake her unless she spilled everything. "Is the baby your boyfriend's?"

The lie she'd promised she'd tell him hovered on her tongue. It would be so easy to claim the baby was Tim's because it was clear that's what he was expecting to hear. She'd lose him. But isn't that what she'd decided was best for all concerned?

She lifted her arm and broke his hold. "This baby is mine. And no one else's."

"Stop evading the truth." He expelled the words through tight lips. His eyes blazed with fury and despair. "Who's the father?"

"What's the point in telling you? You're already convinced it's Tim's." Her head spun. At the moment, the only thing keeping her upright was her stubborn pride. "You need to go."

By some miracle she kept her voice steady. Telling herself this was for the best didn't make the loathing in Sebastian's gaze any easier to stomach. Tears burned the back of her eyes. She couldn't cry. She wouldn't.

Sebastian gathered in an enormous amount of air. His chest swelled with it. The condo was so silent Missy could hear the hum of the refrigerator in the kitchen. Her heart thumped in her ears. At last, he released his breath. His next words shocked her to her toes.

"I'm not going anywhere without you," he intoned. He'd

regained control of his emotions. "My family is waiting for us at my parents' house. We're supposed to be celebrating my mother's birthday."

"Your family is waiting for you." Faint with confusion, Missy shook her head. "I'm not going."

Why would he want to have anything to do with her after what they'd just been through? The answer jumped into her mind a second later. For the same reason he'd stayed married to Chandra despite all her craziness. He was a man who honored his commitments.

"You're going if I have to carry you out to my car."

Convinced he would act on his threat, she picked up her abandoned bowl of melted ice cream and dumped it over her head. She bit her lip to hold back a yelp as the sticky, cold liquid drenched her head and trickled beneath the neckline of her dress. She'd ruined her beautiful new dress, but the shock on Sebastian's face almost made up for the loss.

"Have you lost your mind?" he demanded.

"I lost it four years ago when I came to work for you." A hysterical giggle bubbled up, quickly followed by a ragged sob. Only Sebastian brought out such crazy impulses. The years she'd spent tempering her wild nature might never have been for all the control she exhibited around him.

"Go shower and change, I'll call and let everyone know we're going to be late."

She shook her head. Three chocolate drops stained his beautiful suit. "I'm not going anywhere with you."

"Fine." His expression hardened to granite. "Just answer one simple question before I go. Is the baby mine?"

A crazy sort of calm settled over her. She felt disconnected from her bedroom and from Sebastian. Chip had turned on her like this. She'd believed he cared about her. She'd trusted him and fifteen years later the pain remained fresh.

But her feelings for Sebastian weren't a teenage crush.

She loved him with everything in her and he'd accused her of something horrible.

"Yes," she whispered, a hollow shell waiting to be filled with agony. "The baby's yours. But after this, I'll never be."

Eleven

Missy's pronouncement droned in Sebastian's ears like a dirge as he drove to his parents' house. She'd never be his. That's where she was wrong. If she was pregnant with his child, she was going to find out that mere words would not get him to back off. He just needed a little time to regain control over his emotions.

Finding out that she was pregnant and that she'd intended to keep the truth from him roused every negative attitude he'd ever had about relationships. How many times had Chandra pulled some stunt when she wanted his attention? Too many to count.

But Missy wasn't his ex-wife. He'd been wrong to paint the two women with the same brush. Missy wouldn't deceive him into marrying her by passing another man's child off as his. No, quite the opposite. He wouldn't put it past her to lie to him in some misguided attempt to make things easier for him.

The child she carried was his. In his gut he'd known the truth before the question had surged out of him. He never should have let past mistakes ruin his future happiness.

Cursing, Sebastian stomped on the brakes and stopped inches from Max's car parked halfway up his parents' circular driveway. Distracted driving wasn't like him. But since that first night in Las Vegas, much of his behavior had become unrecognizable.

A collection of familiar cars were parked all around. The party was under way. He was one of the last to arrive. Sebastian listened to the engine cool, keenly aware of the empty passenger seat. This is not how he'd imagined the evening going.

Inside, his mother was the first to greet him.

"Happy birthday." He kissed her cheek and slipped her gift into her hand. "Sorry I'm late."

"Where's Missy?"

"She's not coming."

"Why not?"

Sebastian grimaced. "It's complicated."

"There you are." His father joined them in the foyer. "Where's your date?"

"Not coming." Sebastian had been too busy dwelling on his troubles with Missy to concoct a decent excuse for her absence.

"That's odd. When I spoke to her this afternoon, she was looking forward to it."

"She changed her mind," he said, hoping his bland tone would prevent further questions.

"That's not like Missy," his mother chimed in.

"Not at all," Brandon agreed. "What happened?"

"Nothing." Feeling ganged up on, Sebastian tried to turn the conversation away from him. "Looks like you have a houseful. Am I the last to arrive?"

"We're still waiting on Trent and Amy," Susan said, referring to her husband's brother and sister-in-law. "Come have a glass of champagne and say hello to everyone."

Sebastian would have followed his mother, but a hand on his arm stopped him. He glanced toward his father.

"Do you want me to call her and see if I can get her to come? Your mother was looking forward to having her here."

Irrationally irritated, Sebastian glared at his father. "A phone call from you isn't going to convince Missy to come tonight. She doesn't want to be here." With me. The last two words went unsaid, but Sebastian could hear them echoing in the foyer.

"You might be surprised how persuasive I can be. I got her to stay at Case Consolidated Holdings after you let her quit." Brandon leveled a disappointed look at his son. "I'd hoped if she stuck around long enough you might come to your senses. I can see I overestimated your intelligence."

"Come to my senses?" Sebastian repeated. "What the hell are you talking about?"

"She's in love with you. Has been for years." The older Case nodded knowingly.

His father's words hit him hard. "What?"

"And at long last, you're in love with her." Brandon waved his hand when Sebastian began to speak. "Don't bother denying it. It was all over your face that morning at the hotel."

"I have no idea what you're talking about." But he wasn't completely convinced he believed that. Something had happened between them that first night. "We were together, sure, but it was one night."

Brandon's smile turned sly. "And since?"

"That's none of your business."

"You were ornery and distracted when she was visiting her family. And since she's back, you've had a bounce in your step."

Sebastian couldn't believe what he was hearing. "I don't bounce."

"Well, you sure won't be if you let that girl get away. Smart, beautiful, funny. Good at getting things done. The office ran more smoothly once she came aboard. And she knew how to handle you." Brandon nodded, his expression self-satisfied. "I knew a week after she took the job that she was the best thing that ever happened to you."

And deep down, Sebastian knew it, too.

He rocked onto his toes, thrown off balance as his father clapped him on the back.

"That's my boy. Now, why don't you go fetch her? Give your mom a birthday present that'll really make her happy."

Sebastian thought about his child growing inside Missy and muttered, "I think I already have."

The drive from Missy's house to his parents' house had taken thirty minutes. The return trip seemed to take an eternity. While he negotiated Houston's traffic, he prepared a convincing argument for why she needed to forgive him. He parked in front of her condo and immediately saw her car was missing from her parking spot.

When she didn't answer her doorbell or respond when he knocked, he knew in the time it had taken him to come to his senses, she'd left. Next he tried her cell phone, but she wasn't picking up. Only one place made sense for her to have gone. Home.

And that's where he intended to follow.

The day after her big fight with Sebastian, Missy pulled into her father's driveway around ten in the morning. After he'd left, she'd been too upset to sit in her condo and rehash the mess she'd made of things. Instead, she'd taken a shower and headed for Crusade.

Three hours out of Houston, she'd decided to stop for the night. Her family wasn't expecting her until the next day, and when she'd fled Houston, she hadn't considered that her six-hour drive would put her at her father's house around one in the morning. Besides, after exhausting herself with anxiety and recriminations, she wasn't in any shape to drive that far in the middle of the day, much less at night.

Heart thumping too fast, she stared at the car parked in her father's driveway. Sebastian's Mercedes stuck out like a couture gown at a country dance. What was he doing here? She opened her door as family members poured out of the house. Sebastian led the way.

"Where have you been?" He jerked the car door from her hand, opening it wide, and dragged her from the seat. His hands explored her face, arms and shoulders. His gaze traced her forehead, cheeks and nose as if to reassure himself she was okay. "I left you a dozen messages. Why didn't you call?"

"Because I turned off my cell. A dozen messages?" Her traitorous heart danced for joy at his concern, but she pulled away from his touch. "What are you doing here?"

"When you didn't show up or call we all thought something had happened to you," Sebastian explained, cupping her face in his hands. "Where have you been?"

"I was tired so I stopped at a motel and slept." His somber, worried expression was beginning to blur the reasons why she'd left him in the first place. "How did you know I was coming here?"

"When I went back to your house last night and found you gone, I figured you'd head home."

"But why are you here?"

"I came to apologize."

"You're apologizing?" That didn't sound like Sebastian. What was the catch? "What if I'm not accepting?"

"Why wouldn't you?"

She looked around the tall man blocking her view of the group clustered in front of her car and spied her father standing behind him, a wide grin on his face. Her brothers and sisters-in-law were all standing too close for her to have this conversation with Sebastian.

"If you don't know, then there's no use in telling you."

Missy reached into the car and pulled out a duffel filled with clothes. To her annoyance, Sebastian plucked the bag from her hands and grasped her by the elbow.

"You obviously have something to get off your chest. Let's go inside and talk."

"No." She twisted her arm free. "No more talking. Look around you, Sebastian. This is where I'm from. My family doesn't have money or power. We have love. We have trust. We have each other's backs. And that's enough."

"I don't get what you mean."

"I don't care about your money or your fancy friends. Love. Trust. Commitment. That's what I want in a relationship."

Missy snagged her bag and strode into the house. She didn't realize that she'd left everyone outside until she reached the stairs to the second floor and the silence pressed in on her.

Turning, she peered through the front picture window and spotted Sebastian getting into David's truck. Where was he going with her brother? Her father entered the house.

"What is the matter with you?" he demanded. "That boy drove all night to get here and he's been fretting like a dog with fleas when you didn't show. Why are you acting like he's the enemy?"

For a second Missy didn't know how to react. Her father never scolded her. That had been her mother's job, and after the stroke stole her voice, her brothers' responsibility.

"I don't know why he came."

"He came because he loves you."

Her heart jerked. "Did he say that?"

"Not in so many words."

Not in any words.

"He's not in love with me," she said, flinching away from the stab of disappointment.

"Then why does he want to marry you?"

"He doesn't." A loud thump rang out as she sat down on the worn wood stairs. "What gave you a crazy idea like that?"

"He asked my permission."

Suddenly she couldn't breathe. "He did?" Who did that anymore? The traditional gesture was so sweet and so unlike Sebastian that Missy couldn't wrap her head around it. "Or is it just what you hope he'll do?"

"I'm not so addled that I don't know when a man's asking for my only daughter's hand in marriage." Her father sat beside her and took her hands in his, rubbing them to restore warmth. He smelled like soap and barbeque sauce. "In case you're wondering, I told him yes."

"I wish you wouldn't have done that."

Missy rested her head on his shoulder like she'd done as a child. Her father had always been her comfort zone when having four older brothers got to be too much for her to handle. Or when her mother tried to mold her into the polite, refined young lady a pastor and his wife could be proud of.

"It's done. Can't be undone. Is there a reason you don't want to marry him?"

She took a moment before answering. Sebastian's accusation had hurt. He'd shaken her trust in him and that wasn't something that could be repaired overnight. Besides, the original reason for avoiding a relationship with him hadn't changed.

"I don't fit into his world. He has money and lots of well-connected friends. I'm just a small-town girl who's been working as his assistant for four years. There's nothing sophisticated or interesting about me."

"So, you're afraid."

Her father had been counseling engaged couples for years. He'd probably seen it all. No use trying to deny the truth.

"Terrified."

"I don't know him well, but unlike that young man you dated in high school, Sebastian doesn't strike me as the sort who'd feed you to the wolves."

"No," Missy agreed. "You don't know him well. He's not

marrying me because he loves me." She puffed her breath out in a huge sigh. "I'm pregnant."

Her father sat in silence for a long moment. When he spoke, a deep sadness filled his voice. "Tim's?"

"No." She shook her head, the burn of tears blurring her vision. "Sebastian's. That's why he wants to marry me. It's why he married his first wife. He's honorable."

"Do you love him?"

"Yes. But I'm not going to let him make the same mistake twice."

"I don't think he views marrying you as a mistake."

She twisted her hands in her father's grasp until she held him. She squeezed gently, thinking of all the people he'd touched both physically—with a gentle hug, a comforting hand on the shoulder during a moment of grief—and with his wise sermons and thoughtful counsel.

"He can be rather thick-headed that way."

Laugh lines deepened at the corners of her father's dark-brown eyes. "I can see he's going to have a tough time convincing you to marry him."

"Tougher than you know. He's terrible at negotiating."

The front door opened and Matt's wife, Helen, entered, followed by David's very pregnant wife, Abigail. They carried bowls and trays.

"What's going on?"

"It's Memorial Day weekend," Helen explained. "We're barbecuing."

Missy got to her feet. "Do you want some help?"

"We've got it covered."

Abigail winked at Helen. "We wouldn't want you killing Sebastian with your cooking."

Of all the household tasks Missy had mastered after her mother's stroke, cooking was not one of them. And it wasn't as if she got much time to practice. Sebastian kept her working until seven most nights. She usually grabbed take-out on the way home.

She headed upstairs to drop off her duffel bag. Passing David's old room, she spied Sebastian's suitcase in the corner. He was staying here? In the room next to hers? How was she expected to get any sleep knowing he was on the other side of the wall?

Emotions churning, she sat on the window seat that overlooked the garden in the backyard. Her mother had planned and lovingly maintained each and every bed from the vegetables to the roses. After she'd had her stroke, Missy tended the garden while her mother looked on. At first Missy had resented the weeds that seemed to sprout overnight. The task of keeping the numerous beds in perfect order had pained her with its tedium.

Eventually, however, she began to find the repetitious chore soothed her restless nature. She'd read up on the various types of plants and dreamed that when she moved into her own house, she'd spend many free hours creating colorful plantings around her property.

"We're heading over to bring the boys some lunch. Want to come?"

Helen and Abigail hovered in the hallway.

"Sure." She snatched up the battered Stetson she wore only when in town and followed her sisters-in-law downstairs. "What are they doing today?"

"Repairs on the Taggets' roof," Helen said. "Last week's thunderstorm did quite a bit of damage to a dozen homes. It's been tough getting to everyone who needs help."

"Nice of your boss to pitch in," Abigail added. "Or should I call him your boyfriend?"

Missy pretended as if she hadn't heard the sly question. "Sebastian's working with them?" Is that why he'd been dressed in a T-shirt and jeans earlier? She'd been too agitated by his presence in Crusade to notice how he was dressed, but now that she thought about it, she remembered he'd looked damned sexy in a snug cotton shirt that stretched across his chest and scarcely contained his biceps. "I didn't realize he was handy."

"Apparently he worked construction during college," Helen said.

How had she not known that? She'd worked for the man four years. And yet, how much had she discovered about him in the past couple of months? As much as he'd learned about her? Or had her determination to keep him at bay prevented him from getting to know her in turn?

Missy's pulse fluttered as Helen's SUV stopped in front of a storm-battered house. More than just the roof had suffered from the high winds. Half the front porch was missing and a pile of wood stacked next to a gaping hole in the front yard hinted at a tree that was no more.

A dozen men swarmed the roof and yard. Missy had little trouble spotting Sebastian's tall form as he jumped off a ladder and headed her way. She snatched her gaze from the worn denim riding his narrow hips and wrapping his powerful thighs. She'd never seen him in jeans before and found the view disconcerting.

His expensive business suits gave him the air of an aloof multimillionaire. Fascinating to look at but remote. The casual clothes made him much more approachable. Touchable. She wanted to hook her fingers into his belt loops and tug him close enough for a long, slow kiss. Heat bloomed in her cheeks as he stopped beside her.

"Hello, Missy."

"Hi." Her mouth had gone too dry to offer more. The clean scent of sweat, soap and something uniquely Sebastian was so tempting, she had to shove her hands into her back pockets to keep from reaching out to him. "Thanks for helping, but you didn't need to."

He, too, wore a hat. The wide brim shadowed his eyes, forcing her to guess at his mood.

"I'm happy to pitch in."

"I didn't know you could handle a hammer."

"Figured me for a spoiled rich kid, didn't you?"

Missy hunched her shoulders. "Can you blame me?" Surrendering to temptation, she took his hand and turned it palm up so she could trace the lines and contours. She discovered rough spots she'd never thought about before, old calluses that revealed he hadn't spent his entire life behind a desk. "You don't have a workman's hands, but they're not exactly soft, either." Not like Tim's hands. He'd never been one for physical labor.

"You'd better eat. We're only breaking for fifteen minutes." David held a sandwich in front of Sebastian's chest and gave Missy a meaningful look. "Why don't you get Sebastian a bottle of water?"

"Sure." Missy sent her brother a meaningful look of her own and released Sebastian's hand. When she returned a second later, her brothers had formed a crowd around Sebastian, blocking her from conversing with him.

Why were they keeping her and Sebastian apart? Was it to protect her or him? Watching the camaraderie between the five guys, she decided her brothers had come down on Sebastian's side. Resentment bubbled. Even they didn't think she was good enough for him.

And why was she so close to tears? Maybe it was because she agreed with them.

Twelve

Sebastian waited until Missy had driven away with her sisters-in-law before he returned to work. Repairing roofs hadn't been the plan when he'd trekked halfway across Texas; but, now that he was here, he remembered how much he enjoyed the satisfaction of a job well done.

The afternoon flew by. A pleasant ache entered his muscles as he and Missy's brothers accepted the homeowner's thanks and packed up the leftover materials.

"We really appreciate your help," Matt said, slamming the tailgate shut on his pickup.

David nodded. "Never would have gotten it done that fast without you."

"I enjoyed it." Sebastian joined Matt in the truck and leaned his arm on the open window. "How many more projects you got?"

"How many weeks can you stay?"

Sebastian laughed but gave the question serious consideration. How long had it been since he'd taken time away from the business to do something he enjoyed? Probably the last vacation had been his honeymoon. And he wouldn't exactly call that fun.

The truck sped through town as Matt headed back toward the parsonage. Sebastian removed his hat and let the wind dry the sweat from his brow and temples. He liked Missy's family. Discovering her father was a religious man had caught him off guard at first.

Why hadn't she ever told him about such an important part of her? What was there to hide about her family? From what he could see, there was nothing to be ashamed of. Each brother was happily married with kids. They had successful careers, good standing in the community.

What else didn't he know?

For four years she'd dressed and behaved in a manner he could only call conservative. Nothing flashy about her clothes or her lifestyle.

Then, in Las Vegas she'd unveiled a different side of herself he'd never dreamed existed. He loved both women. And now, after spending time with her family, he'd become that much more determined to keep her in his life.

Sebastian saluted Matt as he drove away. Hat in hand, he entered the house, eager to talk to Missy. Earlier, when she'd taken his hand and traced the lines on his palm, the simple touch had aroused so much more than his libido. If her brothers hadn't been standing nearby he'd have taken her in his arms and kissed her until she promised to love, honor and cherish him until death did they part.

Not that he was convinced that she'd have him after what he'd said to her.

The turn-of-the-century house contained an empty stillness as he entered. Wood floors creaked beneath his step as he headed for the back door. He paused in the kitchen for a glass of water and caught sight of Missy in the backyard, hoe in hand, tackling the weedy flowerbeds. He stepped onto the back porch to better admire the wiggle of her rear end in

denim shorts as she dropped to hands and knees to attack the
weeds crowded too close to the perennials to remove with
the tool.

He released a sigh. The woman was flat out delightful no
matter what angle she presented. Although he admitted a keen
appreciation for the sight of her round backside thrust into the
air. Grinning, he started down the steps for a closer look.

"You all done with the roof?" She straightened to a kneel-
ing position and smudged her forehead with dirt as she wiped
sweat from her brow.

How long had she been aware of him? Did she sense his
nearness the same way he noticed hers? As if some invisible
cord connected them to each other?

"We finished half an hour ago." He sat down beside her.
"Looks like you have your work cut out for you."

"No one has time to keep it up since I left." She returned to
her weeding. "Gardening was my mother's love. She designed
and planted all these beds. After her stroke, she couldn't take
care of them anymore so I took over." She attacked the inva-
sive plants as if they personally offended her. "I used to hate
working in the garden. It would take hours to weed even a
single bed. The stupid things seemed to grow ten inches overnight. Mulching helps, but they still find a way in."

"Some things are like that, finding ways to thrive where
they're not wanted." He longed to touch her, to get her to take
down the wall she'd erected to keep him at bay.

"My mom was the most giving and kind person on the
planet. Everyone loved her." She stabbed at the soil with her
trowel, loosened a weed's roots from its hold, and flung it
aside. The act seemed cathartic. As if she was ridding herself
of stuff that bothered her. "She and I never got along. I suppose that makes me sound like a bad person."

She'd never talked about her mother except to say she'd had
a stroke around the time Missy had turned fifteen and died
almost ten years later.

"My dad and I don't, either," Sebastian said. "It's not unusual to get along better with one parent than another."

"My dad loved me unconditionally when I was growing up. It was my mom who was always trying to turn me into someone different."

"Different how?"

"Less tomboy, more young lady." Missy snorted. "I don't know why she expected me to act like a girl when all I wanted to do was run with my brothers and do everything they did." She drove the trowel into the dirt and sat back to dust off her knees. "See these scars? I got those jumping my bike off the ramp my brothers built in the parking lot behind the church. Busted my arm, too." She shook her head. "But do you think they got into trouble for daring me to try the jump? Nope. I got yelled at for doing something dangerous."

She wrapped her arms around her legs and set her chin on her knees. "Then there was the time when I almost drowned down by the lake because I dove off the dock and went in too steep and hit my head. That was my brothers' fault, but I got banned from the lake for the rest of the summer."

Sebastian couldn't stop a chuckle. "Sounds like you were lucky to survive childhood. I gotta admit, I never pegged you for a tomboy."

"I gave it up when I turned thirteen and figured out boys didn't date girls that could do more tricks on a bike or a skateboard than they could." Her grin came and went. "It was about that time that my mother really had her hands full with me."

He could see where she might have attracted a lot of male attention. "You were a little wild?"

"I was all about acting like that stereotypical daughter of a minister. You know, the one who behaves badly because life at home is so restrictive? I felt smothered by expectations of how I should behave, by how small the town was. My future stretched out in front of me like a west Texas highway. Empty, flat and endless. Some days I thought I would explode if I didn't get out of here."

It wasn't a stretch to imagine her full of energy and frustration.

While Sebastian threw away the pile of weeds Missy had pulled, she gathered her gardening tools and put them away in the shed. They entered the house through the back door and headed upstairs to clean up for dinner.

"My dad told me what you asked him," Missy said as she reached her bedroom door. The way her remark came out of nowhere told Sebastian how much it had been on her mind. "It's nice of you to offer, and all, but I can't marry you."

"Any reason why not?"

"You're marrying me because I'm pregnant."

"In part." He cupped her face and held still until she met his gaze. "But that's not the only reason."

"No one expects you to do the right thing," she said, applying pressure to his chest.

"*I* expect me to do the right thing." He made sure she saw that he meant every word. "Besides, I don't want to stay a bachelor forever. I built my house with a family in mind. I want you and our baby to be that family."

She shook her head. "This is not the way I saw my future."

"How is it so different? In Las Vegas you resigned because you wanted a husband and children. You will soon have one. Why not the other?"

"Sure, but I never considered marrying you."

"Really?" Doubt and laughter tangled in his voice.

"Really." Her scowl told him she meant what she said.

"My dad thinks you're in love with me."

Her mouth popped open. Outrage brewed in her hazel eyes. 'I won't deny having certain feelings," she said, her tone tart. 'But even if I was madly in love with you, I'm not sure marriage between us is a good idea."

"If you were madly in love with me?" he teased. "You mean you're not?"

"It really doesn't matter if I am or not."

"It matters to me."

"They'll say I seduced you. That I got pregnant on purpose. I'm the one who's going to be looked at as a gold digger."

"No one will dare say anything to you." He kissed her long and slow to soothe her worries, keeping up the gentle pressure until she sagged against him. Only then did he release her lips and begin nibbling down her neck.

"Maybe not, but they'll be thinking it." She tipped her head to offer him better access. "I won't be accepted by anyone."

He never dreamed he would have to convince a woman that marrying him was a good idea. "That's nonsense."

"Is it? Up until five weeks ago, I was your executive assistant. Face it, Sebastian, I'm the last woman in Houston you'd have picked to marry."

Was she? If she'd said that before Las Vegas he might have agreed with her. Since then she'd become his obsession. "That's not true. Stop telling me all the things you think I need." His ex-wife had been shallow and showy. He'd sworn the next time he married it would be to a woman with depth and concern for more than herself. "You're warm, sensitive and real." He turned over her left hand and traced her lifeline the way she'd done earlier to him. "As much as I appreciate a glossy cover, what I can't get enough of is what's written on the pages between."

She tried to take her hand back, but Sebastian tightened his grip. Her lashes fluttered as he plied her palm with a soothing massage until her shoulders relaxed.

"I don't fit into your world."

"Stop saying that. I'm not your high school boyfriend."

"You accused me of seducing you to make you believe another man's child was yours."

"That was a stupid reaction to things that happened in my

past. I've regretted it every second since it happened. I swear I've learned my lesson. I'll never hurt you again."

"I want to believe you."

Her continued hesitation was scaring him. Sebastian knew it was time to pull out the big guns. "Maybe this will help."

He scooped something out of his pocket and slid it onto her ring finger. Against her dirty palm, the enormous diamond sparkled like a miniature star.

Groaning, Missy closed her fist, hiding the ring. "It's gorgeous."

"It's an Emma Case original," Sebastian said. "I had her design it especially for you."

"You had it designed for me?" Her resolve began to waver. Emma took weeks from design to execution. That meant that Sebastian had been thinking about proposing long before he found out she was pregnant. "Why are you doing this to me?"

"What?" His gray eyes were as dazzling as the diamond clutched in her palm. "Torturing you with expensive engagement rings and marriage proposals?"

"Yes, that."

"Because I don't want to live without you."

Hope surged in her. "You don't?"

"Of course not." He dusted her lips with his. "I love you."

"You do?" She didn't think she'd ever heard three more wonderful words.

A growl rumbled from his throat. "What do you think I've been saying?"

Missy bit back a flippant reply. She'd been wrong about so much. By not embracing her strength and not trusting Sebastian to keep her from harm, she'd nearly walked away from the love of her life.

"I love you." She launched herself against Sebastian's body, pressing her face against his chest. "I love you," she repeated, her declaration fierce and sure. "Marry me before I do something stupid."

Chuckling, he released the loose knot she'd bound her hair into. The strands rushed forward to consume his fingers as he framed her face and gazed down at her. Missy met his grin with one of her own as he lowered his head and kissed her.

Sebastian tugged her into the bathroom and got them out of their clothes. As hot water poured over them, his hands skimmed her body, his touch equal parts reverence and passion. Missy trembled beneath his gentle kisses, her blood heating to a quiet simmer as he toweled her dry.

"Your room or mine?" she quizzed, opening the door to the hall.

He came up behind her and slipped his arms around her. "Which room is closer?"

Voices filtered up the stairway toward them, followed by the thundering feet of excited children.

"You have way too many family members," he groused, dropping his chin onto her head. "Shall we get dressed and go tell them the good news?"

"You know my father and your mother are going to fight over where we should get married." She looked up at him. Her heart expanded as she realized this man was going to be hers for the rest of her life.

"That crossed my mind."

"What do you want to do?"

"I don't care as long as it happens sooner rather than later."

"I'm glad to hear you say that." She smiled. "Did you know it's only an eighteen-hour drive from Crusade to Las Vegas? If we leave now we could be there in time for lunch."

"Or, we could fly and be there in time for a late dinner." He nudged her inside her bedroom. "After we swing by a wedding chapel, of course."

"Of course." Missy grinned as he left her to go dress and pack.

* * *

Five hours later, Mr. and Mrs. Sebastian Case checked into the same hotel that had hosted the leadership summit. As they headed toward the elevators, Missy gazed with longing at the casino.

"We have a bridal suite waiting for us," Sebastian said.

"Just one spin of the wheel." She smiled at him. "For old time's sake? Please."

"One spin." Sebastian followed her to the roulette table and changed a hundred dollar bill for chips. "Black or red?"

Missy took the chips and put them on red. As the silver ball spun round, she leaned against Sebastian and for a second it was only them.

"Fifteen black," the dealer called.

"I lost?" She couldn't believe it.

"Lucky at cards, unlucky at love." Sebastian drew her away from the table. "Looks like your luck has changed."

"It has indeed," she said, snuggling against his side as they headed upstairs to start their honeymoon. "And I couldn't be happier."

* * * * *

MILLS & BOON®

Let us take you back in time with our Medieval Brides...

The Novice Bride – Carol Townend

The Dumont Bride – Terri Brisbin

The Lord's Forced Bride – Anne Herries

The Warrior's Princess Bride – Meriel Fuller

The Overlord's Bride – Margaret Moore

Templar Knight, Forbidden Bride – Lynna Banning

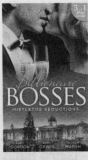
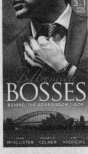

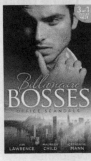
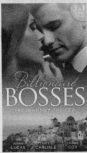
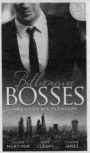

The World of
MILLS & BOON®